CHICAGO BLUES

Forge Books by Hugh Holton

Presumed Dead
Windy City
Chicago Blues

HUGH HOLTON

CHICAGO BLUES

March 15, 1997

To Virtua,

*My cousin, best
wishes on the night of that
flat tire.*

Hugh Holton

A TOM DOHERTY ASSOCIATES BOOK
NEW YORK

CHICAGO BLUES

This book is printed on acid-free paper.

A Forge Book
Published by Tom Doherty Associates, Inc.
175 Fifth Avenue
New York, N.Y. 10010

Forge® is a registered trademark of Tom Doherty Associates, Inc.

Library of Congress Cataloging-in-Publication Data

Holton, Hugh.
    Chicago blues / by Hugh Holton.
      p.   cm.
    "A Tom Doherty Associates book."
    ISBN 0-312-85984-8
    1. Police—Illinois—Chicago—Fiction. 2. Chicago (Ill.)—Fiction. I. Title
PS3558.O4373C48   1996
813'.54—dc20   95-42568
                                      CIP

First Edition: April 1996

Printed in the United States of America

0 9 8 7 6 5 4 3 2 1

I would like to dedicate *Chicago Blues* to my sisters Marcia Ann and Betty Jean; my nephews Aaron "Reggie," Brandon, and Craig; my nieces Judy, Monday, Rhonda, and LaVeda; my uncles Walter and Clifford; my cousins Deborah, Nedra, Ernestine, Frieda, Berniece, Oliver, Leonard, Wanda, Gilbert, Herman, and Elaine; my grandparents Oscar, Rebecca, Walter, and Edna, my great-grandfather Isaac Ginn; and all the members, living and dead, of the Holton, Ginn, Watts, Hampton, and Jack families.

Acknowledgments

Again, I would like to thank Robert and Susan Gleason for all their help and for continuing to be my very good friends. A very special thanks to Mrs. Barbara D'Amato for her assistance as a writing instructor and for teaching me that the book is never done when the writing is finished. And to Mark Zubro and Susan Dunlap, my traveling companions, who accompanied Barbara and me on a 5,000-mile book-signing tour in the spring and summer of 1995.

—Hugh Holton
Chicago, Illinois
August 1995

Cast of Characters

THE POLICE
Commander Larry Cole
Sergeant Blackie Silvestri
Detective Lou Bronson
Detective Manfred Wolfgang Sherlock
Police Officer Judy Daniels
Chief of Detectives Jack Govich

THE FBI
Special Agent Reggie Stanton
Special Agent-in-Charge of the Chicago Office Dave Franklin
Deputy Director William Connors
Special Agent Robert Donnelley
Special Agent Tom Prentiss

THE MOB
Antonio "Tuxedo Tony" DeLisa
Wally Boykin
Art Maggio
Attorney Frank Kirschstein

SIGNIFICANT OTHERS
Lisa Cole
Rachel DeLisa
Senator Harvey Banks

PART

I

"Next time this will be you, DeLisa."
—R. Stanton

MARCH 4, 1994
8:47 P.M.

I t was raining. The streets had developed a mirror-sheen slickness and there were few cars and even fewer pedestrians traveling on this night. On South Stony Island Avenue cars traversing the six-lane thoroughfare threw a mist up from the pavement, severely limiting visibility.

In the southbound lanes of the 8200 block, a dark brown, four-door Buick pulled to the curb and parked in front of a Land of Lincoln real estate office. The driver extinguished the headlights, but the windshield wipers continued flapping.

Charlie Butcher, a heavyset man with reptilian eyes, was driving. Angelo Cappeletti, a thin, nervous man with a cadaverous face, sat in the front seat with Butcher. Simon Jones, an obese black man with a shaved head, was the lone rear seat passenger.

The radio was playing softly. Cappeletti reached over and turned it up. The blues singer was Anna Carey, who'd often been compared to Anita Baker. Her voice was low, and she was singing about Chicago.

Cappeletti hummed along with her.

> *Its North Side leaves you grievin'.*
> *Its South Side leaves you bleedin'.*
> *It's cheatin' and it's lyin'.*
>
> *It's the gun's eye-view of dyin'.*
> *View of dyin'.*
> *View of dyin'.*
> *View of dyin'.*

Butcher reached over and switched the radio off.

The three men stared through the rain-streaked windows across Stony Island at a storefront office. The sign on the plate glass window proclaimed, HARVEY BANKS—UNITED STATES SENATOR—STATE OF ILLINOIS—CHICAGO OFFICE. Beneath the sign was the quotation, THE PEOPLE ARE THE POWER! H. BANKS.

Despite the rain, the three men in the Buick were able to see the shadowy images of people moving around inside the office.

"Do you know what you're supposed to do?" Cappeletti demanded of their passenger.

"I know what to do." The black man's voice rose barely above a whisper. "Could you let me out on the other side of the street?"

"Oh, for chrissakes!" Cappeletti exploded.

Butcher raised a hand, silencing his partner. "We can't drive any closer to that office. It would be too obvious and we might get noticed. A little walk in the rain will do you good."

"Especially the way your black ass smells," Angie added, sarcastically.

Jones tensed at the insult. Butcher spun around to watch him in case he made a move on the big mouth Angie. But the black man's anger only went as far as a glare cast at the back of Angie's head.

"That wasn't necessary," Butcher said to his partner.

"The hell it wasn't," Angie sneered. "I can barely breathe in here."

Butcher's eyes tightened into angry slits. "You apologize to Mr. Jones right now, Angie, or I'm turning this car around and driving back to Oak Park. Then you can personally explain what went wrong to Mr. DeLisa."

Angie's gaunt body curled inward to form a question mark. The "I'm sorry" he uttered was said so softly Jones couldn't hear him clearly, but it was enough.

"Okay," the black man said with a fatigued sigh. "I'll bring him to the place we agreed on. You guys promised to make it quick."

"It'll be quick, Si," Butcher said. "Damn quick."

As Butcher and Cappeletti remained facing front, the back door opened and the overhead light went on momentarily. Slamming the door, Jones shuffled down the sidewalk. He pulled his coat collar up around his neck. Waiting at the corner until a couple of cars passed, he crossed to the parkway. The men in the Buick watched him every step of the way.

"He did stink, Charlie," Angie said defensively. "Smelled like he hasn't bathed in a week."

Butcher turned to face his partner. "That wasn't B.O., stupid. That was the smell of fear. It was coming off of you as much as it was coming off our fat, black friend."

Cappeletti started to say, "What about you?" But he'd heard Butcher had killed a couple of guys who said things he didn't like. So Angie Cappeletti kept his mouth shut and instead checked the magazine of his Uzi machine gun.

Butcher had a twin of Cappeletti's firearm on the floor under his seat. He didn't need to check it. He'd done that before they started. Now all they had to do was wait for Jones to bring Senator Harvey Banks out of the office so they could tail them to the place they'd arranged. Then the two killers were going to blow the senator and his betrayer to pieces.

2

MARCH 4, 1994
8:50 P.M.

Senator Banks's office, Naomi speaking," the secretary said answering the telephone in the outer office of the storefront. The place was wood-paneled and originally had been a beauty shop. Besides her desk, there was a reception area with a cheap imitation leather couch with matching chairs, and a fragile cocktail table piled with year-old copies of *Ebony* and *Jet* magazines on top. The bodyguard sat on the couch. He and the secretary were the only occupants of the outer office. Senator Banks was in his inner office alone.

The secretary's name was Naomi Bowman. She was a five-foot-nine-inch, twenty-seven-year-old black woman. She had straight black hair hanging to the small of her back, ebony skin and a stunning figure. She was a secretary in Senator Banks's northern Illinois office and served as the night receptionist whenever he worked late in Chicago, which was most of the time.

Being employed by the senator had given her a certain degree of prominence. Her looks had gotten her amorous propositions from politicians, prominent businessmen and even a well-known black movie star. But she only had eyes for one man and now that man sat on the couch across the office. She was so engrossed in staring at him she found it difficult concentrating on the call.

"I'm sorry, ma'am," Naomi said into the telephone. "I didn't quite catch the last part."

The object of Naomi's attention was reading a copy of *Ballantine's Illustrated History of the Violent Century; War Leader Book Number 11—SKORZENY* by Charles Whiting. He was particularly absorbed with a photograph on page fifty-seven showing Benito Mussolini with a group of German SS commandos, who had just rescued the Duce from Gran Sasso in September of 1943. In the background there was a paratrooper, whom Naomi's love interest recognized. In doing so he said quietly, "Uncle Ernst."

Naomi hung up the telephone after advising the caller to write the senator in care of his Washington, D.C. office. She knew the bodyguard had said something, but she hadn't been able to hear it.

"What was that, Reggie?" She had a way of drawling her words to make them drip with honey. Some men thought it sexy. On Reggie it was wasted.

Reggie Stanton's head came up from the book and he stared across the office at Naomi with eyes that took her breath away. Stanton was a light-complexioned black man with a head of curly light brown hair and glacial bluish-gray eyes under long blond lashes. His nose and lips had a decidedly Negroid cast, which gave the face character. But those observing him always came back to the eyes. Some, like Naomi, found them sexually exciting. The majority found them terrifying.

Before he could answer, Simon Jones knocked on the window.

Naomi pressed the buzzer under her desk, which released the lock. Jones entered with water dripping from his shaved skull. He glanced briefly at Naomi before noticing Stanton. When he did, a look of fear fell over his face.

"I need to see the boss right away," Jones said to the receptionist.

"Certainly, Mr. Jones. Why don't you have a seat and I'll tell the senator you're here?"

Jones bristled. "I don't have time for this shit now. You know who I am. I'll announce myself." He started for the inner office door. Stanton's voice stopped him.

"Don't do that, Mr. Jones."

Jones halted, but did not turn to face Stanton, who had not moved from the couch. Five seconds passed and no one in the office made a sound.

"Call the senator on the intercom, Naomi, and tell him Mr. Jones is waiting to see him."

"It's urgent," Jones said.

Stanton's lips stretched making his cheeks swell slightly. This was his way of smiling, but few could tell. "Everyone who comes to see the senator has urgent business, Mr. Jones. But I'm sure Naomi will convey the imperative nature of your call to him."

However, Naomi didn't switch on the intercom until Stanton swung his eyes from Jones back to her.

"Yes?" The senator's voice cracked over the speaker.

"Mr. Jones is here to see you, sir."

"Send Simon in, Naomi."

Jones started for the door, but Stanton's voice stopped him again. "The senator's had a full day, Mr. Jones. Don't keep him long."

When the door shut behind Simon Jones, Stanton stood up. He was six feet even and weighed two hundred and ten muscular pounds. At the age of thirty-seven he possessed nineteen-inch biceps, a thirty-one-inch waist and twenty-eight-inch thighs. Naomi had often fantasized about what he looked like with his clothes off.

Stanton crossed to the front window and looked out at the rain-swept street. Carefully, his eyes examined the darkness.

"It sure is a nasty night, ain't it, Reggie?" Naomi said.

Without turning from the window he replied, "Did you smell anything when Mr. Jones came in?"

"Smell anything?" she said with confusion. "Naw. He just smelled wet to me."

Stanton was still staring out the window. He didn't comment.

"Why? Was I supposed to smell something?" she pressed.

He turned around. "How would you like to go out for drinks and a late supper with me after I get the senator home?"

"Oh, Reggie, I think that would be just delightful. I thought you'd never—"

He cut her off. "But you've got to do a couple of things for me."

"Sure."

"First, I don't want you to let anyone else into the office unless they're personally cleared by me. Now listen closely. I mean no one and that includes cops either in uniform or men flashing badges through the window and claiming they're cops. Do you understand?"

There was an urgency about him that frightened her. His voice had never risen above a conversational tone, yet something had happened to him since he went over to stare out the window. Something quite terrifying which was affecting every square foot of space in the office.

She managed a weak nod. Suddenly, the prospect of being alone with this man was no longer as attractive as it had been in her fantasies.

"Second, after I go into the senator's office I want you to ignore anything you hear from inside."

"Anything like what?" He was really scaring her now.

"Anything like Mr. Jones screaming."

Then Stanton crossed to the senator's inner door and slipped inside.

3

MARCH 4, 1994
8:55 P.M.

A ll of it," Harvey Banks said with amazement. "That would really be a coup!"

Simon Jones sat across the desk from the black United States senator. Jones was sweating profusely and breathing heavily, which added credence to the story he'd just told.

"He said he's willing to tell it all, Harv." Jones used the senator's first name because they had been teenage members of the Cook County Third Ward Young Democrats over forty years ago. "He said no cops and no reporters. Just you and me."

Harvey Banks got up from his desk and walked over to the bar. He poured half a tumbler of straight J & B scotch for Jones and a shot of Remy Martin cognac for himself. As he turned with the glasses, Jones added, "It might be good to lose that crazy bodyguard of yours while you talk to this guy."

The senator smiled as he handed Jones his drink. "Reggie's my shadow, Simon. Sometimes I even think he's capable of getting inside my head. And I've never felt such a sense of security. It's almost as if he's invincible."

"But he looks like a cop, Harv. He could queer the play with this guy."

"I am a cop, Mr. Jones. In fact, I'm with the Federal Bureau of Investigation," Stanton said from across the room. Neither the senator nor Simon Jones had heard him enter.

"C'mon, Harv!" Jones protested. "This shit is supposed to be confidential."

Harvey Banks turned and cast a questioning frown at his bodyguard. "I want to talk to Simon alone, Reggie. If you need to see me you'll have to . . . "

Banks's voice dropped, as Stanton charged across the office. His normally cold gaze had assumed arctic proportions. In horrified amazement the senator watched his bodyguard pull a dagger from his sleeve. Stanton grabbed Jones by the back of the neck and jabbed the tip of the dagger under his chin.

"What in the hell are you doing?!" the senator screamed in shock. Blood began running down Jones's neck.

"Probably saving your life, sir," Stanton snapped, twisting the dagger. "Now, Mr. Jones, you want to tell me about it?"

"I don't know what you're talking about." Jones's voice had become a high-pitched rasp.

"Reggie, stop this!" the senator demanded. "Stop this at once!"

Stanton ignored Banks and focused his attention on Jones. The bodyguard's voice was calm as he said, "This blade is eight inches of tempered steel and it's sharp enough to shave with. If you don't tell me the truth by the time I count to three, I'm going to drive it under your chin up through your brain."

Senator Banks rejected the option of physically intervening in the attack.

Stanton counted off, "One."

The senator's hands shook so violently it took him two tries to get 911.

"Two."

"Chicago Emergency, Holland."

"Three!"

With his eyes shut and sweat pouring down his face to mix with the blood running into his collar, Jones said, "Two of DeLisa's men. Butcher and Cappeletti. They're outside with guns. Want me to lure you away from here."

Banks still held the telephone in his hand. The policeman on the other end was talking. The senator dropped the receiver back on its cradle. He stared at his bodyguard and the man who had once been his best friend.

"Why are you helping them?" Stanton demanded.

Tears were now mixed with Jones's sweat and blood. "I owe DeLisa a lot of money. He threatened to kill my wife. Burn my house down. Mutilate me."

"Let him go, Reggie," Banks said quietly.

Abruptly, Stanton released Jones and stepped behind the captive's chair. The knife vanished back up the bodyguard's sleeve.

"Why didn't you come to me, Simon?" Banks said.

Jones refused to look at him. "I was afraid."

A sadness descended over United States Senator Harvey Banks. He looked at Stanton.

"Senator," the bodyguard said crisply, "you must do exactly as I say."

With one final look at Jones, Banks said, "Of course."

4

MARCH 4, 1994
9:07 P.M.

H e's taking too long," Cappeletti said. "Something's wrong."

"Banks is nobody's fool," Butcher said. "There's the chance he won't go for it at all."

The door to the storefront office opened and Jones came out followed by another man. The heavy rain made surveillance difficult, but Banks's Burberry trench coat and black fedora were easily identifiable.

The two men got into a blue Mercury with orange U.S. Senate license plates, which was parked in front of the office.

"Hold it," Cappeletti said, as Butcher reached for the gear shift lever. "Jones is driving."

"Big fucking deal," Butcher said, turning on the lights and guiding the Buick out into traffic. He drove to the cross street that would enable them to follow the Mercury.

"Didn't Mr. DeLisa say that Banks didn't like anyone to chauffeur him around?" Cappeletti said.

Butcher made the turn and stayed a block behind the Mercury. "Did you see Banks get in that car, Angie?"

"Yeah, I saw him, Charlie, but—"

"Shut the fuck up, Angie. You're starting to make my ass hurt."

Cappeletti did as he was told.

5

MARCH 4, 1994
9:10 P.M.

The Mercury traveled north on Stony Island to Seventy-first Street and turned east. The Buick followed. The Buick was forced to drop back two blocks, because of the sparse traffic on the street running beside the Illinois Central Railroad surface tracks. But with Jones driving the Mercury, Butcher wasn't concerned.

At Yates the Mercury turned left, crossed the I.C. tracks and entered the gates of the South Shore Cultural Center. After the Mercury passed under the ornate arch and disappeared onto the grounds, the Buick hesitated a moment before extinguishing its lights and following.

A colonnade led up to the main building. A parking lot was in front of this building. The Mercury was parked at the edge of the lot. When the Buick pulled up, the Mercury was empty.

"I don't like this," Cappeletti said.

"Relax, Angie. Jones is following the plan right to the letter." Butcher reached under the front seat and removed the Uzi. Checking the load he added, "Let's go kill us a senator."

They left the Buick and crossed the dark parking lot. The rain had stopped and the temperature was dropping. Cappeletti shivered as he walked beside his confidently sauntering companion. They entered the clubhouse. The shadows of the cavernous lobby loomed over them as they raised their weapons and listened for any movement or voices in the building. In the main corridor they flattened themselves against the wall. Jones was supposed to lure the senator into the south ballroom. In tandem Butcher and Cappeletti began moving in that direction.

The double doors at the ballroom entrance stood open. The room itself had been cleared and the wooden floor gleamed even in the dim lighting from the overhead night lights. The stage was at the opposite end of the ballroom. Butcher and Cappeletti both saw the man in the chair at the same time.

It was too dark for them to identify him. They exchanged wary glances.

The plan was for Jones to entice Banks to the cultural center on the pretext of meeting with an informant high up in the DeLisa crime family. The informant had not been identified, but, as the story went, had agreed to testify before Banks's Senate Rackets Committee. The catch—he would only talk to the senator in an isolated location like the deserted cultural center. And, only if the senator came alone with Simon Jones.

Now the assassins could only see the lone man on the stage. There should have been at least two men present: Jones and Banks.

Cappeletti wanted to run. He whispered to Butcher, "Let's get out of here."

The heavyset killer motioned for Angie to shut up and follow him toward the stage.

They crossed the ballroom. At the stage, they found the man's back to them making it impossible to see his face from the dance floor. They split up. Going to the stairs at each side of the stage, they ascended. At the top they carefully approached from opposite sides. With guns leveled they came up on him together.

"What the hell!" Cappeletti blurted out when he looked into the terrified face of Simon Jones. The chair-back had obscured his wrists and they could see now that he had been bound and gagged. Now the stench of fear about him was so great it made Cappeletti gag. Then Butcher died.

The dagger was thrown from the shadows of the stage striking Butcher in the throat. The eight-inch blade reduced his screams to a bloody gurgle and the assassin toppled off the stage, crashing onto the ballroom floor.

Terrified, Cappeletti emptied his Uzi into the shadows. The magazine expended, he pulled a snub-nosed revolver from his waist band and jumped to the ballroom floor. He ignored Jones's grunted pleas for help. He also ignored Butcher's dead body as he sprinted toward the exit.

As Cappeletti ran he glimpsed a hulking shadow leap from the wings of the stage and start after him. The little man stopped at the ballroom entrance, turned and wildly fired three shots back at his pursuer. The shadow dropped and rolled across the floor. Cappeletti fired his last three bullets. His heart constricted when he saw the black silhouette jump back up and start after him again.

Cappeletti raced for the doors leading back to the parking lot. He ran faster than he'd ever run in his life, but could feel his pursuer gaining on him. He reached the doors and was about to fling them open when a terrible pain exploded in his back.

He pitched forward and struck his head on one of the glass door panes. The glass splintered, tearing open the skin of his forehead and cheek. As he fell, blood cascaded across his face; however, the pain in his back wiped out all other sensation.

Cappeletti was lying on his face in the vestibule of the South Shore Cultural Center. He reached around attempting to grasp the source of the pain freezing his body rigid. He touched the hilt of a knife. A knife that had penetrated six inches into his back through the left shoulder blade. A hand reached down to help him.

The blade made a soft sucking noise as it was pulled from Cappeletti's back. It was a great deal more painful coming out than it had been going in. He screamed.

A large, but amazingly gentle hand turned him over. Feeling his own blood pooling beneath him, Cappeletti looked up at the massive figure, clad all in black, standing over him. The face was covered by a hooded mask with only the eyes visible. The wounded man could tell, even in the dim light, that the eyes were light. Either blue or gray.

The man behind the mask spoke. The voice was flat and emotionless. "I aimed for your heart. I missed. I didn't want to cause you any more pain than was necessary. I hope you understand."

Staring up into his assailant's eyes, Angie Cappeletti nodded. Then the man in the black mask stabbed downwards slicing through flesh and the bones of Cappeletti's ribs. When the dagger pierced his heart, the would-be assassin died.

6

MARCH 4, 1994
11:15 P.M.

Rachel DeLisa was in bed, reading. The book was Hemingway's *The Sun Also Rises,* which was required for her third year literature course at the University of Illinois at Chicago. At twenty-five Rachel considered herself old to be an undergraduate, but then this was her third college and there had been a four-year hiatus between her last school and the U. of I.

Rachel had a heart-shaped face framed by a short haircut, which was almost boyish. Her dark eyes and full lashes were inherited from her mother, who had died under mysterious circumstances when she was ten. Rachel was pretty and had a way of smiling that would light up her face with an aura that made her beautiful. She had rounded into full-blown womanhood at the age of nineteen; however, lately she had lost too much weight.

Rachel's mind began drifting from the Hemingway prose written in 1926. Automatically, she thought of Bobby. She wondered if he still thought about her? If he still loved her or whether her father's interference in their lives had turned his love to hate?

She put the book down and slipped her feet into the fluffy house shoes beside her bed. The slippers were pink, very feminine and a perfect match for the pink full-length gown she wore. Her father had given her the entire sleeping outfit for Christmas. She hated it.

Rachel's bedroom was on the second floor of Antonio DeLisa's Oak Park mansion. The room was located in the east wing and had its own bathroom and balcony that overlooked the garden. It was a large room with big closets that held clothes, shoes and accessories that were mostly new and had cost a king's ransom. Since she had been returned here she had yet to wear everything the man she still managed to call "Papa" had bought her. At times, which came more frequently of late, she had considered starting a fire with the Louis Vuittons and Georgio Armanis just to hurt Papa. To hurt him because she knew she could.

Now Rachel discarded thoughts of arson and opened a closet. There, in one corner crowded by the newer stuff purchased from I. Magnin and Saks Fifth Avenue, were some of her old things. The clothing that had been in her suitcase when Charlie Butcher and that ugly little man named Angie had trapped her and Bobby in Boston.

She found her purse. It was a big, leather shoulder bag. Rachel had lived out of it many times during the two years she and Bobby had been on the run from Papa. The purse was deep and had lots of compartments. She searched inside until she found the small photograph. Carefully, she pulled it out.

It was a black and white picture of her and Bobby. They were standing on a dock with the ocean behind them. It was a windy day and Bobby's black curls and her straight dark brown hair blew off their foreheads. It was sunny and they were laughing into the camera. Tears sprung to her eyes as the memory of that long-ago happy day returned.

She sank to her knees on the floor of the walk-in closet and blinked until her vision cleared. She stared at Bobby's face in the grainy photo. He was so skinny, yet he had been so strong for her when she needed him. He had been there through it all. He had been there until . . .

Shouts from outside tore her from the memories. Carefully she returned the picture to its hiding place. If Papa found it he would destroy the photograph the same way he'd destroyed everything else she had with Bobby.

She reached the window in time to see Arthur Maggio, Papa's

assistant, running down the driveway with one of the bodyguards. They were heading for the front gate. Through the wrought-iron fence she could see a dark car parked on the street. They were running toward it. The idea came to her in an instant. Maggio and the rest of them looked confused. Maybe even frightened. Papa did that to people. Something was going on out there. This could be her chance!

Rachel moved as fast as she had ever done in her life and she'd had lots of practice when she was with Bobby. She was out of the night gown and into panties and a brassiere in seconds. Sweat socks replaced the hated furry slippers. Jeans and a turtleneck went on along with a pair of worn running shoes. She snatched her suede jacket from the closet. It was a gift from Papa, but it was fur-lined and she didn't know how long she'd be outside before she could find shelter. Her wallet went into a jacket pocket. Papa's credit cards would be useless, but she had plenty of cash. She dashed to the closet and retrieved Bobby's picture from her old bag. As she carefully stuffed it into her wallet, she vowed she would find him. Then she was ready to go. The quick change had taken less than a minute.

She went to the door of her room and opened it a crack. A peep outside revealed an empty corridor. She could hear angry voices coming from downstairs. She slipped out and silently shut the door behind her.

She moved carefully to the edge of the balcony railing and looked down the spiral staircase. She was directly above the front entrance to the mansion. One of the bodyguards, whom she didn't know, was talking on the telephone in the alcove. Papa had telephones all over the house. Even in the toilets.

"Jeez, Wally, we got problems here. Big problems."

A terrible depression settled over Rachel. The only way she could escape was across the entrance alcove where the man on the telephone now stood. Then she remembered the time Butcher had cornered her and Bobby in that motel in Westport, Connecticut. She had felt the exact same despair that she did now and Bobby had turned to her, winked and said, "Don't worry, sweetheart. This will be a piece of cake."

"Piece of cake," she whispered to herself. But although comforting, the words did nothing to help her current situation. Then Arthur Maggio came back into the house.

Maggio was a tall, gaunt man with graying hair and the expression of a perpetual worrier. From her second floor perch Rachel was able to see that his face was drawn and he looked close to shedding actual tears.

"Is that Vegas?!" Maggio snapped at the bodyguard.

Papa was in Las Vegas. He'd left yesterday.

"Yes, sir. It's Wally Boykin. He's with the boss in the Coronado Casino."

Maggio walked over to the bodyguard and snatched the phone from his hand. "Wally, this is Art Maggio. I need to talk to the boss right away." Maggio listened for a moment and then said, "Goddamnit, I don't care how much money he's winning. I need to talk to him right now. And get him away from that table to take the call in private. Do you understand me?" There was another long pause. "Yeah, I'll be right by the phone."

Rachel watched Maggio hang up.

"I'll take Mr. DeLisa's call in the study," he said to the bodyguard.

"What do you think happened, Mr. Maggio?"

Rachel was able to see Maggio through the bannister railing. His shoulders were slumped and he looked to have aged ten years. Slowly, he shook his head. "They were on a job for the boss. Something went very wrong."

The phone in the study rang.

Rachel watched Maggio turn and run toward the study door. She held her breath and then exhaled slowly when the bodyguard followed.

She slipped over the top step and peered across the alcove. The study door was open. Maggio stood at her father's desk on the other side of a room lined with books her Papa had never read. The mob assistant had the telephone to his ear. His left profile was to Rachel as he stared through the patio windows out at the garden. The bodyguard took up a position just inside the study doors. His back was to her.

Maggio's voice carried. "Yeah, Wally, I'm here. Okay, I'll hold."
Maggio began bouncing up and down like he'd caught some
form of nerve disease or had to make an urgent trip to the toilet.
"Wally says the boss is winning big at the poker table. I sure hate to
spoil his evening with this shit."

As Papa's assistant settled in to wait, Rachel slipped down the
stairs.

Las Vegas, Nevada   7

MARCH 4, 1994
9:15 P.M.

Antonio "Tuxedo Tony" DeLisa sat at a poker table in the
Coronado Hilton Casino on the strip in Las Vegas. The
Coronado was new, having opened that past October, and DeLisa
owned a piece of it through a legitimate investment firm in Chicago.
So far he'd won twelve thousand dollars. But it wasn't winning the
money Tuxedo Tony was enjoying so much; it was the action.

They were playing seven card stud with no limit. There were five
players surrounding the dealer. To Tuxedo Tony's right there was a
Texas real estate tycoon, who wore a Stetson and talked like a refu-
gee from a *Hee Haw* convention. The Texan had dropped close to
five thousand dollars in the past hour and was still losing. Seated
beside him was a seventy-year-old professional gambler from Reno
who had dropped a grand and was waiting for Tony to make a mistake. Next was an aging television actress, who had been featured in
a couple of series over the years. She was behind about three thousand it didn't look like she could afford. Last, at the end of the table
to Tony's left, was a black professional football player, who, as a
running back for a West Coast team, made three million dollars a
year. He had yet to win a hand and was about seven thousand dollars in the hole.

Tuxedo Tony had won his best hands when the football player

called to the last card. Luck had been with Tony tonight, but the football player handled his cards like an amateur and was slugging down the complimentary cocktails as fast as the waitresses could bring them. In Tony's estimation, this was his biggest mistake. When you gambled you didn't drink. That was as much a law of the game as never attempting to draw to an inside straight.

The hand was coming to a close. Tony's seventh card was flipped to him face down by the dealer. He didn't even look at it as he placed his bet. "A grand in the dark."

"The bet is a thousand dollars," the dealer said.

Most of them promptly folded. The gambler took a moment to study his cards. The football player called immediately.

Finally, the gambler reached for a stack of hundred-dollar chips. DeLisa's heart soared; however, his face remained expressionless.

Antonio "Tuxedo Tony" DeLisa was not necessarily a handsome man. He was instead what could be called striking. He was of average height and weighed a slim one hundred and sixty pounds, which he kept under rigid control with lots of racquetball in the winter and tennis in the summer. At the age of sixty-one his once thick black hair was shot with gray, and his sideburns, all the way to his temples, were pure white. His features were those of a peasant, but the eyes possessed an X-ray intense, compelling quality that could make strong men's knees go weak and beautiful women's hearts beat faster.

He had obtained the name "Tuxedo Tony" from his penchant for always wearing either a black tuxedo with bow tie and cummerbund, or a black suit, white shirt and black tie after five o'clock in the evening. Now, at the Las Vegas poker table, he was wearing his trademark tuxedo.

DeLisa was many things: gambler, father and successful businessman. But most of all Tuxedo Tony was a killer. He had gotten where he was in the underworld hierarchy of the United States by murder and he planned to stay there by committing or ordering more murders. Even the murder of a United States senator.

DeLisa never figured out why Harvey Banks had decided to come after him. His illegal enterprises—whores, gambling and a bit of loan-sharking—were victimless crimes in DeLisa's estimation, whereas down there in the black ghetto, where Banks came from, the dope and poverty fed real crime. Violent crime.

At another time in history DeLisa would have made a contribution to the senator's private campaign fund. The one that didn't get disclosed. But the senator was supposedly fanatically honest. Wouldn't take a quarter from a blind man. As DeLisa saw it, a fatal flaw.

DeLisa couldn't afford to let Banks convene his crime committee. Yes, there were other senators, but then they might take a different approach. A few might even be persuaded to leave DeLisa's name totally out of it. That is for the right contribution to the right campaign fund.

"The pot is right, Mr. DeLisa," the dealer said. "Turn up."

Tony snapped out of his reverie. "Aces full," he said, turning over the two black aces he'd been dealt as the first two cards of the hand to go along with the ace of hearts and pair of jacks he had showing. With a supreme enjoyment that he never revealed in his face, Tony watched the gambler's shoulders sag. He had a king-high full house, but that would do him little good now. Tuxedo Tony reached for the pot just as his bodyguard and companion Wally Boykin stepped up beside him and said, "Excuse me, boss."

"Yeah, do excuse me, boss," the football player said, flipping over his hole cards to reveal three fives which went with the fourth five he had keeping company face up with a six, seven and nine of different suits. "I don't think your full house beats my four of a kind."

"Hot damn!" the Texan roared.

"Well, it's about time," the television actress said, shooting a mocking look at DeLisa.

Even the Reno gambler smiled.

The football player began raking in chips. "Goddamn," he said as Tony looked on with outer passivity. "This is almost as good as winning the Super Bowl!" With that he flipped the dealer a five-hundred-dollar gold chip.

"Boss," Wally said, carefully, "you got an urgent call from Chicago."

Gracefully, DeLisa got up from the table leaving his chips in

place. He said an almost cordial, "Deal around me. I'll be right
back."

As the mobster turned to go, the football player called after him,
"Come on back real soon, my man. I think this is gonna be the start
of something big."

"Fucking idiot!" DeLisa whispered so that only Wally could
hear him, as they crossed to the casino manager's office.

Chicago, Illinois   **8**

MARCH 4, 1994
11:22 P.M.

Arthur Maggio's palm was sweating making the phone slippery
in his grasp. He flinched when DeLisa's voice came over the
line, *"What is it, Art?"*

"The shipment of glass crystal you had imported from France
arrived damaged, sir."

A strained silence ensued from the Las Vegas end. Maggio
closed his eyes as the acid in his stomach bubbled up, causing a
sharp pain below his breast bone.

"Was the shipment intact or were there items missing?"

Maggio frowned. This was going to be the hard part. The code
utilized so far on the open telephone line told DeLisa that Butcher
and Cappeletti were dead. Now Maggio had to tell the boss that
they had failed to make the hit on the senator as well and that their
dead bodies had been deposited on the street in front of DeLisa's
Oak Park mansion. Even in code Maggio did not relish the task, as
Tony DeLisa was not a man who accepted bad news gracefully.

It was as Arthur Maggio was composing his thoughts into
DeLisa's code that he caught movement out of the corner of his
right eye and turned out of curiosity to see what had caused it.
When he saw Rachel DeLisa sneaking out the front door his emo-

tions ran to stark fear. Maggio knew that losing Rachel, behind the failure of Butcher and Cappeletti to make the hit on the senator, would issue his death warrant.

"I'll have to call you back, Mr. DeLisa," Maggio said urgently. Before the man in Las Vegas could reply, Maggio hung up. He spun on the curious bodyguard still standing at the study entrance. "Rachel just went out the front door. Get her."

The bodyguard ran toward the door. When he reached it he yanked a walkie-talkie from a holster beneath his suit coat. As Maggio watched him go, the telephone in the study began ringing. The mob assistant knew DeLisa was calling back. The Tuxedo would be pissed, but then he would be insane with anger if Rachel escaped again. Maggio ignored the ringing.

For one brief instant Rachel thought she would make it. When she stepped outside, the cold air of the early March night made her hopes soar. Since they had brought her back from Boston, she had never gotten this far alone. Now she was free of the mansion; however, she was still on the grounds.

The gate at the end of the driveway stood open. This was such a surprise that she momentarily rejected going that way. She had learned to disregard such obvious gifts while she was with Bobby. It was too inviting. It had to be a trap.

Conflicting thoughts raged through her mind. The gate was never left open unattended like this, yet they couldn't have known that she was out of her room. Rachel's hesitation was her downfall.

She heard the scratchy, blurted transmission from a walkie-talkie coming from the north end of the house. As she turned to look back at the open gate she saw movement behind the illumination of a flashlight coming fast from the south end of the grounds. She sprinted for the open gate.

It was forty-five yards down the sloping driveway. She was fast in her running shoes, but she could hear the pounding of heavier, faster feet behind her. Despair settled in like a terminal disease. Then the words "piece of cake" echoed through her brain. Like a chanted litany, she began repeating them as she ran.

"Piece of cake . . . piece of cake . . . piece of cake . . ."

The open gate loomed before her and then she was through it out onto the curving, tree-lined street on which Papa's house and her prison were located. The sounds of her pursuers drew nearer, but she had reached a milestone. She was off the grounds.

A giddy exhilaration ran through her. She felt that at this moment she could have sprinted ten miles. Then the ecstasy of her momentary freedom was dashed. One of the dark-suited, stone-faced guards stood on the sidewalk directly in her path. She could almost feel the touch of the one coming up behind her. She tried to veer out into the street, but there was a car parked at the curb blocking her way. With one last burst to reach freedom, she swung toward the car. Then she was grabbed from behind.

Rachel lost her balance and carried her pursuer with her across the pavement and narrow parkway to the passenger side front door of the Buick. They bounced harmlessly against it. She was unable to see the man holding her, but realized instantly that her strength was no match for his. She didn't try to put up a struggle as he held her fast. The "piece of cake" saying died on her lips. It was at that instant that she noticed the bodies inside the car.

They were both sitting upright; Charlie Butcher, whom she hated the most, and the evil Angie Cappeletti. There was blood all over them. A great deal of blood. So much that she knew there was no way they could be alive.

"C'mon, Miss DeLisa," whoever was holding her said. "We've got to go back to the house." He began pulling her gently in that direction.

Rachel resisted. She wanted to look at the men in the car a little longer. There was a note pinned to Butcher's chest. It was printed in black ink on plain white paper. It read, NEXT TIME THIS WILL BE YOU, DELISA.

Rachel began to laugh. Now she was surrounded by four bodyguards and Arthur Maggio. The nearest house on this suburban street was a hundred and fifty yards away. Her laughter was so shrill it easily carried the distance, causing lights to go on at this late hour.

"Get her back inside the house!" Maggio ordered.

A bodyguard controlled each arm as they began forcing her back through the open gate. She was still laughing so hard that tears ran down her cheeks. She kept twisting to look back at the carnage in the Buick. She shouted at the unhearing corpses, "I hope it will be you, Papa! I hope it will be you real soon, Papa!"

Las Vegas, Nevada   **9**

MARCH 4, 1994
9:31 P.M.

Tony DeLisa slammed the telephone back on its cradle after dialing his home for the fifth time and getting nothing but continuous, unanswered ringing. He glared at Wally Boykin. "Something's wrong. The hit went sour. Butcher and Cappeletti are dead. Maggio hung up before he could give it all to me."

The phone ringing made DeLisa jump. He snatched it up. "Yeah?" It was Maggio.

While DeLisa listened to the conclusion of the coded message his face darkened with anger. Boykin was nearly twice as big and half the age of DeLisa, but he looked nervously around the casino manager's office. They were alone. This was none of the manager's business, but Boykin knew it was dangerous being around the Tuxedo when he was angry. Extremely dangerous.

Slowly, DeLisa replaced the telephone. Boykin had never seen him look like this before. He had the expression a night club comic had once described as that of a walking dead man. A man who had been transformed into an emotionless slab of stone with eyes that held the look of death.

DeLisa stood by the phone for a long time. Then he said in a near whisper, "Wally, fix me a drink."

"Yes, sir." The bodyguard leaped to do his master's bidding from the fully-stocked bar running along one wall of the office. "Bourbon on the rocks, boss?"

Tuxedo Tony nodded as he walked around behind the manager's desk and sat down. When Boykin handed him the drink DeLisa sipped it slowly and stared blankly off into space.

Boykin stood by silently waiting with no little degree of anxiety for DeLisa to signal what was on his mind. Finally, Tuxedo Tony said, "Sometimes you got to cut your losses and deal yourself out so you can play again tomorrow, Wally. A new deal at a fresh table can do wonders for that elusive bitch they call Luck."

"Yes, sir," Boykin said obediently. He breathed an inner sigh of relief. The worst was over.

"But the one thing you need more than anything else is someone who is a master at the game."

"Yes, sir."

DeLisa looked up at the bodyguard. "What we need is someone they call 'the Mastermind' to take care of our little problem back in Chicago, Wally."

Wally Boykin was not a moron, but he possessed a low I.Q., which was complicated by little more than a grammar school education. So he wasn't following his boss very well with this "Mastermind" thing. But Antonio "Tuxedo Tony" DeLisa had no such problem. No such problem at all.

London, England   **10**

MARCH 5, 1994
4:00 A.M.

In Room 521 of the Dorchester Hotel, Karl Steiger was packing. The phone rang. He dropped a stack of monogrammed dress shirts on the bed and went to answer it.

"Mr. Steiger," the operator said, *"your call to Monte Carlo can be put through now."*

"Thank you." Steiger's English held just the faintest hint of a German accent.

The phone began ringing at the other end. On the fourth ring a laughing female answered. *"What do you want?"* she slurred drunkenly in French.

"Is this Ernest Steiger's room?" the man in London inquired keeping his voice rigidly under control.

"Ernie, it's for you!"

She dropped the receiver on a hard surface. The loud bang made Steiger jerk the phone away from his ear. "Stupid bitch!" he hissed.

He waited nearly five minutes for his son to come to the phone. It was obvious Ernest was drunk. *"Who the fuck is this?"*

"This is your father, Ernest."

An awkward silence ensued. In the background Karl could hear the raucous sounds of a drunken party. He mentally kicked himself for letting Ernest go off alone.

"Hi, Daddy," Ernest sounded like a little boy who had been caught with his hand in the cookie jar. *"What's up?"*

Karl's jaw muscles rippled, as he fought to control his anger. "You're supposed to meet me in New York later today, or have you forgotten?"

"I'll be there, Daddy. They're just giving me a little going away party here."

There was a knock on Karl Steiger's hotel room door. He snapped his head around and his face contorted in a questioning frown. No one should be calling on him at this hour. At least no legitimate caller.

"Now listen to me, Ernest. I want you to get rid of the women and the booze, get yourself something to eat and catch the next plane to New York. Do you understand me?"

The knock came again. This time with the heavy, knuckle-bruising insistence of the policeman demanding entry. Karl Steiger knew that the police did not come calling in the middle of the night. At least not in England.

"I—" The phone was yanked from Ernest's hand.

The drunk French girl spluttered, *"Leave him alone, Daddy! I'm not through with him yet."*

Ernest managed to retrieve the phone. *"I'll be on the next plane as you instructed, sir."*

"Good!" Karl Steiger slammed the receiver down. He was so angry he trembled.

The knocking was becoming so heavy and insistent the entire door shook. Karl forgot about the incongruity of his thirty-two-year-old son reporting to him as if he were still a child and crossed the room to answer the door. As he did he slipped on his suit jacket to conceal the eight-inch dagger in its specially-made sleeve holster.

Inspector Marks and Sergeant Hastings of Scotland Yard stood out in the hall.

"Didn't mean to wake you, governor," Marks said. "But the chief superintendent told us to make sure we was on time to give you a ride to Heathrow."

Steiger looked from the painfully thin Marks to the brutally-mashed features of ex-pug Hastings. He could smell liquor on them. There had been no arrangements made with Chief Superintendent Gordon Edwards of Scotland Yard to provide him with transportation. In fact, Steiger would have refused any such offer. So Marks and Hastings had come looking for trouble. The anger at his son's weakness and stupidity still coursed through him. Maybe this was exactly what he needed.

"That was very considerate of Herr Superintendent Edwards," Steiger said, deepening his accent. "I was just packing. Won't you come in?"

Steiger stepped back and held the door for them.

Inspector Marks sat down in an easy chair. Sergeant Hastings walked over and stood beside the window overlooking the foggy London street below.

"May I get you officers something to drink? Perhaps a cognac?"

"No schnapps, governor?" Marks said. "Or some good Bavarian lager?"

"Ach," Steiger threw up his hands in a gesture he hoped would be sufficiently German for them. "I am sorry to say I have neither, but there is a bottle of Remy Martin. May I do the honors?"

Hastings came off the wall.

"I'll do it, governor. You continue packing. Wouldn't want you to miss your plane."

A look passed between them which Steiger understood all too well. They had no intention of taking him to any airport. He touched his sleeve. The steel beneath the soft fabric made him smile. He forced the smile into a full grin, as he clicked his heels together and bowed.

"Of course. I submit to the efficiency and promptness of the great Scotland Yard."

"Hell, you should," the sergeant said. "You made us look like bleeding amateurs, you did."

Marks shot Hastings a warning glance. But the man with the putty-shaped features had much more to say. Feigning ignorance, Steiger resumed packing. He never turned his back on them.

"Tell me something, governor," Hastings was pouring cognac into two glasses on the sideboard. "How'd you do it?"

"C'mon, Harry," Marks said, accepting a glass from his partner. "You don't expect a mastermind like the governor here to tell us his trade secrets. That is what they call you isn't it? The Mastermind?"

Their goading was making his disguise of stupidity wear thin, but Steiger was an excellent actor. "They have called me many names during my career, Herr Inspector. Baron, Mastermind, Fritz, Kraut, even Little Adolph. Names never meant much to me. It's the money that counts." This was a lie. His good name and reputation meant more to him than any sum of money. He planned to prove this to these arrogant limey bastards before the sun came up.

At the words "Fritz" and "Kraut" the policemen laughed. Hastings said, "You've got to admit that you do look like an all-German German, governor. I mean you're the spitting image of what old Adolph Hitler called a true Aryan. Blond hair, blue eyes, tall, broad shoulders. Maybe a little heavy in the middle, but who am I to talk." Hastings patted the gut visible under his trench coat.

"His eyes ain't blue, Harry," Marks said. "They're more gray than anything else. Kind of a mixture of colors."

Hastings drained off his cognac. "You'd better wear a coat, governor. It's damp out. We wouldn't want you catching cold."

"Of course," Steiger said, going to the closet. "How very thoughtful of you, Sergeant."

Steiger retrieved his lead-weighted sap from the shelf and slipped it into his trench coat pocket. He stepped back into the room and faced them. He raised his hands to his shoulders once more and said, "Now, I am ready." They didn't notice that his eyes actually sparkled with an icy coldness when he stared at them.

They were in a Ford sedan cruising through the pre-dawn London streets. The instant they left the hotel, Steiger realized they were heading in the opposite direction from the airport. From this point he would play it by ear as to how far he planned to let this charade go.

"So, governor," Hastings was becoming increasingly belligerent. "How'd you do it?"

"Do what?" Steiger said innocently.

Hastings was seated in the back seat behind Steiger. Marks drove. Now the heavy-handed sergeant sat forward and grabbed the back of the German's neck. His fingers dug into the muscles, making Steiger go rigid. Steiger could smell the booze on the policeman's breath as he said, "You know I lost me mum, two uncles, an aunt and me grandpap during the Blitz. As far back as I could remember, I hated anything German. Hell, I can't even stomach the sight of German chocolate cake." To emphasize his words he tightened his grip.

Marks laughed. "Oh, Harry's mad now, governor. You'd better tell him what he wants to know. I seen him snap a bloke's neck with just a twist of one of those mitts of his."

But Karl Steiger did not answer immediately. Instead he focused on the pain just as Uncle Ernst had taught him. He did not fight nor surrender to it. Instead he fed on it allowing the discomfort to nurture his anger to a white-hot intensity. He looked at the street they were passing through. It was deserted and curtained by fog. It was also in the type of neighborhood where screams in the night were ignored.

"I asked you a question, governor." Hastings was attempting to shake Steiger's head like a bull terrier with a rag doll.

"Ease up, Harry," Marks cautioned. "You might be hurting him so bad he can't talk."

Steiger spoke slowly and distinctly. "Fuck you, you drunken, limey bastard!" Then he reached up and grabbed the thumb the policeman had gouged into the muscle on the left side of his neck. With one quick jerk he dislocated it at the joint.

Hastings's howl of pain made Marks slam on the brakes. He spun toward them just as Steiger, still holding the sergeant's damaged thumb, sapped him across the side of his skull. Marks joined his partner in oblivion.

Marks's foot remained on the brake, keeping the car stationary. As a precaution Steiger reached over and slammed the gear shift lever into park. He got out of the car massaging his sore neck. He rotated his head a couple of times to get the circulation going again.

He looked in at the two unconscious policemen. "How'd you do it?" Steiger said, repeating the question Hastings had asked him. Specifically, how had he obtained the release of Lord Rutherford, the kidnapped English banker, without the exorbitantly high ransom being paid or not one hair on the old aristocrat's head being harmed? It had not been easy for him. Marks and Hastings were assigned to the case, but, despite their cop training and experience, had screwed things up from the start. Their mistakes had complicated matters.

The decision now was what to do with Marks and Hastings. Karl decided to use one of Uncle Ernst's favorite methods, but, since Marks and Hastings were English he would vary it slightly.

As he worked, he thought about the case that had brought him to England. Lord Ian Fitzhugh Harcourt Rutherford IV—nobleman, banker and member of one of the oldest houses in England. Could trace his genealogy all the way back to William the Conqueror. Snatched off the street in broad daylight by two men in dark clothing and stocking masks. A third masked man had driven the getaway car, which was a small white van.

Steiger parked the police car across the street from the New

Scotland Yard complex. He shut off the engine and left the ignition key in the "on" position. Glancing once at his still unconscious charges in the back seat, he started to get out of the car when he noticed the haphazard angle of the sergeant's dislocated thumb. Reaching across the seat he grabbed the injured appendage and snapped it back in place. The policeman never stirred.

After turning on the left directional signal, Steiger got out and retrieved his bags from the boot. He walked off into the thick fog. He found a cruising taxi in less than a minute and gave Heathrow Airport as his destination.

At 5 A.M. a pair of constables, returning to Scotland Yard, noticed the Ford parked with its left turn signal blinking slowly. They crossed the street to investigate and found Marks and Hastings naked, bound and gagged in the back seat.

11

MARCH 5, 1994
8:20 A.M.

It's all over the Yard, Chief Superintendent," Chief Inspector Thomas Wainwright said angrily as he briefed Gordon Edwards. "Marks and Hastings claim they were jumped by four men outside an East End pub. They do have some signs of being knocked around a bit and Hastings has a swollen hand, but somehow I don't buy it."

Gordon Edwards was sixty-seven years old, balding, nearsighted, stooped and arthritic. He walked with a cane, never allowed more than one piece of paper on his desk at a time and generally sat in a slouch with his chin on his chest and his eyes closed, making him appear to be asleep. But those who knew the Chief Superintendent realized after only a few brief dealings with him that he had one of the most astute minds in the field of international law enforcement and that his memory was phenomenal.

"Four men? Masks? An East End pub? I don't think so, Wainwright. Something else happened to them. They made up that story as a blind."

"Then I'll throw the book at them!" Wainwright's face flushed with anger providing a sharp contrast to the charcoal gray of his elegantly tailored suit. "False reports, neglect of duty, drinking and the lot! They'll wish they never heard of Scotland Yard!"

Edwards looked up at the chief inspector from beneath bushy eyebrows. Wainwright was not a true policeman in Superintendent Edwards's estimation, but rather one of the new breed of bookish types who had come to Scotland Yard by way of Exeter and Oxford. Never made a good arrest, but could make a computer program sing. Wouldn't know how to properly interrogate a tough suspect, but could quote the breakdown of next year's budget for criminal investigations off the top of his head. In short, a good man to have around to keep the paper flowing, but absolutely worthless as a cop.

Chief Superintendent Edwards cleared his throat noisily and allowed his eyebrows to droop again. "I wouldn't be too hard on Marks and Hastings, Wainwright. The embarrassment of being found tied together in the buff outside the Yard should be sufficient punishment for them. It's likely they ran afoul of Karl Steiger."

"The consultant? What has he got to do with this?"

Gordon Edwards sighed. Wainwright was a good man in his way, but at times he could be terribly tiring. Now was one of those times.

"Sit down, Chief Inspector. We really need to talk."

Unsure of himself, Wainwright took the chair across from Edwards.

The chief superintendent busied himself filling and lighting a worn pipe with a specially prepared shag tobacco. When he had it going and smoke filled the office, making Wainwright cough, Edwards began.

"Karl Steiger is not a consultant, as you called him. He would more appropriately be termed a hired gun, as those American Westerns so aptly label their bad guys. He hires out to the top bidder and guarantees his work. In the years I've known or more appropriately been aware of him, he's worked for Interpol, La Cosa Nostra, the

Surete', the K.G.B., the F.B.I. and the C.I.A., not to mention a host
of other organizations and individuals with the interest and money
to pay his freight."

"A bloody mercenary," Wainwright said, frowning as if the
words put a bad taste in his mouth. "I didn't think the Yard dealt
with such scum."

Wainwright was being insufferable, but then Edwards realized
the chief inspector couldn't help it. The chief superintendent spun
his chair around to look out the window. It was raining heavily,
streaking the windows with streams of water. Edwards smoked and
continued to stare through the glass as he spoke.

"Karl Steiger is not a mercenary, Wainwright. He would be considered more of an organizer or fixer in the most basic terms. He's
called the Mastermind. A brain who knows how to plan operations
with military precision. The nephew of Hauptman Ernst von Steiger
of the Nazi SS. The uncle was a highly-decorated paratrooper with
Otto Skorzeny's outfit that kidnapped Mussolini from Gran Sasso
in Italy in nineteen forty-three. Skorzeny, with Steiger's help,
planned additional kidnappings and other acts of mayhem in a
guerrilla warfare, commando raid fashion during the war. Steiger
was on Skorzeny's planning staff for the Battle of the Bulge infiltra-
tion of German troops in American uniforms behind Allied lines.
After the war Hauptman Steiger was branded a war criminal. He
escaped but was captured in the United States sometime in the late
seventies. He escaped again under mysterious circumstances. I
heard at the time that the F.B.I. could have been involved."

Edwards turned back to face Wainwright. He expected the chief
inspector to be bored silly by tales of a half-century-old war. But the
younger man was listening closely.

"The von Steigers were Prussian aristocrats with a long history
of military service. Junkers they were called. The von Steigers had at
least one member on the general staff of the Prussian Army going
back to the Napoleonic Wars. Not much of an estate to speak of, so
the men kept joining the army and becoming officers. Turned the
strategy of warfare into an art."

"But how does Steiger tie in with the Rutherford Affair?" Wainwright asked.

Edwards puffed pipe smoke into the stale air of his office. "It was actually my idea. We were getting nowhere fast finding Lord Rutherford. We needed someone who would know not only where to look, but who to look for, as far as the kidnapers went."

"It sounds like this Steiger has criminal contacts."

Edwards's bushy eyebrows arched briefly before drooping again. "In his business there's no other way to operate. You see, it's not who you are or what you stand for that interests a man like Karl Steiger. And it has nothing to do with the money he's paid. At least not primarily. It's more of the job, the task, the challenge he faces in planning a strategy and then carrying it out to a successful conclusion. That's what he's so damned good at."

"He sounds like a very dangerous man to me, sir."

Edwards took the pipe from his mouth and stared up at the ceiling. "Back during the war, Otto Skorzeny, undoubtedly with no little help from Ernst von Steiger, reportedly planned a commando mission to kidnap General Eisenhower from SHAEF H.Q. in Paris. The Allies took the threat so seriously they virtually placed the commanding general under house arrest.

"At that point in history some intelligence officer, staff aide, or possibly even a journalist labeled Otto Skorzeny the most dangerous man alive. Now, Chief Inspector, I would say that alias belongs to Ernst von Steiger's nephew Karl."

Chicago, Illinois **12**

MARCH 5, 1994
9:15 A.M.

Y ou can go in now, Commander," the pretty blonde detective seated outside the chief's office said.

Larry Cole put down his Styrofoam coffee cup and stood up. He was in the reception area inside the Detective Division offices on the fifth floor of Chicago Police Headquarters. The commander was six feet one inch tall and weighed two hundred pounds. His curly hair was graying slightly at the temples, but in his late thirties he was still trim and handsome.

Cole crossed to the door marked CHIEF OF THE DETECTIVE DIVISION and knocked. A voice from inside called, "Come in."

Larry Cole had been inside the chief of detectives' office many times during his twenty-two years as a cop, but never while its current occupant had been in residence. Now, Jack Govich looked up from behind his desk and smiled.

"How's it going, Larry?" Govich said standing up and walking around his desk with his hand extended. "You're looking good."

Cole was slightly surprised by the openness of the chief's greeting; however, he took it in stride. Cole sat down in one of Govich's guest chairs.

"Can I get you a cup of coffee?" Govich asked, indicating a pot beside his desk.

"No, sir. I had one outside."

The chief picked up the pot and began filling his own cup. As he did, Cole studied him. Jack Govich didn't really look like a policeman, but rather a successful attorney. His hair was cut in one of those not-one-hair-out-of-place styles, his waist size was the same as it had been when he joined the force thirty-five years ago, and all his suits were custom-tailored. He also had the reputation of being one of the toughest cops and most astute criminal investigators in the country.

Govich got to the point. "The reason I called you down this morning, Larry, is because we have a little situation here at headquarters. I take it you've heard about Charlie Butcher and Angelo Cappeletti getting iced last night?"

"They were dropped on Tuxedo Tony's doorstep. I bet he'll be crying for police protection by nightfall."

Govich nodded. "He's got a wiseass mob lieutenant out there named Art Maggio."

"I've heard of Maggio," Cole said. "Came up through the Arcadio Mob. Changed colors real fast when DeLisa made a move on old Rabbit Arcadio."

"You've got them pegged. Maggio's already braced the Oak Park PD with a demand for a twenty-four hour police detail to protect the Tuxedo when he returns from Vegas."

"What did the Oak Park people say?"

Govich grinned. "They told him to pound sand down a rat hole. DeLisa's got a small army out at that mini-castle he owns. He also never goes anywhere without a bodyguard."

"That makes it simple enough."

"Not quite," Govich opened one of his desk drawers and removed a mini-cassette player. Placing it on the desk blotter he said, "We got a couple of problems with the hits on Butcher and Cappeletti. One is that the F.B.I.'s involved."

"Why?"

"They're telling the Oak Park Police that the two hoods' deaths tie in with an on-going federal investigation. Right now there's a fed named Robert Donnelley and a team of baby feds sniffing around in Oak Park like they're on to where Hoffa's buried."

Cole's brow knitted. "I've heard stories about Donnelley going back to the sixties. He was one of Hoover's main eyes on Martin Luther King. In the seventies he got into dirty tricks and agent provocateur scams against the SDS and other militant groups. A real sweetheart."

"Age hasn't mellowed him either," Govich said. "But there's not a helluva lot we can do about him. He's there, but he doesn't have to know what you'll be doing."

Cole looked questioningly at the chief of detectives.

Govich pressed the Play button on the recorder. The voices came across with startling clarity.

"At the tone the time will be twenty hours, fifty-nine minutes and thirty seconds," a computerized voice announced.

Then, *"Two."*

"Chicago Emergency, Holland."

"Three!"

"Two of DeLisa's men. Butcher and Cappeletti. They're outside with guns."

"Hello, Chicago Police Emergency. Is anyone there? Hello!"

The tape ended.

Govich played it again. After the second time he said, "This call came into the Communications Center last night. This Officer Holland thought it was a crank, but he made a note of the address from the Call Location Identifier. It came from eighty-two thirty-one South Stony Island Avenue."

Cole stared at Govich. "That's Senator Banks's office."

Govich nodded. "And whoever that was talking was being forced by someone to tell that Butcher and Cappeletti were outside with guns. There was more said, but Holland was talking at the same time. I've got the original down in the Crime Lab having them mask out his voice so we can hear the last part."

Cole didn't like the sound of this. "The senator's office is in Area Two, Chief." Cole was the detective commander of Area One.

"Don't get your back up yet, Larry. At least hear what I've got to say first."

Cole waited.

"What do you think someone like our boy Bob Donnelley would do with this tape?"

"He'd leak it to every newspaper in the country and then try to hang some kind of murder or murder conspiracy rap on the senator."

"Exactly!" Govich said leaning forward and emphasizing his words with an index finger pointed at Cole. "There'd be no ifs, ands or buts about it. *Washington Post, New York Times, Chicago Tribune,* the whole nine yards. Before the senator had a chance to defend himself he'd be before a nationally televised Senate subcommittee looking like an Ollie North rerun."

Cole sat in silence for a moment. He tapped the surface of Govich's desk beside the recorder. "I'll bet this is a phony. Somebody's trying to lay a frame on the senator and I bet I know who."

They said together, "Tuxedo Tony DeLisa."

"So, now this is what I want," Govich said. "I'm going to relieve you of your duties in Area One temporarily and put you on special assignment out of this office. You will report only to me or the superintendent, but you can bet your ass the boss won't want to know too much about this investigation, the way the people in this state feel about Banks.

"After you get through in Oak Park go by the senator's office. You know how to handle it, so how you decide to play it is up to you. Whatever you find out is to be reported back to me first. Then we'll evaluate it and see where we go from there."

"Can I call on some of my people to help with the legwork?"

"I don't want any leaks on this one, Larry."

"I'll only pick those I can trust. There will only be a few of the personnel who've been with me awhile. A sergeant and possibly one or two detectives."

"I want to approve anybody you select beforehand. This is going to be a very sensitive operation."

"Of course, Chief," Cole said. He hesitated a moment and added, "Suppose I do find out that Banks had Butcher and Cappeletti killed?"

"Then there's only one thing I want you to do."

"And that is?"

"Make damn sure you can prove it beyond the shadow of a doubt, because we're going to be in shit up to our eyeballs."

"And if he didn't?" Cole said, playing devil's advocate.

"Then you can be damn sure all fingers will be pointed at our pal Tony DeLisa."

13

MARCH 5, 1994
11:18 A.M.

Park there," said Special Agent Robert Donnelley of the F.B.I.
"That's a handicapped zone, sir," warned Agent Tom Prentiss, who was driving.

"We're on official business," Donnelley said, testily. "Now park it, Prentiss."

The young man, who had less than six months in the field and was still referred to as a "baby agent," did as he was told. When Prentiss had applied for the F.B.I. he never expected it to be like this.

Leaving the unmarked Dodge with the F.B.I. OFFICIAL BUSINESS tag behind the sun visor showing, Prentiss followed Donnelley into the Oak Park, Illinois, police station. The baby agent tried to stay six feet behind him in the vain hope that no one would realize he was with Donnelley.

The senior agent was sixtyish, white-haired and thick-waisted. His suits were always either brown, blue or gray with an American flag pinned to the right lapel. His politics could be categorized to the right of ultra-conservative and it was rumored he had a picture of J. Edgar Hoover on his nightstand at home.

At the age of twenty-five, Prentiss looked like a high school freshman dressed up to go out on his first date. He was from Fort Wayne, Indiana, and had always dreamed of becoming a "G Man." That is, until he met Donnelley. Since being assigned to the Chicago office Prentiss had been Donnelley's driver. Not his partner, as the senior agent constantly reminded him, but his driver. Prentiss had yet to figure out why he had been selected for such an onerous task.

Donnelley crossed to the desk sergeant, while Prentiss maintained his distance. Donnelley flashed his ID and snapped, "F.B.I."

The sergeant was a balding, myopic man with a healthy row of bars denoting thirty years of police service on the left sleeve of his uniform shirt. The tag above the right breast pocket gave his name as Reidy.

Sergeant Reidy cast a bored expression at Agent Donnelley and waited.

"I want to see your chief," the fed demanded.

"Do you have an appointment?"

Prentiss could see the back of Donnelley's neck getting red.

"I suggest you get him on the phone right now, Sergeant, or I guarantee you'll regret it."

Prentiss could feel his stomach starting to churn as Sergeant Reidy looked Donnelley in the eye and snickered, which transmitted to the F.B.I. agents quite accurately that he could care less who they were or what they wanted.

Confused, Donnelley turned to look at Prentiss. The baby agent noticed that the senior agent didn't know what to do. Angrily, Donnelley swung back to face the sergeant. Reidy was talking on the telephone.

"This is the front desk. There's a pair of F.B.I. agents out here to see the boss. No, sir. They don't have an appointment."

Reidy listened another moment before hanging up. "The chief's not in, but Deputy Chief Baldwin is. He'll see you when he gets through with his eleven o'clock appointment. Have a seat."

The sergeant indicated a row of five chairs arranged in a U-shape across the lobby. Donnelley was about to argue over the delay, but finally relented.

They crossed to the chairs and sat down. Despite the NO SMOK-ING signs on the wall behind them and at the door when they entered, Donnelley pulled out a pack of Camel filterless cigarettes and lit one with a disposable lighter. As there were no ashtrays available, he flipped his ashes onto the floor.

There was one other person waiting. His head and upper body were hidden behind a *Chicago Times-Herald* newspaper.

"Cops," Donnelley said with a sneer. "A few years ago I was part of the Brass Button Scam that sent thirteen of them to jail. Of course that was in Chicago, but someday we'll get around to Oak Park. You can bet on that."

Prentiss looked around nervously in case any of the cops heard Donnelley. A number of officers in and out of uniform were walking past, but no one paid any attention to the grumbling agent.

"It's easy to make a case against cops. Especially in Chicago," Donnelley said puffing smoke into the air. "You catch one dirty, which is as easy as finding a colored junkie whore on the southside."

Prentiss squirmed. Donnelley was always making derogatory remarks in public about not only blacks, but women, Hispanics and Asians. The baby agent was surprised he'd managed to live so long. He breathed a sigh of relief when he noticed no minority officers or women near them.

Whoever was behind the newspaper continued reading, seemingly oblivious to the federal agents' presence.

"So you get some creep cop taking bribes from gamblers or giving a drug house a play for a snoot full of nose candy and you snatch them up. I like to grab cops in uniform while they're on duty. Took a couple right out of police cars on the street in broad daylight. Threatened to blow their goddamned heads off if they even looked wrong. Used to like to get a nice crowd of citizens around when we did it. Made a helluva cheering section. Then we'd strip their guns off, cuff them and hustle their asses down to the Federal Correctional facility. Locked them up in a detention cell and jacked up the temperature until the bastards were sweating bullets. Then we went to work on them. That's the part I liked best."

Prentiss noticed that whoever was behind the newspaper had gotten very still. Donnelley was enjoying his story and his cigarette so much he wasn't paying attention. Prentiss considered warning him, but then it really wouldn't do any good. Donnelley never listened.

"We bring the thieving cops in and start the third degree," Donnelley chuckled. "You got to figure one of them dumb cop bastards has got to know his rights. They've got to figure we can't push them around and question them without attorneys. But then they're real scared. Ready to crap in their shorts. Figure if you knock them about a bit it might be enough. Figure we might just forget the whole thing and let them go. Stupid jerks."

Prentiss watched the front page of the *Times-Herald* begin to drop. A head of thinning black hair became visible first, followed by a pair of thick eyebrows. Then smoldering dark eyes appeared, staring with open menace at Donnelley. Momentarily, the eyes flicked to Prentiss. The baby agent quickly looked away. The paper continued its descent.

Prentiss stood up.

"Where're you going?" Donnelley said.

"Get some water." Prentiss crossed to the water fountain against the far wall.

He was halfway there when he heard a gruff voice say, "There's no smoking in here, mack. Don't they teach you to read in F.B.I. school?"

Prentiss kept walking. He knew what was going to happen next. Donnelley would ignore the complaint and keep right on smoking. Prentiss had seen him do this in the "No Smoking" areas of restaurants, during airplane takeoffs when the NO SMOKING lights were lit, and once in the reception area of the American Cancer Society.

Prentiss bent over the fountain and took a drink. His mouth and throat were dry. Being around Donnelley usually did this to him. He dallied at the fountain briefly and then turned to go back to his seat. He stopped when he saw Sergeant Reidy and the man with the angry eyes standing over the still-seated, still-smoking Donnelley.

Prentiss took a couple of steps toward them in order to monitor what was being said. He stopped, hoping they would forget he was with Donnelley.

"You've got to leave the building, sir," Reidy was saying with barely-controlled anger. "The signs are quite specific."

"I'm sorry, boys," Donnelley said with mocking condescension. "I didn't see them." He took a long drag of his cigarette and exhaled a cloud of smoke at them.

Prentiss took a second to size up the man who had been behind the newspaper. He was barrel-chested, conservatively dressed in a suit and tie, and tough-looking. In short, a cop, but not the federal variety. Prentiss could only speculate what was in store for Donnelley. It didn't take long to find out.

"I said you have to leave the building, sir," the Oak Park sergeant repeated.

Donnelley waved his cigarette hand in front of them. "Listen, Sarge, I'm with the F.B.I. and I'm not going anywhere until—"

"Give me a hand, Blackie," Sergeant Reidy said to his heavyset companion. Together they reached down and grabbed Donnelley's arms. They yanked him roughly to his feet, making him drop the still-smoldering cigarette, before propelling him across the lobby to the front door. As they passed Prentiss, Donnelley bellowed, "You can't do this to me! I'm with the F.B.I.! This is illegal!" Then they went out the door.

Slowly, glancing repeatedly through the glass doors out at the front of the station, Prentiss returned to his seat. He couldn't see what had happened to them. He noticed the ashes and the still-burning cigarette butt on the polished linoleum floor. He rubbed his shoe over the spot attempting to obliterate the evidence, but all he succeeded in doing was smearing it into a dirty stain.

A few moments later Sergeant Reidy and the cop named Blackie came back inside. They were alone. Prentiss wondered what they had done with his partner. As Blackie returned to his seat he shot a glare at Prentiss. The baby agent smiled weakly and said, "I don't smoke."

Without a word, Blackie went back to his newspaper.

14

MARCH 5, 1994
11:30 P.M.

Larry Cole sat in Deputy Chief Edward Baldwin's office examining the pre-autopsy photographs of Charles Butcher and Angelo Cappeletti. Both corpses had been stripped. There were close-up, full-color shots of their wounds. Cole studied them carefully.

"These are punctures, Ed."

Baldwin, a thin, distinguished-looking black man with silver hair, responded, "According to our lab, they were made with a sharp object, probably a knife or some type of dagger. Butcher's went completely through his throat from front to back. There were two wounds on Cappeletti."

Cole nodded. "Can I get copies of these?"

"Sure."

Baldwin's intercom buzzed. While he answered it, Cole picked up the first photo from the stack and examined it again. This shot was of the dead men seated in the front seat of their car. The sign on Butcher's chest was clearly visible. "Next time this will be you, DeLisa."

Baldwin hung up the intercom phone and whistled softly.

"What's the matter?" Cole asked.

The Oak Park deputy chief chuckled. "Our desk sergeant and Blackie just threw an F.B.I. agent out of the building for smoking in the front lobby."

"Isn't that a bit extreme?"

"It's Chief Cowley's orders. Anyone smoking in violation of posted signs in this facility is to be ejected. Forcibly, if necessary."

Cole stood up. "I'd better get Blackie out of here before you have a major incident on your hands."

"I'd better get out there too. The feds parked their car in a handicapped zone. That's another of Cowley's pet peeves. The desk sergeant has ordered the car towed."

Blackie Silvestri and Larry Cole had been partners on the Nineteenth District tactical team over twenty years ago. Now Cole was Blackie's boss in the Detective Division; however, their friendship had remained the same over the years. Blackie was Cole's Case Management sergeant in Area One. He was responsible for keeping the unit's paperwork flow steady and up-to-date. But above and beyond any administrative abilities, Blackie was the best cop Cole knew. For a job like the one Chief Govich had handed him, Cole not only needed a good cop, but someone he could trust.

They were driving back to Chicago from Oak Park in Cole's dark blue Chevrolet command car. Blackie was behind the wheel. Cole was again studying the photos of the bodies of the two dead mobsters.

"Butcher's wound goes right through his throat," Cole said. "The pathologist said it didn't look like a normal stab wound, but instead like one made by a propelled projectile."

"Like an arrow?" Blackie said.

"Something like that, but he's certain it was a knife."

"Maybe somebody threw the knife at Butcher. I've never handled a case in which it was done, but you see enough of it on television and in the movies. I guess it is possible."

Cole continued staring at the throat wound. "Oh, it's possible for someone who's really good with a knife."

"You ever know anybody like that?"

"I've never seen it done personally, but a few years ago I handled a couple of homicides in which the murder weapon was a knife. The perpetrator was a wizard with it."

"Did you catch him?"

Cole stared blankly out the window. He was lost in a fifteen-year-old memory.

"I said, did you catch him, boss?" Blackie repeated.

Cole came out of his reverie. "No. I was working out of Riseman's office then. The Internal Affairs Division took it from us."

"The suspect was a cop?"

Cole nodded. "I never found out what happened, but I always promised myself I'd go back and look into it. I never found the time."

"You've got to tell me about it sometime," Blackie said, as the skyscrapers of Chicago came into view. "What're we going to do next on this Butcher and Cappeletti thing?"

Cole thought for a moment. "Let's head back to the station, so I can clean up my desk. Did you alert Bronson and Sherlock?"

"They should be waiting for us."

"Good. I've got some legwork I want them to do."

"Then?"

"I'm going to make an appointment to see Senator Harvey Banks."

15

Senator Harvey Banks had spent a sleepless night. After Reggie had left with Simon Jones, he had remained behind, afraid to even look out into the outer office where Naomi sat alone. Reggie was gone for half an hour. When he returned he wore a black, hooded jump suit and black gloves. They talked in the senator's office with the door shut.

"The assassins have been disposed of, Senator," Stanton said. Banks noticed a dangerous excitement about him, raw emotion capable of violence.

"What did you do with them?"

Stanton looked at him with a gaze the senator was unable to meet. "You need know no more about this affair than I disposed of them. They will not trouble you again."

Before Banks could ask more questions, Stanton had helped him into his coat and escorted him out of the office. The bodyguard had instructed a terrified Naomi Bowman to wait for him while he drove the senator home.

Senator Banks lived in a furnished apartment on Lake Shore Drive when he was in Chicago. The home he had lived in for thirty-five years on the southwest side had been sold after his wife died two years ago. He also had an apartment in the Watergate Complex in Washington. He spent as little time in either place as possible because he hated being alone. His marriage had been childless.

Last night, after Stanton had gotten him inside the apartment, was the worst night Banks had ever spent in his life. He hated violence, preferring negotiation and compromise to settle disputes. But then he was a reasonable, gentle man and realized he did not live in a reasonable, gentle world.

Unable to sleep after Stanton left, Banks had paced the living room floor of his apartment. He kept the lights off. After the incident in the office he was afraid to turn them on. So he spent the night in the dark, worrying about what his bodyguard had done to the men sent to murder him. He was also worried about what had happened to Simon Jones. Even though his old friend had betrayed him, he couldn't ignore forty years of friendship.

As the sky began brightening over Lake Michigan, the senator dozed. At seven he awoke to find himself still fully-clothed sitting on the living room sofa. His back ached and his eyes felt gritty, as he shuffled to the front door for his morning newspaper. The *Times-Herald's* headline blasted the message,

MOBSTERS FOUND SLAIN
POLICE BELIEVE GANG WAR IMMINENT

When the senator saw the names Butcher and Cappeletti a chill went through him.

By nine o'clock Banks was in his southside office. His plan had been to cancel all appointments, locate Reggie Stanton and force him to confess as to what really happened last night. He was just picking up the phone to call Stanton when his full-time secretary, Margaret Smith, barged into his office.

"You've got a full schedule of appointments this morning, Senator," she said, placing a typed itinerary on the desk in front of him. "You don't have to be downtown until one, so I've arranged for you to have lunch here in the office."

"I'm not feeling well today, Margaret," he said, replacing the phone. "I think I'll just make a few calls and go home."

"Nonsense." She spun from where she had been picking up the glasses he and Jones had drank from the night before. "You've got the Southside Coalition of Women Against Crime at nine thirty, state senators Steele and Franklin at ten thirty and a bunch of appointments this afternoon. We fly back to Washington on Monday, so you've got to get these things done now."

Banks looked up at her. Margaret reminded him of a Marine drill instructor. If he hadn't known better, he would have sworn even Stanton was afraid of her. But she was smart and knew her business. She was also right. There was a great deal he had to do before he returned to Washington to convene the crime committee.

He massaged his forehead. He had gone without sleep many times before. It was a normal way of life during campaigns. But there was more than just a lack of sleep sapping his strength.

"I can give you some of those ginseng tablets to pep you up, Senator," Margaret said, as she busily straightened up the office.

"Fine," Banks said wearily. "Who's the bodyguard on duty today?"

"It's supposed to be Joe King," she called from his private bathroom, where she was washing the glasses out in the sink. "But he called in sick. Might have a touch of the same thing that's bugging you."

Banks stiffened. "Will there be a replacement?"

When the senator was in town the Chicago Police Department provided part-time security for him. That is, when Stanton wasn't around, which was seldom.

"No need." Margaret came out of the bathroom drying the glasses with a paper towel. "Reggie's already here. I don't know when that boy . . . what in the world is this?"

Her outburst startled Banks. She was standing in front of his desk looking down at the floor. He got up and came around to see what she was staring at.

The senator recognized what it was instantly: Simon Jones's blood. However, there wasn't much of it and what there was had dried to a few miniscule brown stains.

"I just had this carpet cleaned," Margaret wailed. "You can't keep nothing straight around here for five minutes. That Naomi didn't even do the filing last night. I think—"

Banks cut her off. "Get Reggie."

The edge in his voice startled her. He was seldom so abrupt. As she started for the outer office she was determined to have the last word. "I'm going to have a nice, long talk with that Naomi Bowman. She's got to do more than sit around here showing off her behind."

When she was gone Banks sat down behind his desk. He felt powerless and trapped. He'd only felt like this twice before in his life. The first time was the day his father died when he was fourteen. The next was when his wife passed.

"Margaret said to give you these, Senator."

Banks jumped. He hadn't heard the bodyguard enter. After last night he would never be able to see Reggie Stanton in the same light again.

Stanton placed the bottle of ginseng energy pills down on the desk blotter and went to get the senator a glass of water. Banks shook two tablets from the bottle with a trembling hand.

Placing the water in front of him, Stanton said, "You should only take one now, Senator."

Banks shook the tablets around in his hand like dice. Then he returned one to the bottle before swallowing the other and chasing it with water.

Stanton remained standing. "Margaret said you weren't feeling well. I hope you're not upset about last night."

Banks took a deep breath. "Did you see this morning's paper?"

Stanton nodded.

"Those two men are dead, Reggie. They were left in front of DeLisa's house."

Stanton nodded once more. "DeLisa probably had them killed."

"And left them in front of his own house with a sign on their chests?! C'mon, Reggie, why would he do something like that?"

"DeLisa is a cunning, vicious criminal, Senator. Leaving the bodies like that will obviously direct official scrutiny away from him."

"And where will that attention go?" The senator's weariness was beginning to show again, despite the energy pill.

"We could be questioned. In fact, I expect it."

"By the police?"

"Yes, sir. But it would be best if you let me handle it. I'm quite sure no Chicago cop is going to barge in here demanding to see you.

That wouldn't be smart at all. I can answer any questions they might have. After all, I was once one of them myself."

The senator thought for a moment. "What about Simon?"

"Oh, I don't think Mr. Jones will be saying much about what happened last night, Senator."

Banks affixed his bodyguard with a questioning stare.

Stanton quickly added, "I would think Mr. Jones's main concern would be dealing with DeLisa."

The door leading from the outer office burst open and Margaret rushed in. "Senator, Marva Jones just called!"

"What's wrong?" Banks said, experiencing a crushing feeling of foreboding.

"Simon killed himself! He left his car's engine running in the garage last night. They found him this morning."

Banks looked at Stanton.

"I'm sorry, Senator," the bodyguard said. "Mr. Jones must have been terrified of what DeLisa would do if he caught him."

But the look Banks saw in Stanton's face did not support the sympathy of his words.

16

MARCH 5, 1994
12:20 P.M.

The chartered Lear jet bearing Antonio DeLisa taxied to a private hanger at Midway Airport. Quickly, a ground crew rolled a ramp into place and braced the aircraft's wheels. A silver Lincoln Town Car and a black Ford Crown Victoria were parked in front of the hangar. Art Maggio, flanked by two muscular men in dark suits, marched toward the plane.

The door swung open and the head of an attractive stewardess in a blue uniform popped out. She walked down the steps and waited.

Wally Boykin deplaned next. He took a quick look around the deserted corner of the airport and spied Maggio. He visibly sagged with relief. Then Tuxedo Tony DeLisa came off the plane.

Maggio and his escorts arrived at the plane just as DeLisa set foot on the runway. The day was sunny but windy and cool, with temperatures in the mid-forties. In his black suit, DeLisa stood on the tarmac. His men waited tensely for his first words.

DeLisa took in a deep breath, exhaled and turned toward Maggio. He smiled. "You know, Art, every time I come back to Chicago I realize how much I miss this damn town. Vegas is Vegas, but the Windy City is home."

The group turned and, with Maggio in the lead, walked over to the cars.

A hundred and fifty feet away a green panel truck was parked next to an air freight hangar. The truck wasn't noticed by either DeLisa or his men. The interior of the truck was packed with electronic surveillance equipment. Two F.B.I. agents in coveralls sat in cramped positions among the tape recorders, video monitors and directional microphone receivers. They could hear every word spoken between the mobsters and see every movement they made. If they desired they could have monitored DeLisa's heartbeat or scanned the pattern of stubble on Maggio's chin. Everything would be recorded and catalogued as part of the endless investigation being conducted by the F.B.I. of organized criminal activity in Chicago.

Boykin, DeLisa and Maggio got into the Lincoln, while the two bodyguards entered the Ford. The Ford took the lead, as they drove toward the airport exit. When the door to the Lincoln closed, the F.B.I.'s electronic surveillance was terminated. The two agents inside the green van had expected this. DeLisa's Lincoln was equipped with state-of-the-art, anti-surveillance devices.

The agent manning the surveillance camera picked up a walkie-talkie. "Surveillance Six to Surveillance Two. Gingiss One just left the hangar. He's headed for the Cicero exit."

A female voice came back over the instrument. *"Surveillance Two, we copy. We'll pick him up."*

A few minutes later the green van pulled away from the air freight hangar and headed for Cicero Avenue.

"Do we have anything on what happened to them?" DeLisa said.

Despite the easygoing greeting back at the plane, Maggio was still waiting for an explosive reaction from his boss. "We know they picked up Jones. From there they were supposed to go for the senator. That's the last we heard."

DeLisa opened the liquor cabinet in the back seat console between their seats. He removed a small bottle of champagne from a refrigerated compartment and opened it. He filled a glass. He offered nothing to Maggio.

After taking a sip, DeLisa said, "I never thought the senator had that kind of muscle."

"Maybe he doesn't. It could have been one of the black street gangs."

DeLisa thought about this for a moment. That was a possibility, but he doubted it. The black gangs in Chicago had as much to lose from Banks convening a crime committee as he did.

"After we get to the house I want you to take a ride downtown to Kirschstein's office. There's a man I want him to contact for me." DeLisa removed a pen and leather-bound notebook from his inside pocket. "He'll know how to do it. I need to meet with this man sometime within the next couple of days here in Chicago. Kirschstein is to handle the arrangements personally."

DeLisa wrote on the paper and snatched the sheet from the pad. As he handed it to Maggio he said, "How's Rachel?"

The mob lieutenant answered promptly, "She's fine, sir. We got her off to school this morning. Her last class starts at one."

DeLisa smiled. He was pleased.

While Tuxedo Tony continued to sip champagne, Maggio looked down at the sheet of paper. The name written on it was Karl Steiger.

17

A rmand Hagar drove his Harley Davidson motorcycle through midday traffic north on Michigan Avenue. At Congress Parkway he pulled to the curb between two parked cars. He rolled the heavy bike up onto the sidewalk next to a parking meter. Ignoring the pedestrians eyeing him cautiously, Hagar locked the bike and strode into the plaza to a bench beneath the bronze statue of the *Indian on Horseback.*

He sat down on the bench and looked around. The only other occupant of the plaza was a student from the college across the street. The student, a suburban male of twenty, only had to glance at Hagar's shoulder-length black hair, thick mustache and beard, along with the worn black leather motorcycle attire and boots. Then, as quickly as he could, he collected his books and left the area in the opposite direction from where the biker sat.

Hagar grinned. It was not an expression which held any mirth.

18

H e's here," Detective Manfred Wolfgang Sherlock said. Detective Lou Bronson and undercover Officer Judy Daniels moved across the room to look over Sherlock's shoulder.

The police officers were on the sixth floor of Roosevelt University. The classroom they had been loaned overlooked the plaza below. Sherlock was a six-foot-four, twenty-six-year-old beanpole who possessed the face of a choirboy. He had been watching the plaza through a pair of powerful Zeiss binoculars and waiting for Hagar's arrival. Bronson, his balding, late-fifties-aged partner, had been going over the plan with Officer Daniels. Although she listened closely and was as sharp as a tack, Bronson didn't think she was as serious about this assignment as she should be. Now the target of their operation had arrived and there was no more time for talk. They'd have to move and move soon.

"So that's Armand Hagar," Daniels said.

"You can see better through these, Judy," Sherlock said, stepping back and right on Bronson's foot.

"Thank you, Manny."

Sherlock ignored his partner's cry of pain.

"He's a nasty-looking piece of work," she said. "You sure he's not into drugs?"

"He's a killer, Judy," Sherlock said. "Even calls himself a professional hit man."

"I know that," she chided in a scolding tone without removing her eyes from the binoculars. "They say he's stomped a few people to death with those boots. The hair is right, but I can't tell from here."

"Tell what?" Bronson said tightly. He hoped that Sherlock hadn't broken one of his toes.

She continued to stare at Hagar. "If he has facial features like a lion. He's a Leo. Born August seventh, nineteen fifty-one."

Bronson frowned.

Sherlock said, "I didn't know that."

"He's dangerous, Judy," Bronson said. "If he even thinks this is a set-up he won't hesitate killing you."

She stood up and faced him. She was five foot six, well built and had shoulder-length hair, which for today was red. Her eyes were blue, which was also an affectation for the day and the assignment. The freckles splattered across her keen nose and cheeks were also fake. She was dressed in an expensive plaid business suit, turtleneck sweater and medium-heel pumps. She looked like a young professional or possibly a college professor, which for this scenario she was supposed to be.

"Lou," she said, "I wish you'd stop worrying about me. I bet if I were a man you wouldn't be constantly reminding me how dangerous our friend down there is?"

This caught Bronson off guard. He made a half-hearted attempt to defend himself, but she waved it off.

"Look, you guys told me that after today you've got to suspend this investigation because you're going on special assignment for your commander. So leave it to me. I'll make a case on this asshole. I guarantee you that." She picked up a Samsonite attache case from the floor.

Bronson regained his composure. "I'd say this to Superman if he was going undercover with a guy like this. Number one, Hagar never makes a deal on the first meet. Number two, Judy, if you believe nothing else I say, believe this. Armand Hagar's a killer. He's not just someone who has the capability of killing or will kill. He's a man who enjoys killing."

She stepped forward and gave Bronson a quick peck on the cheek. "Don't worry, Lou, after all, I'm not your average narc." She grinned and cocked her head to one side. "I'm Judy Daniels, the Mistress of Disguise/High Priestess of Mayhem."

"I was afraid you were going to say that," Sherlock said.

19

MARCH 5, 1994
1:08 P.M.

Armand Hagar was picking his dirt-encrusted fingernails with a six-inch switchblade. He wasn't concerned about the legions of cops patrolling the Loop. If any of those blue-bellied bastards came up and said anything about the knife or tried to lay any of their pig bullshit on him, he's stick them. Hell, Hagar had killed cops before. Even been caught and tried for stomping an Oregon state trooper. Was acquitted for lack of evidence. No, he didn't sweat cops.

He looked up as a chick in a tweed suit came across Michigan Avenue. She lugged an attache case with her. *Nice,* he thought. Walked with that stuck-up, "I am woman" bullshit arrogance. He sneered when he remembered the schoolteacher in Dallas who had come on just like this. After being chained to a bed and gang-raped by him and a few of his biker buddies for a week her attitude had changed. She was probably still in the asylum.

He watched the stuck-up broad start across the plaza toward him. This couldn't be the mark, but he realized that nowadays anything was possible. With his thumb and forefinger he cleaned a gob of grit from the knife blade. He eyed the woman again. Once, when he'd spent some time with Hell's Angels out in Los Angeles, he'd watched a movie company working in Palo Alto. It was one of the few times in his life when he became so engrossed in something to the point that he didn't start any shit. For hours he had studied the actors and actresses doing their thing for the camera. Later, he realized the one thing he hadn't liked about what they were doing was that it wasn't real. The whole thing was phony. Faked. Every movement, action and gesture had been make believe.

Hagar again eyed the redhead. She walked just like those phonies on the coast. Just a little too practiced with too much motion in her stride and the sway of her behind. "You'd better be real, Miss Muffet," he said to himself, "or it's going to take you a long time to die."

20

I *think you're waiting for me, sir,"* Judy said.

Bronson and Sherlock watched and listened from the sixth-floor post in the university across the street. Bronson was on the binoculars, Sherlock beside him manned the receiver neatly contained in a small suitcase. Judy's microphone had been specially constructed for Chicago Police Department undercover operations by Motorola. It was a miniature transmitter the size of a quarter, powered by a battery a millimeter thicker than a dime. It had a four-block transmittal radius with both receiver and battery concealed in the necklace she wore beneath her coat.

Hagar did not respond, but Bronson could see him looking up at her from his spot on the park bench. "He does look like a lion, Judy," Bronson said. "A lion ready to devour the Mistress of Disguise/High Priestess of Mayhem."

"The man I talked to described you and said you would meet me here at this time."

Bronson had to give it to her. She didn't sound scared.

Hagar remained mute, but continued to stare.

"Manny," Bronson said, "alert the back-up units that Judy's made contact. Tell them to stay on their toes."

"Look, if I've got the wrong party will you at least say so?"

Sherlock received acknowledgments from the two units down on the street backing up their operation. One unit consisted of two detectives in a Commonwealth Edison van; the other, a pair of detectives in an unmarked police car. Both units were ready to move on a moment's notice.

"What's he waiting for?" Bronson said.

"Is something wrong, Lou?" Sherlock abandoned the receiver and walked over to Bronson.

"Get back over there, Manny!" Bronson snapped.

Sherlock jumped to follow the senior officer's order. Tension was developing in the room because of the danger the young undercover officer was in.

"I'm sorry. I guess I made a mistake."

Bronson watched Judy turn and start walking back to Michigan Avenue. The binoculars were powerful enough for him to see the disappointment on her face. His heart skipped a beat when Hagar jumped up and grabbed her left arm from behind. The killer didn't appear to be holding her tightly, but the switchblade was still in his hand.

"I'm the right party, mama."

Bronson turned to look at Sherlock's receiver. The younger cop stared back at Bronson with amusement. The voice coming through from Hagar was high-pitched, almost feminine. It was nothing like what they expected from a human monster like him.

"Take your hands off me!"

"No problem, sweetheart." Hagar let her go and walked past her heading for his motorcycle.

"Let him go, Judy," Bronson said.

"Please," Manny added.

"Wait!" she called to Hagar.

"Shit!" Bronson swore.

Hagar stopped and turned to face her. Bronson noticed that he had massively broad shoulders and a thick neck beneath his mane of dirty hair.

"I'm sorry," she said. *"I'm just not used to being handled like that."*

"Yeah. I can tell. You're a real Mona Lisa."

"Pardon?"

"Let's stop fucking around. You've made the connect. Now we—"

"How can I be certain that you're . . . ?"

"Shut up and listen! If you want to do business with me, we're

going to take a little ride just in case you ain't what you're supposed to be."

"Don't do it, Judy," Sherlock said.

"Forget it, Judy," Bronson added.

"Let him go. Just let him go," Sherlock pleaded.

"Shit, she's going to do it!" Bronson said. Beads of perspiration were forming on his forehead as he stared through the binoculars at the scene unfolding down in the plaza.

This time Sherlock couldn't stay by the receiver. He remained at Bronson's side staring down at the street. "She hasn't moved yet, Lou."

Bronson sighed. "I can see it in her face, Manny."

"I'm not dressed to ride on a motorcycle," she said.

"We're not going far."

Then Hagar and Judy Daniels, aka the Mistress of Disguise/ High Priestess of Mayhem, walked across the plaza to the big Harley.

"Everybody be alert!" Sherlock shouted into the walkie-talkie on their special car-to-car frequency. "They're moving!"

Then he followed Bronson out the door.

The roar of the motorcycle's engine made hearing impossible. Judy was forced to wrap her arms around Hagar, as he raced down the sidewalk and bumped over the curb onto Michigan Avenue. Her attache case was jammed into a saddlebag behind the seat. Hagar smelled and his touch made her skin crawl. However, as the wind whipped through her hair, she felt exhilarated. She promised to test-drive a motorcycle like this one as soon as she got the chance.

21

Detectives Cox and Brown were in the Commonwealth Edison van parked on Michigan north of Van Buren. They watched Hagar and Judy ride past them.

"You're going to have to make a U-turn," Cox, a heavyset black detective, said.

"In this traffic?" Brown, a thin white cop in dark glasses, questioned.

"What do you care? Your life insurance is paid up."

Frowning, the detective forced the van out into traffic. He cut off a Mercedes and a C.T.A. bus. The drivers of both vehicles blasted their horns and shouted curses at the Edison vehicle. A traffic cop, stationed at the Jackson/Michigan intersection, watched the maneuver and swore, "I don't fucking believe this!"

Hagar was stopped at the red light. He was enjoying the pressure of the woman's breasts on his back and the feel of her thighs against his buttocks. He heard the traffic cop's remark. He checked the bike's side-view mirror. He saw the Edison van turning north on Michigan behind him. He studied the van with mere idle curiosity. He was still watching when the traffic cop flagged the van down.

The traffic cop came up to Brown's window. He was already flipping to a blank citation in his ticket book.

"Look, man," Brown said. "We're from Area One Violent Crimes. We're following that motorcycle. Oh, Jesus, don't look!"

But it was too late. The traffic cop turned and stared right at Hagar and Judy.

"Who the hell are you yelling at?!" The traffic cop was angry.

"I'm sorry, officer," Cox said through clenched teeth. "But we're trying to conduct an undercover operation here. Why don't you give us a break?"

The traffic cop reddened. "Why don't you two super-spy, glory boys show me some identification?!"

"Aw, c'mon, man!" Brown protested.

But Cox could see the traffic cop wasn't going to budge. On top of that the light was about to change. Quickly, Cox reached into his back pocket and flashed his badge.

Satisfied, the traffic cop stepped back and saluted them.

Armand Hagar saw the salute.

"Hold on, sweetheart!" he shouted to Judy over the heavy grumble of the motorcycle's exhaust. Then he swung the bike hard to the right, let out the clutch and roared east on Jackson Boulevard into Grant Park.

"Seventy-one Oh Seven emergency!" Cox's voice came over Bronson and Sherlock's radio.

They had made it out of the university building and onto Michigan Avenue. Their car was parked in the alley beside the Fine Arts theater. They had just gotten to the car when Cox transmitted the emergency.

Bronson grabbed the walkie-talkie, as Sherlock put the car in gear. "Go ahead, Oh Seven. This is Seventy-one Oh Four."

"The subject just made a hard right into Grant Park on Jackson. I think he made us."

Sherlock drove out of the alley, scattering pedestrians as he crossed the sidewalk onto Michigan Avenue. He started to turn left, but Bronson stopped him. "Go south to Congress, Manny."

"Suppose he heads north?"

"Listen," Bronson said, turning up the volume on their receiver. They could easily hear the motorcycle's howl. "If he did, we'll lose that signal in a few seconds. If he didn't we can intercept them on either Columbus or Lake Shore Drive."

Without further argument Sherlock turned south.

* * *

"You got friends with the electric company, honey?" Hagar shouted, as they flew east on Jackson toward the lake.

"I don't know what you mean." She was conscious of her skirt billowing up to completely expose her thighs.

"A couple of guys in an electrical repair truck made a stupid turn back there. Looks like they buffaloed a blue-belly, who was gonna give them a ticket. The only way they could have done that is if they were a couple of blue-bellies themselves."

"I'm not following you," Judy said, but she understood exactly what he meant.

They were stopped by another red light at Lake Shore Drive. Dutifully, Hagar braked to a stop. The arrow flashed for northbound traffic on the Drive to turn left onto Jackson. Judy watched a black Chevy that had cop car written all over it make the turn and drive past them. The detectives inside, Martinez and Wozniak, both turned to look right at the motorcycle. Judy could have killed them.

"Boy," Hagar said, "there sure are a lot of blue-bellies out today. Must be something real heavy going down. Right, mama?"

The light changed and he accelerated across the Drive. However, instead of turning, he went straight up onto the sidewalk above Burnham Harbor. A couple, pushing a baby carriage, scrambled out of the way, as the big bike rolled onto the grass throwing up divots of turf.

Judy hung on tight as they rolled down a steep incline before leveling off on a walkway running parallel to the sea wall. She realized that no car could follow them down here.

The receiver went dead. Bronson and Sherlock were at Columbus Drive and Congress Parkway on the west side of Buckingham Fountain. Sherlock stopped the car and turned to stare at his partner. In the past, Bronson always had the right answers.

"Take it easy, Manny," Bronson said. "They couldn't have gotten too far."

"*Seventy-one Oh Six,*" came across the walkie-talkie.

"Go, Six," Bronson responded.

"*We spotted the subjects at Jackson and Lake Shore Drive. We drove past and made a U-turn. By the time we got back to the intersection they were gone. We couldn't tell which way they went."*

"What are we going to do now?" Sherlock said with a note of panic in his voice. "He'll kill her if he finds out she's a cop."

"Go south, Manny," Bronson said with maddening coolness. "That's the only way they could have gone."

"I don't get you."

"I'll explain later. Now move it."

As Sherlock sped south, Bronson said a silent prayer to the patron saint of cops that they were going in the right direction, because right now he was merely guessing.

22

MARCH 5, 1994
1:15 P.M.

For Judy, being on the back of Hagar's motorcycle was like riding a bucking bronco. He drove the bike over sidewalks, up short flights of stone steps and down grassy inclines, as he continued to hug the Lake Michigan shoreline. They were traveling south, but by a circuitous route taking them around the Shedd Aquarium, Adler Planetarium and Meigs Field. The lake front was chilly and there were few sightseers out. Even those they did encounter gave them a wide berth when they saw Hagar's scowl.

Since leaving the Drive no conversation had passed between them. She suspected that he had some particular destination in mind, but she couldn't fathom where. For the first time in the three years she'd been working undercover, Judy was becoming petrified with fear. She only hoped Bronson and Sherlock were close enough to pick up her signal.

The Mistress of Disguise/High Priestess of Mayhem had been in dangerous situations before. Being a narc in a town like Chicago made this inevitable. She had been discovered twice. Once she'd blustered her way out of the situation by screaming that she was a cop and told the whacked-out junkies surrounding her that they were under arrest. They gave up without a fight. The next time wasn't so easy.

Hagar made a sudden turn which caught her by surprise. She almost lost her grip and at that instant actually considered jumping off the bike. But she could have been injured, which wouldn't do her, or the investigation, any good. Also, she wanted this guy. She wanted him bad.

There was a break in Lake Shore Drive traffic. Hagar gunned the Harley across the four lanes of northbound traffic and around the south end of Soldier Field. They were traveling back into the city.

23

MARCH 5, 1994
1:17 P.M.

The receiver gave a brief spurt of sound and died once more. Bronson stared hard at it, as if his will alone would re-establish contact. Miraculously, the howl of the motorcycle's engine blared from the set.

"Got them!" Bronson said.

"Awright!" Sherlock pressed the accelerator to the floor.

They were traveling south on the Drive passing the Museum of Natural History, which was on their left. Bronson alerted the other units to take up parallel routes south from the Loop. He considered alerting every police unit in the area, but doing so would ruin any hopes of them making a case against Hagar. He wrestled with the decision. Perhaps the case was already blown and he was unnecessarily endangering Judy's life. He was still weighing the alternatives when they passed under McCormick Place. At that instant the receiver went silent once more.

"What the hell?" Sherlock said.

"Turn around."

"I've got to go all the way to Thirty-first Street to do that, Lou."

"Then do it, Manny," Bronson snapped, as he reached for the car radio to alert every police car on the southside of the city. "I've been screwing around with this too long as it is."

24

MARCH 5, 1994
1:19 P.M.

Judy had driven down Lake Shore Drive a million times and had been going to Chicago Bears' games since she was twelve, but she never recalled there being a pedestrian overpass between Eighteenth and Twenty-third streets. It was there now and looked to have been there for a long time.

Hagar ordered her off the bike and up the stairs in front of him. Glancing back over her shoulder she looked on in amazement as he muscled the huge motorcycle up the lengthy flight of steps. The overpass went over not only the Drive, but also the Illinois Central Railroad tracks. They came down on a deserted side street two blocks north of the R. R. Donnelley paper mill.

"We're almost there, baby," he said, as he climbed back on the bike. "But now there are no cops around."

She considered making a run for it, but then there was no place to run to.

"Do you mind telling me where we're going?"

Hagar's face remained emotionless. "Get on the bike, bitch!"

"I don't like being called that."

The switchblade snapped open in his hand with a loud click. "Get on the bike or I'll kill you right here."

She had no choice. This was not the time or place to make a move. He was too close. For once the High Priestess of Mayhem found herself overmatched. She climbed on the Harley.

25

". . . where . . . going?"

The receiver wheezed static before going silent.

"Damn," Sherlock said, banging his fist against the steering wheel in frustration. "The set must be malfunctioning."

"No, it's working perfectly," Bronson said. He stared across the Illinois Central tracks. "They're over there."

Sherlock followed Bronson's gaze. They were underneath Twenty-third Street going north. Sherlock felt like a yo-yo. He hit the siren.

26

The mansions were perfectly maintained. The area had been designated the Chicago Historical District. The houses on each side of the cobble-stoned street had been constructed at the turn of the century and were now designated as landmarks. All the early captains of Chicago industry had owned homes here. Swift, Armour, Rosenwald, Rotheimer, Compton and Haggerty. Some of the mansions had been turned into museums. A few were still occupied.

Armand Hagar turned the motorcycle into a narrow breezeway beside the Haggerty House. He motored to the rear where a perfectly maintained carriage house was connected to the main building by a glass greenhouse. Hagar parked the motorcycle by the back door of the mansion.

Judy got off, straightened her skirt and looked around. "What are we doing here?"

"I live here," he said in a voice now devoid of his biker gang snarl. "And you're going to die here." He grabbed her by the back of the neck and forced her toward the rear of the house.

27

MARCH 5, 1994
1:25 P.M.

They met with the other units at Cermak Road and Indiana Avenue.

"Anything?" Cox called to Bronson from the Edison van.

Solemnly, Bronson shook his head. "We've lost her."

"We've got to do something." Sherlock's voice was close to breaking.

"Local district units have been alerted to be on the lookout for a motorcycle with either one or two riders," Bronson said. "Something will turn up, Manny. I can feel it."

"Yeah," Detective Brown said from the van. "That's what I like. A real fucking optimist."

They heard the sirens before they saw the blue lights of the marked squad cars approaching their position. The surveillance detectives could tell that there were at least four of them headed in their direction.

"What in the hell's going on?" Cox asked, as the four cars swept by them.

Bronson keyed his walkie-talkie. "This is Seventy-one Oh Six. What's going on around Twenty-second and Indiana in the Twenty-first District?"

"We have reports of shots fired in the Chicago Historical District area. A woman has supposedly shot a man wearing a black leather outfit," the dispatcher replied.

"Let's go, Manny."

Activating the siren, Sherlock followed the Twenty-first District police cars north from Twenty-second Street. The van and unmarked car were right behind them.

There were ten cops on the street when they pulled up in front of the landmark Haggerty House. The six detectives from Area One left their vehicles and joined the crowd. At the center of the gathering stood Judy Daniels holding a .32 nickle-plated snub in her hand. At her feet lay a silently glaring Armand Hagar. He was clutching his left foot, which was bleeding from the bullet Judy had fired through both the boot and his foot.

"What happened, Judy?" Sherlock asked, unable to conceal his relief.

She looked weary from fear, but managed a smile. "It's a long story, Manny. A very long story."

28

MARCH 5, 1994
2:07 P.M.

R eggie Stanton kept a close eye on Harvey Banks as they rode downtown in the senator's Mercury. State Representative Jim Steele, a glad-handing politician who laughed a lot, was with them. As usual, the senator drove. Steele was in the front passenger seat. Stanton in the rear alone.

"Senator, this crime committee is going to put some of the worst criminal elements in this town out of business. Yes, sir, the streets of Chicago are going to be safe again. I knew the day we elected you we were getting a man who meant business. A man . . ."

Steele was an obese loudmouth who would have made a better nightclub comic than elected official. This was his first term in the State House and he had run against a schoolteacher who was as grim as a hangman and had a penchant for giving long speeches in a flat monotone. He had bored the voters to sleep. Big Jim Steele had kept them laughing and gotten elected.

A couple of times during the drive, Stanton had caught the senator studying him in the rearview mirror. Banks was nervous and maybe more than a little scared. But then it went with the territory. As the bodyguard saw it, things would get a lot worse before they got better.

Their destination was the State of Illinois Building located at Randolph and LaSalle across the street from City Hall. They pulled up at the LaSalle Street entrance to the glass architectural monstrosity. A pair of plainclothes cops were waiting for them. They were part of the senator's local bodyguard detail provided by the Chicago Police Department as a courtesy. Banks remained behind the wheel until Steele had squeezed out of his seat and stepped onto the street. Then he turned to look questioningly at Stanton.

"You're going to be down here most of the afternoon, Senator. A police commander named Cole called for an appointment at the office later today. I scheduled him for four-thirty. I'll be there to meet him personally."

One of the detectives, a pockmark-faced white man with a somber expression, came around to open the senator's car door.

"Suppose he still wants to talk to me?" Banks asked.

Stanton smiled. "I'll take care of everything, sir. Just enjoy your meeting with the State Police."

A crowd had gathered in front of the LaSalle Street entrance to the building. The senator had been recognized. Banks started to say something else to Stanton, thought better of it and got out of the car. Before his foot touched the ground a broad smile was etched on his weary face.

With Stanton helping, the detectives forged a path through the well-wishers across the sidewalk and into the building. Even then the senator shook ten hands and was kissed twice by young women.

Inside, the scene was repeated, but in a less aggressive fashion. The guards managed to get him over to the bank of scenic elevators at the center of the glass-enclosed lobby. As the elevator doors began to close a woman yelled from outside, "We love you, Senator Banks! You're doing a good job."

Banks again flashed his smile and waved at her. When the car rose, Banks slumped against the back railing of the elevator.

"That's true what she said, Harv," Steele said, laughing. "You are doing a good job."

They left the elevator on the sixteenth floor. A State Police captain in full uniform was waiting for them. "Good afternoon, Senator Banks. Right this way."

Stanton stopped the two bodyguards. He watched the captain, flanked by Steele, lead Banks into a conference room down the hall. When they were out of sight, Stanton turned to the bodyguards. "I want you to stay with him until the conference is over, which should be about four. Then take him back to the apartment."

"Suppose he wants to go someplace else?" the one with the pock-marked face said.

"He won't. He's not feeling well. The State Police only want to bend his ear for an hour or so about what a good job they're doing. Don't let it go beyond four o'clock. Then hustle him out of there."

"Yes, sir," they said together.

Stanton returned to the elevator. The detectives entered the conference room before the car came. Back in the lobby, Stanton exited through the Randolph Street doors. Out on the street he walked three blocks east to State and entered the subway. A few minutes later he was aboard a train rushing south over the rails through the darkened tunnel.

Stanton had ridden the subways of Chicago all his life. When he was a boy growing up on the southside, he had played make-believe games. Sometimes he would be Jesse James waiting for the point on the line where his masked gang were in hiding so he could pull his six-gun and make the conductor stop the train. On other occasions he would sit at the front of the first car and pretend he was the engineer. When the train climbed from the subway tunnel to run above ground he would pretend it was a rocket ship soaring high above the Earth.

As the adult Reggie Stanton's mind drifted back through the years, he recalled that he used to engage in these fantasies for hours spent riding the train from one end of the line to the other. He remembered also that back then he'd needed a fantasy because the reality of his existence was a nightmare—at least until Uncle Ernst came into his life.

He looked down at the back of his hand. It was as white in color as any white man's he'd ever seen. That was one of the things he found so confusing when he was a child. If the designation of being black or a Negro was based on skin color, why wasn't he considered white? His grandmother had tried explaining it to him. Uncle Ernst had simply said, *"Es macht nichts."* It doesn't matter.

But to Reggie it did. It mattered a great deal.

The train rumbled into the Thirty-fifth Street station and Stanton got off. Down on the street he entered the Illinois Institute of Technology parking lot on State Street. The lot was manned by an armed security guard twenty-four hours a day. Stanton kept his battleship gray BMW here when he was with the senator.

He flashed his permit at the guard and drove from the lot onto Thirty-third. He turned east and a few minutes later was cruising south on King Drive. In the 4500 block he pulled onto the side drive. Halfway down the block he parked in front of a well-maintained, three-story brownstone. After locking the car and setting the alarm, he crossed the sidewalk to the waist-high, wrought-iron fence. He opened the gate and entered the yard.

Paper and trash had blown over the fence from the street and someone had tossed an empty High Ten whiskey bottle onto the grass. Stanton collected the bottle and the trash. Before going into the house he looked around.

The street that now bore Martin Luther King, Jr.'s name had once been known as Grand Boulevard. It had been aptly named. Back then the mansions stretched from the Loop south to Garfield Boulevard at Fifty-fifth Street. The "swells," as his grandmother still called them, lived there. They were the rich whites who'd made their money during the flourishing years of the Robber Barons at the end of the nineteenth and beginning of the twentieth centuries. That was when America worshiped at the altar of Mammon, when laborers worked for slave wages and the few got rich from the toil of the many.

Stanton climbed the stone steps to the front door. Using his keys, he deactivated the alarm system and went inside.

The house had a slightly stale odor. This was due to dampness which had gotten inside the old walls. He planned to have a contractor come in before summer to give him an estimate on an interior remodeling job. It would be expensive, as all such work on these ancient structures were. For the old mansions north of Thirty-fifth Street subsidies were available for rehab projects. Up in the Historical District north of Twenty-second a great deal of work had been paid for by the city. But south of Thirty-fifth was considered a black ghetto. Stanton had once heard a careless bank manager say that granting home improvement loans down here was like "pissing money down a rat hole."

But Reggie didn't need subsidies or loans. Uncle Ernst had seen to that.

"Reggie?" his grandmother's voice echoed from the kitchen at the rear of the house.

"Yes, Grandma," he called back, "it's me."

He started down the long corridor which took him past the living room with the working fireplace and mantle bearing the photographs of four generations of Stantons; the carpeted staircase with its hand-carved banisters; the dining room with the varnished hardwood table that could seat twelve for one meal; back to the kitchen.

It was a large room as kitchens go. It had rows of wooden cabinets running completely around its circumference and a mosaic tile floor bearing the multicolored design of a giant eagle. A new stainless steel sink, gas range and ice cube–making refrigerator had been recently installed, but the kitchen table was the same formica-topped, aluminum model with the center extension added that his grandmother had purchased new at the end of World War II. It was at this table now that his grandmother, Ida Mae Stanton, and her full-time nurse, Helen Hudson, were seated playing gin rummy.

Ida Mae Stanton was eighty-nine years old, but didn't look a day over sixty. A broken hip, caused by a freak accident on the front steps, made it necessary for her to use a cane to walk. But other than that, she was as spry as a woman of fifty. She was ebony-skinned with coal black hair she dyed religiously and wore tied up on top of her head in a style popular in the 1940s. She still had her teeth and her mental faculties had never been sharper. The only betrayal the years had inflicted on her was her eyesight. She was forced to wear thick glasses because she was rapidly going blind. The eye color was a faint hazel, which set in that ebony face, was as startling as her grandson's blue-gray.

"You would have to come now that I'm finally winning," Mrs. Hudson said, snatching a card from the discard pile and spreading the ten, jack, queen and king of spades.

"One of these days I'm gonna catch you holding those spreads in your hand and it's going to be your behind, Helen."

"Watch your language, Ida," the nurse scolded. She discarded the three of hearts.

"Gin," Ida Stanton said, snatching up the three to make a spread of threes along with fours. She discarded an ace to complete the run.

Helen Hudson was a heavyset, medium-complexioned black woman with short hair and a congenial nature. She always wore a nurse's uniform complete with white shoes and stockings whenever she was working. Even though Reggie paid her the prevailing salary for a live-in nurse, Helen was more of a companion to his grandmother than a nurse.

"How'd you know I was looking for that ace?" Helen demanded.

"You always do it, girl," Ida said counting up her points. "You'll never learn."

Helen revealed the two aces with which she'd been caught.

"That's thirty points you lose," the old woman cackled.

Reggie crossed the kitchen to the refrigerator. He was about to open it when his grandmother's voice stopped him. "You get back here and wash them hands, boy! What's wrong with you?"

With a well-chastised grin, Stanton crossed to the kitchen sink to wash his hands with soap and water. He remembered when he was a child he wouldn't dare go near the icebox unless he washed first. Even Uncle Ernst washed when he was around Ida.

Scrubbed and dried, he walked up behind his grandmother and placed one hand on each side of her. She was still tallying points, but she took a moment to study the palms through her weak eyes. "Over," she said.

He showed her the backs.

"Good."

Before she could return to the cards he gave her a rough squeeze and a wet kiss on the cheek.

"You better go on, Reggie," she said. "You just trying to make up for going in my icebox with dirty hands. If you loved me you'd have give me that kiss the minute you hit the door."

"Yes, ma'am," he said contritely. "I'm sorry."

But Ida Mae was already back to her tally.

"I got fifty, not forty-five, Ida," Helen protested.

"I see it. I know what I'm doing, woman."

Reggie poured a glass of lemonade and turned to look at his grandmother. She was all he had left. He felt a cold hollowness inside himself as he briefly contemplated what life would be like without her. He felt the stab of a still sharp loss. It was five years and he still wasn't over Uncle Ernst's death.

"How's the senator?" Helen asked.

Reggie hesitated for only a fraction of a second. "He's just fine, Mrs. Hudson."

His grandmother's head snapped around. She stared across the kitchen at him. He knew that at this distance all she could see would be a blurred outline of his body, but her gaze was just as hot on his flesh as it had been when he was seven years old.

"It's your turn to cook dinner," she said to the nurse.

"It's not even three o'clock yet, Ida."

"You said you're fixing a roast. That's gonna take at least two hours. I don't want to eat at midnight."

Helen Hudson had been around this old woman and her grandson long enough to know when she was being sent a message. "Well,

I've got to go out to the store if we're going to have it with all the trimmings. Reggie, you staying for dinner?"

"I've got to go back to the office until about seven, but I should be home by eight."

"I'd better get a large pot roast then, so your grandmother won't be able to eat it all up from you."

"You better go on, Helen," Ida warned.

A few minutes later Helen called from the front door as she let herself out. When they were alone Ida said, "What happened?"

Reggie had taken Helen's seat at the kitchen table. He put his lemonade glass down and said, "Two of DeLisa's men tried to kill the senator last night."

"Lord, spare us," Ida whispered urgently. "Were they white?"

Reggie nodded. "But there was a black Judas."

Ida's face constricted into a frown. "Did you handle it?"

"Yes, ma'am."

"Any problems?"

"It shook the senator up pretty good, but he'll get over it."

Ida Stanton stood up slowly. Her bad hip was giving her trouble, but she waved Reggie off when he tried to help. However, she did take his arm to walk from the kitchen to the front of the house.

"Banks is a good man, but he's a politician," she said, as they moved slowly down the long hall. "It comes down to only one thing with them. What they can get out of you."

"The senator's not like that, Grandma."

"Maybe you don't see it, Reggie, but deep down inside they're all the same."

He knew better than to press the argument.

In the living room she pushed him away and walked on her own over to her favorite chair by the window. A copy of the *Times-Herald* was on the cocktail table in the center of the room. He went over and picked it up.

"The two Mafia thugs left on that Oak Park mobster's doorstep were yours, weren't they?" she asked.

"Yes, Grandma," he answered without taking his eyes off the paper.

"Who was the Judas?"

"A man named Simon Jones."

"Will he be a problem for the senator again?"

"No."

Ida Stanton laughed, which caused a cough to rattle deep in her chest. "That old Nazi taught you good."

Reggie's head snapped in her direction. His jaw muscles rippled, but his voice was respectful. "I wish you wouldn't call him that, Grandma."

She chuckled. "Okay, I'm sorry. The way you carry on, folks would think he was your father."

He looked back at the newspaper. "In a way I guess he was. At least the closest thing to a father that I've ever known."

"And I was your mother. So, all in all, I guess you didn't turn out too bad, did you?"

He dropped the paper back on the cocktail table and walked over to her chair. He sat down on the arm and held her. He could feel her frail bones through the cloth of her dress. He kissed her forehead. "And you are the best mother I could have had, Grandma. The best."

29

MARCH 5, 1994
2:20 P.M.

Arthur Maggio sat in attorney Frank Kirschstein's office. Kirschstein was an elegantly-dressed, slender man with curled hair and a penchant for wearing flashy gold jewelry. His office was on the twenty-second floor and was swept daily for secreted electronic listening devices.

"The Tuxedo wants to get in touch with Steiger, huh?" the lawyer said, leaning back in his swivel chair and eyeing Maggio across the desk.

"That's what he said. Wants to meet with him here in Chicago in the next day or so."

"This wouldn't have anything to do with what happened to Butcher and Cappeletti?"

"I wouldn't know," Maggio said flatly. "Of course, you could always ask Mr. DeLisa yourself."

Kirschstein sat up abruptly. "No. No need for that. Just curious. I'll set things up. Get back to you later."

Without further comment Maggio stood up and let himself out of the office. He stepped into the corridor. Two middle-aged women, carrying Bloomingdale's shopping bags, waited for the elevator. He walked to the water fountain at the opposite end of the hall and took a drink. By the time he finished, the corridor was empty.

He took the stairs down from the twenty-second floor to the fourth floor. He encountered no one on the stairwell. The fourth floor of the building was part of an atrium surrounded by balconies extending from the lobby to the fifth floor. A frosted-glass skylight allowed sunshine to filter into the atrium from the air-shaft above it. The air-shaft extended all the way to the top of the thirty-story structure.

On each level of the atrium there were offices and shops. Maggio headed for a bookstore set back in an isolated corner. At the door he stopped and checked the balcony. There were shoppers present, but no one was paying any attention to him. He went inside.

The bookstore was stocked exclusively with paperbacks. One entire rack was devoted to pornographic magazines, the rest to popular novels, spy and detective stories. There was one clerk on duty in the store. He looked like a high school senior dressed up to go out on his prom. His name was Tom Prentiss and he was a special agent with the F.B.I.

"Do you have a copy of *The Day of the Jackal* by Frederick Forsythe?" Maggio asked.

"Yes, sir," Prentiss said tightly. "It's in the back. . . . I mean, uh, the last row."

Maggio gave the F.B.I. agent a hard look. "Get it straight, kid. That way we'll all live a lot fucking longer." He then turned and walked to the back of the shop.

The book rack containing the novels of Frederick Forsythe was situated so that it blocked sight from the front entrance to the rear of the shop. Maggio scanned the titles for a moment before slipping through a beaded curtain into the rear storage room. The room contained stacks of empty cardboard boxes labeled BOOKS in black stencil, a worn desk with a missing leg and a couple of rickety folding chairs. The desk leg was propped up with a stack of books. Cigarette smoke hung thickly in the air. The origin of the smoke was Special Agent Robert Donnelley. He sat behind the desk.

"The surgeon general claims smoking can be hazardous to your health," Maggio said pulling up a chair.

"To hell with her," Donnelley said coughing. "She doesn't know what she's talking about."

"You should know," Maggio said.

"So what's going on with our buddy Tony the Tuxedo?"

"He's been real mellow since he got back from Vegas. Wasn't even upset about Butcher and Cappeletti."

Donnelley frowned. "Doesn't sound like him."

"No, it doesn't."

"Maybe he had them hit?" Donnelley lit another cigarette.

"No way. He wanted Banks dead. It was all set. I was thinking, maybe you people got them on the other end."

"Wasn't us, Art."

"You did have somebody protecting the senator, didn't you?"

Donnelley shook his head. "Nope. I understand he's got some local bodyguards, but that has nothing to do with us."

Maggio studied the F.B.I. man in silence. He'd told him about the planned hit on Banks a week before it was scheduled to go down. He assumed they would have sent somebody to protect him.

"You guys work in funny ways, Donnelley."

"How we work is our business. What have you got that's new for me?"

"The Tuxedo sent me up to see Kirschstein. He wants some guy named Karl Steiger contacted. Didn't tell me what it was about and apparently the lawyer doesn't know."

Donnelley pulled a pad of paper on the desk toward him. "C-A-R-L . . ."

"That's K-A-R-L," Maggio corrected. "Last name S-T-E-I-G-E-R."

Donnelley wrote.

"The Tuxedo wants to meet with this Steiger here in town in the next couple of days. I'm guessing, but I'd say it has something to do with the failed hit on Banks."

"Steiger? Steiger?" Donnelley said. "I've heard that name before, but I can't place it."

"Yeah, it's not real common."

Donnelley tore the sheet with Steiger's name on it from the pad and slipped it into his pocket. "Anything else?"

"Rachel tried to escape again, but we caught her."

"Anything else?" Donnelley repeated impatiently.

"That's it."

Donnelley removed a thick white envelope from his inside coat pocket. He handed it over to Maggio. "Your thirty pieces of silver."

Maggio glared at him. "I don't like that."

"I don't give a shit whether you like it or not," Donnelley's face had turned ugly mean. "We don't pay you for your good will. Just information."

"Suppose the information stops?"

Donnelley smiled. "It won't, because if it did Tuxedo Tony might find out about all the good, inside dope you've been providing Uncle Sam about his operation."

The two men locked eyes for a long time. Finally, Maggio stood up and turned for the door. "You're a real fucking sweetheart, Donnelley. A real fucking sweetheart."

"Ain't love grand?" Donnelley said sticking the cigarette into the corner of his mouth.

Maggio walked through the shop without looking at Prentiss. He slammed the door when he went out. The baby agent watched him storm off across the fourth floor balcony.

Prentiss took off his jacket preparatory to leaving the store. The shop was borrowed periodically from building management for clandestine meetings by F.B.I. agents and their informants. Today the fact that it was in the same building where Kirschstein's offices were located made it doubly convenient.

Being stuck back in the corner of the fourth-floor atrium balcony made the bookstore's operation a financial disaster. The former tenants had been evicted for non-payment of rent. The F.B.I. paid the rent now and the stacks of paperbacks and porno magazines were the property of the U.S. government.

Prentiss was starting for the back room when the front door opened. He turned around. A muscular man with broad shoulders walked in.

"I'm sorry, sir," Prentiss said. "We're closed."

"I only want to get a *Penthouse* magazine."

"I don't think we carry it."

"Sure you do," the man said, walking past Prentiss and snatching the magazine off a rack. "Hey, this edition is two months old."

Prentiss recovered quickly. "I meant to say that we stopped carrying it. If you want you can have that one free of charge."

"Gee thanks, guy. You're alright." The man stared at the automatic on Prentiss's hip. "The book business must be rough nowadays."

Prentiss blanched. "Like I said, we're closed."

"No problem, sport. I'm going, and thanks again for the magazine." With that he left.

A few minutes later, agents Donnelley and Prentiss extinguished the bookstore lights. They walked along the fourth floor balcony and boarded the same elevator Maggio had taken. On the fifth-floor balcony above the atrium at the opposite side of the building, Wally Boykin, Tuxedo Tony DeLisa's bodyguard, watched them go. In his hand he held the January edition of *Penthouse* magazine.

30

L arry Cole and Blackie Silvestri pulled up in front of Senator Banks's office on Stony Island. Cole read the slogan on the front window out loud. "The people are the power." They got out of the car and crossed the sidewalk to the front door. It was locked. Cole looked through the glass. The office was empty and the lights were out. There was a buzzer beside the door. Cole pressed it and waited. No response came from inside.

Blackie checked his watch. "We're early. Our appointment's not until four-thirty."

"Yeah, but I wanted to get the lay of the land before we met with him. Maybe talk to some of the staff."

"Good idea, but this joint is locked up tighter than a drum."

They were about to go back to the police car when a red Toyota pulled to the curb. They watched a tall black woman with a stunning figure step to the street. She didn't see them until she had crossed the sidewalk and was nearly at the front door. When she did look up her shock quickly turned to fear.

"Take it easy, miss," Cole said with a smile, as he flashed his badge and ID card for her inspection. "We're with the police."

The fear did not diminish and actually increased. It was doubtful if she could outrun them in her heels, but she was obviously thinking about trying.

"We're not going to hurt you," Blackie said.

"What do you want?" Her voice trembled.

"We have a four-thirty appointment with the senator," Cole responded.

Her eyes darted to the darkened storefront behind them. "Who made the appointment for you?"

Before Cole could answer his beeper went off. He checked the display. It was his office. He shut the instrument off and turned back to the frightened woman.

"I believe the person I talked to was a Mrs. Smith. I didn't get her first name."

"I don't believe you!"

Cole and Blackie exchanged puzzled glances.

"Is there a phone around here I could use?" Cole asked.

"There's one in the car wash down the street." She began backing away from them.

"C'mon, Sarge," Cole said.

As they walked off, the young woman halted her retreat and stared at them. When they were a quarter of a block away she dashed to the front door of the office, fumbled with a key and struggled with the lock until she got the door open and disappeared inside.

"Talk about paranoid," Blackie said.

"Yeah," Cole looked back over his shoulder. "She's scared to death. I'd like to know who or what frightened her like that."

"Maybe it was us. You come on real hard sometimes, boss."

Cole looked at the sergeant. "Yeah, and you have a face only a mother could love."

The car wash was a small hand operation run out of a converted gas station. A man in coveralls, who was drying a Corvette, waved the policeman to an office pay phone. A teenage girl cashier sat behind a wooden counter bearing an antique cash register. In a reception area in front of the counter two customers sat on a dilapidated couch waiting for their cars. The teenager was watching a soap opera on a Walkman portable television. The look she gave Cole and Blackie told the tale: She'd made them as cops.

Cole went to the pay phone on the wall and dialed his office. Blackie stood over by the counter and squinted down at the small set.

"Did Crystal tell Abe she's married to Mark yet?" Blackie asked the girl.

Her head came up with a jerk. "She tried to, but Abe's mother came in and told Crystal about Mark's father having been an Enright."

"You're kidding?"

"No, I ain't." She crossed her heart. "Mark Fairchild's father was an Enright. That's going to screw things up real good."

Cole hung up the phone. Blackie could tell by the expression on his face that something was wrong. With a parting look at Crystal and Abe on the soap opera, he walked over to join Cole.

The commander waited until they got outside to explain the problems Bronson and Sherlock had encountered on their surveillance of the hit man Armand Hagar.

"So this undercover Daniels shoots the asshole in the foot," Blackie said. "From what I've heard she's lucky she got the drop on him."

"But at the hospital Frank Kirschstein showed up and said he's Hagar's attorney. Claims Hagar is really Andrew Haggerty of the Haggerty department store chain."

They were walking down Stony Island back toward Senator Banks's office. "That doesn't make sense, Boss. According to the reports I read, Bronson and Sherlock have this guy pegged as a killer-for-hire. All they had to do was have him set up a hit with Daniels and they'd have had a pretty good case on him."

Cole stopped suddenly. They were in front of an auto repair shop. Cole was looking south toward the senator's office four doors down the block. Blackie turned to see what Cole was staring at. A muscular black man with a light complexion and sandy hair had gotten out of a BMW parked behind the frightened woman's Toyota. He crossed the sidewalk and entered Banks's office. He did not appear to have noticed the policemen.

"You know him?" Blackie said.

Cole didn't respond.

"Boss, are you okay?"

Cole continued to stare at the front of the office. Then, in a voice that rose barely above a whisper, he said, "Take the car and go to the hospital with Bronson and Sherlock. Keep an eye on Kirschstein."

"What about you? How are you going to get back?"

Cole turned to look at the sergeant. "Don't worry about me. There could be a problem for the undercover cop Daniels."

"I'm not following you."

"She accidentally killed the wrong guy on a drug bust a year or so back. Kirschstein will try to use that to help his client. I'll call you later to see how things work out."

Cole started to walk away. Blackie reached out and grabbed his arm. "Larry, what in the hell's wrong with you? You look like you've just seen a ghost."

Cole stared blankly at Blackie. He responded, "Remember when I told you about the case I handled some years back in which the offender killed by throwing a knife at his victims?"

"Yeah, you mentioned it this morning."

"And I told you there was a cop involved."

Blackie nodded.

Cole turned to look down the street again. "Well that cop just walked into the senator's office."

31

MARCH 5, 1994
4:25 P.M.

Stanton stepped inside the office and turned to look back through the window at the two policemen out on the street. He didn't know the white one, but he recognized Cole. When Margaret Smith, the senator's secretary, had given him the name, it had meant nothing. But then he hadn't seen Cole in fifteen years. At the time Cole had been a sergeant, now he was a commander.

"Reggie?" Naomi said from behind him.

He turned to face her. "I know. There are two cops outside."

"They said they've got an appointment to see the senator." Her voice trembled, but she was making a valiant effort to bring it back under control. "Mrs. Smith told me he wasn't coming back today."

"He's not," Stanton said, crossing the office and pulling off his trench coat. "I'm meeting them for him."

"Reggie, I've got to talk to you. Did you see the papers this morning?"

"I saw them." He turned from the closet just as Cole stepped up to the outside door. "But this is not the time to get into that. Buzz the gentleman in, Naomi."

"Reggie . . . ?"

His face contorted in his weak imitation of a smile. "I said, buzz the gentleman in."

She reached beneath the desk and pressed the button without taking her eyes off Stanton.

Cole stepped into the office and closed the door behind him. He looked first at the receptionist, who would not return his gaze, and then at Stanton standing across the room.

"Commander Cole, how are you?" Stanton said. "It's been a long time."

"Yes it has, Stanton," Cole said. "I have a four-thirty appointment with Senator Banks."

"I'm sorry, Commander," Stanton said, "but the senator has been unavoidably detained and won't be able to meet with you today."

"What about tomorrow?"

Stanton noticed that Cole was studying Naomi. She sat rigidly at her desk staring at her hands. It would actually have been simpler, Reggie thought, if she hung a sign around her neck reading, I'M HIDING SOMETHING! PLEASE QUESTION ME AT ONCE, MR. POLICEMAN.

Stanton cleared his throat to get Cole's attention. "I'm sorry, but tomorrow's out too. Isn't it, Naomi?"

Her head snapped up. She stared at him with total confusion.

"I was telling the commander that the senator's calendar is full tomorrow. Isn't that right?"

She nodded and went back to studying her hands.

Stanton paused a moment to gauge Cole's reaction. He was simply observing them. Not watching, but observing. Taking it all in. Measuring and evaluating. At another time, in another place, with other people, Cole would conduct this investigation in a different manner. Maybe he'd get a little rough. Throw his weight around a bit. But then this was Senator Harvey Banks's office and the Chicago Police Department hadn't sent a commander to simply play detective.

"I only wanted to ask the senator a few routine questions about a case we're working on," Cole said.

Stanton had to give it to him. He was as smooth as silk. No threat in tone or words. Even Naomi appeared to be relaxing a bit.

"Maybe I could help you," Stanton said.

"I'd really like to speak with the senator." Cole paused a moment. "Your name's Reggie, isn't it?"

Stanton smiled. "You have a good memory. Your name's Leonard?"

"Larry."

Stanton snapped his fingers. The unexpected sound made Naomi jump. "Larry, of course. Well, Larry, I don't think the senator's going to be able to see you for awhile, because he's flying back to Washington on Monday. We don't anticipate being back in Chicago for at least a month. Maybe more."

"Then, I guess I'll have to talk to you."

"Good. Why don't we go into the senator's private office?"

Stanton turned to lead the way, but spun back around when he heard Cole talking to Naomi. "I'm sorry we frightened you outside."

"That's okay," she said refusing to look at him.

Then Cole followed Stanton into Banks's office.

"So what can I do for you, Larry?" Stanton said, sitting down in one of the chairs in front of the senator's desk and offering the other one to Cole.

The commander sat down and opened his notebook. "Were you with the senator last night?"

"Yes, I was."

"All night?" Cole looked up to find Stanton staring at him. It made him uneasy. He returned the stare by focusing his eyes on Stanton's forehead just above eyebrow level.

"No. I accompanied him to his apartment about eleven. He drove himself to the office this morning alone."

"What do you do for the senator, Reggie?"

Stanton smiled. "I guess you could say I perform a number of jobs: assistant, bodyguard, all-purpose aide."

"Then you're on his payroll?"

"No. Not exactly."

Cole noticed the bodyguard's stare intensify. "I don't understand," Cole said.

"There's nothing to understand. The senator doesn't pay me. Oh, he pays certain expenses, but those are mostly incidental."

"Then what do you do for a living?"

Stanton was on his feet so fast it startled Cole. He moved like a dangerous snake uncoiling. Before the policeman could even attempt to defend himself, Stanton was already past him. Cole turned around and watched him walk over to the bar.

"Can I get you anything? Non-alcoholic of course," Stanton said.

Cole's mouth was dry. His heart was pounding furiously from the scare Stanton had given him. "A Coke would be okay."

"How about RC?" Stanton opened the refrigerator beside the bar.

"Fine."

Stanton returned carrying two cans of soda. He handed one to Cole, while he popped the tab on the other. Stanton did not return to his seat, but instead took up a position standing against the wall. He was behind Cole, forcing the policeman to turn his chair around to see him. But the bodyguard stood at such an angle the poor office lighting placed his face in shadow. Cole's apprehension increased.

"So you were saying?" Stanton said.

"I asked what you did for a living?"

Stanton did not respond right away. Cole could see the blue RC can move up toward his face. He could also see the outline of the man's head and upper body, but was unable to make out any of his features. The strange blue-gray eyes continued their probing. For a moment Cole considered getting up and walking over to stand closer to Stanton, but then he rejected this. It wouldn't be the smart move at all.

"Tell me something, Commander Cole. How good are you at keeping secrets?"

"It depends on the secret and what it has to do with my investigation."

"You're still all cop. But that's what I always liked about you. It's something one man can respect in another."

Cole stared into the shadow hanging over Stanton's face like a mask and waited. An object flew into the light and bounced on Cole's lap. The policeman flinched, but regained his composure quickly.

Stanton had tossed Cole an identification case. In the office's dim lighting Cole couldn't tell whether the case was black or dark blue. He opened it. The blue scroll-work photo identification card was on one side. On the other a black inscribed gold badge bearing the words, F.B.I. SPECIAL AGENT.

Cole swung his eyes back to the shadow that was Reggie Stanton.

"That is somewhat confusing, isn't it, Larry?"

"It does raise some questions," Cole said, handing the case back. Remaining in shadow, Stanton took it.

"Are you part of some type of official security for the Senator?"

"Not actually official, but let's just say that the U.S. Government has a vested interest in making sure that Senator Banks stays healthy."

"I never knew the F.B.I. to be responsible for bodyguarding elected officials."

"We do whatever the job requires, Commander."

"Do you know an agent named Donnelley?"

"I've heard of him."

"I'm not sure he would share your sentiments about protecting the senator."

"He doesn't have to," Stanton said dryly. "What I'm doing has nothing to do with him."

"Okay, we've established who you are officially."

"Does it have to go into your report?"

"I'm afraid it does."

Stanton crushed the empty soda can and dropped it into a waste basket where it landed with a dull clunk. Then he walked back around to take his seat across from Cole again.

"But you didn't come here to find out about me. You wanted to know where Senator Banks was last night and you now know that I was with him. You mind telling me, one cop to another, what this is all about?"

"I'm investigating the deaths of two men last night. A Charles Butcher and Angelo Cappeletti."

Stanton's emotionless stare was again leveled at Cole; however, by now the policeman had gotten used to it.

"What has that got to do with Senator Banks?"

"A call came into Communications last night at twenty fifty-nine hours. There was no complainant on the line, but in the background a man's voice was heard saying, and I quote, 'Two of DeLisa's men. Butcher and Cappeletti. They're outside with guns.'"

"Sounds like a prank."

"Could be, but then there are some questions we still need answered about it."

"Such as?"

"That call came from this office, Reggie. Our Call Location Identifier verifies that."

Stanton became very still. "At eight fifty-nine last night there was no one here."

"I thought you said you dropped the Senator off at home at about eleven."

"I did, but we weren't here at nine. He had a couple of meetings to go to. You know he's convening a special meeting of the Senate Crime Committee in Washington next week."

"So I heard," Cole said. "Where were these meetings last night?"

"I think you're going to need a lot more than that, Larry. You'll not only need locations, but also times and the names of participants. Why don't I save you some legwork and put that together for you?"

Cole smiled. "I never knew the F.B.I. could be so cooperative."

"Don't expect anything like this from a prick like Donnelley, but seeing how we're old friends, I'd be glad to do it for you. Is there anything else?"

"Have you ever heard the names Charles Butcher and Angelo Cappeletti?"

Stanton rubbed his chin reflectively for a moment. "They do sound familiar, but I . . . wait. Weren't they in the paper this morning?"

"That's right," Cole said with a deadpan expression. "They sure were. What about Tuxedo Tony DeLisa, you ever heard of him?"

Stanton's cold stare returned. "Everybody's heard of Antonio DeLisa, Larry. Remember, I am with the F.B.I."

Cole studied his notebook for a few seconds more before standing up. Stanton stood with him. "Well, Reggie, I guess that's it. You will get that information together for me, won't you?"

"Of course. I'll give your office a call as soon as it comes in. Do you have a card?"

Cole gave the F.B.I. man one of his business cards as they headed for the door.

"Tell me," Cole said, as they were about to step into the outer office, "the last time I saw you was what, fifteen years ago?"

"About that."

"As I recall you were a suspect in a series of vigilante murders on the southside. The I.A.D. even took over the case from the Detective Division."

"That's right. I was cleared on all counts. If I hadn't been, would they have ever let me in the Bureau?"

"I guess not."

Stanton opened the door and they stepped into the outer office. Naomi was still at her desk. She looked up at them through eyes fatigued with fear. Cole caught only a glimpse of her face before she looked away.

"You could have invited your partner in, Larry," Stanton said when they reached the front door. "Me and Naomi don't bite."

"Oh, he's not waiting for me. He had to leave."

"That's strange. I always thought Chicago cops worked in pairs. It's safer that way."

"Not always." Cole unfastened the outer door latch. "If I remember correctly, you always worked alone when you were with the department."

"As a matter of fact, I did. Preferred it that way."

"Sometimes it works out best," Cole said stepping onto the sidewalk. "Give me a call when you get that information. Take care of yourself and a good day to you, ma'am."

Naomi's head came up from her turtlelike pose and she managed a weak smile. Then Cole was gone.

Stanton stood by the door for a long time after Cole had left. Finally, he said to himself, "Smart cop. Real smart cop."

New York City **32**

MARCH 5, 1994
5:30 P.M.

The stretch limousine pulled to a stop in front of the Plaza Hotel in New York City. The uniformed chauffeur jumped out and hurried around to open the back door. Dressed in a white leisure suit, Ernest Steiger stepped to the street. It was a cold, windy day in Manhattan and against the change of elements from the balminess of Monte Carlo, he wore a full-length white cape. His blond hair was slicked back from a high forehead and he wore dark glasses. A bellboy hopped to load his bags on a luggage cart as Ernest swept imperiously into the hotel.

Everyone on the street and in the lobby noticed him pass.

At the front desk a young woman with the practiced smile of the hotel/motel school graduate said, "Good afternoon, sir, and welcome to the Plaza."

He ignored the greeting. "You have a reservation for a Count von Steiger?"

She consulted a computer screen. "That reservation was canceled and replaced by one for a Mr. Karl Steiger and son."

"Incompetence," Ernest hissed.

"I'm sorry, sir. I don't understand."

"Incompetence, is what I said." His shout split the stately quiet of the carpeted lobby. A number of heads turned to stare at him.

The desk clerk's cheeks reddened, but she maintained her composure. "The reservation was canceled—"

"Do you have that cancellation in writing?"

"I don't know, sir. It was—"

"Of course you don't know. How could you? Anyone could simply call up here and cancel my reservation and you would think nothing of it. This is the height of incompetence."

A tall man with silver hair stepped up beside the clerk. "Perhaps I can be of some assistance."

Ernest permitted his dark glasses to drop onto the bridge of his nose. He studied the new arrival through blue-gray eyes under long blond lashes. "And who are you?"

"I'm Mr. Gillespie, the assistant manager."

"Well, Mr. Gillespie, the assistant manager, this woman has canceled my reservation without my consent."

Traffic through the lobby had come to a complete halt. The assistant manager's eyes flicked past the elegantly-dressed man to the interested faces of other hotel patrons. A thin sheen of perspiration spread across his upper lip.

"I'm quite sure we can make arrangements to accommodate you, Mr . . . ?"

"Count von Steiger."

"Yes, of course, Count von Steiger."

"But, Mr. Gillespie, his reservation—," the clerk attempted to explain, but Gillespie cut her off.

"Give him twenty-two ten."

The clerk looked from the assistant manager to the man in white. Twenty-two ten was one of the hotel's best suites.

"He was booked into twelve eighteen before," she said.

"Give him twenty-two ten," Gillespie repeated, dabbing his face with a monogrammed handkerchief. "Boy, take Count von Steiger's bags to twenty-two ten at once. Will that be satisfactory, sir?"

Ernest sniffed imperiously and snatched the room access cards from the clerk's hand. "This should have been done in the first place."

The suite overlooked Central Park. After dismissing the bellboy without a tip, Ernest tossed his cape across a chair and went to observe the view. It was impressive, but wasted on him, due to his dislike of Americans.

By nationality Ernest Steiger was Swiss. No one in the family had actually used the "von" for over a generation. He had long ago relinquished all ties except one to his German/Prussian heritage. Someday he would be the last von Steiger. When that day came he intended to have enough money to live like the royalty his chosen name denoted.

The phone rang. With a frown he turned to stare at it. He let it ring twice more before saying a mocking, "Coming, Daddy." Then he crossed the room and picked up the receiver.

Karl Steiger got off the elevator on the twenty-second floor and followed the numbers to his son's suite. There was a cold grimace on the German's face. He was not happy. Ernest was nearly a day late. This meant a day wasted and they had a meeting to discuss a contract in Chicago tomorrow. Also, Ernest had taken the suite Karl had specifically changed because it was not only expensive, but called too much attention to them. In their business this could be dangerous. Karl sighed as he came up to twenty-two ten. Ernest had always had expensive tastes. It was a trait, among many, that he had inherited from his mother.

"Daddy!" Ernest said expansively when he swung the door open. "It's good to see you." He spoke without an accent and his English was flawless.

Ernest stepped out into the hall and embraced his father. Karl hated such displays of emotion. You hugged women; men shook hands. He struggled out of his son's embrace and stepped into the room.

"Do you really need all this?" Karl looked around the seven room suite with obvious disapproval.

"I can always use the space and I was thinking of entertaining some friends while we're in New York."

Karl turned to face his son. "We're flying to Chicago at nine tomorrow morning. We have a meeting with a prospective client at the O'Hare Hilton Hotel at noon their time."

Ernest made no attempt to hide his disappointment. "We just did a job. Can't we take a little time off?"

"You had time off in Monte Carlo."

"I mean some real time off. A vacation. A month of just lazing around on a beach with beautiful women. Why has it always got to be work with you?"

Karl stared at his son. Ernest had his blond hair and blue-gray eyes, but there the resemblance ended. The rest belonged to his former wife Ursula. Karl had been her second husband. Since their divorce she had been married four times. At the time of the split with Karl, Ernest had been nine. Custody of the boy was never a problem. Ursula hadn't wanted him except on infrequent holidays and for two weeks during summer vacations. But during those short periods she'd easily managed to undo everything Karl had tried to make of his son. In fact, Karl was glad Ernest liked girls, because at one point he was certain his son was beginning to ape his mother's speech and hip-swaying walk.

Whereas Karl and his son's namesake, Ernest, were muscularly built, heavy men, Ernest was lean, almost slight. He also possessed Ursula's features, which were thin and finely-drawn like a brush painting on China. Ernest was pretty, not handsome. Ursula had been born a DeVancourt, which was an old Swiss family of bankers. She had been an only child spoiled into becoming a woman totally lacking in any form of responsibility to anyone or anything. Ernest had picked up her bad habits more naturally than anything Karl had ever tried drilling into him.

"We work when there is a demand for our services," Karl stated flatly. "We play when there is time to play."

Ernest sulked. Another trait he'd picked up from his mother. Ursula could do it for weeks or even months until you either gave her what she wanted or she found someone who would.

"But this is our fourth job in a row, Daddy. Aren't we taking chances?"

God, how he hated it when Ernest whined. But Karl did not shout at him. It was too late for that now. He had stopped the screamed recriminations and even the blows when Ernest was in his teens. They'd done no good anyway. Ernest was as much a man as he would ever be.

But this was his son. The only Steiger left. That meant a great deal to Karl.

He turned and sat down in one of the arm chairs. He examined his son's white cape with open disdain. Then he began massaging his right knee. It was an old wound suffered in the trade, which gave him trouble from time to time, and getting progressively worse as he got older.

"The only chances we take are when you don't do things exactly the way I tell you to do them."

Ernest knelt on the floor in front of his father's chair. He pushed the older man's thick hands away. Ernest's fingers were small and delicate. They were the hands of a musician or an artist. He pushed his father's pants leg up to expose his scarred knee. Expertly he began massaging the knee cap and the cartilage at the sides and back. Karl was forced to grit his teeth against the relief from pain he was experiencing.

Ernest looked up at him with eyes which were cast the same as Ursula's. He knew what pleased his father even though Karl had nothing but disgust for the intimacy of the touch of another man, even if it was that of his own son.

"I was only a few minutes late, Daddy," Ernest purred as he continued the massage.

Karl pushed his son's hands away and stood up. His pants leg was bunched at the top of his calf and he angrily pushed it down. He attempted to forge his face into its most vicious scowl, but the effort failed. Ernest remained kneeling on the floor staring up at him.

"Exchanges in kidnappings can be very dicey," Karl said. "I had the kidnappers believing I could walk on water as far as the British authorities went. I had Rutherford and even the stupid, ugly one ready to go along. When you failed to show, their confidence increased."

"But I took care of it, didn't I?" Ernest said, bounding gracefully to his feet. As a teenager he'd been a gymnast and still kept his wire-thin body in competition shape.

Karl watched him cross the room to the telephone. "Yes, you did, but that wasn't part of my plan. I was forced to discount my fee because of the violence. If Rutherford had been hurt there would have been no fee at all."

Ernest spun to face Karl. "You said 'my' fee. I thought it was 'our' fee?"

"It is our fee, Ernest, but what I'm trying to tell you is that it could have been a great deal more if you had followed the plan."

"So, we can make it up on the next job." With that he picked up the phone and dialed room service.

An impotent rage coursed through Karl as he watched his son. When he was growing up in Germany, had he dared turn his back on either his father, Johann, or Uncle Ernst, he would have been knocked unconscious. But that was then and this was now.

Karl sat back down in the armchair and began massaging his bad leg again. He wondered if he could take Ernest in a fight? As he studied his son's slender body in the white leisure suit, Karl considered the fact that appearances and his mother's tendencies to the contrary, Ernest was as good at dispensing violent death as he and Uncle Ernst had ever been. Perhaps even better, as neither he nor Ernst had enjoyed killing. Karl realized that his son did.

MARCH 5, 1994
4:35 P.M.

R achel DeLisa was being chauffeured home from school by her bodyguards. They didn't look like bodyguards, but instead like students. They rode in a Chevy Blazer. The driver was named Sam. He was an All-American boy–type with sandy hair and a toothpaste-ad smile. The female was Carrie. She sat behind Rachel and was of the girl-next-door, cheerleader variety. Rachel ignored them.

Sam and Carrie were in each of her five classes. They sat either next to her or behind her. At lunch they sat with her at one of the restaurants on campus. When other classmates attempted to approach Rachel, they'd discourage contact. Once, a boy named Ramon had been persistent in his intentions. Sam warned him off, but Ramon refused to back down. On the way to school one morning Ramon was struck by a hit-and-run driver. He would never walk again. Although she couldn't prove it, Rachel believed Papa was responsible for the accident.

Last night's events had made Rachel even more silent with her companions. Occasionally, they attempted to make small talk with her. Lately they'd said less and less when she failed to respond to even their "hellos." But they did talk to each other.

Now they chatted casually.

"Are you going to Jorge's party this weekend?" Carrie asked.

"Yeah. Are you?"

They were turning into the driveway of the DeLisa estate. There were two bodyguards at the gate. Usually, there was only one. Rachel smiled. Papa had gotten the message from whoever had killed Butcher and Cappeletti. This made her smile.

"I'm thinking about it," Carrie was saying about Jorge's party. "Last time things got out of hand and somebody called the cops."

"That's the way Jorge is. Never a dull moment."

As they pulled up in front of the house one of the other bodyguards walked out the front door. He was younger than the usual ones Papa employed and had an extraordinarily pale complexion. As they got out of the Blazer, the young bodyguard staggered to the side of the house and was violently ill.

"What in the hell's wrong with him?" Sam said as they entered the house.

The downstairs hall was empty. The study doors shut. Without a word to her companions, Rachel trotted up the stairs to her room. She was walking down the second floor corridor when she heard a scream. She stopped.

The house was quiet. Too quiet. She took two more steps toward her door when she heard another scream. This time it chilled her to the marrow. The anguish in that voice was as intense as anything she'd ever heard.

She held her books so tightly against her chest she could barely breathe. Slowly, she let them fall to the floor. She stepped over them and walked back to the top of the stairs.

She looked down from the balcony to find the alcove empty. Her companions were nowhere in sight. There were no more screams, but she could hear shouting coming from somewhere down below. She couldn't make out the words; however, the voice was definitely her father's.

A horrible curiosity possessed her. She started down the stairs and crossed the alcove to the study door. She had heard him angry many times before, but this time there was an added fury in his tone. Rachel remembered she had only heard him this angry once before. That was the night her mother died.

She stopped at the study door and listened. No sound came from inside. She could also no longer hear Papa. She grasped the handle and opened the door. Being alone in the house like this was a unique experience for her. Her near escape last night had also been unusual. Perhaps this was an omen of things to come.

Rachel briefly considered another escape attempt, but remembered the two guards at the gate. There was little chance of her getting off the grounds in daylight.

If the study had not belonged to Papa, she would have loved it. Books lined floor-to-ceiling cases completely covering the walls. The desk, chairs and conference table were polished daily with a lemon wax that exuded a fragrant aroma. There was an antique carpet on the floor, which Rachel recalled her mother purchasing when she furnished this room. It was her mother and not Papa who had arranged everything here.

It was as she had this thought that another terrible scream echoed through the house. A scream that sounded as if it originated right in the room where she was standing. Rachel spun around looking for the source of the sound, but there was no one there. The scream came again. She slammed her palms over her ears. She backed into a bookcase and stood trembling as the distressed howl sounded again and again in her head.

Then the bookcase beside her moved.

The entire affair, six feet in width, stretching from the floor to a foot below the ceiling, swung outward like a door opening. One of the bodyguards hurried across the study and through the door Rachel had left standing open. He did not see her.

"Wake this stoolie motherfucker up!"

Rachel jumped when she heard Papa's voice. It was coming from the other side of the bookcase. In all the years she had lived in this house, she had never been aware of any secret passages. The idea fascinated and, at the same time, horrified her.

She stepped around the open bookcase panel and stood before a dark passageway. A flight of stone steps led down into the shadows below. She hesitated.

"Arthur, goddamn your lying heart!" her father screamed. "What else did you tell that fed?"

She heard a muffled whimper. Her legs began moving before the thought registered in her brain. Rachel descended.

The walls were of concrete. The air cold and damp. There was no light on the stairs, but enough illumination for her to see. The stairs led down into a barren room about eighteen feet square. She realized that this was a smaller version of the basement on the opposite side of the house.

There were people in the room. She recognized her life-sized Barbie and Ken doll bodyguards. They stood cringing off to one side, awestruck by what was taking place at the center of the room. There stood Wally Boykin in shirt sleeves. There was an obscene leer on his face. There too was Papa and Art Maggio. They were the focus of all attention.

Later, she would find it hard to believe that her first reaction was concern that Papa had hurt himself very badly. This was because he was covered with blood. But the blood on Antonio DeLisa was not his own, but instead that of Maggio.

The mob lieutenant was suspended by a pair of handcuffs fastened behind his back and attached by their chain to a meat hook hanging from the ceiling. He had been stripped, and his body jack-knifed forward to hang like a side of beef. His torso was flabby and out of shape. His pale skin was covered with blood flowing from wounds all over his body.

Rachel felt the skin of her face begin to burn in embarrassment, as she initially thought that Mr. Maggio, despite the excrutiatingly painful position he was in and his numerous injuries, was experiencing a massive erection. Then she looked closer and found that the wooden handle of some type of instrument protruded from the tip of his penis. Her throat constricted when she saw ice picks, with the same wooden handles as the one sticking out of Maggio, arranged on a table Boykin was standing next to.

Papa had stepped up very close to the hanging man. His ear was cocked an inch from Maggio's mouth. "No, Arthur. No, no, no, no! You're not going to die until I get it all. Now what else did you tell the feds?!"

Once Rachel dreamed that she'd died and gone to hell. In her dream, hell was a horrible place with winged-demons, snakes, fanged-insects and ghouls that reached for her from open graves. The memory of that horror haunted her for years. Now it was erased by the reality she was witnessing.

"Give me another pick," DeLisa said to Boykin.

With the precision of a surgical nurse, Boykin slapped the instrument, handle first, into the mobster's hand.

He studied the bleeding man in front of him carefully before plunging the weapon into his left bicep. Maggio grunted. Rachel felt the room becoming at once hotter and brighter.

DeLisa pulled the ice pick out. Blood flowed from the wound to mix with what had already accumulated on the floor.

"He ain't feeling nothing, Wally," DeLisa snarled. "He's getting used to being stuck. Give me the torch."

Even the leering Boykin hesitated before picking up a small blowtorch from the floor beneath the table. He turned on the gas and lit the flame with a cigarette lighter before handing it to DeLisa. "You want goggles, boss?"

"Hell no," DeLisa said with a laugh. "This will hurt old Art a lot more than it's going to hurt me."

The tortured man was aware of what was going on, as he began moaning deep in his throat. The flesh of his face, although untouched by punishment, hung slack, and saliva ran unchecked from his mouth. He started moving around weakly on his perch. His feeble attempts made DeLisa laugh louder.

"You know what I'm going to do, don't you? I'm going to toast your balls, my friend. Do you remember the last time I did that to someone?"

"No," came the barely audible plea from Maggio. "Please, God, no."

"God ain't got nothing to do with it, Art. It's just between you, me and the fucking F.B.I."

DeLisa began moving the torch slowly toward Maggio's groin. The ice pick–impaled penis stood out at right angles from the dangling body. Feebly, the prisoner attempted to close his legs.

DeLisa began giggling in a low, hoarse tone as Maggio's pubic hair sizzled. The woman who guarded Rachel buried her head in the male bodyguard's chest. Sam looked away. Wally Boykin's face was illuminated with awe, Rachel's with ever-increasing horror.

The hairs caught fire, bringing a scream from Maggio. DeLisa shoved the torch directly into his groin and the stench of burning flesh permeated the small torture chamber. Maggio's screams caught in his throat, and only his mouth remaining open in soundless horror told the tale of his agony. Then another scream was heard.

DeLisa spun from his victim in time to see his daughter collapse on the bloodstained floor.

34

MARCH 5, 1994
6:10 P.M.

Tony DeLisa paced the floor outside his daughter's bedroom. The doctor, who lived two houses away, and the female bodyguard were inside the room. They'd been in with Rachel for forty minutes. Tuxedo Tony was getting impatient.

The door opened. The physician, who looked like a golf pro, came out, followed by the bodyguard.

"How is she?" DeLisa asked.

Although the doctor knew his neighbor had the reputation of being a mobster, he considered him a friend. DeLisa came to dinner at the doctor's home regularly and he and his wife had been here on occasion. He thought of DeLisa as no more than a slightly unethical businessman.

"She's had a tremendous shock, Tony. Did something happen to her today?"

"Something like what?"

The way DeLisa looked at him made the doctor uneasy.

"I don't know, but she's been frightened out of her wits."

"She tell you anything?"

The doctor shook his head. "She babbled and was so agitated I gave her a sedative. What she was saying actually made no sense."

"What did she say, doc?"

He shrugged. "Something about a side of beef having its balls burned off. Weird stuff. I need to know something, Tony."

"What?" DeLisa took a step toward his neighbor. He was wondering how he'd dispose of the doctor's body and explain it later.

"Is Rachel on drugs?"

"Of course not," DeLisa snapped. "She just had a bad dream."

"I don't think a dream could frighten anyone like she's been. She really needs to be in a hospital for—"

"Yeah, sure, doc," DeLisa said grabbing the doctor's arm. "If she wakes up and has problems I'll give you a call. Thanks and send me a bill."

At the top of the stairs he handed the doctor over to Wally Boykin. Then he rushed back to Rachel's room.

DeLisa stood over her bed and looked lovingly down at her face in the repose of sleep. She was beautiful. She was his beautiful little girl. He had loved her since the second she'd come screaming into the world. He bent down and kissed her cheek. She did not stir.

"It's going to be alright, baby. Don't worry. Your Papa will make it just fine."

The female bodyguard stood behind him. Holding his finger up for silence, he tiptoed from the room, motioning her to follow him. With one last glimpse at her sleeping charge, she did.

Out in the hall DeLisa led her a short distance down the corridor before he turned and struck her in the face with his fist. The blow broke her nose and knocked out her upper front teeth.

"Bitch!" he said, grabbing her hair but keeping his voice low for fear of waking his daughter. "Why weren't you watching her?"

The woman was unable to answer as blood and bits of broken teeth clogged her mouth.

DeLisa let her go and started for the stairs. As an afterthought he came back and kicked her viciously in the side. He heard ribs give under his foot. Then he went back to his special room.

"Is he dead?" DeLisa asked Boykin. Both mobsters had changed out of their bloody clothing before the doctor arrived. Now they studied their victim.

"Naw, boss," Boykin said, walking over to Maggio and lifting his chin. "But he's in a pretty bad way. You want me to see if I can wake him up?"

DeLisa thought for a moment. "No. He told us everything he knew. We might as well end it now."

"You want a gun?"

"Are you fucking crazy? My daughter's sleeping upstairs. I thought this room was supposed to be soundproof, anyway."

"That's his fault, not mine, Mr. DeLisa," Boykin said, hooking his thumb at the hanging man.

"Give me another ice pick and that hammer," DeLisa said.

Boykin complied and then watched as Tuxedo Tony DeLisa drove the ice pick through Arthur Maggio's left ear all the way up to the hilt.

35

MARCH 6, 1994
9:57 A.M.

It was raining. Not misting or drizzling, but sky-splitting, earth-shattering, torrential downpour raining. Chief Govich's black Chevy with the buggy-whip antenna pulled off 103rd Street onto the gravel road leading up to the abandoned Amalgamated Steelworks Compound. A hundred feet down the road the car was stopped by a sour-faced policeman whose nylon cap and raincoat were drenched with falling rain water.

The detective driving the car rolled the window down. The rain-soaked cop looked from him to the occupant of the front passenger seat. Recognition dawned immediately and he waved them on.

The black car proceeded to what was left of the Amalgamated Steelworks factory at which six thousand Chicagoans had once been employed. Now the building was in such a gross state of disrepair it was in danger of imminent collapse. A summer storm of near tornado proportions had taken out the east wall two years before. What was left played a waiting game between the wrecking ball and the next storm.

The black car drove into the building following the tire tracks from the road through the space left by the missing wall. Halfway down the length of the block-long structure, a knot of official vehicles was assembled around a 1993 burgundy Cadillac Alante.

Govich got out of the car and walked carefully to avoid the leaks pouring through the sievelike ceiling onto the floor below. The Area Two detective commander, a red-faced beer-bellied man named Tim Shroeder, came over to meet him.

"Mornin', boss."

"Tim," Govich said looking past the commander at the expensive car. The head and shoulders of a body could be seen in the driver's seat through the rear window.

"It's a mob hit," Shroeder explained. He was wheezing slightly because he was a chain smoker. "Guy's really fucked up. Ice pick marks all over him, his prick's been blowtorched and . . ."

"Who is he?" Govich knew the drill. He'd been handling mob executions in Chicago for over thirty years.

Shroeder lowered his voice and stepped so close to Govich the chief could smell the tobacco odor on his breath. "It's Arthur Maggio. Tuxedo Tony's right-hand man."

Govich's face remained passive. "The lab through with the scene?"

"Yes, sir. They just finished before you arrived."

Govich walked past Shroeder to the Cadillac. A couple of detectives were starting to search around the body preparatory to moving it. When they saw the chief and Shroeder coming, they got out of the way.

Maggio was sitting up in the front seat. His nude, mutilated body stood out in sharp contrast against the luxury of the car's interior. Govich merely bent at the waist to look inside the car. He didn't touch anything.

"Whose car?"

"It's registered to a Grace Maggio," Shroeder said. "Probably the wife."

"She is."

The chief took it all in for another minute or two before turning away and heading for his car. Shroeder, wheezing noisily, ran to catch up.

"Tuxedo Tony's developed some very dangerous enemies," Shroeder said. "What is this, three of his guys in two days?"

Govich didn't break stride. "It wasn't his enemies. DeLisa did that himself. It's his style. When you get the body to the morgue you'll find a dead parakeet stuffed in Maggio's mouth."

They reached Govich's car. "That marks him as a stoolie," Shroeder said. "But who was he talking to?"

"It wasn't us, so who's left?"

Before Shroeder could answer, the chief had gotten back into his squad car and slammed the door. He didn't hear the Area Two detective commander say, "The Feds?"

36

MARCH 6, 1994
10:10 A.M.

Antonio DeLisa knotted his black tie and slipped on his black suit jacket. He splashed a dab of Gray Flannel after-shave on his freshly shaven cheeks and prepared to face the new day. He left his bedroom and crossed the hall to Rachel's room. He knocked softly and entered.

The main body of the storm that had rocked the city and suburbs since dawn had passed; however, there were still heavy rumblings from the skies. Despite it being midmorning, the room was in semidarkness because of the overcast day and the shades being drawn. DeLisa could make out the silhouette of someone sitting in the chair beside his daughter's bed. He wasn't able to make out who it was until he crossed the room. The male bodyguard Sam, who usually accompanied Rachel to school, stood watch and it looked like he'd been at it for awhile.

DeLisa frowned when he saw him, but at that moment the mobster had more important things on his mind.

He looked down at his daughter. She was still asleep. He'd been in to see her seven times during the night and early morning hours. Each time she had been unconscious and lying in the exact same position she was now. Once, at about 3:00 A.M., before he had gone out with Wally and a couple of the boys to dump Maggio's body, he'd become so concerned over her lack of movement he had taken her pulse. It was slow, but steady. Tuxedo Tony didn't actually know whether that was good or bad. After the drop he'd called his neighbor the doctor.

"The rest is good for her, Tony. I'm sure there are no complications, but if you want I can look in on her later in the morning."

"Yeah, you'd better do that. I'll see you then."

But all the doctor could tell him after he'd seen Rachel was that she was resting quietly. This made DeLisa roll his eyes. He already knew that.

Now she was still asleep and he didn't like it. But it was getting late and he had business to take care of.

"How long you been here?" he whispered to the bodyguard.

"Since five, Mr. DeLisa."

"She wake up at all?"

"No, sir. Not once."

DeLisa took one last look at her before bending down to kiss her cheek. Her flesh felt cool against his lips. He tiptoed from the room.

Wally Boykin was waiting for him downstairs. He held a black raincoat and black cap for his boss. As he helped DeLisa into them, Boykin asked, "How's Rachel?"

"She's still out cold. What did that quack give her last night, an elephant tranquilizer?"

Boykin did not reply.

"And look, get some women to sit with her. I don't want no young stud sitting up there figuring she's knocked out so he can take himself a piece of ass. I don't want no strange cases of immaculate conception around here."

Boykin's eyes widened in shock. "Gee, Mr. DeLisa, wouldn't none of the boys try nothing like that with Rachel. That would be crazy."

"Crazy, huh?" DeLisa face split open in a snarl. "Would you say that shit Arthur pulled on me yesterday was fucking sane? Look, you find some broads to come in here and stay with my daughter and you put another guy up there to watch Mr. Macho Stud while I'm gone. I ain't through with him for leaving her alone yesterday."

"Yes, sir," Boykin said. "But I thought you wanted me to go with you."

DeLisa started for the door. "Do what I told you, Wally. I'll make the meet with the Kraut on my own. You take care of Rachel."

37

MARCH 6, 1994
10:25 A.M.

DeLisa's chauffeured Lincoln Town Car followed the Ford Crown Victoria through the gates of his estate onto the streets of Oak Park. Traveling bumper to bumper, the two cars headed for the expressway.

The network of federal agents picked up the convoy the instant it left the estate grounds.

"Gingiss One and Two are rolling."

"Can you confirm occupancy of Gingiss One in the Town Car?"

"Negative, but the principal should be aboard. Repeat, the principal should be aboard."

"Chase One, we're taking up position at Green and Highwood Streets. Will follow Gingiss One and Two to the expressway. Copy?"

"Roger, Chase One. Looks like he's headed for the warehouse. We copy."

The convoy proceeded to the Eisenhower Expressway and sped east. The Crown Victoria and the Lincoln were bracketed by nine federal agents in six different vehicles. At this instant in history, mobster Antonio "Tuxedo Tony" DeLisa was as well protected as the president of the United States.

At Laramie Avenue in the city, the DeLisa convoy and four of the federal vehicles exited. In tandem, they sped south on Laramie.

The rain had slackened, but was still falling steadily out of a menacingly dark sky. The cars moved slowly across the slick pavement, maintaining a rigid distance. To a casual observer it would almost seem as if the drivers of all the cars involved, both mob and federal, were aware of each other. In fact, they were; however, the federal agents would have been shocked to learn that Tuxedo Tony knew not only the make, color and year of each of the federal cars, but also each of their license plate numbers. There were informants taking bribes on both sides of this game of cat and mouse.

The Del-Ray Distributing Company was located in the 5200 block of South Laramie Avenue. From a two-story warehouse with six loading bays and two docks, trucks bearing the red and white Del-Ray logo delivered liquor to selected establishments throughout the city. Tony DeLisa was the sole owner and operator of Del-Ray.

The Ford and Lincoln pulled into the parking lot through a gate in the fence. The cyclone fence was eight feet tall with barbed wire on top stretching completely around the property. The federal surveillance cars drove past the gate and kept going south.

Across the street from the Del-Ray Distributing Company was the Blum and Rosenthal meatpacking plant. For a little help in securing a federal contract to supply meat to the military, Blum and Rosenthal allowed federal agents to use their plant by parking two surveillance vans on their property. Tuxedo Tony knew about this arrangement too.

"Chase One to Surveillance Alpha. Gingiss One and Two have arrived."

"Surveillance Alpha, we copy."

Tuxedo Tony's convoy pulled into designated parking places in front of the warehouse. The two bodyguards in the Ford got out first and checked the parking lot and the loading dock area. At the loading dock a van was being loaded with cartons of booze. The driver of the Lincoln got out with an umbrella and opened the back door for DeLisa. Shielding the mobster from the street with their bodies, the three bodyguards escorted him quickly into the building.

"Where's Boykin?" asked the agent monitoring the closed-circuit television in the back of a tractor trailer in the Blum and Rosenthal parking lot.

His partner sat on a stool behind him reading the *Times-Herald*. She frowned and picked up a walkie-talkie.

"Surveillance Alpha to any chase car on the Gingiss frequency."

"Chase Three."

"Lurch is not with Gingiss One today."

"Affirmative. Must have called in sick."

"Neither is Gomez."

"I don't know what to tell you, Surveillance Alpha. Maybe Gingiss One has turned over a new leaf."

The female agent frowned and dropped the mike. "You're a funny man, whoever you are."

"So," the agent watching the screen said, "do we report it?"

"No. DeLisa's there. He's the only one we're being paid to watch."

The rain continued to fall and the forecast was for no letup for the rest of the day. The agent's eyes strayed from the screen to the text book on real estate management he was studying. The van being loaded at the dock was the only place where there was movement on any of the four-color monitors in front of him. He was unable to see who was doing the loading due to the angle at which the van was parked. The agent made a note of the van's license plate number and promptly forgot it.

A burly black man with the build of a Sumo wrestler slammed the back door of the van and got behind the wheel. He jerked the gear shift lever into drive and skidded away from the dock. At the front gate he stopped and waited for traffic on Laramie to clear.

"Smile, Connie. You're a star on the F.B.I. television network," DeLisa said from the back of the van, where he was concealed behind a stack of boxes.

The stocky driver grunted, made a left turn and sped north toward the expressway.

The F.B.I. Surveillance Alpha agents made a note of the van's departure. Tuxedo Tony DeLisa was reported as being physically present at the Del-Ray Distributing Company for the rest of the day.

38

MARCH 6, 1994
10:45 A.M.

Larry Cole reread the summary he had typed on the screen of his computer. He had enough facts to go to the State's Attorney for charging and, with a bit more probing, he could probably come up with sufficient evidence for a grand jury indictment. But did he really have enough to justify getting Senator Banks's name dragged through a murder investigation?

He reviewed the facts. Charles Butcher and Angelo Cappeletti had been killed with a propelled, possibly thrown, sharp projectile. The department had the taped conversation from Banks's office with a man's voice saying that Butcher and Cappeletti were outside. Reggie Stanton, while serving as a Chicago Police officer, had been investigated fifteen years before as a suspect in murders with this exact same MO. Now Stanton was with the F.B.I. and involved in some way with Senator Banks. And Stanton had lied to Cole.

Cole leaned back in his chair and stared at the typed words on the computer screen until they blurred. When Stanton had told him there had been no one in the office at the time the police had received the call, Cole had known he was lying. The Call Location Identifier equipment was carefully monitored and kept in good repair. A citizen's life could depend on the system working properly. Stanton's evasiveness and volunteering to gather the information establishing his and the senator's alibis had confirmed this lie. Cole had decided to go along with him, because at that point he actually had no choice. It would also give the F.B.I. man a chance to tighten the noose around his muscular neck.

Cole was also in a quandary about Stanton claiming to be a federal agent. Hell, he *was* a federal agent and Cole had seen enough official identification to be able to spot a phony. Stanton's was genuine. But how did he figure in with Banks? In with Banks and the murders of a couple of low-life mobsters like Butcher and Cappeletti?

He pressed the Save button and removed the cassette from the machine. He carefully locked it in his desk drawer and picked up his notes. He realized that he had a responsibility to at least keep Chief Govich updated on his progress. Then what? Cole was aware of Senator Banks's plan for the Senate Crime Committee to be convened in Washington next week. If Banks was sincere, and there was every indication that he was, then Tuxedo Tony DeLisa would be out of business in Chicago and persona non grata with the rest of the organized crime families in America. The publicity would make his fellow big city crime lords nervous. It would also be the signal to aspirants to the throne of Chicago Mafia boss that it was time for Tuxedo Tony to "sleep with the fishes," as the movies called it.

But if Banks didn't conduct the committee all bets were off.

Cole was still wrestling with this dilemma between duty and conscience when Blackie knocked on his office door.

"Come."

The sergeant stuck his head in the door. "We're still waiting for you to give us the word, boss."

Cole had Blackie, Bronson and Sherlock standing by in case he needed them to do any legwork for him. A half hour ago he didn't think he was going to need them at all. Then an idea came to him.

"Get them and come in, Blackie."

A few minutes later they were seated in chairs across the desk from Cole. Each had a notebook open and pen poised over it waiting for his instructions.

"First, I want someone to go downtown to Records and look up a series of homicides which occurred sometime in mid- to late July nineteen seventy-nine."

"Sir?" Sherlock's head snapped up from his notes. "Did you say nineteen seventy-nine?"

"That's exactly what I said, Manny."

Blackie frowned. "Pay attention, Sherlock. The boss ain't got all day."

"Lou, you were in Area Two back then, weren't you?" Cole asked.

"Yes, sir."

"Do you remember a series of homicides in which street people were killed with a knife? It was all done vigilante fashion."

Bronson chewed at a thumbnail. "Yeah, I think there were a couple of dope dealers and a prostitute done. Didn't somebody accuse a cop of being responsible?"

Cole smiled. "A cop named Reggie Stanton. Worked out of the Sixth District. The I.A.D. took over the investigation. They might still have a file on it."

"I doubt that, boss," Blackie said. "They're only supposed to keep inactive files for five years."

"But maybe this file's still active. It could have been closed in some type of exceptional fashion because no one could be charged. It could be down there on the twelfth floor of Eleventh and State waiting for us to come get it."

"Okay, I'll take a look at that one myself," Blackie said.

"The last thing I want is for you to find out everything available about Senator Harvey Banks."

The three of them looked at the commander. No one spoke.

Cole didn't see the need to explain. In fact, he felt it better that they know as little about what they were gathering information for as possible.

"I would say that there are plenty of sources we can go to to find out about the senator," Bronson said. "Is there anything you want in particular?"

"No. Just get as much as you can," Cole said. "Questions?"

They had none.

"Then let's get to it."

Blackie remained behind after Bronson and Sherlock left.

"We got a slight problem, boss. That Policewoman Daniels on loan to us from Narcotics."

"Yeah."

"Well, we're gonna be stuck with her for awhile because of the shooting yesterday."

"Says who?"

"The First Deputy's Office. The assistant deputy superintendent wrote it up as a good shooting, but they've extended her detail for a week, so she'll still be assigned here."

"We can always use another warm body," Cole said without much enthusiasm.

"That stuff you gave us to do is fairly routine. Maybe I could take her along with me when I go downtown. She could help me go through the files."

"Won't that be a bit tame for a fast-track, undercover narc like the Mistress of Disguise/High Priestess of Mayhem?"

"Oh, so you've heard of her?"

"Sarge," Cole said, smiling, "everybody's heard of Judy Daniels. If you want, take her along, but no more motorcycle rides."

"Yes, sir."

Blackie reached the door and stopped. "Oh, boss. It just came across the teletype before we came in. They found Art Maggio's body in a car over on the southeast side."

"Wasn't he Tuxedo Tony's right-hand man?"

"The same. But somebody was real mad at him. He had an ice pick in his ear and another up his prick. His balls had been torched and there were fifty odd stab wounds around the body."

"Sounds like something Tuxedo Tony would do. I wonder if they found a parakeet in his mouth?"

"I'd be willing to bet on it," Blackie said before letting himself out.

39

The Del-Ray Distributing Company van pulled into the parking lot of the O'Hare Expo Center and slowly cruised the aisles. When it was certain that no smart federal agent had tumbled to the deception pulled off to evade the surveillance, the van pulled to a side entrance to the Expo Center and parked.

The back door of the van opened and a man stepped out. He wore a cheap dark brown wig that was slightly off-center, a pair of sunglasses with black frames and an orange and green plaid sports jacket. He sported a bushy, sandy-colored mustache that made no attempt to match the color of the wig and a small gold earring in his left ear.

It was still raining and he quickly crossed the sidewalk to the door of the convention hall and entered. Ordinarily, he would have stood out, but when he went through the door he became lost in a sea of humanity that was dressed in a very similar fashion.

Tuxedo Tony DeLisa, in disguise, had joined the Annual Midwest Convention of the National Organization of Auto and Truck Exhaust System Repair Mechanics (NOATESRM). Although few were dressed as outlandishly as he was, there were enough unusual sights so that no one gave him more than a glance.

The main floor of the Expo Center was crowded with conventioneers studying various exhibits of new hardware and tools they could use in their war against excessive air pollution. DeLisa moved along from exhibit to exhibit blending in and twice exchanging comments with a couple of conventioneers about exhaust system improvements.

After making a thorough scan for anyone taking more than a passing interest in him, DeLisa made it to an escalator and ascended to the mezzanine. Noise from the crowd below followed him, but when he stepped off the escalator he was alone.

Playing his role, he looked around the area as if he were a lost hayseed looking for a washroom. When no one appeared to challenge him, he crossed the mezzanine level to an Exit door that could not be seen from the convention floor.

He climbed three flights of stairs, becoming angry with himself when his breathing became labored from the exertion. Since this thing with the senator had been going on, he'd neglected his racquetball.

The door he stopped at was marked with a 4. Carefully, he opened it a crack and looked into the empty corridor beyond. A wall of windows illuminated the area. There were three doors leading off the corridor, one at the far end and two opposite the windows on his right. The second one down was his destination.

Assuming his lost-exhaust-system-mechanic-from-the-sticks shuffle, he stepped into the corridor. The place was deathly silent. DeLisa felt moisture forming on his forehead beneath the cheap wig. He didn't like this, but he figured maybe he wasn't supposed to.

He reached the second door on the right and knocked. There was no response. Nervously, he checked the corridor once more and went inside.

He found himself in an Expo Center meeting room. It was fairly large and capable of seating from two hundred and fifty to three hundred people. What DeLisa particularly didn't like was that it was dark and empty. At least it appeared empty.

He held the outside door open to provide illumination, while he looked around for a light switch. It was after twelve o'clock, which was the time Kirschstein had given him, so he wasn't early. He hadn't liked this setup from the start, but then he had no choice. He couldn't very well invite the Kraut to Oak Park with the feds watching him. Yet this whole thing didn't seem right. It didn't seem right possibly because too many times in his life he had lured people to isolated locations just like this so he could kill them.

DeLisa's hand moved along the surface of the wall until his fingers touched a metal panel. He was extended in a ludicrously awkward position with one leg stretched out behind him while he leaned forward reaching for the switch. He realized he was terribly vulnerable. Anger at his situation came mixed with fear.

His fingers felt the edges of a light switch and flicked it up. He released the door. It slammed shut; however, no lights went on. Tuxedo Tony stood alone in the dark.

"Just relax, Mr. DeLisa," a voice came from right beside him. "You're among friends."

"Friends don't fuck around with the lights!" DeLisa reached inside his waistband for the 9 mm. automatic he had taken from the warehouse before getting into the van.

"Don't touch the gun."

DeLisa froze. He could see nothing, but obviously they could see him.

"Walk straight ahead."

The voice was non-threatening, almost pleasant.

DeLisa didn't move, but he rationalized that if they had wanted to kill him he would already be dead. Then another voice spoke.

"We haven't got a great deal of time for these negotiations, Mr. DeLisa. Either you follow our instructions or you'll be standing in the dark alone."

This voice was deeper and the German accent was noticeable. Now Tuxedo Tony knew who he was dealing with. A bit of his tension eased as he moved forward.

He took slow, careful steps through the dark. He kept his hands raised in front of him like a blind man, but felt nothing but dry, cold air blowing through the ventilation ducts. Once someone moved very close to him before slipping away. DeLisa refused to cry out like a frightened child. He understood these games. He'd played them many times before himself, but he hadn't expected this of Steiger.

"Stop." The German-accented voice brought DeLisa to an abrupt halt.

"If you drop your hands slowly you will touch the back of a chair. I want you to sit down in that chair."

DeLisa did as he was told.

"It would help if you removed your glasses," the other voice said.

He did.

Gradually, he was able to make out a couple of silhouettes sitting in chairs some twenty-five feet directly in front of him. There was illumination from some source, but he wasn't able to make it out at first. Then a single candle, resting on the floor behind them, flickered.

"What can we do for you, Mr. DeLisa?"

"You're Steiger aren't you? Did some work a few years back for Paul Arcadio."

There came no response from the silhouettes.

"Hey, I need to know who I'm dealing with here. I don't lay out deals with nobody in the dark."

"Is that a pun?" The other voice dripped with sarcasm.

"Silence!" the one with the accent snapped.

DeLisa was starting to have a bad feeling about this entire thing. He began inching his hand toward his gun.

"Mr. DeLisa," the one with the accent said. "I am the man whom Mr. Arcadio hired in July of nineteen ninety-one to deal with the problem posed by Mr. DeAngelis of Kansas City. Now please place your hands palm down on your knees and leave them there. My associate is going to relieve you of your sidearm so we won't be distracted any further from our negotiations."

Someone was there in the dark beside him. He was touched quickly, but not roughly. Then the pressure was gone and he was disarmed. He had never been more frightened of anyone or anything in his life.

"Now that we have that out of the way, would you like to tell us why you're here?"

"You're Steiger, right? The one with the accent?"

"We're both Steiger. You may speak freely."

"Okay. I'll do it your way. I want a job done."

"What kind of job?"

"I want a man killed."

"What man?"

"His name is Harvey Banks."

"The United States senator?" There was no added emphasis in the German's tone.

"Y-yes. The senator." DeLisa found it difficult making his mouth work.

"And you do not want it to appear to be an assassination?"

"That's right. Make it look like an accident or natural causes. Whatever you want. You're the Mastermind, right?"

"It will cost you one million dollars."

"What? You gotta be fucking kidding? For a million bucks I could buy the black bastard off."

"Then why don't you do that, Mr. DeLisa? It will make for a happier situation all around. Have a good day."

"No wait!"

Silence came from the shadows in front of him.

"Just give me a minute or two to think."

"Of course, but we can't remain here much longer. It's dangerous for all of us."

DeLisa rubbed his forehead. He never thought it would cost this much. But then this guy . . . he corrected to think, *these guys,* guaranteed results and were good. Whomever had taken that gun off him moved like a ghost.

"Okay. I'll pay the price. A million. How do you want it? Half down and the rest later?"

"You're not buying a car, Mr. DeLisa. You pay all in front, we do the job at our own pace. Our reputation is your assurance that the senator will indeed die."

"That's not good enough." DeLisa fought to control his anger. "I need this job done before Monday."

"Why?"

DeLisa snatched the orange handkerchief from the breast pocket of his blazer and dabbed his face. "The senator's convening this crime committee in Washington. Supposed to have a ton of evidence, but I think he's just blowing smoke. The problem is I got people that are telling me Banks is going to subpoena me to testify. I could have some problems behind that."

"Problems similar to the ones Mr. Arcadio suffered a few years ago?" the other one said.

"Hey, what the fuck are you, some kind of goddamned comedian?" DeLisa said jumping to his feet. "You need to take that shit to one of the casinos in Vegas. Maybe there you'll find someone who'll appreciate it!"

"I'm sorry," the sarcastic one said flatly. "I didn't know you were so touchy."

The one with the German accent interrupted, "You pay the money following the arrangements we outline and the job will be done before the senator convenes the crime committee."

DeLisa sat down. He didn't like laying games in the dark, but then at this point he had no choice. "Okay," he said, "you've got a deal."

40

MARCH 6, 1994
12:32 P.M.

Blackie Silvestri drove the unmarked police car up to Building C of the city's archives warehouse on South Sacramento Avenue. He got out with an umbrella and came around to open the door for Judy Daniels. They huddled together as they hurried into the building.

The I.A.D. files were in locked cabinets that had been carted intact from the twelfth floor of police headquarters. In order to gain access to them, which entailed a not-too-interested male clerk showing them the way and providing a set of keys, they had to produce a requisition signed by their commander. Of course, Cole had obliged.

After finding the appropriate cabinets, they would have to pull the files and carry them half the length of the warehouse to an area furnished with reading lamps, scarred wooden tables and rickety, rusting folding chairs. No files could be taken from the warehouse, but a copy machine was available for use as long as the requisitions authorized duplicates. Theirs did.

Judy had become a completely different person in appearance from the one Blackie had met the day before. The woman yesterday had been the career girl type. A professional. Smart, confident, sexy, but not a sex object. A woman who was comfortable with her own body. The person today was different. This one was a mouse. The librarian or file clerk type. With short hair, enormous horn-rimmed glasses, she was even stoop-shouldered with a funny little bouncy walk she executed with short steps. Boy, Blackie thought, he really had to give it to her. She was one hell of an actress to carry off yesterday's deception when she was really just a little slip of a girl who seemed afraid of her own shadow.

Then, as they drove across the city to the archive warehouses, an intriguing thought struck him. Maybe this wasn't the real Judy Daniels either. Maybe this was just another role the Mistress of Disguise/High Priestess of Mayhem had assumed for his benefit. If it was, Blackie figured, she deserved an Academy Award.

It took them half an hour to find the file. Judy pulled it from the back of the third drawer of a four-drawer cabinet.

"This is it, Sarge," she called to Blackie, who was on his knees in a cabinet two rows away.

They carried the file to the reading area. The material was two inches thick and bound with a thick rubber band. Blackie turned on a lamp and sat down. Judy pulled up a chair beside him. The worn, yellowing manila folder was stenciled in black lettering with: COMPLAINT REGISTER NUMBER 768190—ACCUSED: POLICE OFFICER REGINALD E. STANTON #12111—SIXTH DISTRICT—OPENED: 22 JULY 1979—FILED: 4 AUGUST 1979.

Blackie removed the rubber band and opened the folder. The first sheet was a form headed: COMPLAINT REGISTER SUMMARY REPORT. It contained much of the same information that was listed on the cover with one addition. There was a short narrative box headed ALLEGATIONS. Blackie and Judy read them together.

Officer Reginald E. Stanton #12111—Sixth District—is alleged to have committed the following criminal acts:

1. The murder of William "Big Willie" McCoy, Sr. M/B/DOB 19 May 1936.

2. The murder of Cassandra "Gunslinger" Davis F/B/DOB 20 March 1957.

3. The murder of Pablo "Little Caesar" Martinez M/WH/DOB 5 November 1949.

4. The murder of William "Little Willie" McCoy, Jr. M/B/DOB 19 May 1958.

All acts are alleged to have been committed while Police Officer Stanton was acting in the capacity of a sworn member of the Chicago Police Department.

"Wow," Judy said breathlessly.

"Yeah," Blackie said with a frown. " 'Wow' is right. But I don't get it."

"Don't get what, Sarge?"

"If this Stanton was accused of committing four homicides it wouldn't have been any I.A.D. investigation. The Area Two Detectives would have handled it all the way. If they got anything on him it would have been a simple matter to go out and lock him up."

"Just like that?"

"Cops got no immunity, Judy," Blackie said flipping to the next page in the file. "In fact, maybe we got fewer rights than the average asshole walking the streets."

At that moment Judy's beeper went off. She looked at the display and frowned.

"Your boyfriend checking up on you?" Blackie said.

"No. It's an old girlfriend's number. You think there's a phone around here?"

"Should be one out front."

"I'll be right back."

While she was gone, Blackie returned to the file. The next several pages listed the attachments, which was an index of the numbered documents in the file. There were fifty-six of them. The first four were the results of the criminal investigations into the deaths of the people Stanton was accused of killing. The fifth was listed as "Report of Chief of Detectives William R. Riseman requesting investigation transfer to I.A.D. dated 22 July 1979."

Blackie flipped through the file until he came to Attachment Five. It was a single page report. It read:

OFFICE OF THE CHIEF OF THE DETECTIVE DIVISION

22 July 1979

TO: Superintendent of Police
FROM: William R. Riseman
          Chief of the Detective Division
SUBJECT: Request to transfer active criminal investigations from the Detective Division to the Internal Affairs Division.

1. Per our conversation of 22 July 1979 at 1645 hours, it is hereby officially requested that the following active criminal investigations be transferred from the Detective Division to the Internal Affairs Division for further action. These cases are listed under the following Records Division Numbers:

X-283221
X-283375
X-284100
X-284199

2. Your expeditious approval of this request would be greatly appreciated.

William R. Riseman
Chief of the Detective Division

The question raged through Blackie's mind. Why? He'd been a cop too long not to smell the rat lurking within the pages of this file. Then Chief of Detectives Riseman, with the then superintendent's full approval, had pulled a fast one. They had covered up four murders to protect this Reginald Stanton. Blackie figured that if he looked long enough and hard enough he could come up with an answer to his questions. But first he had to read the entire file.

He flipped back to the front and was beginning the case report on the homicide of one William "Big Willy" McCoy, Jr., when Judy returned.

"Sarge, I think I've got something."

Blackie looked up. "What?"

She spoke in a rush. "That was a friend of mine I went to high school with. She's been on a fast track since we graduated. Her name's Karen Schmidt, but she changed it to Carrie Curtis. She's worked in Las Vegas and Hollywood, but not legitimately. She's a hooker—a high-priced call girl working for Tuxedo Tony DeLisa. She moved back to Chicago a few months ago and went to work at DeLisa's place in Oak Park as a bodyguard for his daughter Rachel."

Blackie sat up straight.

Judy ran her hand through her hair. "Something happened yesterday. She wouldn't tell me what, but it was hard for her to talk. I think DeLisa beat her up. Now she's alone and scared. She wants me to come get her."

"Will she talk?" There was skepticism in Blackie's question. He knew mob types, male and female, well. He'd been around them all his life.

"Like I said, she's scared, Sarge. We help her and get her some protection, she just might."

Blackie picked up the folder. "Let's go."

"I thought we weren't supposed to remove that file from the building."

"I'll bring it back," he said, slipping the file beneath his trench coat and grabbing her by the arm. "They'll never miss it."

41

The Chicago Office of the F.B.I. is located at 219 South Dearborn on the ninth floor of the Dirksen Federal Building. Inside the glass doors at the entrance to the office, a wholesome-looking redhead sat typing routine reports and answering calls coming into the switchboard. When Chief Jack Govich walked in she looked up and smiled warmly before glancing at the black man accompanying him.

"How've you been, Jack?" she said. "Or do I have to call you 'chief' now?"

"You do and I'll bite you."

"Promises, promises."

"This is Commander Larry Cole. Larry, Martha Grimes, the best receptionist in the state."

"You said the country last time."

"I did?" Cole said grinning. "I must have been drunk."

"No. I was the one drunk and you got me that way. I'm pleased to meet you, Commander."

Cole nodded.

She looked back at Govich. "It's too late for lunch and too early for dinner, so I can assume you're not here for me."

"We want to see Franklin."

"Without an appointment? You must be insane."

Govich reached over and picked up her telephone. "Call him and tell him we're here. If he gets huffy, remind him about November of ninety-two."

"You promised you'd never bring that up again," she protested without a great deal of vehemence.

"I lied, Marty. Now call him."

A few minutes later they were being escorted back through a maze of cubicles to a row of offices overlooking Dearborn Street. They were deposited on a pair of vinyl chairs separated by a wooden table piled with F.B.I. bulletins.

A few minutes later a craggy-faced man of fifty, with tousled hair in a style made popular by John F. Kennedy, stepped in front of them. He had a sour expression on his face.

"It's good to see you again, Jack," he said extending his hand.

"Same here, Dave. I'd like you to meet my Area One detective commander. Larry Cole this is Dave Franklin, the special agent-in-charge of the F.B.I.'s Chicago office."

Franklin extended his hand to Cole. The commander noticed the sightless stare Franklin gave him. The special agent-in-charge's mind was somewhere far away from the location where his body now stood.

Franklin had a corner office. The view was of the Kluzynski Federal Building across the street and the Van Buren el tracks running in front of the downtown Federal Correctional Center on Clark Street.

When they were seated, Franklin barely suppressed his annoyance as he said, "This is a bad time for me, Jack. Why didn't you call?"

"I know you're busy, Dave," Govich said with ease. "The commander and I won't be long, but I didn't want to talk about this over the telephone."

Franklin stared blankly back at him. "Talk about what?"

"Tuxedo Tony DeLisa."

Not one muscle of Franklin's face moved. "What about him?"

"You're investigating him."

"So are you."

"C'mon, Dave. It's me. I'm not talking about the limited range bullshit our Organized Crime Division can put together. I mean a major investigation. Round the clock surveillance, wiretaps, electronic bugging, the whole nine yards."

Franklin shook his head. "What is it with you local cops? You figure that we make a major production out of every case. You know the Bureau has a budget too."

"Yeah, tell me about it," Govich said. "I'll bet my next paycheck that a large part of that budget in Chicago is being spent trying to nail Tuxedo Tony."

Franklin turned cold. "Is that why you came up here? To talk about my budget?"

"Take it easy, Dave. You must be working too hard. You never used to get this uptight. Lighten up, for chrissakes."

"Jack, I'm really busy and I'm probably going to be in the office late tonight, so I'd appreciate it if you'd please stop kidding around and get to the point."

Govich nudged Cole's arm. "What'd I tell you about these Feds. Tough as nails. Efrem Zimbalist, Jr., would be proud of this guy."

Before Franklin could explode, Govich said, "Arthur Maggio got hit. We found him this morning. Balls blowtorched, prick skewered with an ice pick, the whole smiel."

"So?" Franklin said. "Another dead mobster. I thought things like that made you people happy."

"He had a parakeet jammed down his throat, Dave. He was a stoolie. Now there's no way an operation like ours can come up with the trump to make a guy like Maggio flip and we didn't have shit on him we could use for pressure, so he wasn't talking to us. That leaves you."

Franklin shook his head. "What about the D.E.A. or the Treasury Department?"

"C'mon, Dave. Maggio would have laughed at them. The only people could run him would have been the Bureau and in Chicago that means you'd have been in charge."

Franklin glanced impatiently at his watch. "So what do you want?"

"We'd like to take a look at the stuff Maggio was feeding you about Tuxedo Tony."

"That's out of the question."

"Why? Maggio's dead. We won't expose your stoolie. Somebody already did that. What I want is to hang a murder rap on DeLisa."

Franklin laughed. "Be serious. You'll never get him dirty that way."

"They said the same thing about Al Capone."

Franklin stood up. "Okay, I'll see what I can do, but no promises."

Cole started to rise, but when Govich remained seated he stayed down as well. Franklin was not pleased.

"There's just one more thing, Dave, then me and Larry'll get out of your hair."

"I'm all ears."

"I'll let the commander explain it."

Cole cleared his throat and looked at the F.B.I. man. He found that Franklin was again giving him that sightless stare.

"We have reason to believe that DeLisa has put out a contract on Senator Harvey Banks."

Franklin's expression did not change.

"The two hit men he sent the other night were found dead on Tuxedo Tony's doorstep."

"I'd say that was a form of poetic justice," Franklin said dryly.

"The killer was very efficient," Cole continued. "No guns. Just a knife. A throwing knife."

Franklin was tuning up to throw them out.

"We were concerned that the senator might still be in danger. At least we were until yesterday."

"Gentlemen," Franklin said with exasperation, "I'm sure this is all terribly interesting and has a lot of relevance to the case or cases you are currently working on, but I've got a lot to do, so if you don't mind. . . . " He opened the door.

The two policemen stood up. "We're sorry for taking up so much of your time, Dave," Govich said, "but we really didn't have a choice." Govich took a step toward the open door and stopped. "Oh, Larry, you forgot to tell him the part about why we're no longer concerned about the senator's life."

Cole stared levelly at Franklin. "That's because Senator Banks has an F.B.I. agent named Reggie Stanton as his bodyguard."

Franklin continued to stare at Cole. His somber expression had not changed, but now his eyes were focused. He was actually look-

ing at Cole for the first time since the commander had walked into
his office.

"The F.B.I. doesn't do bodyguard work," Franklin said.

"This one does," Cole countered.

"Do you know this Reggie Stanton, Dave?" Govich asked.

"I've never heard of him and like I said, the Bureau doesn't do
bodyguard work. This . . . what did you say his name was?"

"Stanton," Cole said. "Reggie Stanton."

"Well, this Stanton is probably an impostor."

"He had official F.B.I. identification," Govich said.

"Undoubtedly forged," Franklin said, making another attempt
to herd them out the door.

"Whatever you say, Dave," Govich said. "You will try to get
that information on DeLisa for us, won't you?"

"I'll call you."

"Nice meeting you," Cole said, following Govich.

"Same here, Commander," Franklin said, as he shut the door
behind them.

They walked to the front of the office and across the reception
area, where Martha Grimes was talking on the phone. They were
about to step into the hall when they heard her say, "Special Agent
Franklin of the Chicago Office is calling for Deputy Director Connors."

Govich stopped and waved to her. She winked back.

"I guess that didn't go too well," Cole said when they reached
the elevators.

"On the contrary, Commander," Govich said. "It went extremely well."

"I don't understand."

"I'll tell you about it downstairs."

When they hit the street Govich said, "You got a rise out of
Franklin when you mentioned Stanton's name. He may not have
looked it, but I've known him a long time. Before he became the
special agent-in-charge in Chicago, he used to come to my apartment for weekly card games. He's got a pretty good poker face, but
over the years I've learned to read him. He reacted to your talking
about Stanton in more ways than one."

Cole waited.

"Besides his face giving him away, he's got Martha calling a guy named Connors in Washington."

"Yeah, I heard her."

"Connors is in charge of a little-known section of the Bureau called Special Operations."

"Never heard of it."

"Few have. You probably won't find it in any F.B.I. directory, but it does serve a purpose."

Cole and Govich were forced to dodge a bus as they crossed Jackson Boulevard in front of the Federal Building. It wasn't until they reached the opposite side that Cole was able to ask, "What purpose?"

"Hard to say. Some agents will tell you it doesn't exist at all. Others speak guardedly when they talk about it and claim the division is staffed by phantoms. I would bet your Reggie Stanton is one of those phantoms."

"But what do they do, Chief?"

Govich's smile was grim. "Whatever's necessary."

42

MARCH 6, 1994
2:45 P.M.

The Forty-seventh Street Chicago Transit Authority bus pulled to a stop at Lake Park Avenue. Dressed in a sweat suit, hooded windbreaker and running shoes, Reggie Stanton got off. With his head bent against the wind-swept rain, he crossed the street to the Illinois Central overpass viaduct. On the opposite side of the viaduct he came out on Lake Shore Drive. He waited for a break in traffic before trotting across the northbound lanes into the park. He stretched and did knee bends for five minutes before starting to jog north along the western shore of Lake Michigan.

For the first mile his pace was slow. This was his warm-up period during which he listened to his body. His exertion was minimal with his breathing deepening slightly. He recalled that years ago he would start off running at a dead sprint. Back then he would run as long and as fast as he could until either he escaped or was caught. He was seldom caught. Then Uncle Ernst had taught him that he no longer had to run.

"You will do all the problems in section B of your mathematics workbook tonight and read the third story in the anthology for to-morrow," Mrs. Reed, the sixth grade teacher, said at dismissal time.

Reggie felt the peril of his eleven-year-old existence descend on him. He was a big boy for his age, and overweight. Not really fat, but plump with a thick middle and double chin. His nickname in the school yard was "White Meat." It was not complimentary.

His eyes swung to the wall clock in the classroom. It read 2:59. The second hand moved rapidly toward the twelve. At 3:00 school was out releasing the sixth graders from the confinement of this pub-lic education institution. They would all be happy except one. In-stead of freedom, Reggie would be propelled onto a dangerous obstacle course where gang members called Disciples and a strong-arm thug named Leo waited to trap him.

As he watched the clock, he became aware of his classmates' stares. Mrs. Reed made him sit in the first seat of the first row by the door. This was because he was her brightest pupil. This also hap-pened to be the best place for him to launch himself onto his escape route. He was also in plain view of each of the fifty black students jammed into the overcrowded classroom. He could feel their eyes on his back. Feel them mocking him, hating him, wanting him to fail simply because he had a lighter complexion than they did and pos-sessed eyes the local bully Bo Ross said belonged to a "Trick Baby."

The bell rang. Bo Ross did a fair imitation of a horse racing an-nouncer, as White Meat leaped for the door. "And they're off!"

The adult Reggie Stanton finished the first mile of his run and in-creased his pace for the second. Now his legs began pumping with a steady rhythm as he cracked the ten-minute-mile pace. He felt the power of his body asserting itself. He was a strong man. *"Mann-haft!"* Uncle Ernst had called him. He ran now for pleasure and conditioning. He could also run in pursuit. He would *never*—he clenched his thickly muscled fingers into fists—*never* run from anyone or anything again out of fear.

Each day White Meat took a different route from the school to his home in the old brownstone on Martin Luther King Drive. Each day he chose a different alley and series of gangways to make his escape through like a rat being pursued by a legion of scrawny alley cats. A different route since January when Leo had taken the Timex watch grandma had bought him for Christmas. He told her he lost it. He heard that Leo still wore it.

White Meat made it from the school on Thirty-fifth Street, around the southern perimeter of the Ida B. Wells projects to Thirty-ninth and King Drive. Now he would have to run from Thirty-ninth to Forty-fifth. Six blocks with potential minefields every step of the way and a no man's land at Forty-third Street.

In January he was almost home when Leo caught him. The thought of the big teenager with the black skin and red-rimmed eyes turned White Meat's stomach to ice.

"Where you goin', White Meat?" Leo said, holding onto the collar of his jacket.

"I'm goin' home. Let me go?"

Leo slapped him hard across the face. White Meat tasted blood. Tears of pain and humiliation welled in his eyes.

"How much money you got on you, White Meat?"

"I don't have no money."

Leo searched him and found thirty-five cents.

"Give me the watch."

"Please. My grandma gave it to me."

"Give me the watch, White Meat!"

White Meat gave him the watch.

He made his way toward Forty-third Street. Four doors west of this intersection was Floyd's Grill and Sandwich Shoppe. Leo hung out there. In order to survive, White Meat had learned a great deal about Leo and the Disciples street gang, who terrorized the entire neighborhood. He knew their hangouts and the times they were there. He knew the streets they traveled and which way to run if he accidentally encountered them. In his mind he was constantly planning escape routes and, if all else failed, hiding places. He faced his moment of greatest peril when he crossed the intersection of Forty-third Street and King Drive.

Today he was lucky. There was no Leo nor any Disciples to threaten him. White Meat made it to the front of the old brownstone where he lived with his grandmother, Ida Mae. Originally, the building had been a mansion, but as the area became ghettoized, it had been cut up into small, one-bedroom kitchenette apartments with common bathrooms on each floor.

White Meat and his grandmother lived on the first floor of the brownstone. They had the largest apartment in the building with a private washroom and exclusive access to the large kitchen with the American Eagle symbol in the linoleum pattern on the floor. Ida collected the rents, which afforded White Meat a certain status that he didn't enjoy on the street. This made the dilapidated ghetto structure White Meat's sanctuary.

Once safely inside, he walked down the narrow hall to their apartment. Locking the door behind him, he stepped into the small sitting room his grandmother kept for visitors. What he found there froze him in place. A heavyset white man, with a scarred face, short crew cut and the coldest eyes White Meat had ever seen, was sitting in his grandmother's chair. There was no one else in the room.

Their eyes locked. In that instant White Meat recognized him and was frightened. He had never seen the man before, yet the eyes staring back at him were exactly the same as his own. White Meat was frightened because of the man's size and the ferocity of his stare. As usual, when faced with the unknown, White Meat resorted to instinct. He turned to run.

It was then that Uncle Ernst spoke to his nephew for the first time. He barked, "Stop."

*   *   *

Running on the lakefront in 1994 Reggie Stanton reached Thirty-first Street and the end of his second mile. He increased his pace to cover the next mile in seven minutes. His body protested, but he pushed himself. Uncle Ernst had taught him to ignore pain. Ignore it or make it work for you. For the last twenty-four years Reggie had followed these teachings to the letter.

White Meat's grandmother came into the room carrying a tray containing a cup of coffee and a slice of cake for their visitor. Visits from white men always meant trouble and this man had shouted at him. White Meat's terror was so great he almost dashed across the room to bury his head in his grandmother's skirts.

But then there was something in the way the severe-looking blond man looked at him and not only held him riveted to the spot, but also transmitted that he had nothing to fear.

"This is . . . ," his grandmother hesitated, " . . . a relative."

White Meat glanced from her back at the man. Of course this was a joke.

"No, boy," the white man said in a voice that filled the cramped room with sound. "I am more than a relative. I am the Uncle Ernst." His accent was so thick they could barely understand him. They would have years to get used to it.

Reggie's breathing came in sharp rasps. He was pushing it and his body rebelled. But he refused to slow down. He blinked the sweat and rainwater out of his eyes and forced his mind back over the years to that time when Uncle Ernst had first come to them. Back to a time when he had hated the man he now thought of with love every day of his life.

"You must never talk about Uncle Ernst to anyone else but me, Reggie," Ida Stanton whispered in gravely serious tones.

"He's not my uncle, Grandma! He's a white man."

She gave him a look which was filled at once with pain, love and pity. "No, Reggie. He's your uncle. He's as much your blood kin as I am."

"Then why don't he take us to live in a white neighborhood? Why we got to live down here where everybody hates us?"

"Because he can't," she'd said. "He can't."

Even though White Meat had thought it impossible, the persecution he suffered increased.

"White Meat's grandma turning tricks with a white man," Bo Ross crowed to the whole playground at recess.

The lie about his grandmother inflamed him. Despite being outmuscled, White Meat attacked Bo. For the trouble he received a split lip, but also the accompanying satisfaction that for once he'd fought back.

On a late spring day, a week before school adjourned for the summer, Leo came after White Meat again. It was warm and White Meat was simply happy to be away from the stares and insults of his classmates. He still bore the scars from his fight with Bo and wasn't being as cautious as he normally was when he approached Forty-third and King Drive. He was crossing the street thirty yards from Floyd's Grill when Leo stepped outside and spied him.

"Hey, White Meat, c'mere."

Forgetting his bravery with Bo Ross, White Meat ran. Leo pursued.

With a terrible despair, White Meat realized that Leo was going to chase him all the way home. This would leave him no time to unlock the heavy downstairs door. That meant he would be caught. Caught, beaten and robbed again. As he ran, tears of fear and anguish flooded his eyes. He was also getting tired and Leo was getting closer. He made it to the wrought-iron fence surrounding the brownstone and was about to surrender when he saw Uncle Ernst working in the weed-strewn yard.

Uncle Ernst stood up when he saw White Meat approaching at a dead run. White Meat slowed down and looked back to see Leo stop twenty feat behind him. The thug took one look at the big German and fled. From that moment on White Meat began to see the white man in a different light. He also began calling him "Uncle Ernst."

The third mile completed, Reggie was beginning to feel stronger now. Getting his second wind. He felt at one with the sky, the air and the rain. He was a force of nature. Something formidable and dangerous. What he was now had begun to take shape that summer of 1970.

Uncle Ernst's accent was so thick that at times neither Reggie nor Ida could understand him. He was not very fluent in English, but he was getting better. Often he would revert to German to make a particular point. As a result, Reggie and Ida began understanding some of his native tongue. Especially the profanity.

"Scheisse!" Uncle Ernst swore after striking his finger with a hammer. He was repairing a shelf in the kitchen.

"Watch your language in this house, Ernst," Ida warned.

Reggie grinned. He understood the German word for excrement.

"Verdammt, do I have to show you everything, boy?" He swore at Reggie for failing to plant flowers properly in the garden Uncle Ernst had begun growing in the front yard. But the child learned a great deal more German than his grandmother. This was because he spent a great deal more time with Uncle Ernst.

"Never run from a fight," Uncle Ernst taught him. "You might end up with scars like mine, but then you'll probably give your share as well. But no matter what happens you'll always be able to hold your head high."

"Where did you get those scars?"

It was when Reggie asked such questions about the past that he would notice Uncle Ernst change. His face would become softer and his eyes would take on a dreamy quality. Once, Reggie had even witnessed a tear roll down his cheek.

"I got them in school."

"They fought you."

"No. We fought, because it was expected. These are dueling scars. They honor me."

"Will I have scars too?"

Ernst looked sternly at his nephew. "Perhaps, but before you get the scars you must first learn to fight."

* * *

Reggie Stanton would begin his fifth mile shortly. At that point Billie would join him. She would be fresh, having only run one mile at that point. She would push him, make it harder on him, taunt him with her speed. He would be ready for her.

"Das was mich nicht toted macht mich starker!" Uncle Ernest would scream when Reggie grew tired during training that first year. "That which does not kill you makes you stronger!" And he was certain Uncle Ernst was indeed trying to kill him.

But during that summer of 1970 he learned to fight. When he returned to school in September he had knocked Bo Ross unconscious for calling him "White Meat." No one ever called him that again. In October Leo was found dead in a vacant lot near Forty-third and King Drive. His neck was broken. The police never found out who killed him. And Reggie Stanton never ran through the neighborhood again except for exercise.

A fog drifted off the lake enshrouding the park. Reggie began looking for Billie, but the visibility was bad. Then suddenly the misty curtain parted and she was there beside him.

"Hi, G.I., looking for a good time?" she said with an exaggerated Vietnamese bar-girl accent.

"Why? You got money to spend, little girl?"

"What you talk, G.I.? Billie number one girl. You pay her, she no pay soul brother."

Reggie laughed.

"You're wheezing, old man." She dropped the accent and dashed out in front of him. "You ain't got it no more."

"I'll show you what I got." He pursued.

Billie Smith was a shade above five feet tall, but powerfully built. She possessed a medium-brown complexion and curly black hair. Like her running mate, she was of mixed blood. Besides the African-American ancestry evident in her hair and coloring, there was the definite stamp of Asian on her features. She had been a war baby left behind in the streets of Saigon after the Americans pulled out. She had been adopted by a white American family and raised from the age of eleven in the United States. She never knew her father and had only vague recollections of her mother. In this regard she was one up on Reggie Stanton, who had never set eyes on either his father or his mother.

Reggie was a freshman in high school. Uncle Ernst was training him to go out for the varsity football team in the fall. The training sessions lasted three hours every day except Sunday. Ernst would have made his charge work on Sunday too, but Ida would not stand for it.

Uncle Ernst permitted Reggie a brief rest period after he'd run ten consecutive one-hundred-yard wind sprints.

"Who was my father, Uncle Ernst?"

"Ask your grandmother."

"She won't talk about him."

"Then why should I?"

"Because he was your brother." Reggie's voice held emotion, but his tone was carefully respectful. Uncle Ernst would not tolerate disrespect in any form.

But despite the tone, Uncle Ernst glared at him. He walked a few steps away from Reggie. With his back still turned he said, "Not my brother. My brother's son."

"Where is he, Uncle Ernst?"

"He's dead, Reggie, like you will be if you don't get back to work."

Billie ran with ease, but Reggie caught her.

"Not bad," she said breathing noisily through her mouth. "At least for an old-timer."

"I'm going to make you pay for that old-timer crack."

Together they continued to run through the fog.

43

The taxi pulled up a block from the Haggerty House on Prairie Avenue in the Chicago Historical District. Karl and Ernest Steiger got out and stood in the rain until the taxi pulled away.

"How quaint," Ernest said, looking around at the faithfully preserved mansions.

"This area is the same as it was a hundred years ago," Karl said.

"Why, Daddy, you sound almost nostalgic."

Karl frowned and snatched up his bag. "I have a respect for history, Ernest. No more, no less."

Ernest picked up the single valise he'd been restricted to when leaving the O'Hare Hilton and followed his father down the street. "You seem to know a great deal about Chicago."

"I lived here many years ago," Karl said. "This is a good town. Lots of interesting things to see and do."

"Then you must have friends here. We should go to some of the places you frequented years ago. I'd like to see them."

"We won't have time for that. After we do the job we're leaving."

"Whatever you say," Ernest said with a shrug.

They went the rest of the way in silence. At the Haggerty House they climbed the stone steps to the front door. Karl pushed the antique bell and waited. A moment later Armand Hagar, who was also known as Andrew Haggerty—the owner of the house and heir to the Haggerty fortune—answered the door.

The Steigers entered the vestibule and turned to face their host. Karl studied the cast encasing Hagar's left foot. Ernest examined his beard and long, dirty hair with open disdain.

"So you're Karl Steiger," Hagar said. "My old man used to talk about you all the time. Said you were a real genius."

"Your father was a good man in the trade himself. I'm sorry he's no longer with us."

Hagar sneered. "I'm not." With that he turned and limped down the hall leading to the rear of the house. They followed him.

"What happened to your foot?" Ernest asked.

Hagar stopped and turned to face the younger Steiger. His expression was not cordial. "I know him," he hooked a thumb in Karl's direction, "from the pictures he took with my old man, but I don't know you at all, pal."

Ernest returned Hagar's glare. "Ernest Steiger. I'm his son."

A dangerous chill developed between the two men. Ernest had no trouble matching Hagar's menace. Expecting violence, Karl stepped between them just as Hagar turned to continue down the hall. He said over his shoulder, "As for my foot, a cop shot me."

They entered a dining room which contained a huge, highly varnished oak table and glass cases containing lighted displays of priceless china lining the walls. Hagar crossed to a door concealed in the wood-paneling. He pressed a switch beside one of the cabinets and the door swung open, revealing an elevator. The Steigers followed their host aboard.

Hagar operated the manual mechanism and the car rose.

"Are you currently under investigation by the police?" Karl said.

"No," Hagar replied.

"Are you under police surveillance?"

"Like he'd know," Ernest mumbled in a voice too low for either of them to understand him.

"No, there's no surveillance. What happened is over. I'm out on bond. I've got a court date in mid-May," Hagar said, matter-of-factly. "You guys got nothing to worry about while you're here."

The elevator came to a halt in the attic. Hagar swung the door open to reveal a small, but expensively-furnished apartment with two bedrooms, a bathroom and a kitchen.

As the Steigers dropped their bags on the polished hardwood

floor and looked around, Hagar said, "This place is secure and I can provide you with anything you need while you're here. Of course, there's a price."

"Of course," Karl said. "Is there anyone else in the house besides you?"

Hagar shook his head. "The rest of the place is nothing but a fucking museum. Got stuff in some of the rooms that my great grandfather used to peddle as junk off a pushcart back before the Fire."

"What fire?" Ernest asked.

"The Chicago Fire of eighteen seventy-one. Where've you been, boy?"

"They don't teach the history of primitive cultures at the Sorbonne."

"The Sorbonne," Hagar said in a falsetto tone, before sneering, "ain't that a bunch of shit."

Before Ernest could shoot back a response, Karl said, "I need to know the full details concerning your trouble with the police."

"No problem," Hagar said, flopping down on the leather couch in the center of the tiny living room. "There are no secrets between us."

Ernest explored the apartment while they talked. He really wasn't interested in how the stupid, filthy American had gotten shot. He was only sorry that the bullet hadn't hit him in the crotch.

Ernest didn't like this place. It was clean, but too small, cramped and spartan. Going to ground in places like these was part of the way his father operated. He had places like this all over the world and some of them were a great deal worse than this cramped attic. Ernest still didn't like it and couldn't figure why they didn't stay in a hotel with room service, a swimming pool and women. But his father had said no. To Ernest, it was almost as if Karl was playing a secret agent in some fantasy.

"So this bitch up and shoots me in the goddamn foot," Hagar was saying. "But me and my lawyer will take care of that. The city's going to pay out a lot of money for what that policewoman did, then me and her got a score to settle."

"You sure you won't need any help the next time you go up against her?" Ernest said, as he took a chair next to his father.

The hatred in Hagar's eyes was intense. "You're gonna step in my shit once too often, man. Then, job or no job, your ass is mine."

"You will both put an end to this stupid bickering," Karl snapped. "You are professionals and I want you to act like it."

Hagar left his smoldering gaze on Ernest a moment longer before looking away. Despite his father's warning, Ernest kept an amused, mocking grin on his face.

"We only have two days to bring this off, so we must operate with dispatch. Ernest?"

"Yes, Daddy." His tone was less than enthusiastic. He was examining his fingernails.

"Are you paying attention?"

"Yes, sir," Ernest said, sitting up a bit straighter, but still exuding a pronounced boredom.

"I'll need you to do some research. Find out what you can about our target and his habits."

"And how would I do that?"

"Perhaps you can use the excellent public library system they have in this city or the morgues of local newspapers. You've done this type of work before. Use your imagination."

"The library," Ernest repeated flatly. "Wonderful."

"We'll need transportation," Karl said looking at Hagar.

"I've got a whole garage full of cars out back. Take what you want."

"No. I'll give you a credit card. It's a phony name, but legitimate in case it's checked. Have rental cars delivered to a location not far from here."

"Make mine a Mercedes," Ernest said.

"The vehicles are to be standard American four-door sedans with no frills," Karl said. "All we need is basic transportation."

"I understand," Hagar said struggling to his feet.

"It looks like there's blood seeping through your cast," Ernest said pointing to the red droplets on the floor where Hagar'd been sitting. "You really should stay off that foot."

Hagar looked down at the blood and snorted. "I can handle it, pretty boy."

"I'm quite sure you can," Ernest replied.

Karl stood with Hagar and handed him a Visa Gold card. "Use this to order the cars. We will require them within the hour."

"You want me to make arrangements for your dinner?" Hagar said.

"No," Karl answered. "We'll get something while we're out. We'll need weapons. Two side-arms. Something small, Walthers or nine-millimeter Berettas with extra clips will do."

"Done," Hagar said entering the elevator.

When they were alone Karl turned to his son. "What's the matter with you, Ernest? Why were you intentionally trying to provoke him?"

"Just having some fun," Ernest said. "Trying to lighten things up a bit. I don't see why we need him anyway. This job seems simple enough."

"No job is simple, Ernest," Karl said tightly. "Someday you're going to forget that and it will cost you your life. We follow procedure. We're in a foreign land. As such, it is not wise to operate without having one of the natives on your side. It's worked as a military intelligence precept for centuries."

Ernest nodded weakly. "I also don't trust your Mr. Armand Hagar. He's a loser. Letting a woman get the drop on him proves that."

"I don't trust him either, but I haven't got time to debate this with you now. We both have work to do."

Ernest didn't answer immediately. Finally, he said, "Do you have the directions to the nearest library, or should I ask our host?"

Heading for the bathroom, Karl called over his shoulder, "Dial Information and ask them."

Ernest noticed the telephone on the end table beside the couch. The bathroom door slammed, followed by the sound of running water.

Ernest crossed to the phone and dialed "O" and got the Information operator's number. He was about to redial when a thought struck him. He looked quickly at the closed bathroom door before dialing the Information operator.

When she came on the line he asked, "Do you have a listing for United States Senator Harvey Banks? Yes, the local office will be just fine. Thank you."

Hagar handed Karl Steiger two sets of car keys. "They're parked over on Nineteenth and Indiana. That's only a couple of blocks from here."

"Chevrolet," Ernest said examining his keys. "How interesting."

Karl shot his son a disapproving look before saying, "We'll be back in a few hours. Should we leave the cars on the street?"

"I wouldn't. Niggers from the projects over on State will have them stripped before dawn. I'll have a couple of mine moved to the Grant Park Garage to make room for you. Just honk when you get back and I'll open the garage doors."

Ernest followed his father out. Before exiting, he said to Hagar, "That's what I always found so fascinating about you Americans. You call this the Land of the Free and still use such quaint little slurs such as 'nigger.' "

Before Hagar could reply, Ernest was gone.

44

MARCH 6, 1994
4:30 P.M.

Larry Cole found the address on North Lake Shore Drive. He pulled into the driveway and was met by a uniformed doorman. Cole flashed his badge.

"You must be going up to fifteen F," the doorman said. "Two cops up there already. Something big must be going on, huh?"

"Is it okay for me to leave my car here?" Cole asked.

"Sure. Just park it behind the other one. There's plenty of room. You know, my ex-brother-in-law was a cop. Worked somewhere on the southside maybe twenty or thirty years ago."

Cole smiled and got back into the car. He parked it behind Blackie's. A few minutes later, after the doorman had followed him all the way across the lobby still trying to find out what happened upstairs, Cole was in an elevator on the way up to the fifteenth floor.

He followed the directory to 15F and used the brass knocker. He didn't recognize the frail young woman who answered the door.

"I'm looking for Sergeant Silvestri," he said.

The woman extended her hand. "How do you do, Commander? I'm Judy Daniels."

"Oh," Cole replied with surprise. He'd expected someone a great deal different.

"Right this way."

He followed her into the apartment. The place was large and expensive. There was a panoramic view of the lake and North Lake Shore Drive. Cole figured that on a clear day someone looking out the windows of this apartment could see all the way to Evanston.

Blackie was in the living room. There was a woman lying there on a brocade couch. Ice cubes wrapped in a thick towel obscured most of her face. When Blackie saw Cole, he motioned for Judy to come over and sit in the chair beside the woman. Then he took Cole into the bedroom and closed the door.

"Chick's name is Carrie Curtis," Blackie explained. "She works for Tuxedo Tony DeLisa. He beat her up pretty bad yesterday, but she's too terrified to tell us why or to even go to a hospital. Says she's scared he'll kill her."

Cole angrily shook his head. "You know I've never seen this Tuxedo Tony face-to-face, but the more I hear about him the more I'd like him to resist arrest if I ever pinch him."

"I know what you mean," Blackie said.

"The girl's not going to be of much help unless she fingers the Tuxedo," Cole said. "Even then we won't have much more than a battery rap on him. It'll be hard to make it stick even with her testimony."

"That's not the reason I called you up here," Blackie said.

"We've got an opportunity to put someone right inside the DeLisa house in Oak Park."

This stunned Cole. He had just left Chief Govich. While they were together Govich told him about all the aborted attempts the CPD and the Feds had made over the years trying to put someone inside the DeLisa organization. The Feds had apparently succeeded for a short time with Art Maggio, but now he was dead. DeLisa was as suspicious as a cat in a dog pound and also homicidally paranoid. Any cop going undercover against him was almost certainly committing suicide.

But Cole let Blackie have his say.

"These calls came in a few minutes after we got here," Blackie said crossing to a telephone answering machine on the night stand and pressing the Replay button.

The machine rewound past three messages each signaled by a beep.

"Carrie, this is Sam." Cole and Blackie noticed the tension in the voice. *"I've got to talk to you. Call me at the mansion."*

There was a beep and then another call from Sam. The tension had increased to the point his voice was close to cracking. *"Carrie, are you there? Look, babe, I got to talk to you. The old man is still pissed, but Wally said we can make it up to him if we find a woman to come out and stay with Rachel. Hell, you used to live in Chicago. You must know somebody. You gotta help me, Carrie. I don't know nobody in this town and they won't let me leave. Please call me."*

The third message was also from Sam. This time he alternated between terror and anger. *"Goddammit, Carrie, I know you're there! What are you trying to do, get me killed? Mr. DeLisa's going to be back any minute and it'll be my ass if I don't get him somebody for Rachel. You could at least pick up the phone and talk to me. Carrie? Carrie?!"* There was a long pause before he hung up.

"You want to hear it again?" Blackie said.

Cole shook his head. "I've got the general idea, but I still don't see what you've got in mind."

"We could send somebody out there to help this guy Sam, Boss."

"Like who?"

"Judy."

Cole stared at Blackie in disbelief. "You're kidding."

"No, boss, I'm not. She's one of the best undercover narcs in the business. She can disguise herself so well that—"

"Stop it, Blackie."

The sergeant fell silent.

"Have you forgotten about yesterday already? Have you forgotten that while on loan to us, the Mistress of Disguise/High Priestess of Mayhem almost got herself killed?"

"I know and I don't blame you for being upset, but yesterday was a foul-up. These things happen in police work. Remember back in seventy-eight when we killed Frankie Arcadio?"

"I remember," Cole said, some of the steam escaping from his anger.

"Well, I got shot that day, boss. Maybe if we'd have followed the rule book and called for back-up and all that other good shit it wouldn't have happened. But it was our decision to make and we made it and stuck by it, for better or worse."

Cole exhaled a long, tension-easing breath. "That was all well and good back then, but this is now and I'm not going to authorize Daniels going undercover against Tony DeLisa. That's final, Blackie."

"Well, it was worth a try."

Cole managed a weak grin. He punched Blackie in the arm. "You're still the best street cop around, but the Feds have got a blanket surveillance on DeLisa. They'll nail him eventually. Our main problems right now are Senator Harvey Banks and the so-called F.B.I. man Reggie Stanton."

"We found the old I.A.D. file on Stanton, boss," Blackie said. "There were four homicides involved. They were transferred from the Detective Division to Internal Affairs by Riseman while he was still chief of detectives."

"Riseman?" Cole said with a frown.

"It's in the case file in black and white with his signature on it. I was going to let you see it when we got back to the station."

"Good."

"Okay, we're going to try and persuade Carrie to go to St. Joseph's and then Judy's got a place for her to stay. Maybe in a day or two we can get her to talk to us."

Cole nodded heading for the door. "I'm on my way back to the Area now. If you run into any problems call me."

After Blackie let the commander out, he walked back into the living room where Judy sat watching her old high school friend. Carrie had not moved.

"He didn't go for it did he, Sarge?" she said.

"No, he didn't. I didn't think he would anyway."

"We still on?"

Blackie looked down at Lake Shore Drive. He didn't think he could ever get used to living this far above the ground. Hell, he didn't even like to fly and he would never sit by the window in an airplane.

"You know this could cost both of us our jobs."

Judy stood up and walked over to him. She was so charged with excitement he could almost feel the electricity flowing off of her. "Nobody would ever have to know you knew, Blackie. If something happens, I'm on my own. I'll even put in for comp time to cover the days off. If something happens they won't be able to implicate you."

Blackie's dark-jowled face turned angry enough to scare her. "Maybe you never heard of me and maybe the cops you work with in Narcotics would go along with some shit like keeping their names in the clear if you get iced. But I'm not. If we do this, we do it together. If something goes wrong, then I'll be in it up to my ass right with you."

"And if it works the way we planned?" she said, softly.

Blackie turned to look back out the window. He stood that way for a long time. When he finally spoke, he said, "Then I only hope Larry will forgive me."

45

The scream of pleasure rose in Billie Smith's throat. Reggie had said he would make her pay for the remark about him being over the hill and he was.

They were entangled in the silk sheets of her oval-shaped water bed on the fortieth floor of the north tower of the twin Lake Point Towers. They were a mile from where Blackie and Cole Daniels were plotting a direct violation of Commander Cole's orders. The sheets were slick with perspiration and she was experiencing with tremendous but frightening pleasure what it was like to be made love to by Reggie Stanton.

Billie had not had a gentle life and she was not a gentle woman. The streets of Saigon were still as much a part of her as was the Medill School of Journalism at Northwestern University where she was studying for her master's degree. She'd had her first sexual encounter with an old papa-san when she was seven. By the time she was twelve she had done things with men that would have shocked the most seasoned American prostitute. At one time she'd thought she would never be capable of experiencing a normal orgasmic reaction with a man—that is, until she met Reggie.

He was not a sensitive lover and he was not a good one either. He made love as if he were engaged in physical combat to the death, which she recalled an old whore in Vietnam had once said that a sexual climax came very close to matching. He attempted to dominate her, even abuse her, and in that she found a rallying point of excitement from which to build. She fought him back and together they engaged in brutal sexual bouts that always left them both exhausted and never without bruises. Billie didn't know if this was love, but it sure as hell was lust.

Now she'd succeeded in exhausting him. His thrusts into her weakened and his breathing deepened to include a whispered rasp at the end of each exhalation. At this point she began to dominate him. She scissored her legs around his buttocks. She could feel the moan begin deep in his chest. She increased the pressure of her vaginal walls on his penis then quickly released it before re-applying it again. This was a technique she'd learned in Saigon to make the tricks finish faster. He knew it and had even managed to resist it once or twice. But now there was no strength left in him. Finally, he surrendered and when she was certain of her triumph she gave herself over to pleasure.

When it was over neither of them moved. The lathery slickness of their bodies served as an adhesive holding them in place. With a grunted effort he lifted himself off her and flopped on his back. He was too close to the edge of the bed and almost fell off onto the floor. She caught his arm and pulled him back. The water bed rocked under their shifting weights.

"You are the strongest woman I've ever met," he said, looking at her through lidded eyes.

"I have to be," she patted his flat stomach above the sweat-matted pubic hair from which his still-thick organ protruded. "If I wasn't, you'd have fucked me to death a long time ago."

For just an instant a frown dented his features. He didn't like it when she used profanity. Most of the time she respected his wishes, but then this was her apartment and in it she could damn well do and say what she pleased.

She bounded off the bed. "You ready to eat or do you want to cool off with a beer first?"

He propped a forearm under his head. "I'm not hungry yet. Just the beer will be fine."

Billie went to the bathroom and showered. After slipping on a silk kimono that exposed more of her than it covered, she headed for the kitchen. She opened the refrigerator and was reaching for two iced-bottles of Heineken when she felt a wave of dizziness sweep over her. She steadied herself and took a deep breath.

Maybe this was too much, she thought. First the run, then they had lifted weights in the spare room she'd converted, at his expense, into a gym. Then sex.

She took a deep breath and the dizziness passed. She removed the beer and ran one of the bottles across her forehead. Its coolness felt good. She closed the door and leaned against it. This was a routine with them twice a week. Maybe once a month, sometimes less, he took her out to dinner and a movie. She liked him, but she was beginning to wonder if they were ever going anywhere? Would they ever be anything more than exercise and sex partners?

She scolded herself. She was starting to think like an American woman. She was starting back for the bedroom when she realized that she *was* an American woman, at least a naturalized one.

He was in the bathroom. She could hear the shower going. She knew he wanted to check in with the senator later. Even though this was supposed to be his day off, he always called to see how Banks was doing.

She bounced onto the bed, rebounding as if she were on a trampoline until she reached the headboard. She placed his beer on the night stand on *his side.* He was very protective of those types of things. Everything had to be in the right place at the right time. He was fanatical about it.

She opened her beer and took a swallow. Not a sip, a swallow. It tasted good. She took another. She cocked her head to listen to the shower. It was still going. Reggie took long showers.

How long had they been together now? A year? No, longer. Closer to eighteen months. They had been lovers almost from that first night, although she'd had to force the issue with him. It wasn't that he was shy. Far from it. Just proper. Proper and careful.

"What do you do for a living, Reggie?" she'd asked, noticing the tailored suits and the BMW.

"I work for the government," he'd replied. "Kind of a security specialist."

"Kind of?"

He had stared at her with those glacial, blue-gray eyes. "Yeah, kind of."

She was unable to find out anything else for six months. Then, within a matter of days around Christmas, she'd discovered it all.

They had gone shopping at DeWitt Plaza. He had been seeing her about once a week. She was considering whether she wanted this arrangement to continue or if a search for someone more consistent and less secretive was in order.

They were standing at the corner of Chestnut and Michigan Avenue when the traffic cop in the intersection spied Reggie. "Hey, Stanton. How's it going?" The cop waved.

"I'm okay, Bryant," Reggie responded self-consciously. "How have you been?"

"Friend of yours?" she asked after they crossed the street.

"Yeah."

But a couple of nights later, Billie was invited to meet his grandmother and the grandmother's nurse, whose name Billie couldn't remember.

After dinner the nurse vanished, leaving the three of them to sip brandy in the charming but ancient living room. Initially, Billie was intimidated by Ida Mae Stanton, but as the evening wore on she developed a definite affection for the old woman. She also found that Ida Mae was very, very proud of her secretive grandson.

"You know Reggie was a policeman, Billie?"

"No, I didn't." Billie looked at Reggie seated beside her on the couch. His face was emotionless, but it was obvious he didn't approve of his grandmother's boasting or of the information she was disclosing so freely to a stranger.

"Sure was," Ida continued. "Top of his class at the Chicago Police Academy. Graduated as class commander, didn't you, Reggie?"

"Yes, ma'am."

Billie smiled. He sounded like a little boy forced to recite poetry in front of his parents' friends.

"But he didn't stay long with the city. Boy's too smart. Mr. Hoover's F.B.I. snapped him up. Made him a special—"

"Grandma!"

Ida Mae stopped. She stared at him. "I ain't biting my tongue no more, boy! You are F.B.I. and I'm proud of it. Your Uncle Ernst was proud too. At least he knew you couldn't keep everything secret."

But Ida Mae had said little more about Reggie or his job.

On the way home that night Billie asked, "Reggie, who is Uncle Ernst?"

He shrugged. "He was my uncle. He's dead."

"Ernst. That's an unusual pronunciation for an American name. It's usually Ernest."

"He wasn't an American," he said tightly.

This did not satisfy her. She wanted to know more. The bits and pieces of information she had discovered about the man she had invited into her bed had intrigued her. Asking him outright would have done her little good, so she decided on subterfuge. She planned to get him drunk.

But he had the constitution of a grizzly bear with a hollow leg. The only one who got drunk was her. Drunk and sick. After she threw up for the fourth time, he stripped off her kimono and stood her under a cold shower.

While she screamed, he laughed and kept repeating a phrase in German. Later, after he had toweled her dry and put her in bed, she asked him what it meant.

"That which does not kill you makes you stronger."

She thought she was going to be sick again. "Where in the hell did you get that bullshit?"

As she faded into blissful unconsciousness, she heard him say, "Uncle Ernst."

The next morning she was so hungover she could barely see. He made breakfast and served it to her in bed. She could do little more than sip the coffee and nibble at a piece of toast, as her stomach was still in an uproar. But as she began to feel more human she noticed that he was unusually subdued, which for Reggie was tantamount to turning into the Sphinx. When he came out of it, he started to talk. To talk about Uncle Ernst.

"My uncle was Hauptman Ernst von Steiger of the *Friedenthaler Jadgverebande*. That was Germany's commando force led by Captain Otto Skorzeny. Their unit name comes from the town of Friedenthal near Berlin where they trained. In July nineteen forty-three Uncle Ernst, under Skorzeny's command, was part of the force that landed in gliders on the mountain fortress of Gran Sasso to rescue Benito Mussolini. It was one of the most impressive military actions of the war, but then Skorzeny's commandos had only just begun.

"The war was going badly for Germany. Hitler was ecstatic and seized the Skorzeny raid as a tool to pump up flagging morale. Otto was an Austrian like Hitler. Him and Uncle Ernst were very popular. Rommel and the rest of the General Staff were in disfavor with the Führer by this time, so Hitler was looking for new heroes. But one raid wasn't enough for Skorzeny to qualify. Hitler planned more. A lot more.

"Otto was not a professional soldier. He was a damned good man, Uncle Ernst used to tell me, but he didn't have the best grasp of operations or tactics. For that he relied on Uncle Ernst, whose family had been planning military strategies since before Napoleon."

Billie, despite her hangover, felt herself being drawn into the strange story. She had never been interested in tales of war. Her experiences in Vietnam had placed her too close to real war for that. But somehow this was different. Later she would understand why.

"Uncle Ernst was your father's brother?" she asked.

He shook his head. "No. My father was his nephew. His name was Karl. He died before I was born."

"And your mother?"

"That's another story," he said. He resumed his tale. "Since Skorzeny and Uncle Ernst had managed to rescue Mussolini, Hitler thought them capable of anything. The man Hitler wanted most in Europe was Winston Churchill, and they were ordered to plot his kidnapping. Hitler figured that snatching him would demoralize the English and rob them of their will to fight. He made it a priority for the commandos, but even Otto and Ernst had their limitations. They were forced to finally abandon their plan in favor of more realistic military objectives. They had some success, but by then the war was lost.

"Hitler was still looking for some miracle to turn the tide. He talked about super weapons and divisions which no longer existed. The generals listened to him, as they had no choice and the Führer came up with one last bold plan. In December nineteen forty-four he threw everything he had left into a massive counteroffensive through the Ardennes in Belgium. Skorzeny's commandoes came to play a very big part in the Battle of the Bulge. Their part in it caused Uncle Ernst to end up a hunted man for the rest of his life.

"The plan was to drop Skorzeny's commandos in American uniforms behind Allied lines to cause confusion. Of course, any soldier caught disguised in the uniform of the opposition was subject to being shot as a spy. Some were. Uncle Ernst dressed himself as an American colonel and with only one man, who was a sergeant and spoke fluent English, parachuted behind the Allied lines in France. They commandeered an American jeep and drove right up to the villa at Petit Trianon outside Paris. This was the headquarters of the Supreme Allied Commander. There he and his driver blustered their way inside, and, while confusion over what was going on in Belgium reigned, kidnapped General Dwight D. Eisenhower."

The shower stopped. Billie had finished her beer. She eyed his bottle, which was beaded with frost. She considered drinking it, but she didn't know how he'd take it. He had never struck her or hurt her intentionally, except during their mutually combative love bouts. But then she refused to take him lightly. Not after what he'd done to Chuck Nelson.

The bathroom door opened and Reggie stepped out. He was nude except for a bath towel draped around his middle. He was a massive slab of muscle from neck to ankle, but he didn't move with stiff, bodybuilder awkwardness. Each action was natural, almost graceful. She noticed something else as well. He possessed a coiled-spring tautness capable of exploding in any direction instantaneously like the strike of a snake.

The only other time she had seen anyone with such a dangerous trait was when she was a little girl in Vietnam. After the Americans pulled out, squads of Vietcong guerrillas had begun filtering out of the hills. Many of them had been in the jungle so long they were never able to adjust to civilization again. Some were dangerous to be around. Reggie reminded her of these men.

He picked up his beer and drained it in one long, continuous pull. She liked to see him do that. It thrilled her. He was a real macho man. But he didn't like that term. He preferred something German. *Mannhaft,* he'd called it.

"You said something about dinner," he said, controlling his belch so that no sound came out of his mouth.

She slid off the bed and walked over to him. She pressed her body against him. She was nearly a foot shorter and the top of her head didn't even reach his chin, but she wasn't interested in his face right now.

"Billie, I'm hungry."

She assumed her fake accent. "Vietnamee girl taste good. You try, you like. Vietnamee girl number one."

He dropped his arms around her and squeezed until she yelled. She let him go.

"I thought one lesson was enough for you," he said.

A little more pressure and she was certain he would have crushed her ribs. She straightened her kimono. "Once is never enough for me."

"Feed me and I'll see what I can do for you," he said, sitting down on the edge of the bed and picking up the phone.

"How do you want your steak?" she called from the kitchen door.

"The usual," he said as he dialed.

"Baked potato and salad?"

"Whatever."

She remained there staring at him. It was always like this. They made love like maniacs, then he would hop up, shower and act like she was an afterthought. A whore who had just serviced him. Sometimes this angered her deeply. But she had learned that this was his way. And after what he told her about his life, she'd understood why. Also, she had found that in the long run it was better to be with him than without him.

She turned to go back into the kitchen when he said into the phone, "What's all that noise, Naomi?"

Billie paused, not really eavesdropping but curious about the tautness of his tone. She had never heard it before.

"When did he schedule a press conference?"

She turned around. He was angrier now than she had ever seen him before. The muscles and veins of his upper body stood out in sharp definition.

"Then why didn't someone tell me?!" A pause. "What time?" He checked his watch. "Who's there? No, I mean security. Get one of them to the phone right now."

Billie was glad she hadn't been the one to screw up.

"King, this is Stanton. What's going on there?"

There was a long moment while he listened.

"Okay, watch everything and never let him out of your sight. I'm on the way."

46

MARCH 6, 1994
6:00 P.M.

Special Agent-in-Charge Dave Franklin of the F.B.I. sat in his office on the ninth floor of the Dirksen Federal Building. He was watching the videotape from the surveillance on the Oak Park estate of Antonio DeLisa for the week beginning March 1 and ending at four o'clock that afternoon. He was particularly interested in a segment for March 3. The on-screen time read 11:17:30 P.M.

DeLisa's house was on a hilltop with a sloping lawn, a winding driveway and a twelve-foot, wrought-iron fence visible from the angle from which this shot was taken. The sidewalk and street outside the grounds were also visible. For four hours and thirty-two minutes prior to this time, there had been no movement in the area. Then all at once things started happening.

The surveillance operation was set up in a house directly across the street from DeLisa's. The occupant, a banker who'd been caught laundering money for a Colombian drug cartel, had been persuaded to take a lengthy Florida vacation in return for a little help from the F.B.I. in quashing his indictment. Surreptitiously, the surveillance team had moved in and set up shop. They were certain that DeLisa was unaware of their presence. Franklin didn't believe this for a minute.

However, right now Tuxedo Tony was not Franklin's primary concern. He was more interested in what was taking place on the television screen.

The caption was in full color and enhanced by an infrared lens. The brown Buick rolled slowly into the picture and stopped when its front wheel hit the curb. The engine was off. Two men could be seen sitting up in the front seat. They had the rigid, motionless postures of mannequins or, more appropriately, corpses. There was no one else in the frame and nothing moved.

Franklin watched the video timer run: 11:18:00; 11:18:15; 11:18:-30. There was nothing happening on the street nor any movement from the house. 11:19:00; 11:19:15; 11:19:30.

He picked up the Surveillance Event Log. The entry at 2320 hours was neatly printed: "Brown late model four-door Buick pulled up in front of the Gingiss residence. Two occupants remaining in the front seat."

11:20:00; 11:20:15; 11:20:30.

"What are you guys doing in there?" Franklin asked the unanswerable question to the motionless screen.

Finally, at 11:21:45 the front door of the mansion opened and a man looked out toward the street. The camera zoomed in on him. It was Arthur Maggio. He turned and yelled something to someone inside the house. Then all hell broke loose.

The surveillance tape was also equipped with audio, so Franklin was able to hear part of the conversations between the panicked mobsters.

Two of them ran from the house down the driveway.

"Watch yourself, Lenny," a sharp-faced bodyguard warned his broad-shouldered, ex-pug–featured companion.

"Jeez, it's Angie and Charlie. Aw, man, look at the blood!" Lenny cried.

"Get Mr. Maggio."

"Oh, Jeez."

"Lenny, pull yourself together and go get Mr. Maggio right now!"

There was a great deal of confusion for the next few minutes. At 11:27:42 Rachel DeLisa appeared outside the house. Franklin watched the replay of her escape attempt. He heard her scream, "I hope it will be you, Papa! I hope it will be you real soon, Papa!" before they hustled her back inside the house. Maggio had taken charge and began barking orders. He forced the reluctant bodyguards away from the Buick and told them to go back inside as well. Before following them, the mob lieutenant looked up and down the street, as if attempting to spot whoever was responsible for the carnage left on DeLisa's doorstep. His last glare was right into the camera lens. Franklin stared back impassively at the video replay.

According to the F.B.I.'s surveillance records, Maggio called the Oak Park Police at 11:42:46 P.M. This was after he made his report in code to DeLisa in Las Vegas. Franklin had these conversations on tape. In fact, he possessed a great deal of information on Antonio "Tuxedo Tony" DeLisa. Information which had cost the F.B.I. millions of dollars. Information that up to this point told them no more than the fact that DeLisa's daughter hated him and someone had dropped a rather nasty package on the mobster's doorstep.

Franklin was also aware that there was a gap in the tape he'd been watching. This morning, March 6, from 3 to 6 A.M. the F.B.I. equipment recorded nothing but static. It hadn't taken the special agent-in-charge any great feat of deductive reasoning to figure what was going on.

Arthur Maggio was last seen alive by agents Donnelley and Prentiss at one of the Bureau's downtown business fronts. Maggio's 1993 Cadillac was noted on the surveillance tapes as entering the grounds at 16:15 hours on March 5. There was no record of the dead mobster leaving the grounds, yet his car, with him in it, was found twenty miles away.

So one of the agents on the surveillance had either rigged or erased the tape and Franklin planned to find out who the turncoat was.

But that wasn't his most pressing problem at this moment; the assassin who'd taken out Butcher and Cappelletti was. Now, thanks to Jack Govich and Larry Cole of the Chicago Police Department, Franklin had a pretty good idea as to the identity of the assassin.

He was about to replay the tape when his intercom buzzed. He answered using the speaker phone.

"Deputy Director Connors is on line three for you, sir."

"Thank you." Franklin left the speaker phone on and punched line three. "Bill, this is Dave Franklin. How are you?"

"Fine, Dave." The deputy director's voice possessed a hollow ringing noise due to their conversation being encoded at the point of origin and decoded at the point of reception. Anyone listening in would hear nothing but indecipherable gibberish spoken between the two men.

"How are things in Chicago?"

"As best as can be expected. We're still gangbusting out here."

Connors chuckled. *"Good luck. You've probably got more of that type of thing than you can handle."*

"We don't have any problem with the hoodlums, Bill, but we have developed a bit of a situation with one of your assets."

"Oh?" Connors voice had suddenly become somewhat less than friendly. Franklin knew the deputy director didn't like discussing his "assets" with anyone but the director.

"Reginald E. Stanton is in Chicago and has become involved in a local police investigation. He is a possible suspect in the double homicide of two of Antonio DeLisa's henchmen. By the way, Bill, a throwing knife was used to dispatch the two dead Mafiosi."

Connors said nothing. Not even his breathing was audible over the secured line.

This did not alarm Franklin. He still had more cards to play.

"Stanton's been questioned by a police commander named Cole. At the time of the interrogation Stanton identified himself as one of our agents and displayed official identification."

There was a noise from Connors's end, but it was too faint, with the scrambler distortion, for Franklin to catch. But he made an accurate guess. Either Connors had hissed a curse with his head turned away from the speaker or he'd struck something hard with his fist. Despite his silence, Franklin knew that the deputy director's asshole was puckering right about now.

"He also," Franklin went on, making an effort to narrate his report in a cool, professional voice, "has reportedly told this Commander Cole that he has been assigned to officially bodyguard Senator Harvey Banks of Illinois."

The special agent-in-charge of the Chicago Field Office of the F.B.I. had no more to tell. Connors provided no immediate reaction from the Washington end. Seconds ticked by to become a full minute.

Connors was not well liked in the Bureau. He'd even been accused of being a sycophant. Never much of a field agent, he had managed to rise through the ranks to become a deputy director by ingratiating himself with every administration that had occupied the house on Pennsylvania Avenue since he'd been with the Bureau. He currently operated in the shadows with virtual impunity and was said to have re-introduced black bag operations and dirty tricks back into American law enforcement at the federal level. Needless to say, Dave Franklin had no use for him.

"Have you verified any of what you've just told me?"

"I felt that any attempt by my office at verification would give credence to the police allegations. I denied Stanton's involvement with the Bureau, but did no more. I assumed Headquarters would want to deal with it from that end directly."

When Franklin finished, he smiled. This was basic F.B.I. procedure. In such cases, you always left decisions about verification or further investigations in cases like this to the brass operating out of the J. Edgar Hoover Building in D.C. The deputy director had simply been attempting to trip Franklin up.

"I'll take care of everything," Connors said, breaking the connection.

Franklin turned off his speaker phone. He leaned back in his chair and smiled. He said into the emptiness of his office, "I'm sure you will, Mr. Deputy Director. I'm sure you will."

47

MARCH 6, 1994
6:07 P.M.

Maureen Taft, the political affairs reporter for the *Times-Herald,* exited the Dan Ryan Expressway at Stony Island Avenue and sped north. She had received the call forty-five minutes ago that Senator Harvey Banks was holding a six o'clock press conference. She had raced from the news room to her car and driven right into the jaws of rush hour traffic.

Banks was hot copy and she'd developed a fairly good relationship with him. She would be damned if she would let some other paper scoop her or be forced to cover the press conference from a videotape borrowed from one of the television stations. Because of this she sliced back and forth through the congested traffic lanes, drawing blasts from the horns of offended motorists. She also used the shoulder of the road as often as she could, while keeping one eye on the rearview mirror for the state police.

With a couple of minutes to spare she pulled up outside Banks's office. There was no space at the curb, either legal or illegal, for blocks. She started to chance double-parking her Honda next to the ABC Minicam van, but at that instant a marked police cruiser turned off a side street and pulled in behind her.

"Shit!" she swore, as she floored the accelerator and raced off down the street. She found a spot two blocks away and ran, as fast as her high heels would carry her, back to the office. She reached the front door at 6:10. The press conference had already started.

Maureen managed to squeeze inside the outer office, which was jammed full of reporters from every media outlet in the city. She was a medium-height, attractive brunette with a slender figure. A few years before she had entertained the idea of pursuing a career as a television newscaster, but somehow she didn't consider that real journalism.

Her height and lack of muscle made it impossible for her to shove through this mass of humanity; however, she had never let such things stand in her way before. She began looking around for some way she could either get through this crowd or at least obtain a better vantage point from which to view the proceedings.

She inched her way around the perimeter of the crowd and at one point she lost her balance and came dangerously close to falling through the plate glass window. She made it to a corner and was forced to stop, as the shear magnitude of the task was exhausting. Muffled by the crowd, she could hear the senator speaking.

" . . . is an insidious violation of the rights of the people of this state and particularly of the city of Chicago, who have a right to live their lives in a productive, peaceful manner free from the oppression of the lowest forms of human vermin. . . ."

"Give 'em hell, Harv," she whispered, as she slipped around a couple of freelancers. Usually, she wouldn't have given them the time of day, but they had her out-positioned, so she was forced to whisper sweet apologies and flash her most winning smile until she was past them. Then she forgot them quicker than yesterday's news.

But she was no closer to the heart of the action than she had been when she started. Banks was still speaking. When he finished, the Q and A session would begin. For her story to really sing she needed to ask at least two questions. She would later write, "In response to this reporter's inquiries, Senator Banks said . . ."

However, Banks couldn't recognize her if he couldn't see her and at the rate she was going it was doubtful if she was going to be able to do anything about that. She was about to give up when she saw her salvation.

The receptionist's desk had been shoved against the wall to provide more space in the cramped office. A pair of black trouser-clad legs were visible standing on top of it. Maureen could tell there was room for someone else up there. She planned to be that someone.

She pushed, shoved and elbowed her way across the room until she reached the desk. She tried to climb up on it, but there wasn't enough space for her to maneuver. She bumped the sound man for the NBC Minicam crew. He turned and gave her a dirty look. She managed a weak smile before attempting to climb up onto the desk again. This effort was no more successful than the last.

She was about to give it one last try when a powerful pair of hands reached down, grasped her wrists and pulled her up. When her feet came to rest on the desk surface, she looked into the face of a blond man with a pale complexion and keen features. She was certain she'd never seen him before, even though his eyes were shielded behind tinted aviator glasses.

"Thank you," she said.

He gave her a silent salute. They turned their attention back to the press conference.

Senator Harvey Banks was bathed in the combined lights from four Minicams. He was wearing a tailored blue pin-striped suit, white shirt and maroon-patterned tie. His gray hair looked to have been cut recently and he appeared rested. On his right stood one of his secretaries, whom Maureen had seen before. In fact, the reporter and her blond companion were standing on the secretary's desk. Flanking the senator and the young woman were two heavyset men in neatly-pressed but inexpensive business suits. The bodyguards were black and stared back at the unblinking lights with passive menace. She'd been around long enough to recognize them as cops.

Maureen recalled that there was usually another bodyguard with the senator. A lighter-skinned black man. She remarked to herself once that he was a good-looking hunk; however, he gave her the creeps when he looked at her. He wasn't here, so Maureen quickly forgot him.

Banks had been reading from a prepared statement. Now he looked up and directly into the cameras. Skillfully, he paused to heighten the drama of the moment. The thirty-odd people jammed into the room became still.

"What I say now is directed at one man, who singularly represents the worst in our society. I need not call his name for he knows who he is. If you are listening, sir, I have this to say to you. Chicago will not be a clean, crime-free town until you and the vermin you call your associates are rotting in jail. I plan to put you there along with anyone else who attempts to undermine the freedoms and protection which this great nation affords all its citizens. I will put you there using all the resources of the people of the United States of America. I will put you there because this great Land of Lincoln's legacy charges me with the duty to do so. I shall give no quarter in this crusade and will expect none to be given to me."

The senator paused a moment before saying, "Questions?"

Bedlam erupted. Ten questions were shouted at once. The seasoned politician he was, Harvey Banks started with the major media representatives first. For the next thirty minutes he answered questions from the network crews and major dailies at a three-to-one ratio over the smaller publications and freelancers.

Maureen Taft got three questions answered by Banks. He also quipped at how much she'd grown when he saw her towering over everyone else from her desk-top perch. The press conference was a major success. A major success for not only Harvey Banks and Maureen Taft.

48

MARCH 6, 1994
6:30 P.M.

The senator felt alive again. In the past twenty-four hours he'd experienced a complete rejuvenation to the point he had spent the day traveling through the city with the intensity and energy he usually reserved only for campaigns. The shadow of what had occurred two nights ago was still with him, but then he had yet to be directly touched by it. He also realized that his spirits had begun to soar because Reggie Stanton wasn't around.

"Senator, is the unidentified party you mentioned Tuxedo Tony DeLisa?" a reporter from the *Sun-Times* asked.

"I will identify the individual I was referring to during next week's committee hearings."

"Senator, do you believe that Antonio DeLisa has ties to the Mafia?" a reporter from the *Tribune* demanded.

"My, my, Tony DeLisa is popular with you people." This drew a laugh. "I don't know what Mr. DeLisa's affiliations are, one way or the other, but I will say this: we will be looking not only at affiliations, but also individual criminal activities."

An ABC reporter was next. "Will your Senate hearings be focusing exclusively on organized criminal activity?"

"The crime committee will be examining evidence of criminal activity over a wide spectrum of our society, but we will be particularly interested in any individual or group operating an ongoing criminal enterprise in Illinois."

"Senator Banks!" Maureen Taft's yell drowned out the rest.

He looked up to where her head nearly touched the ceiling. A man in dark glasses stood behind her, but Banks was unable to see him clearly.

"Yes, Maureen." He had always liked the feisty reporter.

"Can we assume that the majority of the evidence your committee will be exploring is connected to Antonio DeLisa's activities?"

Banks held out his arms in a gesture of surrender. "For that, ladies and gentlemen, you'll have to wait and see what develops in Washington next week. Good night."

With that the senator turned and walked into his inner office. Naomi Bowman followed. The two police bodyguards stood shoulder to shoulder, blocking anyone from following Banks.

Inside the office Banks went to the refrigerator and removed a can of soda. He popped the tab and turned around to face his receptionist. He toasted her with the can. "So, what did you think?"

"It went great, as always, senator. You had them eating out of your hand."

He walked around behind his desk. "Well, I want to keep them doing just that until this thing is over. Maybe it'll get some of our law enforcement authorities interested in taking a closer look into DeLisa's activities."

She remained standing across the room. She stared down at the carpet.

"Naomi?"

She looked up at him. There was a great deal of anxiety on her face.

"Is there something wrong?"

She opened her mouth to speak, but no sound came out.

"Naomi . . . " There was a knock at the door.

She spun away from him to answer it. One of the bodyguards spoke to her. The noise of the news people dismantling their equipment and rushing out to file their stories carried to the senator. Naomi closed the door and came back across the office.

"It's the *Times-Herald* reporter, Maureen Taft. She'd like to see you."

"I don't think I should be granting any exclusives on this. It wouldn't be fair to the others."

"She told Detective King that she wants to introduce you to a foreign reporter."

Banks eyebrows shot up. "A foreign reporter?"

"Yes, sir. There's a man with Taft. He doesn't look like a reporter to me, but then I'm not much of a judge of such things."

He focused his attention back on her. "What's troubling you, Naomi?"

She took a deep breath, held it a moment and then released it slowly. "Why don't you see the reporters first? Then we can talk."

"Okay," he agreed. "But as soon as I'm through I want you to level with me."

"Yes, sir," she said, managing a smile.

Naomi returned to the office door and spoke to the guard. A moment later Maureen Taft came in, followed by a slender blond man dressed in black. He carried a wire-bound notebook and wore tinted glasses.

"Maureen!" Banks came around the desk to embrace her. "How's my favorite scribe?"

She giggled. "You're still the charmer, Senator. Don't forget to remind me to vote for you next time."

He laughed. "You know if I thought you really meant that I'd be crushed, but of course you're kidding."

"You know I am," she said. "You're the best political copy we've had in this town in many a year. We've got to keep you around."

Banks looked at her companion.

"Senator," she said, "I'd like to introduce you to Mr. Helmut Strahlman of the German Bild . . . ?"

The newcomer smiled. "That's the *Deutschland Bild Zeitung,* Fraulein Taft. *Zeitung* means newspaper in German," he said in excellent English, spoken with just the faintest trace of a German accent. "I am visiting briefly in your country and wanted to do a piece on a prominent American elected official. I was fortunate to discover that you were holding this evening's excellent press conference."

"I'm glad you enjoyed it, Herr Strahlman," Banks said with a bow. "How long will you be staying in America?"

"Only a few more days," he replied. "I expect to conclude my business here very soon. May I make a request, Herr Senator?"

"Of course."

"I know that you must be fatigued after such a long and arduous press conference, but if I could have just a few more moments of your time it would mean so much to my readers back home."

Maureen Taft waited expectantly. This would be an exclusive for her too.

A true politician, Banks couldn't resist. "Definitely. Let me offer you some refreshments. I'm glad to be able to extend our American hospitality to you."

"And me?" Maureen asked.

"I guess you can stay too, Miss Taft, but would you let Herr Strahlman—"

"Please, Herr Senator, call me Helmut."

"Okay, Helmut. Let him ask the questions, Taft."

"Goodie!" she said, as the polite German reporter held the chair for her.

Naomi Bowman left the office as Ernest Steiger, in the guise of Helmut Strahlman of the *Deutschland Bild Zeitung,* took the seat beside Maureen Taft.

49

MARCH 6, 1994
7:12 P.M.

Tuxedo Tony DeLisa sat in his office at the Del-Ray Distributing Company on South Laramie. The mobster had decorated the room himself and the result was as cheery as a coffin. All the furnishings were of either chrome or black leather, the carpet and walls were gray, and the only picture in evidence was a black and white, full-face photograph of Rachel. As if displaying disapproval of her surroundings, she was not smiling.

The lights were turned low and a television cast distorted flickering beams into the room. A glass of twenty-five-year-old brandy in his hand, Tuxedo Tony stared glumly at the screen. He was not a happy man.

There was a soft knock on the office door. DeLisa turned his head to look in that direction, but said nothing. A few seconds passed and the knock was repeated. Still he made no sound. Finally, a third knock was followed by the door opening a crack.

Very carefully, one of DeLisa's bodyguards looked in. The man, although standing well over six feet tall and weighing two hundred and fifty pounds, seemed ready to withdraw in an instant if the Tuxedo threatened violence.

"Boss," the bodyguard said in a whisper, "Mr. Kirschstein's here."

DeLisa looked back at the television screen. On it a faggoty-looking, blond teenage boy was talking animatedly to a fluffy-looking teenage girl, who was making a career out of showing off her dimples. DeLisa had to admit that the broad with the dimples had a nice ass. He tried to remember when was the last time he got laid. He couldn't.

The bodyguard still stood with his head sticking beyond the edge of the door like a turtle looking out of its shell. He knew better than to repeat his message. He was about to leave when DeLisa spoke.

"Send the shyster up."

DeLisa had not spoken in a very loud tone of voice, but it was loud enough for the bodyguard to hear. He let himself out and went to get the lawyer. DeLisa continued to stare at the television.

Down below in the warehouse, attorney Frank Kirschstein waited. Two of DeLisa's men stood guard over him.

"He wants to see you," said the bodyguard who'd delivered the message, jerking his thumb at the wooden staircase leading from the warehouse floor to the administrative offices above.

Kirschstein hesitated.

"I wouldn't keep him waitin' if I was you. He's in a bad way."

The lawyer's mouth was dry, but his palms were soaking wet. On legs with knees possessing the consistency of silly putty, he walked to the staircase and ascended.

When Kirschstein knocked, DeLisa called, "Come in." DeLisa's voice sounded as if it came from inside a tomb.

The lawyer opened the door and entered.

"Did you hear what that black bastard said?!" DeLisa roared, pointing at the television set.

Kirschstein couldn't answer right away. His gag reflex was spasming, threatening to disgorge the contents of his stomach all over the mobster's carpeted floor.

"That sonofabitch talked about putting me in jail!" DeLisa jumped up and stormed around the office with his brandy glass in hand. He stopped abruptly and said, "Wait a minute."

The mobster went back behind the desk and snatched up the

television remote control. He turned on the VCR unit. It took two
tries for him to begin replaying the recording he'd made earlier of
the senator's press conference. Senator Harvey Banks appeared on
the screen.

Kirschstein took a few tentative steps across the office. The nervous spasming in his gut had stopped. On the opposite side of
DeLisa's desk, the lawyer halted. He could see the television set, but
he was watching his host instead. DeLisa was totally engrossed in
what Banks was saying.

The tape ended.

"Did you hear that? Who does he think he is? Is it legal for him
to go around threatening me like that?"

Kirschstein had regained some of his composure. "I don't think
he actually called you by name, Tony."

DeLisa's glare froze the lawyer in place. "He didn't have to call
my fucking name, counselor. Who in the hell do you think he was
talking about, Santa Claus?"

DeLisa's eyes remained on Kirschstein for an agonizingly long
five seconds. Finally, he looked back at the screen and said, "Go fix
yourself a drink, Frank. You look like hell."

Kirschstein walked over to the bar. He considered pouring himself a bourbon, but instead took a bottle of club soda from the refrigerator and poured its contents into a glass. He took a sip before
returning to the desk, where DeLisa sat watching the videotape
again.

"Well, I'm going to take care of our friend the senator," DeLisa
said. "He won't be convening any crime committee next week."

"Steiger?" Kirschstein said.

"Yeah." Abruptly, DeLisa shut off the set and swung to face the
lawyer. "They charged me a million bucks for the job."

"They?"

"The Mastermind's got a kid. A real snotty little punk. Kept
making smart-assed cracks."

Kirschstein didn't comment.

"But I been thinking on this thing since I got back this afternoon. No matter how the Steigers pull this one off, there's gonna be

heat. Lots of heat. There'll be enough do-gooders and conspiracy nuts running around to make things real uncomfortable for a lot of people. The way I see it, I'm gonna be the prime, number one suspect. I'm gonna have cops, both Feds and local, coming out of my ears for years. Unless I can give up the real killers."

"Suppose the Steigers talk?"

"Aw c'mon, Frank. I thought you was supposed to be smart? I'm not talking about giving them up alive or, for that matter, even in one piece. But I do want to make sure they're tied in tight to Banks's death. The cops won't like closing the case with a couple of stiffs, but if we play our cards right they won't have a choice."

Despite himself, Kirschstein shook his head. "This Karl Steiger's supposed to be the best, Tony. It won't be easy getting the drop on him."

DeLisa was again glaring at the lawyer. "He's only a man, counselor. Just like Paul Arcadio, Sol Levitsky and Art Maggio. You cut 'em, they bleed; you rip their fucking hearts out, they die. Steiger's a man just like they were."

Kirschstein averted his eyes, sipped his club soda, but could not help thinking: "So are you, Tony. So are you."

50

Karl Steiger found the house near the University of Chicago campus. He parked the rented car on the narrow two-lane street and walked to the address he'd been given. Utilizing rigid discipline, he kept his mind focused on the task he had come here to complete. With every fiber of his being he attempted to ignore where he was and how close he'd come to places that were as much a part of him as either his arms or legs.

The house had a flight of steps leading up to the front door. Climbing the steps, Karl considered how much these Chicago mansions tended to resemble each other. The house he was about to enter was very similar in basic architectural style to the Haggerty House over in the Historical District. The thought intruded before he could block it out. *It was also very similar to Adele's house over on the street they used to call South Park.*

Gritting his teeth until his jaw muscles ached, he pressed the doorbell. The sound of chimes could be heard echoing inside. He waited.

"Yes?" The voice came from an intercom speaker beside the door.

"My name is Anderson," he said using his adopted alias. "I believe Professor Engstrom telephoned about my visit."

Silence followed.

He was about to ring the bell again when the Judas window opened and a furtive, suspicious pair of eyes stared out at him.

"What is Professor Engstrom's first name?" an aged female voice demanded.

"Klaus."

"And what university did he attend?"

"I don't know. He must be eighty years old now. How . . . ?"

"I know how old he is," the woman snapped. "If you don't know what school he graduated from, then tell me where was the last place he taught."

Karl Steiger was growing tired of this stupid game. There were other places he could go to get what he needed, but this was his first choice. He decided to play along a bit longer.

"Oxford."

"What was his specialty?"

"The study of snakes, spiders and bugs."

"That's not funny!" the woman rebuked him. "If you're here to play games you've come to the wrong place."

"Sorry. Dr. Engstrom studied herpetology."

Karl could hear the sound of locks being undone. The door swung open to reveal the rest of his interrogator. She stood barely five feet tall.

"Actually, he studied zoology," she said. "Herpetology is one of its branches and it goes beyond simply studying snakes, spiders and bugs. Come in."

He followed her into the house.

She was quite old, with a curved spine that made her walk with a bent-over, round-shouldered shuffle. Her hair was snow-white and thinning on top. Her skin was wrinkled and liver-spotted. There were enormous bags under her eyes, but it was the eyes themselves that told him about her. They were as clear and sharp as those of a woman of thirty. They revealed that she was not only very much alive, but seriously interested in life. Despite her age, it was obvious she had something to live for, something that continued to drive her on from day to day.

She led him into a spartanly-furnished living room. Karl noticed the coating of dust on everything and the lack of any type of personal mementos, such as photographs, knickknacks or even an ornamental ashtray. She did not live in this room. She probably seldom even passed through it.

"You said your name was . . . ?" She turned around to look up at him.

"Anderson."

"A lie, but it doesn't matter. I am Eloise Vollmer Stritch. This is my home."

"How do you do?" Karl said, taking the woman's surprisingly strong hand.

"You are German?"

He nodded.

"So am I." But before he could comment, she held up her hand. "Don't give me any of that Deutschlander crap. My grandfather was beaten to death over in the stockyards area when World War I broke out simply because he was German. My grandmother was forced to move after it happened. In the new neighborhood she became Dutch."

This angered Karl, but he said nothing.

"What do you want, Mr. Anderson?"

"I need a fast-acting undetectable poison, one that can either be ingested orally or injected with equal potency. I don't want it to leave any traces an autopsy can uncover."

Eloise Vollmer Stritch laughed sharply. Actually, it was more of a cackle. "C'mon."

He followed her across the living room, down a hall, through a kitchen with a sink filled with putrefying dishes, onto a porch. She unlocked a back door that led into a small rear yard enclosed by a six-foot-tall wooden fence. They crossed the yard to a brick building that was much newer than the main house. This building was a single-story affair without windows. As she fumbled with a ring of keys that she then utilized to unlock the door and deactivate a sophisticated burglar alarm system, she cackled again. He was starting not to like this.

The interior of the building was hot. It was also, unlike the house they'd just left, antiseptically clean.

"You'd better take off your coat, Mr. Anderson, or you'll melt in here."

He gratefully did as she instructed, but still found that he was beginning to sweat.

The place was dark, but this was quickly remedied when she flipped a light switch by the door. Fluorescent overhead lights that stretched across the ceiling illuminated every square inch of space. Karl could see that this was a laboratory by all the electronic equipment, test tubes, beakers and Bunsen burners in evidence. There was also something else.

The usually confident Karl Steiger froze when he saw the occupants of the numerous glass-enclosed cages lining the walls. Each of them, from the small hand-sized model to the larger bathtub-sized crates, contained either live snakes or spiders. He knew enough about the field of herpetology to recognize some of what he saw; however, everything was made easy for him by the labels in English and Latin above each cage.

Keeping his distance as Eloise Vollmer Stritch thumped away from him down the center of the laboratory, he read a few of the labels: Fer de Lance, Green Mamba, Mojave Rattlesnake, Coral Snake, Bushmaster. And his presence had aroused the cages' occupants. Dozens of pairs of unblinking eyes, attached to narrow heads and slithering bodies, came to bear on him. Some were stirring lazily, others violently coiling as if to strike at him right through the glass.

With an effort Karl straightened his spine and remembered the old saying, "That which does not kill you makes you stronger."

He realized with a growing apprehension that any one of the things in these cages could indeed kill him. Kill him very dead.

Eloise had taken a seat on a stool at the other end of the lab. "Stop bothering my babies, Mr. Anderson, and come over here and sit down. I don't have all night."

With all the nerve he could muster, Karl walked over and took a stool facing her. As he looked on, she reached down and opened a wooden box lying on the laboratory table beside her. From it she removed a black tarantula that was larger than her hand. With another cackle that exposed stained, but even teeth, she placed the hairy spider on her shoulder. Like a trained pet, it perched there, barely moving. Then she looked at him and said, "You're prepared to meet my price for what you want?"

"Of course," he said, unable to keep himself from staring at the tarantula, which seemed to be staring right back at him.

"Then I'm certain I can help you, as long as you give me a hand extracting the venom. I'm not as strong as I used to be and some of these critters can get damned mean at times."

Karl sincerely hoped she was joking.

51

MARCH 6, 1994
7:30 P.M.

So you see, Helmut," Senator Banks was saying, "an elected official in this country must wear many hats along with providing a myriad of services to his constituents."

Ernest Steiger held up his hand. With an embarrassed grin, in keeping with his disguise as Helmut Strahlman of the German *Bild Zeitung,* he said, "The English of the senator is very good. Would you please to spell for Helmut the words mir . . . mir . . . ad and con-sti-tu . . . ?"

The senator and Maureen Taft laughed.

"I'll help you with those later, Helmut," she said.

"You must excuse me for using such words, but it's a habit of mine," the senator said.

"You know when you do that," she said reflectively, "you sound a lot like Harold Washington."

The senator looked at her and smiled. "I take that as a compliment."

"This Harold Washington," Ernest said, "I have heard of him. Was he not a senator, like you?"

"He was a United States congressman," the senator explained, "but he will probably be best remembered as the mayor of Chicago."

"Ya, the Herr Burgermeister," Ernest said with a broad grin, as he scribbled more notes on his pad. They were now one big, happy family. Trusting and relaxed. No bodyguards in sight. He turned his head to the side, so he could see the door out of the corner of his eye. It was securely closed and the noise the reporters had been making had ceased. That meant they were gone. The two bodyguards and the receptionist would probably be the only ones left. A plan began taking shape in his mind.

His father had taught him that Uncle Ernst had called situations like this "God-given opportunities." He could carry out the contract right now, which would mean he would have to kill not only Banks, but the Taft woman and anyone left in the outer office. It wouldn't be simple, but he could do it.

The Beretta Haggerty had given him was in the car. He didn't want to risk bringing a gun into the press conference in case of a frisk. But he did have his sleeve dagger.

Maureen Taft was saying something. He turned his head to look at her. She mouthed words he didn't hear. The senator laughed.

Without knowing what they were laughing about Ernest smiled. Banks resumed talking.

The dagger was in a sheath strapped to his left forearm. He could pull it, stand and throw it at the senator. He would need to hit him in the throat to silence any screams. At this distance, with his skill, he couldn't miss. While the senator strangled on the steel and his own blood, Ernest would take care of the girl.

The need to move with blinding speed would be essential. In completing the knife toss, he would have to step sideways and strike the reporter a disabling blow. He wouldn't be able to cut this too fine, as all she would need do was get off one scream. That would bring the bodyguards down on him.

He casually turned his head to look at her. She had a habit of tilting her head to the left. This would expose the right side from forehead to chin. A blow to the temple would stun her long enough for him to get in a better position to snap her pretty neck. If the deaths of the senator and the reporter were carried out in silence, he would then deal with the guards and the receptionist.

"Helmut," Maureen said, "the senator asked you a question."

"I am sorry, Herr Senator. I was pondering something you said about Herr Washington. Now is not the time, but perhaps later you could clarify it for me. What was your question again?"

Banks asked him something about Germany. With a smile, Ernest answered and placed his notebook on his lap. He slipped his right hand beneath it. The fingers of his left hand pressed the release clasp. The handle of the dagger slid into his palm. He tensed. In an instant it would be over.

The minute change in the air pressure transmitted to Ernest that someone had opened the office door. He froze in place. Sliding the dagger back into its sheath, he waited, continuing to stare at Banks. The senator looked up and the reporter turned around.

"Good evening, Senator," Reggie Stanton said from the other side of the office. "I hope I'm not intruding?"

52

Rachel had tried to stay asleep, but that was no longer possible. She felt groggy, sore and disoriented, but she was aware of where she was. She had awakened twice last night and three times during the day, but had managed to slip back into oblivion. Once, when she awoke and saw daylight filtering through slits in the blinds, Papa was there. She remained motionless as he bent to kiss her. She endured his touch and dozed off once more. Later, the chair beside her bed where the bodyguard had been stationed throughout the night was empty. Her hopes of being left alone were dashed when she heard him talking to someone named Carrie on her telephone.

She slept again and more time passed. Each time she regained consciousness, it became harder to escape back into that dark world where there were no memories, that place where she could escape Papa and his evil.

Finally, she forced her eyes open. It was dark. The chair where the bodyguard sat was again empty. She turned her head to look around and a wave of dizziness swept over her. She shut her eyes and tried to swallow. Her throat was sore and her tongue dry.

Someone cradled a hand beneath her head and lifted her into a sitting position. A glass touched her lips. Liquid flowed into her mouth. A sweet, cold liquid. She tried to drink more, but the glass was pulled away.

"Sip it slowly. Too much will make you sick."

Her eyes still closed, Rachel followed the instructions. She was drinking lemonade, the best lemonade she'd ever tasted. Finally, she'd had enough. She was lowered back to the bed. She took a moment to gather her courage and opened her eyes.

A shadowy figure stood over her in the dark. She could tell it was a woman by the size and the sound of the voice.

"How do you feel, child?"

A heavy despair descended on Rachel and she turned her head away attempting to bury it in the pillow. Tears filled her eyes.

"Now, now, don't do that."

The voice was soft, concerned, almost . . . Rachel rejected the thought, but it pressed to the forefront of her mind demanding recognition. Motherly? Could her mother have sounded like this?

A hand touched her shoulder and pulled. Rachel did not try to resist. She was helped into a sitting position in the bed. The woman embraced her. It had been a long time since she'd experienced a human touch from someone she didn't hate. She felt the warmth of the woman's body, the aroma of a sweet, flowery perfume, and the roughness of some type of beaded pattern on the front of her blouse. Like a troubled child, Rachel allowed herself to be held. She was rocked back and forth like an infant. A slight whimper escaped from her lips, followed by a sob. She began to cry. Emotion made her body shudder as she left herself go.

The bedroom door opened and a bodyguard appeared silhouetted in the hallway light behind him. "What's going on?" He sounded more frightened than demanding.

The woman stopped the rocking and spun her head around. She still clutched Rachel to her breast as she spat, "Get out!"

The bodyguard jumped as if her words were gunshots. He shut the door behind him.

Rachel tried to see her protector's face, but the room was too dark. She didn't really care what the woman looked like, as for just a few moments she felt safe in her arms. But she was curious.

She finished her cry and was allowed to lie back in the bed. The woman busied herself fluffing the pillows and straightening the bed covers.

"Do you think I could have some more lemonade?" Rachel asked.

"Of course."

There was the sound of ice cubes tinkling against glass followed by the soft rushing of liquid being poured.

"Can you hold it?" the woman said.

"I . . . I think so." Rachel reached out her hand through the dark and took the glass. She held it to her lips and drank it all. She handed the empty glass back.

"Are you hungry?"

"Yes. I guess so."

"What would you like to eat?"

"I don't know. I don't think I could hold anything down that was too heavy."

"Maybe some hearty minestrone soup and a couple of slices of bread with butter?"

Rachel found herself smiling. She'd never had any relatives other than Papa. At least none that she knew. But Bobby had an aunt who reminded her a lot of this woman. Especially by her concern. This was something Rachel had always sought in life. Someone to be concerned about her. Someone to be concerned about her other than Papa.

"I think I could handle that," she said, concerning the soup and bread.

The woman stood up.

"Wait," Rachel called to her.

The woman stood in the shadows at the foot of Rachel's canopied bed.

"Who are you?"

"My name is Angelina Lupo," she answered. "I am your new guardian."

With that the woman turned and crossed to the door. In the darkness Rachel could make out a thick figure and hair drawn back from the forehead into a bun at the back of her neck. Rachel also noticed that she limped.

Tuxedo Tony was in a very foul mood when his chauffeured Lincoln pulled up in front of the Oak Park mansion. In the downstairs alcove he was met by Wally Boykin.

"How'd it go, boss?"

DeLisa handed over his black coat and hat. "Good. How's Rachel?"

"She was still asleep a little while ago, but—"

"Goddamit, get that fucking doctor on the phone! I want him over here right now!"

The woman's voice came from the top of the staircase. "Rachel doesn't need a doctor. She just needs something to eat and a good hot bath."

DeLisa stared up at her, his mouth open in shock. She stared back at him impassively. Boykin expected his boss to explode. Instead, Tuxedo Tony remained motionless for a long time.

Boykin cleared his throat. "This is Mrs. Lupo, boss. Sam Sykes found her for us. She's got real good credentials."

DeLisa still didn't move. Slowly, he took in the severely tied-back black hair shot through with streaks of gray, the thick eyebrows and heavy peasant features, which were very much like his own. He looked at the black dress and heavy, thick-soled shoes. He finally looked at the eyes.

Hers, like his, were black pools seemingly capable of flashing a burning flame from within. DeLisa only glanced at them a second before looking away. They reminded him of someone he'd rather not think about at this moment.

"Is Rachel awake?" he asked.

"Yes." Mrs. Lupo's voice was accented, but not with an Italian inflection. Instead she spoke in the flat intonations of the Chicago South Side native. A southsider from the area of the Italian enclave on Taylor Street, where Antonio DeLisa had grown up.

Mrs. Lupo came down the stairs, walked past DeLisa and headed for the kitchen.

53

The instant he stepped inside the senator's office Reggie knew that something was wrong. The blond man, seated in front of the desk, was too rigid. Tensed, as if ready to uncoil and strike at the senator. Reggie was unable to see the man's hands, but realized he was doing something that had nothing to do with writing. Reggie realized that he was too far way to make a move without endangering the senator. Somehow he'd have to get the blond's attention.

"I hope I'm not intruding?"

The blond man did not turn around, but Maureen Taft did. Finally, the senator looked up. There was a frown of annoyance on Banks's face.

Reggie started across the office. He kept his attention focused on the blond.

Banks stopped him. "Wait outside, Stanton."

Reggie halted. He still couldn't see the blond's face. Reggie looked quizzically at Banks. Confused, he said, "Senator . . . ?

Maureen stared at Stanton. The blond man still didn't turn around.

The door opened. Reggie glanced over his shoulder to find King and Hill, the on-duty bodyguards, standing behind him. He realized he could take them easily, but they weren't his primary concern at the moment.

"Senator, you've got to—" Reggie said.

"Just leave." Banks pointed at the bodyguards and said, "Get him out of here."

Reggie was confused. A hand grasped his upper arm. "C'mon, Stanton," King said. "You heard the senator. Let's go."

Reggie didn't budge and continued to stare back at Banks. "What's going on, Senator?"

"I don't need you anymore, Stanton. The fact is, you scare me."

A terrible pain clutched at Reggie's gut. He hadn't felt like this since Uncle Ernst died.

"Let's go, Stanton," King said, attempting to pull him from the room.

Reggie pirouetted toward King and slipped from his grasp. Now they stood face to face. The bodyguard reached for his gun.

"You'll never get it out of the holster," Reggie said.

Slowly, King dropped his hand to his side. The other bodyguard stood by looking confused. Everyone in the office froze.

Reggie turned back to look at Banks. "We need to talk, Senator. If you don't want me around anymore, I guess that's your decision. You're the man. But we still need to talk. I'll call you tomorrow."

Banks didn't respond. Maureen and the bodyguards stared at Stanton. The blond man had yet to turn around.

Reggie remained a moment longer before turning for the door. As he crossed the outer office, Naomi handed him a message.

It read: CALL ME AS SOON AS YOU CAN, GRANDMA.

Fear jolted him from shock. He snatched up the phone on Naomi's desk. While it rang, Reggie looked back at the inner office. Banks, Maureen Taft and the bodyguards were staring at him. Finally, the blond man turned around. For an instant Reggie's eyes locked with those of the stranger. He felt the same jolt of recognition as he had that day, years ago, when he'd first looked into the blue-gray eyes of Uncle Ernst. Then, King slammed the door.

Ida Mae Stanton answered the phone.

"What is it, Grandma?"

"Mr. Webster called. He said you must come at once."

Reggie stiffened. This was his operational code.

"Are you okay, Reggie?"

"Yes, Grandma, I'm fine. I'll take care of Mr. Webster."

Hanging up the telephone, Reggie Stanton took one last look at the closed door to the senator's office before leaving.

54

Mama Mancini's Pizzeria was doing a brisk business. Located on Taylor Street, a short distance from the Presbyterian/St. Luke's Hospital complex, the restaurant was popular and had been on the same corner for fifty years. Waiters and waitresses clad in white aprons, red vests and black bow-ties hustled back and forth between the red-checked, cloth-covered tables and the kitchen, carrying steaming platters of pizza and ice cold pitchers of beer. At the entrance, a line had formed with patrons waiting for available space. Some of the potential customers were waiting in the bar, where Jimmy Mancini, the owner's nephew, and two bartenders were filling drink orders as fast as they could.

"A scotch and soda with a twist, a Manhattan and two Miller Lites," Jimmy said, filling the orders of four nurses squeezed into a corner of the U-shaped bar.

Jimmy was a rotund man with the imperious features of a Caesar and a grossly out-of-style ducktail haircut. He was well liked by the regular trade, even though at times he could get a little fresh with the ladies. Now, he was winding up to tell the nurses an obscene joke about his idea of the ideal woman when the phone rang beneath the bar.

"Mancini's."

His ruddy complexion turned a shade or two lighter when the caller identified himself. "Yeah sure, Mr. DeLisa. Hold on."

Jimmy hit the Hold button and punched an in-house line. "Ma, he's on line two."

* * *

In the restaurant's office behind the kitchen, the owner, Grace Mancini, picked up the telephone. At the age of seventy-eight, Mama Mancini possessed gleaming silver hair and a face patterned with wrinkles. However, her eyes were still bright and alert. On occasion, when the restaurant became extremely busy, she would pitch in and outwork those much younger than her.

"Hello?" Her Italian accent was thick.

"Mama, this is Tony DeLisa. How are you?"

"I'm fine, Antonio. How are you and how is that beautiful daughter of yours?"

"We're real good, Ma. Rachel's in school. She goes over there to the Illinois Chicago campus."

"Then why don't you have her come by and see Mama sometime? You forget that me and your mother were best friends in the old country? Now that you a big man, you no come see Mama, even on her birthday."

"Yeah, Ma, I know, but I been real busy lately. Look, next year me and Rachel will be there on your birthday with bells on."

"Not next year, Antonio. September sixteenth this year. I'll be looking for you. Don't let Mama down."

"Right. We'll be there. But look, uh, that's not the reason I called."

"Yes. What is it?"

"You know a woman from the neighborhood calls herself Angelina Lupo?"

"Know her? Antonio, Angelina's my niece. If you come around once in awhile and saw the people you grew up with, you'd know that."

"Your niece? I didn't know you had any nieces, Ma. Thought you was an only child?"

"Maybe you forgot that I was married to Carmine Mancini for thirty-seven years? Maybe you also forgot Carmine had five brothers and six sisters? What's the matter, Antonio, you not been eating so good or something? You're too young a man to lose your memory like that."

There was a pause from DeLisa's end. Then, *"Tell me something, Ma. Which one of Carmine's brothers was Angelina's father?"*

"Not his brothers, his sisters. The second oldest girl Maria. Angelina was their third child. Maria married Vincente Lupo, who owned the hardware store over on Loomis. You do remember that, don't you?"

"Yeah, I guess so." Again, DeLisa hesitated. *"Okay, Ma. thanks a bunch. I'll be in touch."*

Mama Mancini hung up the telephone and looked at the man seated across from her. Blackie Silvestri patted the back of her hand and said, "You did great, Ma. Just great. But he sounded suspicious."

She grunted. "That Antonio. He's like his father before him. Evil and suspicious. He'll come to the same bad end."

"He's going to call back," Blackie said as a warning.

"Don't worry. I'll be ready for him." She paused. "But, Cosimo, you tell Mama something."

Blackie flinched at the use of his first name. Mama was one of the few people who refused to call him "Blackie."

Mama Mancini ignored his distress. "That little girl you brought in here earlier. How she gonna pass for Angelina? My niece is a forty-seven-year-old spinster. I was happy to get her to go away on that cruise, but if Antonio asks anybody but me, he's gonna know that she's not my Angelina."

Blackie managed a smile. "As long as Angelina Lupo stays gone the week she's supposed to, there won't be any problems. As far as appearances go, I don't think DeLisa's going to be able to tell who the real Angelina is, even if he had the girl I brought in earlier and the real Angelina stand side by side."

"Now you the one talking crazy, Cosimo. But I'll tell you one thing about my Angelina."

Blackie waited.

"She's the spitting image of Antonio's mother. Other than his Rachel, I think Antoinette DeLisa is the only woman he ever loved."

55

The Coles were watching a movie on a cable channel and Larry "Butch" Cole, Jr., had fallen asleep. The six-year-old was sitting up on the couch next to his father in the living room of their southside home. Lisa sat on the floor with her legs curled beneath her. Larry, Sr., tapped his wife on the shoulder and pointed to their sleeping son. Quietly, she stood up and took the child in her arms. He never awoke as she carried him up to bed.

Cole grabbed a handful of popcorn from the bowl on the table, chewed and chased it with a lukewarm swallow of beer. He tried to focus his attention back on the movie, but he'd seen it before and hadn't liked it that well the first time around.

His mind kept returning to Senator Banks, Stanton and the I.A.D. file Blackie had given him. When Cole left Area One at about six he'd stuffed it in his briefcase.

Lisa returned and stared at the remains of the pizza they'd eaten most of during the movie. "Do you want me to heat some of this up for you before I put it away?"

"No," Cole said. "I've had enough."

Before beginning to tidy up, she looked at her husband. Then she walked around behind him and began massaging his shoulders and neck. "You look exhausted, honey."

"I'm okay," he managed. His eyes were closed and he was enjoying her machinations. He purred, "You do that much longer and I'll be too sleepy to read this old file."

"You're not going to work tonight?" she said, removing her hands from his neck.

"Got to." He reached down and opened his briefcase, which rested on the floor beside the couch. From it he removed the I.A.D. file.

She shook her head. "You're not going to read all that tonight, are you?"

"I'm going to give it a try." He stood up. "I probably already know most of what's in it anyway." He headed for the den.

"How old is it?" she asked, as curiosity forced her to follow him.

"Fifteen years. I was a sergeant working out of Riseman's office back then. I never knew how they closed it. Now I plan to find out."

Cole's den was small but comfortable. The walls were polished wood, the desk an antique rolltop, and the chair a leather recliner. Shelves, containing novels and texts on police procedure, lined the walls. On a stand, near the window, was an IBM PC. A vinyl couch, covered with an afghan, rested against the far wall.

Turning on the overhead light, Cole sat down at the desk. He was pulling the thick rubber band from the file when Lisa asked, "May I join you?"

He stifled a yawn. "Of course. As a matter of fact, why don't I take a nap and let you read the file. Then you can summarize it for me when I wake up." He had spoken in jest.

She smiled at her husband and realized how much she loved him. Only she wished he wouldn't work so hard. "If I thought it would help you I would." Then she began searching the bookshelves until she found a novel she hadn't read. Carrying it over to the couch she sat down and tucked her legs beneath her.

Then both of them began reading. The study door was left open in case Butch woke up.

56

R eggie Stanton called his grandmother from the airport.
"I've got to fly to Washington right away, Grandma. I'll be
back as soon as I can."

"What's the matter, Reggie? You sound strange."

"I'll tell you about it when I get back."

A few minutes later he boarded United Airlines Flight 290
bound for Washington, D.C. When the plane became airborne, he
stared out at the lights of Chicago receding into the night. He ordered a cognac from the stewardess and attempted to relax and forget the scene back at the senator's office. As he did so his mind
drifted back over the years to the beginning of the life he now led. A
beginning which found him in the uniform of a Chicago police officer.

PART

"That which does not kill me makes me stronger."
—Friedrich Wilhelm Nietzsche

57

S tanton, you're assigned to Beat six twenty-three tonight working ten–ninety-nine. The commander gave Williams and Johnson the night off," Lieutenant Barry "Biff" O'Hara announced
from the podium at the third watch roll call in the 6th District squad
room.

The salt-and-pepper sprinkled head of Officer Kenny Collins
snapped in Stanton's direction. The kid was a rookie barely out of
the police academy. Collins had been his training officer. He figured
that O'Hara was joking. A pretty cruel joke, but Biff had been
known to play cruel jokes before. Collins only hoped O'Hara
wouldn't take it too far.

When Collins turned back to face front he found O'Hara staring
at him. The look the lieutenant gave him revealed that indeed this
was no joke. He was sending the rookie out to work alone on Commander Charles Howard's personal beat. In Kenny Collins's estimation this was very bad.

"Okay, if there's nothing else, hit the streets and remember, boys
and girls, we're low on moving violations, so write those tickets,"
O'Hara said, dismissing them.

Reggie Stanton stood up, placed his uniform saucer cap squarely
on his head and picked up his briefcase. He was turning to follow
the rest of the officers to the radio room to pick up his walkie-talkie
when Collins stopped him. The senior officer waited until everyone
had cleared out of the cramped, un–air conditioned room before he
spoke.

"Why's Biff pissed at you, kid?"

Reggie was as fair as he would be fifteen years in the future. The only difference was that his frame held thirty pounds less of the muscle he would put on over the next decade and a half. But even at the age of twenty-one he possessed a measure of silent menace.

"I didn't know he was," Reggie said.

A couple of officers coming off duty entered the squad room to check their mailboxes.

"Meet me in the parking lot," Collins said, walking away.

A few minutes later they met between two blue and white squad cars; Stanton's 623 and Collins's 611.

"Twenty-three's the rawest beat in the district, Reggie. Williams and Johnson have got a rep for being tough cops and they make their share of pinches, but they also spend a lot of time looking the other way. They don't do that for free."

"I don't understand," Reggie said.

"C'mon, kid," Collins scolded. "I thought you said you grew up in this town?"

Stanton stared blankly back at his training officer. The rookie's eyes still made the veteran uneasy. Not nervous, just uneasy.

"Okay," Collins said with a sigh, "I'll spell it out for you. Twenty-three's a little East St. Louis right in the middle of two of the most affluent black communities in Chicago. On the west is Chatham, on the east Avalon Park. In a strip of eight blocks, running right through the middle of the beat, there are more bars and liquor stores than for any comparable area on the southside. There are pool halls, rib joints and cheap motels. That's the legitimate, licensed stuff. You also got more prostitutes, gamblers and dope dealers than they've got on forty-seventh Street."

Reggie simply stared at Collins. Then the rookie looked as if he had smiled, but the faint swelling of his cheeks revealed little about what was going on behind those pale eyes.

"Look," Collins said, urgently, "I'm telling you this for your own good, Reggie. You fool around with the wrong people on six twenty-three and you could get hurt."

"But I'm a policeman, Kenny," Reggie argued. "What can they do to me?"

Collins groaned. "Kid, it ain't the lowlifes you've got to worry about. 'The Strip' is Commander Howard's personal property. Williams and Johnson are what is known in the graft game as 'bag men.' You mess with anything they control down there and it'll be your ass."

At that instant a third squad car pulled into the parking lot and skidded to a stop beside them.

"Shit," Collins hissed under his breath when he saw who was behind the wheel.

Sergeant Polly Markham, the green-eyed terror of the district, glared at them. "You boys are flirting with a reprimand if you don't get your butts in those cars and head for your beats right now."

Collins jumped to do her bidding. Reggie moved quickly, but without the degree of fear the sergeant thought he should. As Collins gunned his car from the lot, he knew that Markham would be after the kid from now on and there was nothing Reggie would be able to do to stop her.

58

JULY 7, 1979
3:45 P.M.

Officer Reggie Stanton drove from the station lot toward his beat. This was his third tour of duty on the afternoon watch since his graduation from the police academy. His grandmother had attended the ceremony, but Uncle Ernst had stayed home. He seldom left the house for any reason and being around that many cops would have made him nervous. Reggie understood.

So far he liked the 6th District. The neighborhood where he lived in the 4400 block of King Drive was recovering slowly from being one of the worst ghettos in the city, but was still a long way from the opulence of the homes in Chatham and West Chesterfield. Homes that were owned by black people. Reggie would have liked to move his grandmother and Uncle Ernst out here away from the old neighborhood, where just about every night gunshots echoed through the streets and the howl of police sirens could be heard until dawn.

He used a beat map to find his way north to the geographical Area designated Beat 623. He knew the streets, since they were laid out with the same names as the ones in his neighborhood thirty blocks north. It wouldn't take Reggie long to learn the rhythms of the beat. Then he would know how best to police it.

Uncle Ernst had a great deal of money. In one of the four bank books he kept he had once shown Reggie a balance in a New York investment account of over a quarter of a million dollars. Reggie had been shocked when he saw the names on the passbook as being those of Ida Mae Stanton and Reginald E. Stanton.

"The money is yours," Uncle Ernst said. "You can do with it as you please."

Reggie's first thought was to move away from the urban jungle where he'd been born and learned to survive. Uncle Ernst smiled sadly when he heard Reggie's plan. "You can go, Reggie. Take your grandmother with you. Start a new life."

"You've got to come with us."

Uncle Ernst shook his balding head. "They still hunt me. I am safe here. I will die here. I run no more."

"But we can hire lawyers and take your case to court," Reggie argued. "The Second World War ended nearly fifty years ago."

"They will never acquit me, *mein Sohn,*" Ernst said with a sad smile. "I was too clever. Even though I let Eisenhower go when I discovered the Battle of the Bulge, and thus the war, was lost, I engaged in the acts of a spy. Then the general became president and put a price on my head. I doubt if I would ever even see a trial. That would make the humiliation of the great man public. I will die as a fugitive war criminal before any type of trial could take place."

"But Eisenhower's dead," Reggie protested.

Ernst chuckled. "But *they* haven't forgotten."

"Who are you talking about?"

"Your Gestapo."

"There is no Gestapo in America, Uncle Ernst."

"But there is, Reggie," Ernst said, solemnly. "There is."

Officer Stanton turned the police car from State Street onto Seventy-ninth and drove east. Both sides of Seventy-ninth were lined with retail stores, cleaning establishments, shoe shops and restaurants. This was a thriving business district, but it was not part of his beat. This was the area west of Beat 623. From what he had heard even before Kenny Collins talked to him, what went on over east was due to some type of silent, mutual agreement between the police, the homeowners and shopkeepers in the legitimate area to keep the open corruption exclusively on "the Strip." Reggie was now about to get his first glimpse of his new clientele.

Years ago Uncle Ernst purchased the old mansion on King Drive, moved the remaining tenants to other housing and had the old structure renovated. The only occupants were Uncle Ernst, Reggie and Ida Mae. The renovation took six months. During this time they lived amidst the noise of banging and sawing, along with the plaster dust, on a constant basis. However, when the house was finished, it was as if they'd entered a time machine and been transported into the past of Chicago, circa 1890.

The brownstone had been faithfully restored to its original state. After spending one night there, the three of them vowed to never leave.

Stanton thought there were few things that could shock him, but when he drove across Cottage Grove he was certain he'd entered another world. The cleanliness of the storefronts and quiet streets only a couple of blocks back was erased by vulgar squalor. This was a slice of crime-infested ghetto living at its worst. Every other storefront was a bar, each block had at least four liquor stores, and barbeque and cheap carry-out restaurants proliferated. There was at least one pool hall and pawn shop every two blocks. Also, as Collins had told him, six cheap motels were there with signs advertising "transients welcome."

In the neighborhood where Reggie lived, the people were poor;

however, this was not the case on "the Strip." New Cadillacs, Lincolns and a couple of Rolls Royce Silver Clouds lined the cracked curbs. Men and women wearing custom-made clothing and sporting expensive but garish gold jewelry strutted up and down the filthy sidewalks.

To Officer Reggie Stanton the scene was at once bizarre and shocking. It also angered him deeply. He had seen pimps, whores and dope pushers before, so he had no difficulty recognizing the occupations of those parading on the street. But he had never before seen such human vermin bred in these large, uncontested numbers. He knew the reason for the infestation was that the proper insecticide had not been applied to this form of pestilence. At least not until today.

He intended to make a full sweep of the beat before starting the delousing, but the traffic on Seventy-ninth Street backed up, then slowed to a dead halt. He was unable to see what was causing the problem, as the line of cars in front of him stretched for at least a block. Flipping his mars lights and siren on, Reggie pulled out into the opposite lane, forcing a couple of oncoming cars to pull over to give him room. He made his way down the block without incident.

The obstruction causing the traffic back-up was a lavender 1979 Cadillac Eldorado convertible. It had been customized with what were called "gangster" whitewalls, skirts over the rear wheels and leopard-skin seat covers. The car was double-parked in front of a tavern sporting the neon sign out front which read BIG WILLIE'S.

Stanton pulled his squad car in front of the Cadillac and got out. He put his cap on and slipped his night stick into the ring on his gun belt. Opening his citation book to a blank formset, he walked back to the Eldorado.

He stopped the traffic in the westbound lanes to ease the backed-up eastbound traffic flow and a few moments later Seventy-ninth Street was clear. No one had appeared to move the double-parked car. Stanton began recording the license plate number of the Cadillac on the citation.

"Hey, man!" a male voice shouted from inside Big Willie's. "What the hell are you doing?"

Stanton realized the shouting was being directed at him, but he wasn't about to acknowledge it. Not from some drunken idiot in a bar and not while he was wearing this uniform. He walked around the Cadillac to record the city sticker number.

"Goddammit, can't this son of a bitch hear?"

Uncle Ernst had taught him how to handle situations like this. Taught him better than the instructors had at the police academy. He kept his back turned and studied the reflection of the entrance to the bar in the Cadillac's side window.

"Take it easy, Little Willie," a woman said. "This cop just new. Howard'll set him straight quick enough."

Stanton could detect no movement from the open door of the tavern from which the voices had come. A crowd began gathering on the sidewalk. There were a few comments made by the onlookers, but everyone was apparently waiting for "Little Willie" to make his move. He finally did.

A thin, short black man, wearing a white hat with an enormous brim, a black silk shirt open to the navel and four ropes of gold chains around his neck, appeared at the tavern entrance. A tall, chunky black woman, wearing a skirt so short that it completely exposed her thighs, tottered out of the bar behind him.

Stanton figured the man to be Little Willie. He watched him approach.

The little man walked straight up to Stanton. "Hey, Mr. Cop, do you know what in the hell you're doing? I get on the phone and drop one dime and your ass'll be transferred to . . . ."

Stanton turned around. Little Willie looked into his face and backed up.

"Could I see your driver's license, sir?"

"You not writing me no ticket, man," Little Willie said. "Don't you know who I am?"

Stanton stepped closer to him. "I'm going to ask you one more time, my brother. Let me see your driver's license."

The little man had horribly bloodshot eyes, which Stanton knew came from a combination of excessive drinking and regular narcotics use. He was flying right now and, if Stanton had caught him behind the wheel of the Cadillac, he would have been jailed for driving under the influence. But right now all he intended to do was cite him for obstructing traffic.

The crowd size had increased. The woman, who had followed Little Willie out of the tavern, now stood behind him. She looked drunker than he did.

Little Willie sneered. "Hey, baby," he said over his shoulder to the woman. "Did you hear what this half-white, nigger cop just called me?"

"Naw, baby. What'd he call you?" She glared at Stanton.

"Brother." With that he let out a loud, long laugh contagious enough to infect the crowd.

Stanton's face remained emotionless as he reached for the walkie-talkie microphone clipped to the leather thong looped through his shirt epaulet. He keyed the mike and said, "Six twenty-three."

The dispatcher answered.

"Would you send me a squadron, an assist car and a tow truck for prisoner's property to ten fifteen East Seventy-ninth Street?"

As the dispatcher acknowledged the request, Little Willie sobered a bit. "You not towing my car, man."

"Oh, but I am, my brother," Stanton said. "And guess what? You're under arrest."

At that moment all hell broke loose on Seventy-ninth Street.

59

JULY 8, 1979
12:05 A.M.

Ernst Steiger set up the chess board on the bar in the basement. Down here was his domain and, although Ida forced her way in occasionally to mop the floor and dust the ancient relics the old German hung on the walls as mementos, he was pretty much left alone. Alone with his nephew.

The chess pieces arranged, Ernst went behind the bar that he had built with his own hands to resemble the one in the old von Steiger hunting lodge in the Austrian Alps. He drew a stein of cold beer from the tap. The beer was Budweiser, since he had never gotten used to the so-called imported German beers so popular in the United States. He checked the cuckoo clock over the bar. Reggie would be home soon.

Ernst decided to have a shot of Schnapps with his beer. He poured the clear liquid into a shot glass and downed it. He took a swallow of beer. The familiar taste brought back memories, some of which were good and some not so good. He had learned long ago to take each of them the same. He recognized that the past was as dead as Adolph Hitler and the Third Reich.

He considered another Schnapps, but then this would dull his wits and make it easier for Reggie to beat him at chess. He realized that too much beer would accomplish the same result, only over a longer period of time. He put the beer stein down beside the chess board and crossed the basement to the work area.

The basement of the brownstone on King Drive was L-shaped and spacious. The leg of the L, containing the bar and recreation area, was fifty feet long by thirty feet wide. The longer leg of the L, which served as his and his nephew's workroom, was seventy-five feet in length and thirty feet wide. It served as a combination gymnasium and target range. It was here that Ernst von Steiger had taught Reggie everything he knew.

Ernst walked past the weights, wrestling mats and the Universal apparatus to the target range. It could be used to practice with firearms and daggers. The walls were insulated to contain the sound. Here Ernst had taught Reggie how to use conventional firearms, but Ernst personally preferred the dagger. It took greater skill and perhaps even an exceptional talent to use one effectively. Karl had been good, but Reggie was phenomenal.

At Friedenthal in 1943, Hauptmann Ernst von Steiger had instructed Skorzeny's commandos in the use of the dagger as a silent weapon of death. In 1979, Ernst stepped to the table where the razor-sharp but worn practice daggers were arranged, picked one up and remembered his instructions to the fresh-faced young commandos assembled for training back in that late spring and early summer.

"Your SS training has no doubt exposed you to the commando tactic of slipping up behind an enemy soldier, silencing him by grabbing his mouth and nose, and then killing him with a puncture thrust to the kidneys, followed by slashing his throat from ear to ear."

In the empty basement of the brownstone, Ernst silently demonstrated the grab, thrust and slice motion in exactly the same manner as he had done in 1943. He glared into the vacant basement as he had done at the troops on the training field.

"And how many of you have ever killed a man using this method?"

There were no takers.

Hauptmann Steiger jumped forward and grabbed the Schmeisser machine gun of a lieutenant. He held the weapon over his head. "This is easy to use. You don't even have to be accurate with it. You simply keep spraying the target until you kill it or run out of bullets."

He flipped the machine gun back to its owner. "But when you cut a man's throat you have to be careful of certain things. One, there will be a great deal of blood, so you've got to remember to keep your mouth closed or your victim's act of dying will drown you. Also, keep your eyes closed. A shower of blood can shock the senses into locking up on you, endangering not only your comrades, but also your mission. A quick kill can also result in a sudden release of the bowels and bladder. This method can be silent, but then it can also be very messy."

A few of the commando trainees had gone pale. When Ernest had first explained to his nephew the complications that came with slitting a man's throat at close quarters, Reggie's eyes lit up with fascination.

"There is another way to kill silently with a dagger," Haupt-

mann Steiger explained. "You can stand at a distance of fifteen meters from your target and . . ."

He spun and hurled the dagger across the fifteen-meter span at a
pistol silhouette target. The weapon pierced the target's heart area
and imbedded itself in the corkboard backing.

The whistle of a second dagger split the air impaling the center of
the silhouette target's throat.

Without turning, the German asked, "How far?"

"Twenty-two meters, Uncle Ernst," Reggie replied from behind
him.

Now Ernst turned. His nephew wore a jacket over his police uniform. "That is good, but you can do better."

However, Reggie was the best Ernst von Steiger had ever seen
with a thrown dagger. Better than Karl, better than himself and better even than the old Austrian Gypsy Julio, who had taught three
generations of von Steigers the art of the Whistling Dagger of
Death.

60

JULY 8, 1979
12:45 A.M.

Ida Mae Stanton had her hair up in rollers. She was clad in her
nightdress and housecoat when she heard Reggie come in. She
knew he'd go right to the basement to be with Ernst. She slipped on
house shoes and went down to the kitchen. She always felt a certain
thrill walking through the brownstone after Ernst had it remodeled.
Despite the overall deterioration of the neighborhood they lived in,
the black woman, who had been born dirt-poor as Ida Mae White of
Omaha, Nebraska, felt that she had finally made it. She lived like a
"swell," as the rich were called when she was growing up.

In the kitchen she began making ham and cheese sandwiches on rye bread. Ernst would have Reggie drinking beer by now, but that didn't mean that the boy couldn't eat a sandwich and have a nice glass of cold milk after working all day. She even made a couple of sandwiches for Ernst.

She placed the sandwich platter, an unopened bag of potato chips and a glass of milk on a tray. She carried it to the door, leading off the central hall, that led down to the basement. As she descended, her chest once more swelled with pride over her grandson's accomplishment. He was a police officer. She'd never thought she'd see the day when a member of her family would be with the law. But she understood this to be the way of nature; all things change.

"Checkmate," Ernst crowed.

They were seated at the bar. Reggie's head was bent over the chess board as he studied the pieces with his usual intensity. Ernst rarely beat his nephew.

Reggie looked up as she approached with the tray. "Good evening, Grandma. What are you doing up so late?"

"I wanted to fix my boy something to eat. Didn't want him staying up all night playing chess with this old reprobate on an empty stomach."

Ernst bristled. "Tell me, Reggie, what is this 'reprobate' she calls me?"

"It's nothing, Uncle Ernst," Reggie said, lightly, but he didn't smile. Ida noticed that he never smiled. At times this worried her.

She set the tray down on the bar and shoved the chess board over to the side. A couple of Ernst's chess pieces were knocked over. "Watch it, woman!"

She ignored him.

"I can't eat all this, Grandma," Reggie said, looking at the tray.

"You can give him some if he's not too busy drinking."

"I have to drink," Ernst countered, "to be able to endure your cooking."

Reggie picked up a sandwich and bit into it. Ernst did likewise. But the young policeman returned his half to the tray after one bite. Ernst devoured his. Reggie opened the bag of potato chips and chewed one listlessly.

"What's the matter, Reggie?" Ida asked.

Uncle Ernst was starting on his second sandwich. Now he stopped in midchew and looked from Ida Mae to his nephew. Reggie's face was as impassive as ever, but they knew him well enough to see that he was going through some type of problem.

"I got in a little trouble at work," he volunteered. "The district commander is talking about suspending me."

"Why?" they asked as one.

"It's a long story." He spent the next thirty minutes telling them.

"I knew things in this town hadn't changed that much," Ida spat. "Dope dealers, pimps, prostitutes and cops all in bed together. Makes me sick to my stomach."

"Can you not go to this commander's superiors, Reggie?" Uncle Ernst said. "Maybe they don't know that he's crooked and will take some action against him."

"I don't have any proof that he's doing anything wrong, Uncle Ernst. He simply showed up at the station and took the guy's father I arrested into his office. I don't know what happened in there."

Ida's anger flared. "But when this Commander Howard came out he ordered that Sergeant Markham to release your prisoners and told that Lieutenant . . . ?"

"Lieutenant O'Hara," Reggie said. "They call him Biff."

"Well, he ordered this Biff to get a complaint against you."

"It's called a Complaint Register Number, Grandma."

"What did they accuse you of?" Ida said.

"Brutality. They said I beat up this Little Willie McCoy," Reggie explained. "He's got some bruises, but nothing serious, and he did resist arrest."

"Ach, brutality," Ernst swore. "In America you do not know the true meaning of the word."

"Well, Reggie ain't done nothing wrong," Ida said, "and those people he arrested are lowlifes. It sure looks like your commander is doing something he shouldn't be doing."

Reggie remained silent for a moment before adding, "This Little Willie McCoy's father is named Big Willie McCoy. Kenny said they are two of the biggest dope dealers in the town."

"Who is this Kenny?" Uncle Ernst asked.

"He was my field training officer."

"The lazy one?"

"He's not so bad," Reggie said. "At least he'd talk to me after it happened. When the other officers found out the commander was mad at me, they began avoiding me like I had the plague."

"This Chicago Police Department has no spirit," Uncle Ernst said. "They turn on their own. The superior officers must take care of their men. Treat them like their children. They cannot turn their backs on their own to consort with the enemy. To do so is the most severe form of treason."

Ida sneered. "This is still Chicago, Ernst, and despite Reggie's light skin and gray-blue eyes, they consider him as black as the white establishment does."

"The people he arrested were also black," Ernst argued.

"But his commander and the other two, trying to get Reggie in trouble, are white."

"Stop it," Reggie said, quietly. "I've had a bad enough day as it is without you two getting into a fight."

They lapsed into silence for a time. No one spoke until Ida said to Reggie, "There must be something you can do."

Her grandson's eyes came up to meet hers. What she saw in them chilled her. She had seen this exact same look on her dead father's face many years before when he'd gone out and killed a man for insulting her mother back in Omaha.

"Yes," he said, softly. "There is something I can do. I'm going to clean up Commander Howard's strip on Seventy-ninth Street."

"How?" she demanded.

"Any way I can," he said with a damning formality.

"Good," Ernst said, banging the surface of the bar with his fist and making everything on it—chess pieces, sandwich tray and glasses—jump. "For that you will need a plan. A master plan! That is my specialty."

At that instant Ida Mae Stanton realized that the big German knew a great deal more about her grandson than she did.

61

William "Big Willie" McCoy was a physically imposing man. He stood six feet six inches tall and weighed 245 pounds. He kept himself in rigid condition by working out at the Windy City Health Club in the Loop five times a week. He had a medium-brown complexion with facial skin scarred by severe acne suffered during adolescence. His features were arranged in sets of points and Vs giving him a pronounced demonic look. He liked this, because it frightened people. In his business he needed to make people afraid of him.

Big Willie was one of the largest purveyors of vice activities in Chicago. He didn't have a territory, as most of his competitors did, but instead a street. The eight blocks on East Seventy-ninth Street belonged to him. Down here he was mayor, governor and president. He could also be judge, jury and executioner. By cunning, force and the threat of force, he'd obtained the tacit consent of the communities surrounding him to run *his* street as a "red light" district. This kept him off the surrounding streets. In fact, it was in his best interests to make sure he kept those areas crime-free. It kept the neighbors from complaining and rivals nonexistent.

But to operate his "ongoing criminal enterprise" at the all out, open and notorious level he currently enjoyed, he needed the cooperation of local public officials. In this regard Big Willie owned Commander Charles Howard and had clandestinely financed the political campaigns of the last two aldermen elected in this ward.

Big Willie McCoy was successful. He had more money than he could ever spend, a stable of tender young things whose only desire—for the right price—was to please him, and he enjoyed exalted status among his peers. By all external indications he should have been a happy man. He was not.

Now, on this humid Friday evening, he sat in his apartment above the tavern. He had a ten-room house in the Beverly area, but he spent most of his time in the apartment on Seventy-ninth Street. The reason for his dissatisfaction with life was seated across from him in the living room. As Big Willie looked on, Little Willie snorted a line of cocaine off the surface of the mirrored cocktail table.

"You know that shit costs money?" Big Willie said with a frown.

His son's eyes were at half-mast. He melted back onto the couch and turned toward his father. His head drooped to one side. "And it is some good shit too."

Angrily, Big Willie crossed the room and snatched a bottle of expensive scotch from the sideboard. He dropped ice cubes into a glass and poured the scotch over them. He swirled the contents around briefly before taking a long pull.

"Hey, Pop," his son called from the couch. "Fix me one too."

"Since when did I become your goddamned waiter, boy?"

Little Willie stared at his father. "I'd make you a drink if you asked me."

"And when's the last time I asked you?"

"Shit," Little Willie said, slapping his thighs and pushing himself up off the couch. "I don't remember and I really don't give a shit." He headed for the door.

Big Willie slammed his glass down on the sideboard and leaped across the room to intercept his son. He spun him around and pinned him against the wall. He shoved a muscular forearm under his chin and applied pressure until Little Willie's eyes bulged and veins popped out on his forehead.

"I'm tired of you disrespecting me, boy! I'm tired of you lying around here on your ass all day snorting shit you don't pay for and getting drunk! I'm tired of you, period!"

For just the briefest second, Big Willie seriously considered crushing his son's windpipe and ending his aggravation once and for all. He knew he could do it easily enough, as he outweighed the younger man by at least a hundred pounds. But then Little Willie was his only child. At least the only one he owned up to.

Despite the pain and difficulty he had breathing, Little Willie never took his eyes off his father. Through them he transmitted his contempt and lack of fear. This disconcerted Big Willie. Realizing that he didn't have the guts to kill his son, he released him.

Little Willie slumped against the wall, coughing and gasping for breath. His father walked away from him back to the sideboard and picked up his drink. The older man felt angry, impotent and ashamed. He heard his son say, "The next time you put your hands on me I'm going to kill you."

The sound of the door opening and slamming heralded Little Willie's exit.

The lord and master of the eight blocks of corruption on East Seventy-ninth Street finished his drink and poured himself another.

"Sounds like they had a fight," F.B.I. Agent Bob Donnelley said around a burning cigarette.

Agent Bill Gallagher sat across from Donnelley. Gallagher was eating a hamburger. "They're always fighting. I'd say that before the summer's over, one of them will kill the other for sure. My money's on the old man."

Donnelley and Gallagher were conducting a surveillance of the entire eight-block stretch on Seventy-ninth Street under the McCoys' influence. They were on the top floor of the six-story Cutler Building on the northeast corner of Seventy-ninth and Cottage Grove. The office they used reputedly was being rented by a black dentist named Walter Mason. However, Dr. Mason was in reality an F.B.I. agent imported from the Richmond, Virginia, office because there were so few black agents in the Chicago office. During the day Mason saw no patients and if someone showed up with an emergency, which had happened once, the phony dentist would refer them to Dr. Price, a legitimate dentist on the third floor.

An around-the-clock surveillance of "McCoy's Strip," as it was code-named by the Bureau, was being maintained. Donnelley and Gallagher, along with the rest of the agents assigned to the surveillance, were not interested in the drug sales, prostitution or gambling. Instead they were looking into the official corruption at the police and local elected-official level, which permitted the operation to exist.

They possessed the most sophisticated spy cameras and recording devices available, and also had certain places, such as William McCoy, Sr.'s apartment, his bar and his home in Beverly, bugged. They had listening devices in certain "preferred" rooms of the motels, the main gambling house and in one of the pool halls where William McCoy, Jr., hung out.

So far they had enough evidence to secure the indictments of seven 6th District police officers. But the F.B.I. wanted more. They wanted the local aldermen and Police District Commander Charles Howard. Although Howard's name had been mentioned during a number of recorded conversations, he had never been seen on "the Strip." But the Bureau was patient and had lots of money and time, so they could afford to wait.

"Junior's out on the street," Donnelley said, looking at the video monitor. He pushed a button and the camera zoomed in on William McCoy, Jr.

A woman entered the shot. She was walking toward McCoy.

"Hey, Bill," Donnelley said with definite excitement in his voice, "it's Gunslinger."

Gallagher dropped the remains of his hamburger and dashed across the room. He wiped mustard and ketchup off his mouth with a paper napkin, ogling the screen.

"Would you look at that?"

"I'm looking," Donnelley said, forgetting the cigarette he had burning in an ashtray.

The woman was tall and voluptuous. She walked with a sensuous sway, exuding sex appeal with every move. She had long black hair and the features of a Native American. Donnelley and Gallagher had watched her hopping in and out of cars on the Strip since they started this surveillance in February. More than once they had individually and silently speculated what it would be like to come down here on an off day in disguise and pick her up. But that was as far as either of the agents went with their fantasies. At least as long as the surveillance continued.

Agent Mason had told them her street name was "Gunslinger." How he found that out was never disclosed. Nor did the two agents ever determine what the name stood for. Now, their eyes were glued to the monitor as she walked up to William McCoy, Jr.; however, they could not hear the words spoken between her and McCoy, because they were out on the street.

"How you doin', Little Willie?" Gunslinger said.

"I'm gonna kill that old man someday," he snarled through clenched teeth, staring up at the windows of his father's apartment over the bar.

She caught on. "What happened? You and Big Willie get into it again?"

"Yeah. He's always on my case and I'm getting tired of it." Little Willie turned from looking at the apartment window and looked Gunslinger up and down. "What you doing now?"

"Working, as usual. You know that."

"Let's go down to the Riviera and party. I got some blow and I might even pop for a bottle of champagne."

"Big Willie said I can't do no more freebies. Not even with you."

"I'll pay."

"I want it up front."

"Bitch, do you know who I am?!"

"Yeah, I know who you are and I also know that you ain't getting nothing if you don't come up with a hundred bucks."

In the surveillance post, Donnelley frowned. "What does this guy do, argue with everybody?"

"They must be haggling over the price," Gallagher said, squinting at the monitor.

"How much do you figure she charges?" Donnelley questioned.

"How in the hell would I know? But whatever it is he's paying. See if you can pick up how much he gives her."

Donnelley manipulated dials on the monitor console. The lens zoomed in, enlarging McCoy's hand. They saw him give Gunslinger a hundred-dollar bill.

"She's got to give him change for that," Donnelley said.
"Don't bet on it."

The Riviera Motel was in the next block. As Little Willie and
Gunslinger walked toward it the hidden eye of the F.B.I. camera
followed them. A man in a dark-colored jump suit, dark wide-
brimmed hat and sunglasses stepped from the alley beside Big Willie's Bar and also followed.

"You kind of tense tonight, Little Willie," the prostitute said.
They crossed a darkened side street and began angling across the
motel parking lot.

"Look," he said testily, "I paid you for a piece of ass. I don't
need no street whore trying to get inside my head."

Gunslinger had been holding his arm as they walked. Now she
dropped it and stepped away from him. His hundred-dollar bill appeared in her hand.

"I fuck who I want," she spat, "when I want." She balled up the
bill and threw it in his face before turning to go back the way they'd
come.

He grabbed her arm. "You ain't going nowhere except into that
hotel with me, bitch."

"Let me go!" She fought to pull away from him. "I ain't doing
nothing with you now or ever."

Little Willie reached into his waistband and pulled a .25 caliber
automatic. He shoved it under her chin.

They became aware of another presence in the dimly-lighted
parking lot.

The man stood less than fifteen feet away, but his face was
shrouded in shadow. He was dressed like the other hustlers on the
street, but then there was something different about this one.

The F.B.I. agents picked up on the danger. "Do you think we
should call the local cops?" Gallagher asked when he saw McCoy
pull the gun.

"Naw," Donnelley said. "It won't do any good. By the time the
CPD gets here, somebody down there is going to die."

* * *

"You're a pretty big man down here, my brother," the man standing in the shadows said to Willie.

"Who the fuck are you, man?" Little Willie shouted.

"I mean, you go around pulling guns on people, scaring women, and nobody can do anything to you. That's really impressive for such a simple-minded, ugly little man."

Little Willie pushed Gunslinger away from him and pointed the .25 at the shadow. "I don't take shit off nobody, motherfucker."

The man continued to speak in a maddeningly calm tone, as if he had no concern about the gun. "You figure you'll get away with killing me too, but I don't think so. Not this time, my brother. It's time to pay some dues."

"Shoot him, Willie!" Gunslinger screamed. "Don't let him talk to you like that. Shoot him!"

In a blur of motion the dark figure thrust his right arm up in a sharp, underhand gesture. A projectile flashed across the space separating Little Willie and the man he'd planned to kill.

Gunslinger heard a dull thud. She'd first thought Willie'd said something. Then his gun clattered on the asphalt. There was a confused look on his face. He lowered his head to stare down at his chest. The prostitute saw the knife buried in his sternum.

Little Willie tried to speak, but no words came out, only a strangled cough. He dropped to his knees and vomited blood.

Gunslinger screamed—then went for Willie's .25.

"Don't do that, miss," Little Willie's killer said. "I don't want to hurt you."

"You son of a bitch!" she shouted, rising with the pistol in her hand and sighting in on the killer, who remained in the shadows. She never got off a shot.

62

Little Willie McCoy and Gunslinger Davis were buried together. Big Willie, displaying a flair for the dramatic and bizarre, had his son and the prostitute dressed as an East Indian prince and his bride. Sparing no expense, Big Willie hired live elephants and horses to pull the custom-made wagon, which had been converted into a hearse. The coffins were constructed of glass and each body festooned with diamond jewelry and gold chains. The services were held in a large tent set up on a vacant lot at the edge of the Strip. The occasion drew thousands of spectators.

That night, a week after the slayings, it rained. The curious came from miles around to stand four to eight abreast in lines stretching the entire length of the Strip. The police were called on for crowd control and even Commander Charles Howard put in an appearance dressed, however, in civilian clothes. Reggie Stanton was one of the uniformed officers assigned to this event.

"Would you look at this?" Donnelley said from his surveillance post in the Cutler Building.

Gallagher stood behind him and lifted a bottle of Coca-Cola in salute to the scene below. "To the royalty of the ghetto."

They continued to stare at the crowd in silence. Finally, Gallagher said, "What are we going to do with that tape?"

Without taking his eyes from the monitors, Donnelley replied, "We talked about this already, Bill. I told you we can't do nothing with it."

"Jesus, Bob, we've got a guy killing two people on film. It doesn't seem right that we just sit on it."

Donnelley turned away from the monitors and looked directly at his partner. "We're not just sitting on it. Every inch of tape we have is part of the Bureau investigation into official corruption in Chicago. When the time comes, we turn it over to the director and let him decide what to do with it."

Gallagher avoided looking at Donnelley. "It just doesn't seem right to me."

"What's the matter with you? A colored dope dealer and a whore get iced during a street mugging and you want to compromise a multi-million-dollar federal investigation? C'mon, man. That guy should be given a medal."

Gallagher looked past Donnelley at the monitor screens displaying the funerals William McCoy, Sr., had turned into a circus. He could see that the people down there didn't care about the dead, so, he figured, why should he?

But there was someone who cared and, in fact, cared very deeply about what had occurred the week before. At that moment that person was in the back of a white stretch limousine being chauffeured down the Strip toward the tent where the funeral services were to be held. The limo was escorted by a marked police car driven by Sergeant Polly Markham. She had the lights and siren going.

Big Willie McCoy sat in the rear seat of the limo. He was dressed completely in white and carried a gold-headed, diamond-studded cane that had a white barrel. The head of the cane could be unscrewed to unsheath a twenty-four-inch, tempered-steel sword. He carried a .32 caliber, ivory-handled, gold-plated revolver in his cummerbund.

"Look at this shit," he sneered. "Don't these people have no respect for the dead?"

The man seated beside Big Willie was a wiry Hispanic of medium height. He had thick black hair combed back from a high forehead, a pencil-thin mustache and high cheekbones. His eyes were shielded by wraparound sunglasses and through them he looked stonily and emotionlessly out at the world. His name was Pablo "Little Caesar"

Martinez and he was an enforcer for the Diablo drug cartel, which supplied Big Willie's dope.

Martinez didn't comment about the crowd's disrespect for the dead. He didn't think that McCoy wanted him to.

Sergeant Markham's police car forged a path in front of the funeral tent. The Cadillac pulled in closely behind it.

A uniformed policeman wearing a nylon raincoat jumped to open the back door of the limousine. Big Willie came out, followed closely by Little Caesar. The crowd applauded, distracting Big Willie from paying attention to the door-opening cop. If he'd taken the time, he would have looked right into the face of Reggie Stanton.

Inside the funeral tent a roped-off area had been reserved for Big Willie, surviving members of the McCoy Family and a few of the more prominent members of the black Chicago underworld. In a high-backed chair, which had been outfitted to resemble a throne, sat Big Willie. He surveyed the crowd of onlookers filing past the glass coffin bearing the remains of his son and the prostitute. McCoy exhibited no emotion. Beside him, appearing equally inscrutable, sat Little Caesar.

Big Willie leaned over and whispered something to Caesar. The enforcer got up, slipped under the restraining rope and walked to the entrance to the tent where Sergeant Markham stood. He whispered something to her. She nodded and left. Caesar returned to his seat. No communication passed between him and Big Willie McCoy. The services continued.

Commander Charles Howard sat in the front seat of Sergeant Markham's squad car. The wipers steadily slapped torrents of water off the windshield. They stared out through the falling rain at the officer directing traffic in front of the funeral tent.

"You can say one thing for him," Howard said. "He is enthusiastic."

"That's Stanton. He's the one who arrested McCoy's kid."

"Oh," was Howard's only comment.

She turned to him. "Are you going to meet with McCoy?"

"Why not?"

She reached out and grasped his hand. "Do you think that's wise?"

He refused to look at her. He pulled his hand away. "He's a citizen in the community I serve. It's my job to be responsive to him."

"I still don't think you should do it."

He frowned. "You don't have to think, Polly. I can do enough of that for both of us."

She looked hurt. He ignored her.

"Drive over to the tavern."

Still pouting, she turned on her mars lights, goosed the siren a couple of times and attempted a U-turn. Stanton jumped forward, stopped the traffic and cleared the way for the sergeant's car. As they passed, he saluted. They ignored him.

They met in Big Willie's apartment over the tavern.

"Asking me to come here wasn't the best idea you ever had, McCoy," Howard said.

Big Willie sat on the couch in the exact spot where his son had been sitting the week before. "You're here, ain't you, Commander?"

Howard stiffened. "I think it would be better if we dispensed with last names and titles."

"Whatever you say, Chuck." A grin passed between Willie and Caesar. The policeman glared at them.

Two blocks away Gallagher and Donnelley tensed. This was the break they had been waiting for. Commander Charles Howard was involved in a face-to-face meeting with William McCoy, Sr.

Unnoticed by the feds, the policeman directing traffic in front of the funeral tent was relieved. He walked to his squad car parked in the motel lot where Little Willie and Gunslinger had died. He got in and drove down the Strip.

The F.B.I. agents were glued to the speakers broadcasting every word spoken in McCoy's apartment.

"I want the bastard who killed my son. I don't care how much it costs or what you have to do, but I want him."

"It's not that simple," Howard said. *"There's an official investigation into this thing being handled out of the Chief of Detectives' Office. Your little fiasco out there tonight with the tent and the elephants is going to keep the heat on."*

"What do you think?" Gallagher said.

"Shut up," Donnelley snapped. "He hasn't said anything yet."

On the monitor screens the police car drove past Sergeant Markham's squad car, which was parked in front of the tavern, and made a right turn to disappear into the alley behind Big Willie's.

"Listen, baby," Willie roared. "I don't give a shit about downtown. I got some people over at City Hall who I pay more than I pay you to stay cool. Who I want is whoever killed my son and I'm not talking about putting the bastard in jail. I want him delivered here to me alive and in one piece. I'll do the killing myself."

"And you expect me to find him for you?" Howard said.

"Naw," Willie said, mocking the policeman. "You just a cop. I ain't giving you nothing that's beyond your talents. Little Caesar has got a line on the knife man. It's somebody new, but I bet he's got some ties to you cops."

Howard laughed. "You're trying to tell me you think a cop iced your son?"

"You think that's so funny maybe I should ice you," Willie shouted, slamming his fist on the coffee table.

Howard backed up and reached for his shoulder-holstered .38.

A 9 mm. automatic pistol appeared in Caesar's hand. He leveled it at the cop just as the noise of glass breaking came from the rear of the apartment.

The three men froze.

"Caesar," Big Willie whispered. "Check it out."

Howard started for the front door.

"Freeze right there, cop," Willie ordered. "You ain't going nowhere until we find out what's happening here."

Howard stopped, but looked anxiously from the dope dealer back at his planned escape route.

McCoy stood guard over the cop, while Caesar moved silently toward the rear of the apartment.

* * *

"What in the hell are they doing?" Gallagher asked.

"Something's happening, Bill," Donnelley said. "I can feel it."

The F.B.I. agents waited. Seconds ticked by. Then there was the sound of a metal object clattering on a floor. A metal object that sounded like a gun.

"Caesar? What's happening back there, man?" McCoy's panicked voice carried over the F.B.I. speaker. *"Caesar? Stay put, cop. I mean that. Caesar? Cae . . ."*

"What in the . . . ?" Howard said with breathless awe.

"Get some help up here quick, man! Whoever did this has got to be out back. Caesar's been knifed just like Little Willie. It's the same bastard who killed my boy."

"What does that note say?" Howard asked.

" 'McCoy, get off Seventy-ninth Street while you still can,' " McCoy replied. *"Now get somebody back there to get the bastard who did this!"*

There was the sound of Howard's footsteps and then a door slammed.

"What in the hell happened down there?" Gallagher asked.

Donnelley was amused. "Sounds like our knife thrower nailed Caesar."

While Donnelley was still talking, a police car pulled from the alley behind Big Willie's bar and turned onto the Strip.

63

JULY 17, 1979
9:25 A.M.

Commander Charles Howard was told by his secretary that Sergeant Larry Cole was waiting to see him. Howard's hands trembled as he dialed the number of a functionary high-up in the mayor's office. When his clout answered, Howard gushed, "They sent a sergeant from Riseman's office to see me."

"So?"

"They're after me. I told you I've had the feeling I was being watched for some time now. McCoy's too bold. He's running things wide open down there."

"Have you talked to the sergeant yet?"

"No. I called you first."

"Riseman's office doesn't investigate cops. Internal Affairs does. Talk to the sergeant. Find out what he's got to say. If he doesn't have a subpoena or a warrant for you, call me back."

Before Howard could shout that the last remark wasn't funny, his clout hung up.

The commander composed himself. What a mess. But then his house was paid for and his youngest son would be graduating from high school in June. He had enough of the bribe money he'd taken from McCoy to put the kid through four years at Notre Dame. He figured if he could just hold on one more year he'd have it made for the rest of his life.

Thoughts of Sergeant Polly Markham's demands began intruding on his future plans. He quickly forgot about her and, for that matter, his son too. He straightened his tie and unlocked the door to summon the sergeant.

Cole was not offered a seat when he entered Commander Howard's office, so he took one. He had been cautioned to beware of the 6th District C.O., who was rumored to be as crooked as Frank Nitti. Cole planned to do just that, but then they'd have to get the ground rules straight first.

"Chief Riseman has assigned me to coordinate the murder investigations of William McCoy, Jr., Cassandra Davis and Pablo Martinez. I'll be working with Area Two Detectives and providing the chief with daily progress reports."

Yes, he could see that Howard didn't like this. Cole had intentionally left out any mention of him and the 6th District, as far as the investigation went. The commander could complain to his superiors downtown, but coming on hard with a supervisor working directly for the chief of detectives would cause a lot of attention to be directed toward Howard. Crooked cops didn't relish attention. At least the smart ones didn't.

Howard smiled. "Haven't I heard of you, Cole? Didn't you kill a mobster or something a year or so back?"

Cole returned the smile. "A couple of Rabbit Arcadio's boys. His chief lieutenant Salvatore Marino and the Rabbit's nephew, Frankie."

Howard slapped his palm down on top his desk blotter. "That's right! Man, you have to be a pretty tough guy to have carried that off."

"I was lucky, Commander."

"Yeah, but to stay alive in this business we all have to be a bit lucky."

"I guess so."

"So that's why I don't get it."

"Don't get what, sir?" Cole asked.

"Why they sent a heavy-hitter like you out for a few routine homicides. I'd think you'd be working on crime up on Lake Shore Drive instead of out here on the South Side. I mean, what are we talking about here, Larry? A couple of known dope dealers and a prostitute with a three-page rap sheet. Give me a break. If headquarters started looking into every killing like that they'd have to cut their three-hour lunches and cocktail hours short."

Howard laughed at his last remark. Cole graced him with a tolerant smile.

"I don't think it's who they were that interests Chief Riseman," Cole said. "It's the way they were killed."

"They were knifed, for chrissakes! That's got to happen ten times a day in this town."

"They were killed by someone throwing daggers at them," Cole said, quietly. "Someone with enough skill to make a single throw fatal in each case."

"A dagger's still a knife, Cole."

"And the way it was used, Commander," Cole concluded, "could indicate that you have a serial killer on your hands."

Howard looked as if he was going to be sick.

* * *

An hour later Cole was in the Crime Lab examining the knife they had taken from the throat of Pablo "Little Caesar" Martinez. The department's weapons expert, a studious young woman named Joyce Sheridan, explained her findings.

"Although that weapon is old and quite worn, Sarge, you'll notice that it's balanced perfectly for throwing."

Cole hefted the blade in his hand. He didn't know much about knives, so he couldn't tell whether it was balanced properly or not.

Sheridan continued. "It's of German manufacture and I'd say it was made either before or during World War II."

"Is it difficult to learn to use one of these?"

"A contemporary assassin would never use something like this. It's too unreliable."

"But our perpetrator never misses, so in his hands it's as reliable as a gun."

"True," she said, "but the time and patience needed to learn such a skill would be truly awesome. Almost not worth it."

"Almost?" Cole questioned.

She shrugged. "People devote such time to painting, learning to play a musical instrument or to some other hobby. Not to murder."

"But someone could learn to be very good with one of these if they took the time to practice and . . . ?"

"And had the right teacher," she interjected.

He thought about this for a moment. "So I'm looking for one of a kind?"

"Sarge, you're looking for one in a million."

Cole drove down on the Strip. From what he'd heard he had expected it to be a lively, bustling place. It was early afternoon and Seventy-ninth Street east of Cottage Grove was virtually deserted. He pulled his car to the curb across the street from Big Willie's bar. A woman wearing a red wig, tight jeans and six-inch spiked heels lounged against the wall of the building. Her exposed cleavage indicated what she was advertising, but she took one look at Cole's unmarked police car and vanished inside the bar. Cole figured there had to be a better way to approach this investigation.

* * *

"Somebody who knows the area?" Commander Howard asked with a frown.

They were again in Howard's 6th District office. Cole had just requested Howard's assistance in investigating the three homicides.

"The only thing I'm looking for, Commander," Cole said, "is a killer. Anything else is none of my business."

Howard's brows knitted. "What else do you think is going on down there, Cole?" The commander's voice was neutral, but on the chilly side. Cole had the weight of the chief of detectives behind him, but he figured he could finesse this without ruffling Howard's feathers too much.

"I really don't know, Commander," Cole said, innocently.

Howard studied the sergeant carefully for a moment before saying, "Wait in my secretary's office. I'll get someone to show you around Seventy-ninth Street."

The early afternoon roll call was breaking when Cole stepped into the district secretary's office. A number of the officers coming out of the squad room to begin their third watch tour gave the detective sergeant suspicious glances. Inside the secretary's office, three police officers and a lone civilian seated at desks shoved into the cramped room ignored Cole completely.

He had been waiting for about fifteen minutes when there was a knock on the outer office door. A light-skinned young black officer with blue-gray eyes stepped inside.

"Sergeant Cole?"

Cole stood up from the chair he'd taken beside the door. "Yes?"

"I'm Officer Stanton," he said hesitantly. "The commander's assigned me to work with you."

"Good," Cole said, extending his hand. "Let's go."

"So how long have you been working six twenty-three, Reggie?" Cole asked as they rolled away from the station in the unmarked car. Cole was driving.

"A couple of weeks."

Cole's head snapped around to look at his passenger. "A couple of weeks?"

"Yes, sir. I really haven't learned a lot in that time."

"Son of a bitch," Cole said.

"Sir?"

"Nothing. Well, I guess it's you and me, Reg. Let's see if we can go catch ourselves a murderer."

The sergeant had expected this remark to perk up the young officer. It did not.

They started in the Riviera Motel parking lot. It was as deserted as the rest of the Strip.

Cole held a schematic drawing of the crime scene in his hand. The areas where the bodies were found were clearly marked. The position from which their killer had thrown his knives was estimated. Cole walked over to this position. Stanton watched him closely.

"What would you say this distance is, Reggie, maybe ten or twelve yards?"

"About that."

Cole looked around and shook his head. "I don't get it," he said more to himself than the young cop.

"Don't get what, sir?"

"They had a gun. All he had was a couple of old knives. You'd have thought they had the edge."

"Not necessarily," Reggie said with conviction. "A weapon is only as good as the person using it."

Cole smiled. "Where did you learn that, in the police academy?"

"No. My uncle told me."

64

They drove over to Big Willie's bar. Cole rang the bell and they waited at the downstairs door beside the tavern entrance. A wiry-lean black man with mean eyes and a bad disposition came down the stairs. He peered out at them through the glass pane in the door. Cole noticed Stanton tense.

"You know this guy?" Cole asked.

"His name's Bart Williams. Him and Vince Johnson are the regular crew assigned to six twenty-three."

Cole held up his badge so that Williams could see it. Finally, he opened the door. "What can I do for you, Sergeant?" There was noticeable contempt in his voice.

"I'd like to talk to Mr. McCoy."

Williams looked at Stanton. "What are you doing here, rookie?"

In an even voice Stanton replied, "Commander Howard assigned me to show the sergeant around the beat."

Cole noticed that Stanton, unlike most rookies, was not intimidated by the veteran officer. In fact, while Stanton continued staring at him, Williams was the one becoming tense. "C'mon," Williams said over his shoulder.

In the apartment there were two men besides Williams. The shoulder holster, housing a large nickle-plated automatic, was strapped to a pot-bellied cop whose disposition was a match for Williams's. Cole figured this to be Officer Vince Johnson. The man stretched out on the couch needed no introduction. The gold jewelry and flashy clothing identified him as Big Willie McCoy.

"Sergeant Cole has got the rookie showing him around the beat," Williams said in a voice tinged with sarcasm.

"How'd you like the tour, Sarge?" Johnson said with a whiskey-scarred voice.

"Interesting," Cole replied, before addressing the man on the couch. "Are you Big Willie McCoy?"

"That's right," Big Willie said.

"I'd like to ask you some questions about the deaths of your son, Miss Davis and Mr. Martinez."

Williams laughed. "Miss Davis! Shit. Gunslinger would probably turn over in her grave if she heard somebody call her Miss Davis."

"Shut up, Williams," McCoy spat. "You and Johnson get the fuck out of here. And learn to show some respect for a brother wearing stripes. Then you won't have to spend the rest of your lives kissing Howard's racist ass."

When Williams and Johnson were gone McCoy said to Stanton, "Aren't you the cop who arrested Little Willie?"

Stanton nodded.

Cole hadn't been aware of that.

"Hear tell you slapped the shit out of him."

"I only used the necessary force."

Big Willie snorted. "Probably did him more good than the ass whippings I gave him."

They watched McCoy's eyes well with tears, which he quickly blinked away.

"You brothers want a taste?"

"No thank you," Cole said. "We're on duty."

McCoy stood up and walked to the sideboard. As he poured scotch into a glass he said, "I didn't think there were any cops like you boys left. You probably don't take bribes either."

Cole and Stanton didn't dignify McCoy's statement with a comment.

They were driving off the Strip.

"The thing that's really got me going is the Martinez murder," Cole said.

"Why?" Stanton was driving the car and keeping his eyes straight ahead.

"The assassin climbed the fire escape behind McCoy's place, used acid to burn through the lock and pried open the back door. McCoy is in there with Martinez, so the offender could have taken them both just like he took McCoy, Jr., and the prostitute. But he doesn't. It looks like the only reason he killed Martinez is that he got too close. Maybe even caught a glimpse of our killer. Also, our killer left one of his knives, which he didn't do at the scene of the first two murders."

"Could there have been someone in the apartment the assassin didn't want to kill?" Stanton asked.

"Like who, Reggie?"

Stanton shrugged. "I know that Commander Howard was in the area that night. Maybe he was up there with McCoy."

Cole studied Stanton's rigid profile. "If I'm reading you right, you're saying that you think the killer is a cop."

"I didn't really say that, Sarge."

"But you meant it, right?"

"No, sir, I don't think so."

The rookie said little else for the rest of the night.

There were five F.B.I. agents in the sixth-floor Cutler Building surveillance post watching Cole's unmarked car drive off the Strip. Except for the eavesdropping equipment, the former dentist's office only contained a scarred wooden table, a couple of metal folding chairs, a hot plate and a refrigerator. Gallagher and Donnelley had been relegated to subordinate positions, while an agent wearing heavy horn-rimmed glasses and a gray Homburg studied the monitor screens. When the car was gone he turned to look at the two agents who had accompanied him on the flight from Washington.

"I'd say that the officer in uniform was definitely our knife thrower. Our computer analysis has verified the facial and physical characteristics on the tape of the murders of McCoy, Jr., and the Davis woman. It's a perfect match."

The blond agent stepped over to the window and looked down at the deserted strip. "So he was also the same one that did the job on Martinez?"

"Yes, sir," the Homburg answered.

"Motive?"

"Our understanding is that he had a run in with McCoy, Jr. The woman could have simply gotten in the way, which forced him to ice her too."

"What about Martinez?"

"He might have been after the old man and Martinez was a mistake. Odds are he'll try for McCoy, Sr., again."

"That still doesn't give us a motive."

Donnelley could no longer contain himself. "That cop's a whacko if you ask me."

The blond turned to glare at Donnelley. "Nobody asked you."

Donnelley lowered his eyes and fell silent.

The agent in the Homburg shrugged. "With all due respect, sir, Agent Donnelley could be right. The cop could be psychologically unbalanced. He kills with ease and without compunction. He's probably motivated by some illusion of embarking on a noble quest, which might be to clean up that cesspool down there. Also, I'd say that he's going to kill again and soon."

The blond nodded. To Donnelley the look on the agent-in-charge's face was one of anticipation. Still studying the street below, the blond agent said, "We'll just have to wait and see."

65

After dropping Stanton off at the 6th District station, Cole drove back downtown. In his cubicle in the Chief of Detectives' Office, located on the fifth floor of police headquarters, he typed up a supplementary report detailing what he had learned so far. It was a mere page and a half in length.

With no other duties left for him to perform, he signed out and headed for the police gym at Thirty-fifth and Normal, a stone's throw from White Sox Park. In the locker room he stripped, donned a T-shirt, shorts and running shoes. A few moments later he was back on the street. He ran north from the gym up to Thirty-third Street and then turned east. The outbound leg of his run would take him to Thirty-first and Indiana, which was a mile and a half from the gym. The return trip would give him a total distance of three miles. Not world class, but an adequate aerobics program to help him keep in shape.

Cole ran with ease. After the first eighth of a mile his body drifted into cruise control, freeing his mind to go back over the case he was working on.

Cole realized that everything about it was wrong. The murder weapon was wrong, the places where the murders were committed were wrong, and the cops were wrong. At least all the cops with the exception of Reggie Stanton.

Cole liked the young officer; however, at times he seemed tense and at other times sure of himself to the point of arrogance. A dichotomy? Definitely, but in police work Cole had learned to recognize such contradictions, accept them and then deal with them as best he could. Who had said that? Cole remembered that it had been his former partner Blackie Silvestri, who was currently on vacation in Italy with his wife Maria.

Cole jogged across the Dan Ryan Expressway and entered the western end of the Illinois Institute of Technology campus. It was eighty-three degrees and humid on this warm July evening and he had broken a sweat. At State Street he turned north again.

There was something about the three homicides that Cole couldn't quite fathom. Was it the absence of a clear-cut motive? Every crime, especially homicides, had motives. Why were Little Willie, Gunslinger Davis and Caesar Martinez killed? A gang war? A rival making a move on Big Willie's operation? A vigilante intent on cleaning up Seventy-ninth Street?

The vigilante theory occurred to him just as he reached the outer marker of his run and started back. It was also the most logical one he'd come up with so far. The Strip was an abomination, with dope sales, prostitution and general lawlessness carried on in an open and notorious fashion, while the cops were as crooked as the Wicked Witch's nose. The perfect breeding ground for a vigilante.

Cole began formulating a profile of his vigilante. Young, idealistic and extremely dangerous. Someone who didn't mind killing, even if one of his victims was a woman. Someone on a self-appointed mission, who could throw a knife with the accuracy and devastating results of a marksman with a gun. Someone so good they could overcome an opponent with a firearm.

"A weapon is only as good as the person using it."

It took the jogging policeman a moment to remember where he'd heard that. It was a quote from Reggie Stanton attributed to the young cop's uncle. The alarm bells went off in Cole's head. As he slowed to a walk in front of the police gym he began making metnal notes. First he planned to find out where Reggie Stanton was on the night of the murders. Then he would attempt to find out if the talented young rookie knew how to use a throwing knife.

66

R eggie Stanton walked into the brownstone on King Drive and froze. He could see his grandmother and Uncle Ernst seated on the couch in the living room. Uncle Ernst was handcuffed. Standing over them was a man wearing horn-rimmed glasses and a Homburg hat. He held a .357 magnum revolver pointed at Uncle Ernst's head. Reggie dropped his hands to his sides, as the emotions of rage and fear warred within him.

"Please come in, Officer Stanton," said a voice from inside the room. Reggie couldn't see the man who'd spoken.

With no other options available, Reggie stepped into the living room.

There were three of them. He could tell they weren't local cops. The blond man who'd spoken was seated in a corner armchair. He flashed official identification contained in a dark blue case.

"We're with the F.B.I., Stanton," the blond explained. "I'm Special Agent Connors."

Reggie said nothing to the intruders. His mind was racing in an attempt to come up with a plan to deal with this situation without getting his grandmother and Uncle Ernst hurt.

"We're not here to cause you or your family any grief," Connors said, "but then whatever happens here will be up to you."

Reggie still didn't speak.

"Agent Klein," Connors said to a gray-haired man standing beside his chair, "disarm Officer Stanton before he does something foolish."

The man moved carefully behind Reggie. He frisked him and removed Reggie's off-duty snub-nosed Colt from the belt holster beneath his jacket. He also found and confiscated the dagger strapped to his left calf. Agent Klein missed the one anchored at the small of Reggie's back; however, this knife was smaller than the other one and would do little good against three guns.

Agent Klein handed the weapons to Connors. While the F.B.I. agent studied the dagger, Reggie turned to the captives held at gunpoint on the living room couch.

"Did they hurt you?"

His grandmother shook her head in the negative. There was slight swelling under Uncle Ernst's left eye. Seeing it made a cold rage begin pulsing through Reggie Stanton. Someday he planned to kill these three men and would enjoy doing it.

Uncle Ernst said, "I'm okay, but I curse myself for letting these . . . people," he eyed the agents with the same fierce rage his nephew exhibited, ". . . get the drop on me."

"Don't worry about that now," Reggie said, turning to face Connors.

The agent looked up from his study of the dagger and smiled mockingly at Reggie. "You're pretty good with this, Officer Stanton. I've seen your work on television."

Reggie stared unblinkingly back at him.

"You're a phenomenon," Connors continued. "I doubt anyone in the world could have pulled off what you did with the exception of Hauptmann Ernst von Steiger of the Nazi SS. The war criminal."

"*Sweinhund!*" Ernst hissed straining against the handcuffs binding his beefy arms.

Reggie focused the full laser-intensity of his eyes on Connors. The agent returned the gaze without flinching.

"You were right, Uncle Ernst," Reggie said without taking his eyes off Connors. "There is a Gestapo in America." Then he addressed the F.B.I. man. "What do you want?"

Connors laughed. "You've got a knack for cutting to the heart of the matter, Officer Stanton." He fingered the sharp edge of the dagger's blade for emphasis. "My needs are simple. In return for your uncle's continued freedom and my assurances that he, your grandmother and you can lives your lives just as you did before, I want you to complete your mission. You are to kill Big Willie McCoy, Sr., just like you did his son, the prostitute and the dope cartel's assassin."

A frown creased Reggie's features. "Why?"

Connors's face adopted an expression which was almost as inscrutable as Reggie's. He responded, "I want to see you at work. Call it an audition."

67

JULY 22, 1979
2:50 P.M.

In an attempt to normalize activity, Big Willie sponsored a street party. Seventy-ninth Street was blocked at both ends of the Strip. At McCoy's expense free food and drinks, including booze, were distributed to anyone who wanted them. Of course the illegal stuff—

prostitution and narcotics sales—operated at their normal levels and prices. Because of the festival, these illicit enterprises were being conducted in an open and notorious fashion.

On the sidewalk in front of Big Willie's tavern a picnic table with a huge umbrella awning had been set up. There Big Willie held court while being guarded by 6th District cops Williams and Johnson. Music from loud speakers blared from inside the tavern. As the day wore on into late afternoon every pimp, pusher, whore and street hustler on the Strip stopped at the table to pay homage to McCoy. Like a king, he enjoyed each felicitation. He felt powerful again.

Big Willie didn't often use drugs. He'd seen too much of the devastating effects they had on his customers. But for this occasion he snorted a little nose candy to keep his mind off his son's death. That, and a half bottle of scotch consumed in the ninety-degree heat, had him flying. Flying into a very foul mood.

"Where the fuck's Howard?"

Williams turned to look at McCoy's sweat-drenched face. "You know he ain't coming down here with us poor colored folks, boss."

"Go get Markham," McCoy said nodding toward the Cottage Grove barricade where Sergeant Polly Markham was stationed along with two patrol officers.

"Hey, Willie," Johnson said, "lighten up, man. No need to get yourself in a lather about nothing. Have another drink."

Johnson began pouring scotch into Willie's glass. The mobster jerked forward and slapped the bottle out of the cop's hand. Both bottle and glass shattered on the sidewalk.

"You two pieces of dog shit don't give no orders around here! Now go get the sergeant like I said."

Heads turned in their direction. The two cops followed orders and hurried over to the barricade. Big Willie yelled to the bartender inside the tavern to bring him another bottle of scotch. He never took his eyes off the barricade where Williams and Johnson stood talking to Sergeant Markham. It took five minutes for them to convince her to come with them. When she did finally agree she didn't come alone. As they trooped back to his table Willie noticed that a uniformed officer accompanied the trio. He didn't recognize the cop

until he was almost at the table. It was the same one who had been
with Sergeant Cole the other day. Willie recalled that his name was
Stanton.

"What do you want, McCoy?" Sergeant Markham demanded.

McCoy looked up at her and sneered. "I want a lot of things. I
want to know where your chickenshit boss is and I want to know
who in the hell gave you permission to call me by my last name without a 'mister' in front of it?"

Her green eyes widened in shock. "Who are you talking to? I'll
call you whatever I want. You don't own me!"

"Listen, bitch," McCoy said struggling to his feet. "I ain't taking
shit off you or—"

"Take it easy, Willie," Williams said nervously.

"Hey, Sarge," Johnson joined in, "we need to cool this."

Stanton stood behind Markham. He moved almost impercepti-
bly to stand unobstructed beside McCoy.

"Who are you calling a bitch?" Markham screamed.

"I'm calling you a bitch," McCoy shouted, lunging at her.

She took a step backward. Williams stepped between her and
McCoy. Johnson moved toward McCoy, but Stanton got to him
first. The young policeman attempted to restrain the bigger man,
but McCoy easily threw him off. Stanton fell back into the table
before losing his balance and falling to the ground. Johnson and
Williams found themselves caught in the middle of a fierce battle.
Although drunk, McCoy swung his massive fists with devastating
results landing more blows on Johnson and Williams than on Sergeant Markham. She drew her nightstick and used it like a club. She
too hit Johnson and Williams a great deal more than she did
McCoy.

Stanton jumped to his feet and grabbed his walkie-talkie. "Six
twenty-three emergency! Officer needs assistance at ten fifteen East
Seventy-ninth Street!" Without waiting for a response he waded
into the battle.

Three of the more aggressive street people decided to give
McCoy a hand. The two gangster pimps and the dope pusher were
knocked unconscious almost before they could throw a punch.
Later they would say that it was the light-skinned black cop who hit

them. They would also remark that he had the fastest hands either of them had ever seen outside a professional boxing ring.

Police cars rolled onto Seventy-ninth Street from all over the 6th District. Before he could be restrained and cuffed by Stanton, Markham and the forced-to-take-sides Williams and Johnson, McCoy had blackened one of the sergeant's eyes and split her lower lip. She had landed a number of blows from her nightstick about the mobster's head. One, a wound above the right temple, bled heavily, obscuring one side of his face.

When the cops showed up in force the street people reacted. Rocks and bottles filled the air to knock mars lights off squad car roofs and smash windshields. In turn many of the cops, who had been unable to do anything about this criminal haven in their district prior to this, responded violently. Missile throwers were chased, run to ground and beaten bloody. A pimp in an iridescent red suit, who'd knocked a policeman's hat off with a rock, was grabbed hand and foot by two burly cops and tossed through the plate glass window of a pool hall.

Lieutenant Biff O'Hara finally showed up and began attempting to get things back under control. At this point it simply meant keeping the cops from carrying out further acts of vengeance against the inhabitants of the Strip.

"What in the hell's going on here?!" he shouted at a bleeding, battered Polly Markham.

"This sonofabitch hit me!" she yelled pointing at McCoy. The mobster had been forced back into his seat at the umbrella-canopied table by Reggie Stanton. The young cop stood guard over him.

O'Hara turned to make some conciliatory remark to McCoy. He found the handcuffed, bloodied lord of Seventy-ninth Street crime glaring at him with wild-eyed, silent fury. O'Hara fixed his aging features into a contrite mask. "I'm sure this misunderstanding can be worked out, Mr. McCoy. There are disputes in even the closest of families."

McCoy remained as unmoving as the Sphinx.

O'Hara noticed there was a great deal of blood on McCoy. The entire front of his shirt was soaked with it.

The lieutenant stepped closer and examined McCoy's head

wound. The blood had almost obscured the quarter-inch of metal protruding from his parietal bone. It had been driven home with a great deal of force and caused instant death when it penetrated McCoy's brain. Later, when it was removed, it was found to be an exotic weapon the CPD weapon's expert Joyce Sheridan would call a "needle knife."

"This man is dead," O'Hara said, as he continued to stare at the corpse.

68

JULY 22, 1979
11:39 P.M.

Connors and his two agents were waiting outside the 6th District station when Reggie got off. The F.B.I. men were driving a gray Ford with a buggy-whip antenna. The one with the Homburg and horn-rimmed glasses drove. Reggie got into the car without saying a word.

"Let's go for a ride," Connors said to the Homburg.

The car pulled away from the station.

"You know," Connors said to a stonily-silent Reggie Stanton, "I watched you sanction McCoy through binoculars and we've reviewed the replays at least twenty times, but I've never been able to catch you in the act. I mean, you moved like a ghost. I've never seen anything like it." He addressed his two buddies in the front seat. "What about you guys? You ever seen anyone with Officer Stanton's skill?"

Their pair of "no, sir's" came together.

Reggie kept his eyes straight ahead.

"Hauptmann von Steiger taught you well. He must be very proud of you."

"So my 'audition' was a success," Reggie said. "Does that mean that you're now through with my family?"

"That's going to be a bit of a problem, but we can work something out," Connors said, turning to look out the side window at the passing sights of South Halsted Street. "Everything that happened—McCoy, Jr., the whore, the dope dealer and McCoy, Sr.—is on tape. That tape is part of an official F.B.I. investigation into official corruption in Chicago. What I do with it is my business."

Reggie's jaw muscles rippled. "I did the last one because you told me I had to."

"Reggie, Reggie. C'mon! I'm on your side. We can work this out. We can even keep your name out of the mud that's going to get splattered on just about every cop in your precinct."

"We call them districts," Reggie said in a voice barely above a whisper.

"Pardon?" Connors said with a frown.

"In Chicago, we call them districts, not precincts."

"Whatever you say, Reg," Connors said. "You see, all I want to do is help you, Hauptmann von Steiger and your grandmother."

"The only way you can help us is to leave us alone."

Connors paused a moment. "Oh, we'll leave you alone, Reggie. You won't have any problems from me and the Bureau. That scum you killed were lowlifes. You did the world a favor in my book. No, you won't have any problem from us. Of course, I can't speak for the Chicago Police Department."

Reggie turned to look at Connors. The F.B.I. man's face was shrouded in shadow.

The future deputy director feigned surprise. "Oh, didn't you know? That buddy of yours, Sergeant Cole. I think he suspects you of doing the first three murders. He went into the pre . . . I'm sorry, I meant the district, before you came out. He's probably looking into this thing with McCoy, Sr. From the reports I've seen, Cole's done a pretty good job of investigating the four homicides. And I'd be willing to bet that you're his number-one suspect right now."

Reggie's voice was barely audible. "What do you want?"

"Why, Reggie," Connors said, "all I want for you is every American boy's dream. I want you to become a 'G man.' "

PART 3

"DeLisa's in this thing up to his eyeballs."
—L. Cole

69

During the night and early morning hours Lisa Cole and her husband had switched positions. Now, as the chirp of birds became audible in the pre-dawn darkness, she sat at the desk reading through the final pages of the I.A.D. file charging then Police Officer Reginald E. Stanton of the 6th Police District with misconduct by committing the murders of four people.

Larry was sound asleep on the couch. His mouth was open and his soft snoring carried across the room to her. However, it did not distract her. In fact, she was so absorbed in the case report on the homicide of William "Big Willie" McCoy that her attention couldn't have been diverted by a 747 landing on the street in front of their house.

"A needle knife," Lisa whispered to herself.

She looked up from her reading at her still sleeping husband. In his report he'd described the weapon, that had dispatched Willie McCoy, Sr., into eternity, as "a special dagger constructed of tubular steel, nine inches in length, shaped like the needle of a syringe. Driven into the parietal bone above the temple with tremendous force, it caused blood to flow from the hollow handle in a continuous stream. The damage to the brain, however, was what killed the deceased."

The sun was coming up. She noticed that while he'd slept, Larry's hand had become constricted into a clawlike shape. She knew that this was the result of an injury he'd suffered three years earlier. It bothered him from time-to-time, particularly when the weather was bad or he was very tired. He had been working much too hard lately, but it was difficult for her to persuade him to slow down. He enjoyed police work too much for that.

Lisa left the file on the desk and crossed to the couch. She knelt on the floor and gently grasped his constricted appendage. Despite the brilliant work of a surgeon at University Hospital, scar tissue was still visible from the wound inflicted when Steven Zalkin had driven a nail through Larry's palm. She began massaging the muscles and tendons. As she worked he moaned in his sleep and his features twisted into a grimace, but he did not wake up. In a few moments she had the circulation going again and the hand relaxed into a natural position. Lisa released it and went back to the I.A.D. file.

Following Larry's supplementary report on the murder of Big Willie McCoy there was only one report remaining in the thick file. It was a single, carelessly typed page. It contained numerous typos, strike-overs and spelling errors. Compared to Larry's report, this one was crude.

IAD

4 Aug. '79

TO: Asst. Dep. Supt.
  IAD
FROM: Inv. Gary Croft #7214
SUBJECT: Close report—C.R. 768190.

A review of al applicable repots. re: this investigaxon, and interview of witnesses, the repoxting inv recommends this case be closed excepttional for lack of evidence.

Gary L. Croft #7214

APPROVED:

"And I'm the Queen of Sheba," Lisa said in disbelief.
She couldn't understand Investigator Croft's report. It was obvi-

ous from the investigation Larry had conducted that Officer Stanton was a strong suspect in the four murders. She wondered who this Croft had interviewed? Why wasn't his report approved by a superior as all Larry's had been? Why had Chief of Detectives Riseman taken the investigation of Stanton away from Larry?

Lisa closed the file. She was so enthralled by what she'd read and the questions it posed that she briefly considered waking Larry up and asking him. But he needed his rest. Her questions could wait until later.

70

MARCH 7, 1994
5:32 A.M.

The sun was coming up as Ernest Steiger drove the rented Chevy across Cermak Road and turned north onto Indiana Avenue. A few minutes later he pulled into the driveway of the Haggerty House and honked the horn. Armand Hagar's face appeared at a first-floor window. There was a hum as the gate across the driveway was opened by remote control.

Ernest drove the car back to the garage. The garage door was also opened with a remote and Ernest drove the Chevy inside. He parked beside the twin of his rent-a-car and shut off the engine. Before getting out he looked at his reflection in the rear view mirror. His eyes were red-rimmed but held the glint of sly satisfaction. He had spent the night with Maureen Taft at her condominium overlooking Lincoln Park. He had gotten little sleep. When she had attempted to doze he had awakened her with another item from his repertoire of sexual tricks. He had finally left her as the sky began brightening. He wondered if he would have time for another session with the pretty but sexually naive reporter. She had so much to learn and he was an excellent teacher.

Ernest got out of the car. Hagar was waiting for him at the back door.

"Boy, you're really going to get it," Hagar said. "Your daddy's been up pacing the floor all night."

"Get out of my way," Ernest said softly.

The shabby man with the cast on his foot didn't move for a full ten seconds. Ernest tensed for a fight just as Hagar stepped to the side. There was a leer on his face.

"I sure hope he don't whip your ass, Ernie."

Ignoring him, Ernest walked into the house. He crossed the kitchen and found his way to the dining room. As he rode up to the attic in the secret elevator he resolved to kill Armand Hagar when this job was over.

Hagar limped through the kitchen into the dining room and listened until the elevator mechanism stopped humming. Then he hopped as fast as he could to the staircase leading up to the second floor. Another secret compartment was hidden in the paneling beneath this staircase. He grimaced as he activated the mechanism which caused one of the panels to slide back. His foot was giving him hell, but the bleeding had stopped. He was trying to keep his weight off of it, but he had so much to do today and he'd gotten little sleep last night.

Inside the small compartment was a receiver hooked up to a tape recorder. The device was equipped with headphones. He put on the headphones as the tape spools began spinning silently. The receiver was voice-activated. The voices he was listening to came from the attic he was renting to the Steigers.

Karl Steiger was beside himself with anger, but he used his iron will to keep himself from exploding at his son. He didn't want to broadcast his feelings to their host by shouting. He was unaware of the fact that the small apartment was bugged.

"Where have you been, Ernest?"

The young man sauntered across the attic and flopped down on the couch. He emitted an exhausted sigh before responding, "I've been doing research on our target, as you instructed me to yesterday."

"I told you to check Banks out by using local libraries. Unless I'm mistaken, the Chicago Public Library doesn't stay open all night."

Ernest shook his head and said a matter-of-fact, "I had a drink with the senator in his office last night and have an invitation for lunch with him at noon today in a restaurant in a hotel in someplace called Hyde Park."

Karl's stare was emotionless. "Start from the beginning and tell me exactly what you did last night. I want all of it, Ernest."

The young man sat up, rubbed his hands vigorously across his face and began his report. During the narration Karl's expression did not change, although Ernest could tell he was pleased.

When his son's report was concluded, Karl turned and crossed the room to pick up a small black cloth pouch lying on an antique wooden table. He returned to where Ernest was seated. Opening the pouch, Karl extracted a glass vial. A murky liquid was visible inside of it.

Ernest frowned through his fatigue. "What is that, Daddy?"

"This substance is composed of a number of things. The sweat from a poisonous South American toad, the venom from a South Seas blowfish and a couple of other nasty poisons. My contact calls it 'Lucifer's Cocktail.' It will kill in under a minute if taken orally. At the time of death it will appear that the subject had a heart attack. It is doubtful whether even the most sophisticated autopsy would reveal its presence in the stomach of the deceased. Do you think you can get close enough to our target to put it in either something he eats or drinks?"

Ernest nodded in silent admiration of his father's ingenious selection of the means of assassination. During his narration of the events of the previous evening in Banks's office, Ernest had left out any mention of his aborted plan to kill the senator right then and there.

"We'll be in a public restaurant," Ernest said. "I'll need some type of diversion. Wherever the senator goes he's always the center of attention." He studied the vial his father held. "Will the poison dissolve in a liquid or have a noticeable odor or taste?"

"Your best bet would be a solid food dish," Karl explained, as he removed the top from the vial and sniffed the contents. "It doesn't have a pronounced odor. This smells more like rubbing alcohol than reptile venom. A spicy food dish should be the trick."

Ernest grimaced. "I really don't know what reptile venom smells like anyway and I don't think Banks will either."

Karl recapped the vial and said, "You must remember, Ernest, 'That . . .'"

" '. . . which does not kill you makes you stronger.' You've been telling me that all my life and I still don't believe it. But one thing I do know." He pointed at the vial his father was returning to the cloth pouch. "That will definitely kill."

Karl looked at his son and then back at the pouch. "I hope so, Ernest. I sincerely hope so."

In the ground floor hallway Armand Hagar took off the headphones and closed the secret compartment.

Washington, D.C.   **71**

MARCH 7, 1994
DAWN

Reggie Stanton rode in the back seat of a Capital taxi cab. The skinny black driver, whose chauffeur's license identified him as Mustafa Sharif, looked skeptically at his passenger, whom he'd picked up at Washington National Airport and had given him an address near First and F Streets in one of the more dangerous parts of town.

The Washington weather was considerably warmer and more humid than had been the case in Chicago. During the drive Reggie removed his top coat and laid it on the seat beside him. He relaxed and watched the streets of the nation's capital change from the opulent cleanliness of the buildings from which the United States government was run to the black ghetto comprising most of the city.

The streets of the ghetto were dimly lighted and filthy. Despite the early hour of the morning, small gangs of men and women stood on street corners smoking or passing bottles sheathed in paper bags from hand to hand. As the cab drove past them, suspicious eyes followed it.

The driver was becoming very nervous as they approached the address the fare had given him. He would have refused the trip if it hadn't been for the D.C. taxi ordinance, which forbade him from turning down a trip. Now all he wanted to do was drop the guy off and get the hell out of this area.

The house was a ramshackle wooden affair with no lights visible from inside. The passenger said a curt, "Wait for me," before bounding out of the cab.

The driver would have sped off without his fare, but the passenger had left his coat on the back seat. There was only one street light working and at this hour of the morning the dark shadows of the buildings took on a quality of pronounced menace.

After fifteen minutes the driver was sufficiently frightened to put the cab in gear and drive off when the passenger climbed back inside. The driver noticed that he carried a cloth bundle.

"Take me to the Vista Hotel."

The driver tried to acknowledge this new location, but his mouth and throat were too dry for him to do so. He did manage to bob his head up and down a couple of times before racing away from the dark urban jungle.

"Do you have a reservation for a James Collier?" Reggie asked the clerk in the lobby of the downtown Washington hotel.

The desk clerk looked sleepily at the early morning arrival. The janitors were mopping the floor. Traffic outside the hotel was nonexistent. The clerk noticed that the muscular black man had no luggage with the exception of the cloth pouch he carried protectively under his arm.

The clerk punched computer keys to check the reservation records. The name James Collier came up in bold letters on the screen. The words PRIORITY GUEST flashed beside the name along with the letters V.I.P. and F.B.I. The clerk came fully awake instantly.

"Yes, Mr. Collier. We have your reservation."

The clerk recalled the procedure he was supposed to follow. He placed the computer cursor over the F.B.I. and pressed the Enter key. The screen changed to reveal a list of room numbers. He took the top number—606—and prepared an access control card for Mr. Collier.

Silently, he handed the card to the guest. Other than his name, the black man didn't have to provide any further identification or security for the room. As the guest walked away, the desk clerk shivered. He was wide awake for the remainder of his shift.

Outside the sixth-floor elevators Reggie stopped and listened. There was no sound or sign of movement on the floor. As he traversed the corridor he stayed close to the wall. At the door to 606 he inserted the access card and entered.

The room was clean, cool and empty. After checking the bathroom and closet, Reggie turned on the lights and opened the cloth pouch. Inside were three sharpened, highly-polished throwing knives in various sizes. Accompanying each knife was a spring-loaded sheath with straps for securing it to his body. He strapped one to his right forearm, another to his left calf and the third and smallest to his belt at the small of his back.

Next he carefully checked the room. A Smith and Wesson Model 1006 10 mm. automatic pistol and three full ammunition clips were taped under the sofa. He loaded the pistol, slipped it into his belt beneath his suit coat and returned to the corridor outside his room. He checked the sixth floor once more and, finding it secure, picked a spot where the lighting cast an area beside a potted plant in shadow. He removed the covering over the closest ceiling light and, using his handkerchief to protect his fingers, unscrewed the bulb. Then he stepped back against the wall and waited.

The agent came twenty-two minutes later.

He was overweight and moved clumsily. He came off the elevator and stomped toward the door to 606 with a single-minded concentration. He was not aware of Reggie until the black agent stepped up behind him and pressed the muzzle of the pistol against the base of his skull. The fat agent's arms jerked upwards as if they were attached to puppet strings.

"Easy, Stanton," he said, breathlessly. "I'm a friend."

"Shut up," Reggie said, shoving his access card into the agent's upraised palm. "Use this and walk inside. No games."

Obediently, the agent complied.

Reggie shoved him face down on the bed and dropped a knee into the center of his back. The air escaped from the trapped agent's lungs with a grunt, but he made no attempt to resist. Reggie removed his gun, which was a twin of the Model 1006, his extra bullet clip, his identification case and everything from each of his pockets to include a ballpoint pen and his car keys. All items were dumped on the floor with the exception of the gun. Reggie then performed a thorough body search, which left the agent disheveled and obviously skeptical of Reggie's sanity.

"Hey, man," the fat agent said, rearranging his clothing after Reggie let him up. "Who do you think I'm with, the K.G.B.?"

Reggie backed six feet away from the agent and aimed both pistols at him. The fat agent froze.

"We're friends with the K.G.B. now," Reggie said, "or haven't they told you yet?"

"So why the toss?"

"Maybe you're with the Gestapo."

"Huh?" the agent said with confusion.

"Don't worry about it. What do you want?"

"I've got a message for you from Deputy Director Connors."

"Why didn't Connors come himself?"

"It's late, man. After all, he is a deputy director. He's not coming out at this early hour."

"So you're his messenger boy?"

The fat agent didn't like this, but he wasn't in a position to make an issue of it. "Connors wants you to meet him in the restaurant on the second level of the hotel at 9 A.M. sharp."

Reggie stared at him. It made the fat agent nervous and he looked away. "Is that all?"

"Isn't that enough?"

"He could have told me that on the telephone. That would have saved you from losing any sleep."

"It's basic procedure, Stanton. I'm the night duty officer over at Justice anyway."

"Okay, Mr. Night Duty Officer, pick up your things and get out of here."

The agent moved quickly, shoving his belongings back in his pockets. He was hastily rearranging his clothing when he said, "What about my gun?"

"I'll hold onto it for you."

The agent frowned. "That could get me in trouble."

The look Reggie gave him forced all of the blood from the fat agent's face. "If you are in this room five seconds from now I guarantee you'll be in more trouble than you could ever imagine."

The agent literally ran from the room.

Reggie chained and locked the door before extinguishing the lights and crossing to the couch on the far side of the room. He sat down and settled in to wait with both automatics held loosely in his hands. The safeties on the guns were off. The room began to brighten as the sun rose over Washington. Reggie checked his watch. It was 6:30.

Reggie ran the encounter with the night duty officer over in his mind. It wasn't like Connors to send messengers to meet with his "assets." Plus, the agent had been not only stupid, but also clumsy. He definitely wasn't Bureau Special Ops material. Then why had Connors sent him?

Reggie jumped up and crossed to the bathroom. Turning on the overhead lights, he field-stripped the automatic he'd found in the room. Using his small dagger, he expertly dismantled the firing mechanism. His eyes glinted with an icy coldness when he noticed the gun had no firing pin.

He quickly performed the same procedure on the fat agent's gun. It also had had its firing pin removed.

Reggie didn't know what type of game Connors was playing, but then of one thing he was certain; breakfast would be his most important meal today.

MARCH 7, 1994
6:45 A.M.

J udy Daniels, in her disguise as the matronly Angelina Lupo, was dozing. She was seated in a chair beside Rachel's bed and had drifted off sometime before dawn. Now, after having gone without sleep for nearly twenty-four hours, her slumber deepened and she began dreaming.

She was back in the courtyard in the Chicago Historical District with the knife-wielding Armand Hagar. As she had done in reality she reached for the gun in the holster strapped to her inner thigh. Unlike what had happened in the world outside of her dream, the gun was not there. The terror jolted her; however, she remained asleep. Hagar's ugly, bearded face loomed inches from hers. His knife blade gleamed brightly, almost blinding her with its brilliance. Then he stabbed her in the heart.

She recoiled from the thrust and jerked awake. She lost her balance in the armless, straight-back chair and would have fallen to the floor if Rachel hadn't caught her.

For just a brief instant Judy didn't know where she was. In fact, she also wasn't sure who she was either. It came back to her in a rush.

She righted herself and stared at Rachel. The girl looked frightened to the point of outright terror. She also appeared very curious.

"You were having a bad dream, Mrs. Lupo," Rachel said. "I didn't know whether to wake you up or not."

Judy ran her hands over her make-up and checked to make sure her hair and body padding were in place. Everything was fine. But Rachel was still staring at her.

"What is it, child?" Judy said, employing the Taylor Street accent.

Rachel frowned. She was still clad in her nightgown and looked deathly pale with visible circles under her feverish eyes. "You said something while you were asleep."

Judy composed herself. "Yes?"

"You called a name. I think it was 'Blackie.' "

Judy didn't respond.

Rachel touched her fingers to her forehead. "It wasn't so much the name, Mrs. Lupo, but the way you said it."

"I don't understand what you mean."

Rachel shook her head. "I don't really know. Your voice was different. It was as if there was someone else here in the room with me." Her eyes swung around frantically, as if she was looking for a ghost.

Judy forced Angelina Lupo's matronly smile onto her disguised face. "You need some breakfast and a nice walk in the fresh air."

Rachel frowned and said a halting, "Papa . . ."

"Yes? What about your papa?"

"He doesn't like me to go outside."

"Nonsense," Angelina Lupo said, as she stood up and limped toward the door. "First I will fix your breakfast and then I will speak to your father."

There was a guard outside Rachel's bedroom. He was a heavyset, pockmarked-faced man with oily hair. He stood and nodded solemnly as Mrs. Lupo went by. She nodded back. She could feel his eyes on her as she walked to the staircase and descended.

There were two more bodyguards stationed in the central alcove. Both had small black attache cases resting on the floor beside their chairs. She recognized these cases as the type and size used to conceal Uzi submachine guns. The bodyguards nodded to her. She returned the silent gestures with a nod of her own.

She continued to the kitchen, where she'd made Rachel a bowl of soup last night. She was tense, but this was effectively masked by her disguise. As long as she was Angelina Lupo and kept making them believe that she was, then Judy Daniels would remain alive. One slip would sign her death warrant.

A skinny bodyguard, sporting an elaborately-styled hairdo, was coming out of the kitchen as she approached. He was younger than the others and actually looked out of place among this nest of hoods and hardcases in the employ of Tuxedo Tony DeLisa. The bodyguard was in shirtsleeves and the huge revolver he carried in a shoulder holster made him look even more lost.

"Good morning, ma'am," he said with a shy grin.

"Good morning, young man," she said with a severity she felt her position in this household warranted.

He stood back and held the door for her. She nodded to him as she walked into the kitchen. Then she stopped dead in her tracks.

Seated at the kitchen table facing her sat Armand Hagar. "Good morning," he snarled.

Chicago, Illinois   **73**

MARCH 7, 1994
7:00 A.M.

Lisa Cole shook her husband awake. Bleary-eyed and stiff from having slept on the couch all night, Cole came awake slowly.

"Chief Govich is on the phone for you, Larry."

Cole was completely awake by the time he picked up the receiver. "Yes, Chief."

He listened for a long time. Lisa sat at his desk in the den watching him. He noticed the I.A.D. file open in front of her. He glanced at his watch before saying, "Sure I can be there, Chief. Right. Noon. The China Gate Restaurant in the Hyde Park Hotel."

After hanging up he said to his wife, "The superintendent got a call from Senator Banks last night. He wants to talk to me about the deaths of Butcher and Cappeletti. He's invited me to lunch."

"Do you think it has anything to do with this Reggie Stanton?"

Cole stifled a yawn. "I don't know, but at noon I'm going to find out."

"He's dangerous, Larry." she said pointing to the file she'd spent most of the night reading. "The reports of what he was accused of doing back in nineteen seventy-nine are scary."

"Yeah," was his simple reply. "They are."

Washington, D.C. **74**

March 7, 1994
7:15 a.m.

Reggie Stanton had reconnoitered the Caribe Cafe on the second level of the Vista Hotel. The Vista View Bar was one level above the restaurant on the other side of the atrium. It was closed at this early hour of the morning, however, the windows of the bar were tinted, giving the interior an intimate atmosphere when the place was open for business. The windows on the lobby side of the bar provided an excellent view of not only the Caribe Cafe, but also the main entrance to the hotel.

A set of F.B.I.-issue lock picks had not only gotten Stanton inside the bar, but also enabled him to shut off the burglar alarm. He had selected a convenient but sufficiently spartan position from which to maintain a surveillance of the area below without succumbing to sleep. He had taken up watch an hour and forty-five minutes prior to his scheduled breakfast appointment with Connors. An hour and fifteen minutes of that time remained when one of Connors's Special Ops agents, codenamed the Rattler, sauntered into the lobby.

At the sight of the toothpick-lean, weather-seared cowboy, Stanton tensed. The Rattler being here meant that Connors was expecting trouble. The cowboy hated Stanton, as they'd had a run-in some years before, which the Rattler had barely survived. He had sworn to someday kill Reggie. Perhaps, Reggie thought, Connors had told him that today was the day.

The Rattler went to the front desk first. He was dressed in a conservative business suit and plain-toed oxfords, and his hair was slicked back from a high widow's peak. But his western heritage was etched into his every movement and gesture. When he turned from talking to the desk clerk he looked up into the atrium. For a moment his eyes came to rest right at the window behind which Reggie sat watching him. Reggie knew he couldn't be seen, but then the Rattler was supposed to be very good. Finally, he turned away and strolled across the lobby and climbed the steps to the second level. He made an external examination of the Caribe Cafe, which had opened for business at seven. He reconnoitered slowly, carefully checking distances and lines of sight from a number of vantage points. Reggie figured that the Rattler was probably deciding where he wanted Connors to sit. The deputy director would undoubtedly arrive early, so he could pick his seat. If their plans went off on schedule Reggie would be at their mercy. He didn't plan to let this happen.

From his post behind the tinted glass, Reggie watched the Rattler stop a middle-aged waiter. The cowboy extended his hand and the waiter took it. When the exchange was concluded, the waiter slipped the bill the Rattler had given him into his vest pocket. Then he led the cowboy back through the restaurant. They passed out of Reggie's view.

He figured they were going to check the kitchen and any possible escape routes located there. Reggie stood up and headed for the service exit from the Vista View Bar. The exists from the restaurant and the bar led out into an alley behind the hotel. Reggie made the decision to eliminate one of Deputy Director Connors's assets.

MARCH 7, 1994

7:20 A.M.

There is always tension during an undercover operation. Sometimes such tension reaches unbearable limits and the undercover officer cracks under the strain. Judy Daniels had been in tight situations before, but what she was going through now was ridiculous.

The table in the DeLisa kitchen was in the center of the room. The sink and stove were on one side, the refrigerator on the other. In order for Judy, in her disguise as Angelina Lupo, to fix Rachel's breakfast, she had to travel back and forth between the refrigerator and the stove. This forced her to walk past Armand Hagar, seated at the kitchen table, a countless number of times. And each time she found him staring at her with hostile curiosity. He was trying to figure out where he'd seen her before.

She had managed to fry six strips of bacon and shove a couple of pieces of bread into the toaster. Coffee was percolating in a coffee pot on the stove and would be ready soon. She had a carton of eggs open on the sink beside the skillet she had fried the bacon in. After draining the grease she considered frying the eggs over easy, but she didn't think her nerves would hold up sufficiently for her to crack the shells without breaking the yolks. She decided to scramble them, but for this she would need a mixing bowl. This would require her to again cross the kitchen to retrieve one from the cabinet above the refrigerator.

She steeled herself and turned around. Hagar was staring at her. Somewhere she'd read that the best defense was a good offense. She decided that there was no time like the present to test this precept.

"Would you care for a cup of coffee, young man?"

His eyes reminded her of a shark's. Cold, dead and unblinking. He didn't answer immediately. When he did, he said, "That would be nice, Mrs., uh . . . ?"

"Lupo," Judy answered, crossing to the cupboard and removing two cups along with a mixing bowl with hands as cold as ice.

"Mrs. Lupo," he repeated. "Say, haven't I seen you someplace before?"

Judy placed a cup and saucer down in front of him. She was so close she could smell the rancid odor of his unwashed body. She returned to the stove before responding, "I don't know."

The chrome coffee pot was situated at an angle from which she could see his reflection. He hadn't moved and his eyes never left her. The distortion, caused by the chrome surface, enhanced the peril she felt. The reflection made him look like an alien creature with a narrow head and enormous eyes.

"You a member of the Tuxedo's family?" he asked.

Judy cracked two eggs into the bowl. A large piece of one of the shells dropped into the bowl. Fear was starting to make her giddy. No one should have to be going through what she was at this moment. What she needed to do was walk out of here right now and turn her badge in to the first cop she saw. Then she'd go out and get a nice tame job like big-game hunter or Arctic explorer.

Then she remembered that she was Judy Daniels, the Mistress of Disguise/High Priestess of Mayhem. She turned around and looked directly at him. "If you have any questions about me, why don't you ask Mr. DeLisa? I'm sure he'll clear up any confusion about my identity for you."

His face underwent an instant transformation. His arrogance vanished and he dropped his eyes. He did not look up at her again.

She poured a cup of coffee for him. "Sugar is on the table, the cream is in the icebox."

She returned to fixing Rachel's breakfast, discovering that she also had developed an appetite. She cracked an extra egg into the mixing bowl.

The kitchen door opened and a muscular young man in a tight-fitting knit shirt came in. "Good morning, Mrs. Lupo," he said expansively, extending his hand to her.

"Good morning," she said. He was Sam Sykes, the bodyguarding companion of her friend Carrie.

"Armando, my man," Sam said. "How's it hanging?"

"Okay, Sam," Hagar said glumly.

Sam got himself a cup from the cabinet and poured coffee into it from the pot on the stove. He took a seat across from Hagar and said, "What happened to your foot?"

Judy could no longer see Hagar because Sam had moved her image-reflecting pot, but the words needed no visual aid to interpret the fury of the speaker. "A lady cop shot me."

"Do tell," Sam said. "Must've been a heavy set."

"Not as heavy as the one the Tuxedo's got going down today in Hyde Park."

Judy poured the eggs into the skillet.

"Does it have anything to do with the two Germans I heard Wally talking about?" Sam asked.

"The same. They're gonna do a little job for the Tuxedo. Then somebody's going to do a job on them."

The door opened again and Tony DeLisa walked in. There was a broad smile etched on his face. "Good morning, Mrs. Lupo. I hope you slept well."

She did not return DeLisa's smile, but forged her face into a pleasantly tolerant expression. "I sat through the night with Rachel. It was her sleep I was concerned with, not my own."

"And she looks very good this morning," DeLisa said. "Maybe just a bit pale. She should get more sun."

"I mentioned that to her. After breakfast I planned to take her for a walk."

"Good idea," DeLisa said, turning to the two men seated at the table. In the blink of an eye his face changed from one of cordiality to that of open menace. "You boys talk too much."

"Gee, Mr. DeLisa . . ." Sam began by way of apology, but he never got the chance to finish.

DeLisa was standing behind Judy. When Sam opened his

mouth, the mobster spun suddenly and grabbed the hot steel coffee pot. He swung it at Sam's head, spraying a mist of hot coffee around the kitchen. Hagar, the walls and the refrigerator were splattered with the dark liquid. Sam saw the attack coming and threw up his hands to protect his head and face. DeLisa upended the pot, pouring its scalding contents over Sam.

The scream tore through the kitchen. The pot empty, DeLisa began beating Sam with it. With each blow he swore at the scalded man. "This is for not doing your job yesterday! This is for opening your big mouth today! This is for—"

"Stop it!" Judy yelled.

DeLisa's hand halted in midswing. He glared at her with a fury that she initially thought would lead to violence. Then as suddenly as it had come, the insane anger melted into something Judy thought was very close to fear. Without a word, DeLisa dropped the empty pot and stormed from the kitchen.

Chicago, Illinois **76**

MARCH 7, 1994
8:15 A.M.

Blackie Silvestri was in the real Angelina Lupo's apartment above Paoletti's Drug Store on Taylor Street. He was seated on a plastic-covered couch beneath a window affording him a view of Taylor Street all the way from Mama Mancini's Pizzeria to the Presbyterian/St. Luke's Hospital complex on the other side of Ashland. The one-bedroom apartment was cluttered but neat. It was obviously a woman's place, with lots of lace, flowery patterns and cute knickknacks everywhere. Blackie noticed that Angelina's tastes were very similar to his wife Maria's. That is, the real Angelina Lupo. It was becoming distressingly evident that he knew very little about the woman who was currently impersonating the resident of this apartment out at the Oak Park estate of Tuxedo Tony DeLisa.

Blackie checked the street once more for the Mistress of Dis-
guise/High Priestess of Mayhem. There was no sign of her. It was
possible that she was dead. He hadn't seen or heard from her since
she got in a cab in front of this building last night in route to Oak
Park. Blackie began chewing nervously on his thumbnail.

The plan was for her to spend the first night getting the lay of the
land, then asking to leave so she could pick up some things from her
apartment for a longer stay. As she had nothing with her but the
clothes on her back, they'd figured this a reasonable request to make
of even someone as notoriously suspicious as DeLisa. Of course,
they realized the Tuxedo might not go for it at all. Judy had called
this "an acceptable risk."

"To hell it was!" Blackie said into the emptiness of Angelina
Lupo's apartment. If something happened to Judy he'd have to explain it to Commander Cole. What would he say? How would he
explain the direct violation of Cole's order? What would this do to
their twenty-year friendship?

"Sarge?" Manny Sherlock's voice came over the walkie-talkie
snapped to Blackie's belt.

"Yeah, Manny. Go ahead."

*"There's a guy in front of Mrs. Lupo's building. He looks kind of
odd to me."*

Blackie looked down at the street, but was only able to see the
shoulders and back of a man's head from his vantage point. He
didn't look to be doing anything but simply standing on the street as
if he was waiting for someone.

Lou Bronson's voice broke in. He and Sherlock were stationed
at strategic locations so that they could cover all the approaches to
the building. *"Blackie, he's stopped a couple of people and asked them
questions. He looks familiar, but I can't place him."*

"Manny, head this way and see if you can get him to question
you."

"Ten-four, Sarge. I'm on the way."

Blackie saw the tall, gangly detective stride off a side street a
block east on Taylor Street. The sergeant's mouth dropped open
when he noticed that Sherlock had adopted a disguise for the sur-

veillance. What was Judy Daniels doing, making them all go crazy?!

Manny had his hair swept back from his forehead into a ducktail held in place with what appeared to be an entire jar of Vaseline. He wore an oversized pair of sunglasses, a size-too-large leather jacket, tight jeans and boots with an inch-high heel. And he not only dressed the part, but was acting it for all he was worth. As Blackie looked on in horror, Manny was doing a very, very bad imitation of a hip street walk. It came across as something between Paul Newman's Rocky Graziano shuffle in the movie *Somebody Up There Likes Me* and a kangaroo hop.

"Lou," Blackie said, trying to keep from screaming over their closed frequency, "what in the hell is he doing?"

Bronson coughed before responding, *"Gee, Blackie, I don't know what he calls himself doing now, but he was very impressed with the Mistress of Disguise. Maybe he's practicing."*

"I'll practice him."

Blackie looked down at the man standing in front of the building. He hadn't moved, but was looking in the direction from which Sherlock was approaching. Blackie figured he probably couldn't believe it either.

The sergeant took a moment to study the curious stranger standing in front of the building. He was a big guy with a square head and he was wearing an expensive trench coat against the chill of the morning. The way he stood and carried his shoulders gave him an air of menace. Blackie felt a suspicious tingle begin at the base of his spine. Then Sherlock walked up to the man.

The ludicrously disguised detective pulled a bent filter-tipped cigarette from the inside pocket of his jacket. *"Hey, bro, you got a light?"*

Oh, my God! Blackie thought. *Nobody's going to believe that accent.* Manny sounded like a suburban yuppie imitating street talk.

"Yeah, partner," the man said, stepping forward, but keeping his back turned to Blackie. *"Sure thing."*

A cigarette lighter snapped open over the walkie-talkie speaker. Blackie saw smoke billow into the air between the two men on the street. Then Manny broke into convulsive coughing.

"Take it easy, partner," the man said, slapping Manny on the back.

"No problem," Manny gasped, *"this shit is just too heavy. Want a hit?"*

"Smells like straight tobacco to me."

"It is, but it's some heavy tobacco."

Blackie rolled his eyes at the ceiling. He couldn't believe this was happening.

"Tell me something, partner," the man said.

"Yeah, bro, shoot. I owe you for the light anyway."

"You know a woman who lives around here named Angelina Lupo?"

Blackie tensed.

"I know a chick name of Angie, man," Manny said, puffing smoke furiously without inhaling. *"She lives down on Racine. Chick's nineteen and gonna have Freddie Lucchesi's baby."*

"Nah, partner. This is an older woman. Forty-five, maybe fifty. Lives on the second floor here over the drug store."

"Oh, that Mrs. Lupo. Yeah, I know her. She's related to Mama Mancini. Best pizza in town."

"That's the one. Tell me, have you seen her around lately?"

"Let me see." Manny paused for a dramatically long moment that nearly succeeded in stopping Blackie's heart. *"I think I saw her yesterday. Yeah, it was yesterday."*

"Oh." The man in the trench coat sounded skeptical. *"Mrs. Cabroni down on Loomis said she heard Mrs. Lupo went on a cruise that left on Wednesday and that she's not due back until next week."*

"I can't help what Old Lady Cabroni says, bro. She's kinda touched in the head." Blackie watched Manny tap a forefinger against the side of his skull. The sergeant had to give it to the fledgling undercover officer, he was starting to get good. *"But I seen that Mrs. Lupo yesterday. Now I gotta go. A chick's waiting for me. Stay cool."*

The man watched Manny saunter away and shook his head from side to side as if either rendering a disapproval of the undercover detective or negating what he had just been told. For his part,

Manny did his funny walk to the next corner before, to the tremendous relief of Sergeant Blackie Silvestri, disappearing from view.

The man stood a moment longer staring off down the street before turning around. Blackie recognized him instantly. It was Wally Boykin, Tuxedo Tony's personal bodyguard. He entered the building. Blackie knew exactly where he was headed.

Washington, D.C. **77**

MARCH 7, 1994
9:15 A.M.

F.B.I. Deputy Director William Connors walked into the lobby of the Vista Hotel. He was flanked by three agents who were not part of his Special Operations section, but were on loan from the Washington, D.C. Field Office.

The quartet proceeded directly to the stairs leading up to the Caribe Cafe on level two. They were met at the entrance by a slender maitre'd, who smiled and said, "Good morning, Director Connors. Your guest is already seated."

Connors frowned. He looked across the restaurant at his usual table. Reggie Stanton was seated there alone. Connors's eyes flicked quickly around the area. There was no sign of the Rattler. Of course, the deputy director admitted to himself, if the cowboy was doing his job right he shouldn't be seen. In fact, Connors was surprised that Stanton was still alive.

He turned to his escorts. "You men stay out here. Take no action unless you receive a direct order from me to do so."

The agents nodded and dispersed around the restaurant entrance attempting to look inconspicuous, which made their presence all the more evident.

Connors crossed the restaurant. He wore a broad smile when he walked up to the table. "How are you, Reggie? It's been a long time."

Reggie remained seated. "Seven months."

Connors sat down and looked at the fruit plate and cup of black coffee in front of the black man. "You're eating kind of light, aren't you?"

"I was waiting for you to arrive before I went to the buffet."

"Let's go."

The Caribe Cafe's breakfast buffet was set up along the back wall. Stanton permitted Connors to walk in front of him. The tables they passed were filled with midmorning diners. At the buffet they joined a line waiting to serve themselves from the steaming trays. After making their selections the F.B.I. men returned to their table. They began eating in silence. After the waiter refilled their coffee cups and water glasses Reggie asked, "Do you have an assignment for me?"

"No. We need to talk about how you spend your time in Chicago."

"I thought how I did that was my own affair?"

Connors gave him a humorless smile. "You know better than that, Stanton. Anything you do that connects you with the Bureau causes problems. I thought you learned that after you beat that guy up a year or so ago. If it hadn't been for us, you could have been charged with attempted murder."

Reggie stopped eating. "His name was Chuck Nelson. He was the former boyfriend of a lady friend of mine. He hit her and I came to her defense."

"And he ended up in the hospital with four cracked ribs, a broken arm and a ruptured spleen. Was Billie Smith worth all that?"

"Why don't we leave her out of this and get to the real reason you summoned me to Washington."

Connors took his time buttering a biscuit. "You always cut to the chase, Reggie. No small talk or chit-chat. Just the facts, ma'am."

Reggie didn't respond.

"What's going on with you and Harvey Banks?" Connors demanded.

"I keep an eye on the senator. Again, it's on my own time."

"But you're not supposed to be doing it as an F.B.I. agent."

"I am an F.B.I. agent," Reggie countered.

"Yes, I guess you are," Connors said dryly. "You've even got official identification from what I hear. I'd like to know where you got it."

"That's a long story."

78

Mike Thomas was a prelaw student at Howard University. To supplement his income he worked part-time at the Odds-n-Ends Souvenir Shop directly across the Vista lobby from the Caribe Restaurant. The shop was directly below the Vista View Bar.

The souvenir shop dealt with national capital memorabilia from ashtrays to replica dolls of first ladies. Mike was cleaning a glass display case when he looked across the atrium and saw the three F.B.I. agents in front of the restaurant entrance. He had never eaten at the Caribe because he couldn't afford to, but the vice-president had been there once. A small army of Secret Service agents had accompanied him. He recognized the three agents as official types and wondered who they were guarding. It was as he had this thought that he heard loud tapping noises coming from the rear of the shop over by the postcard racks. Frowning, he went to investigate.

Mike was crossing the shop when something struck him directly on top of his head. Startled, he looked up and three drops of liquid landed on his forehead and shoulders. He staggered back against a counter and stared up at the ceiling. The acoustical tiles directly above him were wet and the accumulation of moisture was soaking through to drip on everything in the store. At first he thought it was water, then he caught the aroma. He opened his mouth and let a couple of drops fall on his tongue. He savored the taste for a moment before smiling. The Odds-n-Ends Souvenir Shop was raining beer.

79

The three F.B.I. agents were bored. They didn't like this kind of duty, especially for a prick like Connors. Everyone in the Washington office knew about the deputy director and his shadow section. However, few spoke of it and those who did were openly critical. Some agents in the know figured that the day was coming when Connors would be up to his chin in shit and find himself on television before a senate committee attempting to explain what he'd been doing for the last twenty years with taxpayers' money.

"He could have let us come in and sit at a table," one of the agents grumbled. "Then we could have at least had a cup of coffee while he has his meeting."

Another agent, the thinnest of the trio, who looked as if he hadn't eaten a decent meal in years, stared across the restaurant at the table Connors and Stanton were seated at. "Who is this guy, anyway? He sure doesn't look like an agent to me."

"I don't know," said the third agent, who possessed the cynical frown of the veteran cop. "But he took Levering's piece this morning. It's gonna cost him some time off without pay."

"Serves him right—" the first agent was saying, but the thin one cut him off.

"Would you look at this?"

They followed his line of sight to the opposite side of the atrium, where prelaw student Mike Thomas staggered out of the Odds-n-Ends Souvenir Shop. The young clerk looked as if he'd just taken a shower with all his clothes on.

As the F.B.I. agents looked on, a building maintenance man in a gray utility uniform rushed up to Thomas.

The cynical agent said, "They got a major flood in this joint, boys. The way that kid looks, the ceiling in that place is going to collapse in another minute or two."

The agents had become so engrossed in the drama taking place across from them that they forgot about the deputy director and his breakfast guest.

"I don't understand you, Stanton," Connors said, shoving his empty plate away. "The Bureau has been damn good to you. But every time I turn around you're trying to crap all over us."

Reggie remained composed, but his voice held tension. "You got a real short memory, Connors. If you recall, I was blackmailed into the F.B.I."

Connors bristled, "And if we hadn't taken you in you'd have gone to jail for murder."

The diners around them became agitated, which interrupted their argument. Connors stopped a passing waiter. "What's going on?"

"There's nothing to be concerned about, sir," the waiter said. "There seems to be a leak in the shop across the way. It isn't affecting the restaurant."

Connors looked in the direction the waiter had indicated, but he didn't notice anything amiss. He was just turning back to Reggie when a loud crash echoed through the hotel atrium. A couple of women screamed. A busboy crossing the restaurant carrying a tray piled with dirty dishes was so startled that he dropped the tray. All eyes in the atrium were drawn to the origin of the sound, which was caused by one of the Vista View Bar windows exploding. A huge beer keg had smashed through the window and plummeted to the lobby floor below. As it fell, everyone saw the body tied to the keg with a ten foot length of rope. The body followed the keg down to smash onto the tiled surface. Screams and shouts echoed through the lobby.

In the instant it took the two objects to fall, Connors recognized the body as that of one of his shadow agents, code-named the Rattler.

* * *

"Let's go!" the cynical F.B.I. agent shouted. Without hesitation the three men sprinted for the stairs.

A clerk and a couple of curious bellhops approached the twisted body and what was left of the keg.

"Don't touch anything!" the cynical agent shouted as he and his companions ran toward them.

They stopped when they saw that the body tied to the keg had been bled white long before the fall. The keg had smashed open to reveal a lather of foam inside. The F.B.I. men looked up.

The cynical agent said to the thin one, "Go back and stay with Connors. We'll go up there and take a look."

A few moments later the building maintenance man was confronted by the two agents, who forced him to accompany them to the Vista View Bar. They discovered that the door was unlocked.

Inside, the smell of beer was overpowering. The footing was precarious as the floor was awash with gallons of the flowing liquid. Across the bar by the smashed window was a table tilted at an odd angle. The agents sloshed over to it, while the maintenance man hung back by the door.

"Smooth," the cynical agent said. "Real smooth." Wrapping his hand in a handkerchief to prevent leaving prints on the surface, he touched the tabletop. It swung freely back and forth like a child's seesaw. "The body's tied to a full keg of beer. The table is rigged to swing freely back and forth on a fulcrum. The body's on this side by the window, the full keg on the opposite end. A hole in the keg starts the beer flowing out. When the keg gets light enough it rolls down with enough force to pass over the body, smash the window and fall. It drags the body along with it."

"I don't get it," the other agent said.

"Don't get what?"

"Why go to all this trouble? That guy was already dead. You can see the blood even with all this beer."

The cynical one shrugged. "I don't know. Maybe it was a diversion."

The other agent looked across the atrium through the smashed window of the bar. "What's he doing?"

They both looked across at the Caribe Cafe. There, standing at the empty table previously occupied by Deputy Director Connors and his guest, stood their thin companion. His arms were extended in a helpless gesture as he shook his head and mouthed the word, "Gone."

They had lost Deputy Director William Connors.

Chicago, Illinois **80**

Wally Boykin climbed the steps to Angelina Lupo's second floor apartment. There were doors to four apartments leading off the narrow corridor at the top of the stairs. He knew the Lupo woman's was marked with the letter A. This letter was also above her name on the mailbox downstairs.

He stood in the hallway and listened. Down at the far end, behind the door marked with the letter C, came the sounds of classical music. There was nothing else stirring on the floor.

He crossed to her door and examined the lock. He hadn't expected much in the way of security. Down on Taylor Street there wasn't much crime. The people didn't tolerate it. They didn't call the cops either. Miscreants were treated with extreme prejudice. This didn't apply to Wally Boykin, because he worked for the biggest miscreant basher of all.

Removing a set of lockpicks from his pocket, he went to work. He was inside in less than thirty seconds.

What a dump, he thought as he stood inside the entryway studying the old furniture. This Lupo broad was very Old Country. Reminded him a lot of an aunt he once had. There were framed photographs, mostly in black and white, arranged on the mantle above the fake fireplace. He started with them.

He didn't recognize any photos of the young Angelina Lupo.

There was a resemblance in some of the later pictures, but . . . ? He recalled the image of the woman back at the DeLisa house. Somehow they didn't match. The pictures were close, but that's all they were.

"So, you're gonna take this shit back to the Tuxedo," he mumbled to himself. "Yeah, and your ass will be on its way to the morgue before nightfall."

DeLisa had sent him to check her out, not comment on how photogenic she was. He considered taking one of the pictures with him, but then rejected this. The Tuxedo didn't tell him to take anything from the apartment. At least anything like this.

The bedroom was furnished just as he expected it to be. There was a shrine to the Blessed Virgin and a crucifix hanging over the bed. A thick, well-thumbed Bible rested on the nightstand. Boykin stared at the religious relics from across the room, but he didn't go near them. Religion wasn't his thing.

He went to the closet, opened the door and glanced in at the rack of old-style dresses hanging there. A sweet, cloying perfume drifted out. He slammed the door.

He turned to the chest of drawers next to the closet. Opening the top drawer he found an odd assortment of jewelry and a stack of letters bound with a rubber band. The top letter bore the return address and logo of the Pickfair Travel Agency located in the Loop. He removed it from the stack.

It was postmarked the twelfth of February and had been opened. There was a single sheet of typed stationery inside, which also bore the Pickfair Travel Agency logo. Boykin read it out loud.

"Dear Mrs. Lupo, your deposit for the vacation cruise on the Southern Star Line has been received and space reserved for one. You are booked on Flight three fifty-three leaving Chicago O'Hare bound for Miami on March fourth, nineteen ninety-four at twelve fifteen P.M. You will board the Bahamian Princess in Miami for a seven day cruise to commence at dusk on March fifth. You will be returned to Miami on March eleventh and be provided with air transportation back to Chicago."

There was brief mention of how pleased the Pickfair Travel

Agency was to be serving her and they hoped she would use them again. Boykin didn't read that part too carefully as he said, "Bingo, the bitch is a phony."

Taking the letter with him and leaving the drawer open, Boykin left the bedroom. He entered the living room noticing that the front door now stood partially open. He hadn't locked it when he came in, but he distinctly remembered closing it. He stiffened and pulled a .32 automatic from a shoulder holster beneath his coat. He angled across the living room, attempting to see who was out in the hall. He stopped when the door swung open and the goofy kid with the duck-tail haircut walked in. The mobster took one look at the snub-nosed .38 he carried and opened fire.

Boykin fired four rounds knocking the kid backwards into the hall. The roar of the gunshots in the confined space partially deafened Boykin. So it was that he barely heard the shouted "Freeze!" coming from the entrance to the bedroom behind him. Without hesitating, the mobster swung his automatic around to point at the source of the sound. He never made it.

Blackie Silvestri had been hiding in Angelina Lupo's closet. When he heard Boykin reading the travel agency letter, Blackie knew he had to stop him and when the first shot rang out he shoved the door open.

The mobster spun around, gun raised. Blackie, .357 magnum at arm's length, pulled the trigger six times. From a distance of eight feet he hit Boykin once in the head, twice in the chest, twice in the stomach and once in the hand opposite the one in which he carried the gun. The mobster was knocked backward onto Angelina Lupo's plastic-covered couch. Before he hit the polyethylene, Boykin was dead.

Blackie took the gun from the lifeless fingers and turned around. The blood froze in his veins when he saw Manny Sherlock lying in the hall. Blackie whispered, "Oh, my God, no."

81

E rnest," Karl Steiger said, gently shaking his sleeping son's shoulder, "get up."

Ernest came awake instantly. "What time is it?"

Karl walked from the bedroom and said over his shoulder, "A little after ten. I bought you some coffee and there is bread, fruit and cheese if you are hungry. After you shower we will go over the plan."

Ernest leaped from the bed, dropped to the floor and snapped off a hundred push-ups. Flipping onto his back he did a hundred sit-ups. On his feet he did deep knee bends until his thighs ached. Sweating, he went to the bathroom to shower and shave. When he came out he found his father had laid out an outfit for him. He frowned.

Karl was sitting on the living room couch studying the pages of a steno notebook. Without looking up he said, "That's the type of clothing a young German reporter wears. Not your designer jeans and custom-made French boots."

"My boots were made in Spain," Ernest said, as he pulled on the wash-and-wear slacks. There was also a striped button-down-collar shirt, knit sweater and corduroy jacket with patched elbows. Black socks and a pair of black loafers completed the ensemble. "All these things are new. Won't that arouse suspicion?"

Karl looked up. "This is America. The land of conspicuous consumption. There is no need to worry about things we ordinarily would be concerned about in Europe."

Ernest put on the sweater and then tried the coat. They fit perfectly. He was forced to admit that the clothing wasn't half bad. His father had pretty good taste.

"We need to go over the plan for this operation."

Ernest took a seat across from his father. Karl placed the notebook on the table between them and turned it so his son could see the top page. On it Karl had sketched a route for Ernest to take from the Haggerty House to the Hyde Park Hotel.

"You will drive the rented car to the hotel, but I have acquired alternate transportation for our escape. We will not return here after the job is completed, but will go right to the airport. Our flight to Mexico City leaves at four."

"Mexico City?"

"You said you wanted to spend some time lying around on a beach with beautiful women, didn't you?"

"Yes, I did," Ernest said, making no attempt to mask his surprise.

Karl turned back to the notebook. He flipped to the next page on which was drawn a detailed diagram. "The China Gate Restaurant is on the eighth floor of the hotel. You will allow the attendant in front of the building to park your car. You will then proceed into the lobby. There is a special elevator for restaurant patrons. Do you know what you are supposed to do when you meet the senator?"

"Yes, sir."

"As soon as Banks ingests the liquid you are to excuse yourself from the table and leave the restaurant immediately. There is a stairwell here," he pointed to a neatly drawn square on the diagram. "Use it instead of the elevator. I will cover your escape and meet you outside. A black Mercedes will be parked on Hyde Park Boulevard a block away from the hotel. We should reach it before the senator collapses."

Ernest nodded. "I understand."

"Questions?"

"No, sir."

Karl stood up. Ernest rose as well. Karl placed a hand on his son's shoulder. *"Waidman heil,* Ernest."

"Good hunting to you also, Father," Ernest responded.

In the secret compartment beneath the stairs on the first floor of the Haggerty House, every word spoken by the Steigers was recorded.

82

Attorney Frank Kirschstein sat in Tuxedo Tony's study going over the books containing the records for the week's take. DeLisa was with him, which made the lawyer nervous. He had heard about the scalding of Sam Sykes this morning. On top of that, the income from the illegal operations controlled by DeLisa was down. Kirshstein expected an explosion from the mobster at any second.

"What is the percentage drop from the Mannheim Road book?" DeLisa asked.

"Thirteen percent this week," Kirschstein said. "Twenty-two percent since the first of the year."

"What about Cicero?"

Kirschstein consulted some figures on a computer printout. "Not too bad. The gambling is a point or two over last week, but still low for the year. The whores are in the toilet though. It's almost as if they've been on strike since December."

"It's that pimp Geno Allegretti," DeLisa said with a sneer. "Figures I got too much on my mind with this Senate Committee thing. I think me and Wally'll pay him a little visit tonight. How's the take on the South Side?"

There was a knock at the study door. The heavyset bodyguard, who was assigned outside Rachel's bedroom, stepped into the study. He waited until DeLisa acknowledged him.

"Your daughter and Mrs. Lupo are back from their walk."

"Good," DeLisa said with a faint smile.

"Mrs. Lupo said she wants to see you," the guard added. "I told her you was busy."

DeLisa looked down at the printouts and ledgers on his desk. "This is all bad news, Frank. Everybody thinks I'm through so they're either skimming or holding out on me. We can go over this stuff later." DeLisa stopped to check his desk clock. It was 11:45. "By then it'll be all over and everyone will know where I stand." DeLisa looked up at the bodyguard. "Go get Mrs. Lupo."

83

MARCH 7, 1994
11:47 A.M.

A sharp wind blew off Lake Michigan and high cirrus clouds hung in a deep blue sky. Maureen Taft, the political affairs reporter for the *Chicago Times-Herald,* stood in front of the Hyde Park Hotel. The wind caused her eyes to tear and her hair billowed behind her, but she stood her ground. She was waiting for the man she knew as Helmut Strahlman of the *Deutschland Bild Zeitung.* The man she had spent the night with.

When he'd left her that morning, she had been asleep. Awakening shortly after ten, she found no note nor anything else left behind to tell her how to get in touch with him. However, she was certain that he would call later. Then something about him began bothering her.

Last night, after Stanton had been ordered out of the office, Senator Banks had called an end to the interview that Helmut had been conducting. Banks was leaving the office, flanked by his bodyguards and Naomi Bowman, when Helmut said, "Herr Senator, perhaps before I leave Chicago you could give me the finish of the interview?"

"I'm sorry," Banks said, "but I leave for Washington the day after tomorrow. I really won't have the time."

"But I already have so much. If you would give to me perhaps the half an hour. Even fifteen minutes more, I would be so grateful."

Banks thought for a moment. "Okay, tomorrow at noon. The China Gate Restaurant in the Hyde Park Hotel. I can only spare you a few minutes."

"Danke, Herr Senator, *Danke."*

So Maureen knew where he was having lunch. Now she waited under the canopy of the Hyde Park Hotel, as a tall man wearing a black trench coat came around the corner and began walking toward the hotel entrance. "Commander Cole," Maureen called to him.

Cole stopped. "Hello, Maureen. You covering a story or just slumming?"

"I'm interviewing Senator Harvey Banks over lunch in the China Gate Restaurant." Of course, this was not absolutely true, but she was sure Banks would let her sit in on Helmut's interview, just as he'd done last night.

The policeman frowned. "I'm here to see the senator too. I didn't know there would be press around."

Maureen glanced away from Cole in time to see Helmut emerge from his car.

"Helmut."

He looked at her with a blank expression. It was as if he had never seen her before. Then he smiled. Snatching the ticket from the car hop, he crossed the sidewalk, took her in his arms and kissed her passionately.

She was conscious of the amused cop standing a few feet away. Cole was about to turn and continue into the hotel when Helmut released her. It took her a moment to catch her breath.

"Please wait, Commander."

Reluctantly, Cole stopped. "I have an appointment with the senator, Maureen, and I don't want to be late."

At that moment another car pulled up in front of the hotel. A middle-aged man, wearing a snap brim hat over close-cut blond hair got out and took a ticket from the car hop. As he crossed the sidewalk, Maureen marvelled at how much he resembled Helmut. However, Cole's impatience quickly made her forget him.

"Well, since we're all going to the same place we can ride up in the elevator together," she said stepping between the German reporter and the American cop. She took each of them by the arm.

The Hyde Park Hotel was a relic. More of an apartment house than an actual hotel, most of the building's tenants had lived there for years. The lobby was an antique monument to the past with Persian carpets, marble pillars and an immense staircase leading up from the main lobby to a glass-windowed restaurant, which provided a view of Lake Shore Drive.

Traffic through the lobby was light with the majority of those entering or leaving the hotel heading for the elevators on the east side of the building. There were four ornate brass, double-door elevators located there. Three were for hotel residents and their guests. The remaining one had a red and gold sign above it decorated with an ornate Chinese arch and the words, CHINA GATE RESTAURANT—EIGHTH FLOOR—NO OTHER STOPS.

Maureen, Helmut and Cole crossed to this elevator. There were two people also waiting to ride up to the restaurant. One was a well-built young black woman in jeans and the other was the man with the snap brim hat, whom Maureen thought resembled Helmut. Neither of them turned around.

"So, we're all going up to see the senator."

"I didn't know you would be lunching with us today, Maureen," Helmet said. "If I had, we could have driven here together. As it is, I want to take you to dinner tonight."

"I bet," she said with a fake pout. "You don't even know my phone number."

He recited the seven digits without hesitation.

She smiled. "You do know it. How sweet."

Cole attempted to disengage himself from the reporter, but she tightened her grip on his arm.

"Helmut, I want you to meet one of the toughest cops in Chicago. Detective Commander Larry Cole, Herr Helmut Strahlman, a reporter from Germany."

A slow smile spread across Helmut's face as he stepped forward and took the policeman's hand. "It is very pleasant to meet you, *Herr Kommandur.*"

The man in the snap brim hat turned and looked curiously at

Cole. The commander returned this gaze. The man quickly turned back to face front.

"Cops always draw curious stares in this town, Helmut," Maureen said. "I guess it goes with the territory."

84

They stepped off the elevator into a narrow corridor with walls painted enamel red and the woodwork accented with gold filigree in the shapes of Chinese characters. The black woman in jeans led the way followed by the man in the hat and, finally, Maureen, Helmut and Cole. Because of the narrow width of the corridor the reporter was forced to release one of her escorts' arms. Cole was granted his freedom and gratefully dropped to the rear.

At the end of the corridor they were forced to turn right and proceed a short distance to a reception desk, where a stunningly beautiful Oriental woman wearing a high-neck white dress with a split running from the top of her thigh all the way down to the hem, waited for them. Maureen caught Helmut leering and pinched him.

The receptionist flashed a dazzling smile. "Welcome to the China Gate Restaurant. How many in your party?"

She seated the black woman and the man in the snap brim hat separately before returning.

"We're with Senator Banks," Maureen said.

"Of course," the receptionist said. "He told me he was expecting more guests. Right this way."

The senator's table was in the center of one of three dining rooms. The table had enough space for ten, but only two people were seated there; the senator and Naomi Bowman. Seeing them approach, Banks stood up and, ignoring the reporters, said, "You must be Commander Cole."

"Yes, Senator," Cole responded.

"Miss Bowman and I have something important to discuss with you." Banks looked past Cole at Maureen and Helmut. "Something that I don't want disclosed to the press right now."

Before Maureen could comment, Helmut said, "Senator, I want only to ask you one or two more questions to complete the interview I started last night. I can wait until you conclude your business with the *kommandur.*"

Banks appeared momentarily uncertain before turning to Cole. "Commander, I hate to impose on you like this, but I would prefer disposing of my interview with Herr Strahlman first and then we can discuss our business over lunch."

"No problem, Senator," Cole said. "Is there someplace I could wait?"

The receptionist had remained at the table until the guests were seated. Now Banks said to her, "Kim, would you show the commander to the bar? Tell Mr. Fong that anything he wants goes on my tab."

The receptionist nodded. "Right this way, Commander."

"See you around, Maureen," Cole said, "and nice meeting you, Helmut."

When they sat down Banks said, "As you can see I don't have much time."

As Ernest Steiger pulled a notebook from his pocket, a white-jacketed waiter approached the table. "May I get something for your guests, Senator?"

Banks looked about to tell him no, but Ernest said quickly, "Perhaps we could have some tea and an appetizer, Herr Senator, since Maureen and I won't be staying long. In my country it is traditional for friends to break bread before parting. I've also heard that the Chinese food in America is very spicy. I would like to try a bit of it and perhaps share it with you and the ladies."

Banks looked about to protest but his political instincts took over and he said, "Give us the China Gate appetizer, Mr. Lee. I'm sure our German friend will find enough hot stuff on it to last him all the way back to Europe."

"*Wunderbar,* Herr Senator," Ernest crowed. "*Wunderbar.*"

Karl Steiger was seated at a table overlooking the lake. His waiter approached.

"A cocktail before lunch, sir?"

"A snifter of Remy Martin," Karl said.

Steiger opened the menu and made a brief show of studying it before looking over the top edge to see his son being escorted to the senator's table. The women and the policeman were still with Ernest. Steiger didn't like this.

He had requested this particular table from the receptionist, because it gave him an unobstructed view of Banks's table. He had never seen the senator in the flesh before, but he had watched him on television last night.

The waiter came with his drink.

"Would you like to order now, sir?"

"Give me a moment," Steiger said, studying the menu.

"Yes, sir." The waiter turned and walked away.

Steiger watched the receptionist escort the policeman from the table. Ernest and the woman sat down. Ernest pulled his left earlobe which signaled to Steiger that they didn't have much time.

The German reached into his right jacket pocket and pulled out two Kennedy half-dollars. He placed one on the table and held the other in his hand. The one he held was clipped to a wooden clothespin. He arranged the clothespin on the table in front of him so that the end with the coin affixed protruded over the edge. He removed a disposable lighter from his pocket and held the flame under the coin. He held the menu up in front of him as a shield to block anyone from seeing what he was doing.

The waiter came with their appetizer. To Ernest it looked like a meal for four. The food was on a lazy Susan as large in circumference as a manhole cover. Each dish was contained in its own section on the tray. There were spare ribs, fried shrimp, egg rolls, chicken wings and a boiled shrimp dish in a red sauce. The waiter set small white plates and forks in front of each of them, bowed and vanished.

"This looks delicious," Ernest said, referring to the boiled shrimp. "What is it called?"

Banks smiled. "It has a very difficult to pronounce Chinese name, but let me warn you, it's very hot."

"I must try some." Ernest began spooning the dish onto his plate. He speared a shrimp with his fork and took a bite. The taste was sensational, but the instant it touched his tongue he felt the sharp tangy aroma sear through his sinuses. He snatched up a glass of water and took a long pull.

The senator chuckled. "I told you it was hot."

"Do you eat this regularly?" Ernest said, feeling a slight numbness on the surface of his tongue.

"Every chance I get," Banks said.

Ernest scratched his chin and said, "Then we must all try some."

The timing was exquisite. Ernest gave the operational signal just as Steiger's waiter approached his table. Keeping the menu up, the German snapped off the lighter and pocketed it. He released the hot coin from the clothespin and dropped it beside the other one. The waiter reached the table just as Steiger got to his feet. "Which way is the men's room?"

"It is located in the entrance corridor, sir."

"Bring me another drink and when I get back maybe you could recommend something for lunch."

"I would be happy to, sir."

Steiger was about to turn away when he added, pointing at the table surface, "That money was there when I sat down. Must be a tip your last guest left."

The waiter's eyes widened in surprise when he saw the coins. As he reached for them, Steiger started across the room.

The scream tore through the restaurant. All eyes turned in the direction of the sound. Steiger's waiter jumped around holding his burned hand and spewing a torrent of Chinese. Two waiters rushed up to him followed by the receptionist in the Suzie Wong dress, who spoke sharply to the injured man. He became silent instantly, but continued to bounce from foot to foot holding his hand.

From across the room, the foursome at Banks's table looked on.

"What do you suppose that's all about?" Maureen asked.

Naomi watched, but maintained the same silence she had since the reporters arrived.

"Looks like that young waiter hurt his hand," Banks said.

The excitement over, the diners returned to their meals.

The senator placed the boiled shrimp on his plate along with ribs, eggs rolls and chicken. When the lazy Susan was rotated to Naomi and Maureen they also spooned some of the spicy shrimp onto their plates.

"Watch it, ladies," Banks said. "You saw what it did to Helmut."

Both of them nibbled at the hot shrimp, but it didn't appear to have the same reaction on them as it had on Helmut. The only thing they chased it with was hot tea.

Banks first ate a rib and half an egg roll. Finally, he picked up one of the boiled shrimps and popped it in his mouth.

Ernest stood up. "Excuse me, but I must use the men's room."

Banks merely nodded, while Maureen and Naomi continued to eat. The phony reporter walked casually toward the front of the restaurant without looking back.

85

MARCH 7, 1994
12:07 P.M.

At one time early in his police career, Larry Cole had found bars attractive. In fact, there were "cop" bars, which catered exclusively to off-duty policemen. In the old 19th District, where he had served as a rookie and broken in on the tactical team as Blackie Silvestri's partner, the local cop bar was called the Cell Block. It developed such a notorious reputation for rowdyness and frequent accidental shootings that the city revoked its liquor license. Since then Cole stayed away from bars. So it was that he was not enthused about being forced to wait for Senator Banks in the China Gate's cocktail lounge.

The bar itself was an oblong room across the corridor from the receptionist's station. The subdued lighting made it difficult to see until his eyes became adjusted. Then he was surprised to find it half full, mostly with solitary patrons hunched very seriously over their glasses.

Mr. Fong, an Asian of indeterminate age, nodded silently when Cole requested a glass of plain orange juice on the rocks. Seconds later a tall glass, filled to the brim, was placed on a cardboard coaster in front of the policeman. Fong stood by until Cole tasted the drink before bowing and turning to wait on another patron.

Easy listening music drifted through overhead speakers and, as there was nothing else for him to do, Cole sipped his juice and listened to Anita Baker croon a love ballad.

Despite over twenty years on the force, Cole had never gotten accustomed to waiting. He had been a disaster on surveillances and had once vehemently argued with a police academy instructor over the wisdom of waiting out a hostage taker. Now he wasn't particularly happy about cooling his heels while Banks jawed with the press. But he was certain that he was about to learn something very important about the mysterious deaths of Butcher and Cappeletti, as well as F.B.I. Agent Reggie Stanton. One look at Naomi Bowman's face told him that.

Over breakfast that morning, Lisa had reminded him how he had gotten pulled off the Seventy-ninth Street homicides fifteen years ago. As she did so, the events of the summer of 1979 came back to him.

The morning following the death of William McCoy, Sr., Cole was called into Chief Riseman's office. When he arrived, there were two men seated outside the chief's door. Cole instantly recognized them as feds. One wore horn-rimmed glasses and held a gray Homburg hat on his lap. Cole was unable to recall much about the other one except he was heavyset and sported a blond crew cut.

Riseman was not alone. The assistant deputy superintendent in charge of the Internal Affairs Division was present.

"Sit down, Larry," Riseman said. "We want to talk to you about one of your cases."

For the next thirty minutes Cole had been questioned about the Seventy-ninth Street murders, which Riseman had personally assigned him to investigate. Occasionally, Riseman and the I.A.D. deputy exchanged meaningful looks or merely nodded, but they made no comment until the then detective sergeant finished his report.

The I.A.D. deputy was the first to comment. "It'll never stand up in court. Everything you've got is circumstantial, Cole."

"Begging the deputy's pardon," Cole said, tightly, "but give me another day and I'll be able to do one of two things."

The two high-ranking cops waited.

"I'll either nail Reggie Stanton for the four homicides or clear him completely."

In the China Gate cocktail lounge fifteen years later, Larry Cole recalled that he never got the chance to do either one, because Riseman had taken him off the case. There had been no rationale given, but sergeants didn't argue with CPD division chiefs. At least not more than once.

Somehow Cole couldn't help but wonder now if the presence of the two feds seated outside Riseman's office that day had something to do with the decision to take him off the case. However, recent events made the picture come more sharply into focus. The F.B.I. was there then and Stanton was with the F.B.I. now, apparently engaged in some type of covert operations and dirty tricks unit. Perhaps what Banks and the scared-bloodless Naomi Bowman had to tell him would make it all clear.

Cole's musings were interrupted by the sound of the waiter's scream. He leaped off the bar stool and ran to the entrance leading back into the restaurant. He was able to see the senator and his party seated at their table looking in the direction of the commotion. As Cole glanced over at the injured waiter, who was talking animatedly to the receptionist, he noticed the German reporter pouring something into one of the dishes on the senator's table. Cole also noticed that the reporter seemed totally oblivious to what was going on across the dining room.

As there didn't appear to be any crime taking place, Cole was about to return to his seat when the big man, who had stared at Cole downstairs, walked past the bar on his way to the exit. Cole didn't give him another thought.

A few moments later, the leggy receptionist led the injured waiter into the bar. Curiously, Cole watched as she and Mr. Fong examined the injured man's hand. Then Fong turned and headed back down the bar. As he passed, Cole asked him, "What happened?"

Fong turned an inscrutable gaze on the policeman. "Customer in restaurant play joke on young waiter. Give him hot coin. Burn hand very bad. Maybe need go to hospital."

Cole got up and walked over to where the receptionist still stood at the end of the bar with the waiter. Over her shoulder Cole was able to see the injured hand. There was a bright red circle at the center of the palm and the tips of his index finger and thumb were starting to blister. Something about this bothered the policeman. It was a cruel prank, but Cole couldn't fathom the reason for such a senseless practical joke.

Cole looked up just as the German reporter walked past the cocktail lounge. He too was heading for the exit. Although Maureen Taft wasn't with the man called Helmut, Cole wondered if the interview was over. He was about to take a look for himself when another waiter rushed into the bar. Running up to the receptionist, who was still attending the injured man, this waiter began spewing a torrent of Chinese, but Cole did catch the name "Banks." Cole raced to the senator's table.

Banks was still alive, but just barely. Maureen Taft and Naomi

Bowman were dead. The senator was sweating profusely, his eyes were glazed over and his breathing came in short gasps.

"Come over here and help me!" Cole shouted to a heavyset man seated at a nearby table. Together they lifted Banks out of his chair and laid him down on the carpeted floor. Cole snatched off Banks's tie and unfastened his shirt collar. He was about to apply cardiopulmonary resuscitation when the receptionist rushed up with an oxygen bottle attached to a breathing mask. Without a word, she dropped to the floor and applied the mask to the senator's face. Cole began vigorously applying chest pressure, as she turned the oxygen tank on.

As he worked, Cole studied the senator's face. The eyes were devoid of life and he was not moving. The receptionist and the cop continued working until the paramedics arrived ten minutes later, but by that time Harvey Banks was dead.

Washington, D.C. **86**

MARCH 7, 1994
1:30 P.M.

F.B.I. Deputy Director William Connors opened his eyes and the cement floor beneath him tilted. His head spun and he was nauseous.

"Sit up and breathe deeply," said a voice nearby. "It will help you recover more quickly."

With an effort, Connors complied. After a few breaths, the disorientation and queasiness passed.

He was in a library. A library in what appeared to be a damp basement. Books lined every inch of three walls with the last wall constructed of barren bricks from which a metal faucet and a couple of deep wash tubs protruded. A dank odor hung in the air indicating that this place had been recently flooded.

"Are you feeling better?"

Connors focused his eyes on the slightly built black man standing a few feet away. The black man's expression indicated concern. Connors managed to nod his head, which caused a wave of dizziness to sweep over him.

"Would you care for some water?"

Connors managed a weak, "Yes," before closing his eyes again.

There came the sound of water rushing into a metal receptacle. Then there was a presence close to him.

"Here," the black man said.

When Connors attempted to lift his hands he discovered that he was bound. Any remaining vestiges of dizziness evaporated to be replaced by stark fear.

"Where am I?"

"Drink. It will make speech easier."

The black man held the cup to Connors's lips. The water was cold and his thirst nearly overpowering. He drank it all.

"Would you like some more?"

"No."

The black man turned and walked back to the sink.

"Where am I?" Connors demanded.

"You'll be told in good time."

"Who are you?"

The man reached the sink and, without turning around, rinsed the cup and placed it on a shelf. "Again, that will be revealed to you in time."

Connors's anger flared and he strained against the ropes. "Do you know who I am? Do you know that what you're doing is a capital offense?"

A familiar voice came from behind Connors, "He knows."

Although he couldn't see his shadow assassin, Connors said, "Stanton, what in the hell is going on?"

Reggie Stanton walked around in front of him. Usually the deputy director was capable of withstanding the shadow assassin's soul-chilling stare, but in his current situation this was impossible. Connors stared at the floor.

"Thanks for keeping an eye on him, professor," Stanton said. "I'll take it from here."

Without a word, the small black man walked from the room.

When they were alone, Connors said, "Kidnapping is a felony, Reggie."

"So is murder."

Connors shook his head. "I don't understand this. Have you gone insane?"

Stanton folded his arms across his chest and stared down at Connors. "No, I'm not insane. In fact, I'm starting to wise up for the first time in years."

"Kidnapping me doesn't seem very smart."

"Sending the Rattler to kill me wasn't very smart either."

Connors's head jerked up. He braved Stanton's stare. "What are you talking about? What has the Rattler got to do with any of this?"

Stanton shook his fingers at Connors. "You know you are really very good. You say that so convincingly that, if I didn't know better, I might believe you."

"I'm telling the truth, Reggie."

"No. The Rattler told me the truth before I killed him and tied his body to that beer keg. You promised him he could kill me years ago for what I did to him in Texas. He told me you called him yesterday and ordered him to hightail it to Washington. He must have barely beat me into town. But you saw him at your house last night. That's a place I've never been. I wonder why."

"C'mon, Reggie. This is crazy. You know you can't believe anything . . ."

The sound of a door opening behind him made Connors flinch. He attempted to look over his shoulder, but he was unable to see anything but a wall of books.

Stanton looked up, nodded and said, "Relax, Bill, I'll be right back so we can continue our little talk."

Left alone, Connors strained against the ropes. Escape was impossible. He tried to remember how he'd gotten here. He recalled the commotion in the restaurant, the Rattler's body tied to the beer keg falling into the hotel lobby and then . . .

There had been a searing flash of pain exploding in his head. Stanton had hit him. The deputy director tilted his head to the side. The area of his left temple felt tight. It was swollen. There was no pain, but simply a tingling sensation. He was injured, but not critically so. At least not yet. Being helpless in Stanton's hands meant that he was soon going to end up just like the Rattler. His prospects for survival looked bleak.

The house in which Deputy Director Connors was being held belonged to Professor Ronald Hakim. Hakim had earned a doctorate in sociology from Yale in the early sixties and taught at some of the most prestigious institutions of higher learning in the United States. During the sixties he'd been a civil rights activist, during the seventies a black militant. When the eighties dawned on the "Me" generation, Professor Hakim had been discouraged over the disintegration of the groups and organizations which had nurtured his Black Nationalist ideology, but did not dampen his ardor in the pursuit of the civil rights cause of his people. So he became an individual activist of the most intense variety.

Hakim was a letter writer, a learned contributor to leftist publications and a thorn in the side of conservative politicians. Classified a security risk, he was relegated to Connors's shadow section for elimination. Connors assigned Stanton to carry out the sanction. This saved the professor's life.

Professor Hakim was teaching sociology at Roosevelt University in Chicago. It was a simple matter for Reggie to drive downtown to place the professor under surveillance. The assassin managed to obtain a schedule of the professor's classes and had even considered taking one in order to get closer to the target. However, fate had intervened. A seminar, moderated by Hakim, was scheduled at the university. The subject: "Political Thought in the Twenty-First Century." The guest speaker was United States Senator Harvey Banks.

Stanton and Hakim became friends. When the professor took a teaching post at Howard University, they stayed in touch. It was to Hakim's house in the Washington, D.C. ghetto that Stanton had come that morning to pick up his daggers. He had also brought the kidnapped F.B.I. deputy director there.

Stanton climbed a rickety flight of wooden stairs to the first floor of the ramshackle frame house the professor rented. Books were everywhere: sitting on shelves, stacked on the floor and piled on furniture. Hakim was a bachelor, so the place was cluttered but clean. It was also drafty due to insufficient insulation and a substandard heating plant.

The assassin found the professor in the living room. The small man sat in front of an ancient, scarred, black and white television set. Stanton had never heard of the brand name Muntz the TV bore.

"What is it, professor?"

Hakim's eyes never left the small screen. "They have killed our brother in Chicago."

"Who are you talking about?" Stanton asked.

Hakim turned from the set and looked up at the sandy-haired black man towering over him. "They've killed Harvey Banks."

Stanton had to brace himself against a nearby table. "How?"

"They don't know. The senator was pronounced dead at twelve thirty Chicago time. There were two women having lunch with him. They too are dead, so it is obvious there was foul play. There was also a policeman there, but the media isn't saying much about him."

Stanton's face darkened and his eyes took on a look of terrible hatred. With an audible click his sleeve dagger slipped into his palm. He turned to go back to the basement.

"If you kill Connors you'll be making a mistake," Hakim said without moving from his seat.

Stanton kept going.

"We can use him to find out who killed our brother."

Stanton started down the stairs.

Hakim continued to stare at the television.

K arl Steiger drove the rented Mercedes north on Lake Shore Drive toward McCormick Place. Passing under the Thirty-first Street overpass, he pulled into the far right hand lane to take the entrance ramp to the I-55 extension. He glanced sideways at his son. Ernest had donned sunglasses, but there was no mistaking the self-satisfied smirk on his face. If Karl were a different type of man he would have mirrored Ernest's triumphant expression. But his up-bringing and the years in the assassin's business demanded caution.

They followed I-55 to the northbound lanes of the Dan Ryan Expressway. The traffic was sparse as they sped north. Finally, Karl broke the silence.

"That woman could have caused us problems."

"She did," Ernest said. "That cop being there was even more of a problem, but I handled them both fairly well."

His son's confidence angered him. "The operation could have failed simply because you couldn't keep your dick in your pants. When will you ever learn?"

Ernest smiled. "C'mon, Daddy, don't go working yourself up over nothing. They probably think the three of them died of food poisoning."

Karl turned to look at his son. "What do you mean *three?*"

Ernest shrugged. "I couldn't just reach over and pour the stuff on Banks's plate. That would have really been obvious. So I put it in the serving dish. All of them ate some."

Karl switched on the radio. Classical music filled the car. Karl punched the Seek button until he came to a newscast. They listened while the announcer concluded a report about the president planning to introduce a new domestic spending bill.

"See," Ernest said, "there's nothing to worry about."

"Be quiet," Karl snapped.

On cue the radio announcer said, *"And repeating our top story of the hour, Senator Harvey Banks of Illinois has been assassinated in Chicago. According to police reports, the senator was apparently poisoned while eating lunch at the China Gate Restaurant inside the Hyde Park Hotel on Chicago's southside. Also killed, after eating from the same poisoned dish the senator consumed, were* Chicago Times-Herald *reporter Maureen Taft and Miss Naomi Bowman, who was a member of the senator's staff. The police are currently searching for a man who identified himself as Helmut Strahlman, a German reporter visiting the United States. Helmut Strahlman is described as a white male, thirty to thirty-five years of age, blond hair, blue eyes and a fair complexion. He is approximately six feet tall and weighs one hundred sixty-five pounds. When last seen he was wearing a . . ."*

The announcer provided an exact description of Ernest's clothing.

Ernest stared in silent shock at the car radio. He was actually afraid to look at his father.

"If you had only given the poison to the senator they would have had to perform an autopsy to determine the cause of death," Karl said, his voice trembling as he fought to control his fury. "Now with three dead bodies, even the dumbest policeman would surmise they weren't having an epidemic of heart attacks. Then we have to worry about the cop who was there."

"Why?" Ernest said in a weak voice.

"In the lobby of the hotel your lady friend introduced him as a detective commander on the Chicago Police Department."

"That's right. His name was Cole."

"Larry Cole," Karl said. "I took a good look at him before we boarded the elevator and I recognized the type. He probably has the persistence of a pit bull and the guts of a charging rhino. He's on top of this thing, which means he'll have undoubtedly put look outs for you and maybe even me at the airports."

"I don't understand, Daddy. Why you?"

"Just a guess. I walked past him on the way out. I gave the waiter the hot coin. He noticed me when I entered the restaurant. Those are too many coincidences for a good cop to ignore. He'll put it together quick enough. Whereas a few minutes ago I figured we had at least a few hours before any alarm would be given, now I find that we are already being hunted."

"We'll get out of this," Ernest said with more confidence than he felt.

"That remains to be seen," Karl said, glancing up at the rearview mirror. "We are being followed."

Ernest spun around to look out the back window. A Ford sedan with two men in the front seat was tailing them about five car lengths back.

"They've been there since we left Lake Shore Drive," Karl said. "If they were cops it would be all over by now."

"Do you think our client has anything to do with this?"

"Probably. There is no honor left in the world. But there had better be more than just those two."

Ernest smiled. This was the kind of talk he liked. "What kind of hardware do we have?"

"The guns are under your seat."

Ernest reached down and felt around until he touched a perforated metal tube. Grasping it, he pulled it from beneath the seat.

"A Sterling submachine gun," Ernest said. "I haven't seen one of these in years." He removed the magazine and checked its thirty-round capacity.

"There are two of them," Karl said. "They will help us put a severe dent in any plans our friends back there have."

Ernest pulled the second weapon from beneath the seat.

They were traveling north on the Kennedy Expressway approaching Addison. They were a half hour away from the airport, which Karl had already decided to bypass in favor of driving straight to Milwaukee. So far their tail had done no more than follow them.

Karl was driving in the second lane from the east guardrail on an expressway that ran four stories above city streets. The traffic was moderate and the right lane reserved for slower cars and trucks. Now a Mack truck pulling a trailer occupied that lane. Up until now this truck had been keeping pace with the tail car. Then, as they passed Addison, the truck increased its speed and pulled ahead of the tail car. The Ford dropped back and the truck changed lanes to pull in behind the Mercedes.

With mounting horror, Karl watched the lane change. He floored the Mercedes, but a white van slowed in front of them forcing Karl to brake. Before he could maneuver around the white van, the truck behind them accelerated and slammed into the back of the Mercedes.

The impact knocked the Steigers' car forward to slam into the white van. The van driver hit its brakes and the Mercedes slammed into it again. The vehicles were still moving when the Mack truck struck the Mercedes again; however, this time with greater force. The van again slowed and the Mercedes became sandwiched between the two heavier vehicles.

Inside the Mercedes Karl and Ernest bounced off the dashboard and doors. Karl twisted the steering wheel in an attempt to escape the trap, but he no longer had control of the car. Now the Mack truck maintained contact with their rear bumper. The van in front accelerated away as the Mack truck began shoving the Mercedes toward the guardrail separating the expressway from the street forty feet below. The truck driver's obvious intention was to shove them through the guardrail to their deaths.

Karl thought furiously, but Ernest was quicker. He slammed his fist down on the button operating the sun roof. When the panel slid back, he jumped up through it with the side-loading machine gun in his hands. He sighted over the mammoth grill of the truck at the windshield. He could see the driver's silhouette through the glare off the glass. Ernest fired a burst into the truck cab and watched it explode in a red haze.

The truck's speed dropped and it slipped away from the damaged Mercedes. The huge vehicle began drifting into the right hand lane and the trailer swayed behind it. As Ernest looked on, the truck cab struck the guardrail, broke through it and slipped over the edge of the expressway. The trailer skidded across three traffic lanes sweeping cars out of the way as if they were toys. Traffic behind them came to a screeching halt. Then, with the truck cab dangling face down over the street below, the trailer stopped.

Karl managed to bring the Mercedes back under control. He was about to accelerate away when the white van sideswiped them. Ernest was thrown back into the car when Karl skidded to a stop. The side door of the van slid open and a man, brandishing an Uzi, leaped out. He sprayed the driver's side of the Mercedes just as Ernest popped back up through the sun roof and hit him with a burst of rounds. The Uzi wielder was thrown back into the white van.

The van driver leaped from the passenger compartment brandishing an automatic pistol. Before he got off a shot, Ernest stitched him with bullets.

Traffic on both sides of the Kennedy Expressway came to a dead halt. At any moment the police would show up in force. Ernest dropped back into the Mercedes and turned to his father. Karl's eyes were closed and his clothing was covered with blood. Ernest managed to gasp an anguished, "Daddy?"

Washington, D.C.   # 88

MARCH 7, 1994
2:15 P.M.

A tense conference was taking place in the Washington, D.C. office of the F.B.I. The agent-in-charge had been apprised of the disappearance of Deputy Director Connors by his three contrite agents and he was not happy.

"Why did all of you have to go down to the lobby when the body smashed through that window?" the agent-in-charge demanded.

The cynical agent served as spokesman for the group. He shrugged. "We didn't know what we were dealing with, sir."

"Well, we do know now, don't we?"

The three of them refused to look at their boss.

"I'm going to have to call the director and tell him. You know the word will go around that we screwed this up on purpose."

The agents exchanged glances. They had already figured that this would happen. They didn't think it would lead to any formal charges of negligence, but anything was possible.

The agent-in-charge was about to pick up the phone to call the F.B.I. director, but it rang before he could touch it.

"Yes?"

"It's Deputy Director Connors for you on line one," the switchboard operator said.

"Are you tracing the call?"

"No. Should I be?"

"Yes. The man's been kidnapped."

"Nobody told me. I'll start the trace right away."

Waiting a tick, the agent-in-charge punched the flashing button above line one. "Bill, are you alright?"

"I'm fine. How are you?"

The agent-in-charge looked up at his three subordinates. They were beginning to look more like Moe, Larry and Curly. "When my men lost you at the Vista Hotel they suspected foul play."

Connors laughed. *"They had their hands full with that body, so me and my asset got the hell out of there. We went someplace where we could talk things over without all that confusion going on around us. That place was a madhouse this morning."*

"So I heard." The agent-in-charge began considering how fortunate the Boise, Idaho, office would be to get three men of the caliber of the agents standing in front of him.

"But the reason I called you was because of this Harvey Banks thing out in Chicago."

"Yeah, it's all over the news. Somebody poisoned him."

"So I heard. I think I've got someone in my section who can give the Chicago cops a hand in solving it. The agent's name is Reggie Stanton. Of course, he'll be working in an unofficial, advisory-only capacity."

The D.C. agent-in-charge frowned. It wasn't like Connors to be so helpful. In fact, it was very unlike him.

"What I'd like you to do is call our Chicago office and have them act as liaison between my man and the Chicago locals. I'd also like you to arrange priority transportation for Stanton by Air Force jet. Can you take care of that?"

"Yes, sir," the agent-in-charge said. Having others do the legwork for him was definitely a Connors trait.

"Good. And look, I'm sorry about your men being inconvenienced. In the long run, I really didn't need them at all. Give them my regards."

"I will."

"Stanton will be in your office within the hour. I'm sure all the arrangements will be completed by then."

"Yes, sir," the agent-in-charge said.

Connors hung up.

"Is he alright?" the cynical agent asked.

"He's fine. In fact, never better. He's his usual charming self. Didn't even ask about the homicide. Did the prints come back on that body yet?"

"No, sir," the skinny agent said.

"Okay, you guys can go and this time count yourselves lucky. If something had happened to Connors, all of our asses would be in a sling."

As the three agents filed out of the office the agent-in-charge reached for the phone. Again it rang before he could touch it.

"Yes?"

The operator said, *"We managed to trace the deputy director's call."*

"And?"

"He's in a house down on First and F Streets. Doesn't seem like the type of neighborhood he usually hangs out in."

"Maybe he's slumming. Forget the trace and get me Dave Franklin in Chicago."

MARCH 7, 1994
2:45 P.M.

W hat have they done to this place?" DeLisa said, scowling through the windshield of the Lincoln out at Taylor Street. "It looks like fucking Old Town." He momentarily forgot that Rachel and Mrs. Lupo were in the car with him.

All of them were seated in front with DeLisa behind the wheel, Rachel in the middle and Mrs. Lupo by the passenger side door. When Rachel had learned that her father was driving them to pick up some things from Mrs. Lupo's apartment, her face had fallen and she had plummeted into a sullen mood. DeLisa had ordered the seating arrangements. Once inside the car Rachel had slid as far away from her father as possible.

"They call it progress," Mrs. Lupo said. "It is the way of things."

"But they've ruined it," DeLisa wailed. "There's no flavor anymore. Like right there," he pointed to a vacant lot slated for redevelopment, "used to be Constantine's Candy Store. You could buy candy a penny a piece. Jaw breakers, kisses, orange slices, the works. Hell, for a quarter you could get a stomach ache that wouldn't quit for a week. And over there was Elzy's Grocery. Even baked his own bread. What the hell is it now?"

"That's a delicatessen. It's still owned by the Elzy family," Mrs. Lupo said.

"Oh." DeLisa's voice held a note of suspicion. "I thought Demetrio Elzy's kid was killed during World War II. I remember because he always used to cry when my mother brought me around. His kid's name was Tony too."

Mrs. Lupo raised her hands and said with a shrug, "I can't tell you about all of that, Antonio, but the Elzys run the delicatessen now."

"Sure you can," DeLisa said in a demanding voice. "Mama Mancini was always tight with old Demetrio. He had dinner at her house at least once a week for years."

"I didn't say he didn't," she said, developing an edge in her voice to counter his. "But he had more relatives than that son killed during the war."

"Yeah," DeLisa said. "Young Tony Elzy got his in North Africa."

Mrs. Lupo turned and leaned around Rachel to look at him. "I thought it was Normandy?"

A weak smiled played at the corners of his mouth. He nodded. "Yeah, it was Normandy. Must've slipped my mind."

Mrs. Lupo leaned back in her seat. She looked confident and composed; however, Judy Daniels's heart was racing at well over a hundred beats per minute. On top of that, Normandy had been only a guess. What was that they said about a good defense?

DeLisa turned the car off of Taylor onto the street where the apartments over Paoletti's Drug Store were located. He stopped the car when he saw two police cars parked in front of the building. One was a plainclothes detective car, the other a marked unit. An officer sat in the front seat of the marked car. The unmarked car was empty.

"So, what's going on here?" DeLisa said.

"I don't know," Mrs. Lupo responded.

Rachel didn't look up.

DeLisa scanned the street. "Isn't that your address?"

"Yes," she said. "I live right over the drug store. I could go and see what happened. Someone in the building could have been hurt."

"No, you sit tight. We're not going anywhere until those cops clear out."

The car radio was playing soft blues, but DeLisa had it turned so low none of them could hear it. Now, as they settled in to wait, DeLisa reached over and turned it up.

They call it Windy City,
'Cause the wind there has no pity,
Like a freight train roarin' toward you,
Like its whistle blowin' through you,
Through your heart, through your heart,
through your heart.

In silence, the three passengers of the Lincoln listened to the blues singer finish wailing about life on the tough streets of Chicago. Then the news came on.

The top story was about Senator Harvey Banks being poisoned. When Judy heard this, she felt a chill. She remembered the small talk between Hagar and Sam Sykes that morning. Something about, "Mr. D. having a heavy set going down in Hyde Park. . . ."

The next news item got her heart pounding at a trip-hammer pace again. *"Chicago Police Detective Manfred Sherlock was shot while apprehending a burglary suspect on West Taylor Street this morning. The suspect, who has not been identified by police, was killed during a heated exchange of gunfire."*

Judy couldn't see DeLisa's face, but his knuckles were bone-white where his hands tightly gripped the steering wheel. He knew something that she didn't. In turn, she knew that Manny had been working with Sergeant Silvestri. This undercover operation was starting to go sour.

A thin man with the emaciated, round-shouldered shuffle of the narcotics addict rounded the corner off Taylor Street and walked past the Lincoln. DeLisa spotted him and blew the horn before opening the door and stepping to the street. "Denny," DeLisa called. "Denny Bagnola."

The junkie stopped and squinted back at DeLisa. He took a couple of steps back toward the Lincoln before recognition dawned and his face split into a lopsided grin. He came back to the car, moving around to DeLisa's side.

The two men embraced.

"How've you been, Denny?" DeLisa said with more warmth than Judy had ever heard him express to anyone but Rachel before.

"Okay, Mr. DeLisa," the junkie sniffled. "You looking good." Denny looked down inside the Lincoln. "How you ladies doing?"

Rachel didn't answer or look up. Judy merely smiled. DeLisa got back inside the car and rolled the window down.

"So how's it going, Denny? You staying out of trouble?"

"You know I been straight since the last time I got out of the joint, Mr. D. I wouldn't lie to you."

"I know you wouldn't, Denny. Hey, what's with all the cop activity across the street?"

The junkie turned around, wiped his nose with the sleeve of his two-sizes-too-big overcoat and said, "Somebody got caught breaking into Mrs. Lupo's apartment this morning. Cop was supposedly waiting inside and wasted the guy. I heard a cop got shot, but he ain't dead."

DeLisa turned to stare past Rachel at Judy. "So you know Mrs. Lupo, right, Denny?"

"Yeah," the junkie said, bending down to look through DeLisa's open window. "I know her. She's out of town on some trip. That burglar must have been crazy trying a job down here. Hell, Mrs. Lupo related to Mama Mancini."

DeLisa's eyes bore into Judy. Rachel was even staring curiously at her new guardian.

"Tell me, Denny," DeLisa asked in a voice that came out sounding like the snarl of a wild animal, "would you know Mrs. Lupo if you saw her?"

"Sure, Mr. D. I'd know her."

"Is this her?"

Again, the junkie looked inside the car. "This a joke or something, Mr. D?"

"No joke. Is this Mrs. Lupo?"

"Naw. But she looks a lot like her. Like maybe they could be sisters."

"Thanks, Denny," DeLisa said, without taking his eyes off Judy. He shut the window.

Judy reached for her door handle. She felt the muzzle of a gun pressed against her temple. She froze.

"Papa, what are you doing?" Rachel shouted.

"Shut up, Rachel. This lady has a lot of explaining to do. Don't you, dear?" To emphasize his words he viciously shoved the gun barrel into the side of Judy's head. However, DeLisa was in an awkward position, because he had to reach around Rachel to point the gun. The girl's position bought Judy a few extra moments.

Frantically, Judy looked across the street at the police car. The cop inside had his head down, as he appeared to be writing something. He had not once looked in their direction.

DeLisa swung the gun over his daughter's head and stuck it in Judy's stomach. His forearm pinned Rachel in her seat and forced him into an awkward driving position.

"Just one move, bitch, and I'm going to perform a lead hysterectomy on you." He put the car in gear.

"Papa, stop this," Rachel cried. "Just let her go."

He pulled from the curb and drove slowly down the street. Judy's hopes for an immediate rescue were dashed as the police car was left behind. But she had already made up her mind that she wasn't going to die without a fight.

Slowly, DeLisa drove north. Rachel began crying. Judy decided that if he tried to pull into an alley or anywhere off the street, she would first attempt to knock his gun away before opening the door and making a run for it.

The Lincoln reached the Eisenhower Expressway. DeLisa checked the traffic before turning right. They were traveling east onto the University of Illinois at Chicago campus.

Judy checked her captor's face. What she saw was terrifying with meanness and cruelty amplified in his hard eyes. However, there was also confusion present. Tuxedo Tony was lost.

"Papa, please let her go," Rachel pleaded. "I don't want to see anyone else hurt. This isn't right."

"I told you to shut up," DeLisa said, as he stopped for a red light. "What I'm doing is no concern of yours."

"It does concern me, Papa. This is my life too."

The light turned green. A car pulled up behind the Lincoln and when DeLisa didn't move, the driver blew his horn. DeLisa looked into the rearview mirror as the horn sounded again.

"Shut the fuck up, asshole," he said to the horn blower. He studied the intersection in front of him.

"I can't let you do this," Rachel said. "I can't let you do anything to Mrs. Lupo, Papa."

"Rachel, I told you—"

At that instant his daughter grabbed his gun arm and jerked it toward the ceiling. Startled, DeLisa fired a round. The bullet zipped past Judy's face, the sound deafening her left ear as the lead projectile shattered the passenger-side window beside her head.

Daughter and father struggled for the gun, but neither of them had the leverage to gain an advantage in the confining front seat. DeLisa's foot slipped off the brake and hit the gas pedal. The big car rocketed across the intersection, bounced over the curb and crashed into a concrete upright over the expressway.

They were all thrown forward. Judy and Rachel struck the padded dashboard. DeLisa smashed his face against the steering wheel. Blood spurted from the bridge of his nose down over his face. He was barely conscious, but he still held the gun.

Judy hit the door release button and jumped out. Rachel leaped out after her. On the street the undercover police officer paused only a moment to get her bearings before sprinting toward the Congress Line El station at the center of the expressway overpass. Rachel followed her.

Judy found that running was difficult in the orthopedic shoes of her Angelina Lupo disguise. She stopped, quickly reached down and snatched them off. Carrying them in her hand, she ran barefoot into the station.

Inside the station Rachel caught up with her. Judy spun toward the young girl, brandishing one of her shoes like a club.

"Please take me with you," Rachel yelled. "I've got to get away from him."

"Let's go," Judy said, leading the way across the station to the fare collector's booth.

A sour-faced woman occupied the booth.

"Police business," Judy shouted, as she bounded over the turnstile.

"I need to see some ID," the woman demanded.

Judy stopped. "I haven't got time right now, but I want you to hit the alarm bell and get me some help here."

The woman gave Judy an outraged look. "Until you show me a badge, I'm not doing anything."

Judy wasted no more time. She turned to find Rachel still standing on the other side of the turnstile. She looked past her out the station window to see DeLisa, bleeding but still holding the gun, staggering toward the station entrance.

"Rachel, jump now," Judy yelled. "Your father's behind you."

Without hesitation, Rachel bounded over the barrier.

As the two women ran down onto the platform, DeLisa staggered into the office. When the fare taker saw him and the gun, she hit the alarm button.

90

MARCH 7, 1994
3:32 P.M.

Larry Cole stood over Manny Sherlock's hospital bed. Tubes ran to bottles and monitors seemingly from every part of the young detective's body. Manny's eyes were closed and his usually pale face was as white as a sheet. Sitting on the other side of the bed, with her hand resting over the injured policeman's, was Manny's wife Lauren. They had met while Manny was working a case for Cole. At the wedding, Cole had given the bride away.

She looked up at the commander with pleading eyes. She wanted him to say it would be okay. That in the morning it would all be over and Manny could get up and walk out of here. Cole couldn't tell her that. At least not right now.

By rights Detective Manfred Wolfgang Sherlock should have been dead. The bullets of Tuxedo Tony DeLisa's bodyguard had all struck in vital areas. The two in the chest would have pierced his heart if Manny hadn't been wearing a bullet proof vest. The other two had struck outside the vest-protected area. Both had nicked arteries; one in his left leg and the other in his neck. Had the shooting not taken place so close to a trauma center, Manny would have bled to death in the ambulance.

The doctor, who had talked to Cole, was optimistic but guarded about Manny's chances of recovering. "We've managed to stop the bleeding and he's strong, but he's lost a great deal of blood. We've almost had to supply his body with all new blood, because at one point he was pumping it out as fast as we were pumping it in. We're keeping a close watch on him through the night and hope that his vital signs start to improve."

Blackie Silvestri and Lou Bronson stood against the far wall of the private hospital room. Since Cole had entered, neither of them had looked in his direction. Now the commander turned to face them.

"Blackie," Cole whispered, nodding toward the door.

As if he was walking to the gallows, the sergeant pushed off the wall and followed Cole from the room.

Cole led the way down the corridor. Visiting hours were beginning. They passed individuals and couples wearing hopeful but strained expressions as they carried plants and flowers as gifts for patients.

In silence the two policemen walked past the nurse's station, which was manned by a lone, middle-aged woman. Two doors past the nurse's station was a door marked LINEN. Cole walked inside and Blackie followed.

The room was narrow. Shelves stretching from the floor to the ceiling were stacked with folded sheets, pillow cases and blankets. There was the aroma of fresh linen and starch.

"Okay," Blackie shrugged, "I fucked up."

Cole said nothing.

"I guess I screwed up pretty bad, huh?"

Cole made no reply.

"But it wasn't because I just wanted to do things my way, Lar . . ." He swallowed the first name and quickly corrected it to, "I

mean, uh, Commander. I figured you was too close to this thing to
see it as clearly as I could. I mean, you haven't seen how good Judy
is, boss. Last night I couldn't believe it when she made herself up in
the disguise of this little Italian lady from Taylor Street."

Blackie's voice rose in excitement, but Cole's solemn expression
did not change.

"You know I came off the west side, boss. I understand people
like DeLisa. He'd never hurt Judy as long as he thought she was
Mrs. Lupo. In fact, Mama Mancini, you know the lady who runs
the pizzeria, said that in disguise Judy looks just like Tuxedo Tony's
mother."

Still Cole said nothing.

Blackie plunged his hands in his pockets. "So I screwed up. It's
my fault. If I had done what you said, Manny wouldn't have been
shot. If that kid doesn't make it I'll never forgive myself. As it is I'm
going to have a hard time getting over what I did to you. So I de-
serve what I got coming. A suspension, getting dumped out of the
Detective Division, whatever. I got enough time in to retire and I
wouldn't blame you if you never spoke to me again. I wanted to stay
a few more years, but if you don't want me around anymore I'll understand. I just want you to know one thing. I would never do anything to intentionally hurt you or anyone on this job. You people
are like brothers and sisters. . . . No, you *are* my brothers and sisters."

Blackie's voice tightened. This had no visible effect on Cole.

There was a knock at the door. Cole stepped around Blackie and
opened it. Lou Bronson stood out in the hall.

"Chief Govich just called, Commander. He wants you to call
him right away."

Without looking back at Blackie, Cole walked away from the
linen closet.

Bronson looked in at the sergeant. "How's it going?"

"It's not," Blackie said, glumly. "He hasn't said a word. It's
driving me crazy. Any change with Manny?"

"Nope."

"Jesus, what a mess," Blackie said, smacking his forehead so
hard it appeared he was trying to knock himself unconscious.

Cole came back down the hall. He was solemn, but something about him had changed. He motioned Blackie and Bronson back inside the linen closet.

"We might have gotten a break on the senator's murder. It looks like DeLisa's in this thing up to his eyeballs. An hour or so ago there was a shoot out on the Kennedy Expressway. Three men, all members of DeLisa's organization, are dead. The shooter, according to witnesses, used a machine gun fired from the sun roof of a Mercedes. He fits the description of my German reporter from the restaurant. There's not much on the driver of the Mercedes, but I bet he's probably the same guy who set up the diversion in the restaurant. Witnesses say he was wounded in the exchange of gunfire."

"That sounds like a DeLisa move," Bronson said. "Pay a couple of hit men to do a job and then try to do a job on them."

Cole nodded. "Well, we've got the airports, train stations and bus depots covered. The Mercedes was riddled with bullets and damaged from a collision with a truck, so it shouldn't be hard to find. We can check on Manny later. Let's go."

Cole walked out with Bronson right behind him. Blackie remained in the narrow room. The door closed and then swung open again. Cole's head popped in.

"C'mon, Blackie. We don't have all day."

"Yes, sir," Blackie said, leaping for the door.

Cole didn't move. He fixed Blackie with a hard stare. "And from now on you follow my orders to the letter. Understood?"

Blackie's head bobbed up and down. "I won't even take a crap without asking permission."

"You know," Cole said, as Blackie followed him down the corridor, "that's always been your problem. You take everything to extremes."

91

Tuxedo Tony DeLisa had learned long ago to ignore pain. Giving into it was a sign of weakness and he hated weakness in any form. So it was that despite a blinding headache and double vision, he pursued Rachel and the imposter, the woman who had impersonated Angelina Lupo, into the Congress Line El Station.

He wiped blood from his face as he staggered toward the fare booth. He saw Rachel jump over the turnstile. He made it to the fare booth, but was forced to brace himself against the wall or he would have collapsed.

The woman inside the booth yelled something at him. He couldn't understand what she was saying, nor did he care. He forced himself off the wall and into the turnstile gate. The restraining bar would not rotate. He tried to force his way through, but found this to be impossible.

"Let me in," he attempted to shout at the woman in the booth, but his voice came out as little more than a croak.

The woman stared through the wire-mesh grill at him. "You'll have to pay your fare just like everybody else," she said in a stern voice.

DeLisa swung his gun up and jammed the barrel against the grill. "Let . . . me . . . through."

Her hand slammed down on the release lever.

He was forced to negotiate two steep flights of steps before he reached the platform. He clutched the center railing to keep himself from falling as he stumbled down the stairs. As he neared the bottom, he could hear the roar of a train approaching the station. He increased his speed as best he could.

The inbound Loop train roared into the station. He scanned the platform for his daughter and the impostor. There was no one there. That meant they had to have boarded the four-car train. He scrambled down the platform to the last car. He barely made it, as the doors snapped shut an instant after he stepped inside.

All of the passengers were black. A few stared at him quizzically, the rest ignored him. The stares were quickly averted as soon as they noticed the gun. No one moved. Rachel and the impostor were not in the car.

The train lurched forward. DeLisa lost his balance, but managed to sit down in one of the seats before he fell to the floor. His head felt as if it had grown two sizes larger and blood was again running down his face. He searched his pockets for a handkerchief, found one and applied it to the wound. It turned from white to red immediately.

He held the cloth against the bridge of his nose and closed his eyes. He took deep, rapid breaths. The anger inside him simmered. He liked it like this. It would give him the strength he needed to do what he had to do.

He opened his eyes and looked around the car. A couple of passengers had been staring at him. Now they quickly looked away. No one made any attempt to approach him.

DeLisa forced himself to stand. He threw the blood-soaked handkerchief to the floor and staggered toward the door connecting this car with the next. They had gotten on this train. There had been no place else for them to go. So he would search it until he found them. Then he would teach each of them a lesson. Rachel would be punished for disobeying him; the impostor for deceiving him. Of course, the impostor would not survive the encounter.

92

Judy Daniels and Rachel DeLisa had waited anxiously on the deserted platform, praying for a train to come and speed them away before Tuxedo Tony found them. As they jumped into the second car, they saw him run for the last car and make it on board before the doors closed. Now they were trapped on an El train that would not stop again until they reached the Loop.

"C'mon," Judy yelled, pulling Rachel through the empty car.

The train was rolling as they passed from the second car into the first. As they stepped inside they saw a young conductor, who operated the doors and called out the stops. Judy considered approaching him for help, but thought better of it. If he was anything like the woman back at the station fare booth, all she would be doing was wasting precious time and endangering another life.

Judy, still carrying her shoes, walked to one of the bench seats facing the rear of the car and sat down. After hesitating a moment, Rachel sat down beside her.

"I saw Papa get on," Rachel said, staring through the rear door of the car. "Shouldn't we try to get off before he finds us?"

"We can't get off. Look," Judy said, pointing out the window.

The train was passing high over the Chicago River. Jumping would be a rather efficient way of committing suicide.

"But we can't just stay here. He'll find us."

There were only two other passengers in their car. A teenage boy in a Chicago Bulls jacket whose ears were plugged into the headset of a Walkman, and an elderly woman, who was dozing with her arms wrapped around a shopping bag. The conductor had taken a seat beneath his post with his back to the two fugitives. "He won't find us," Judy said. "If you do exactly what I say." "What do you want me to do?" "Just sit still."

93

MARCH 7, 1994
3:40 P.M.

DeLisa moved carefully through the third car. There were more people here than in the last car. He kept the gun down at his side, so few of the passengers noticed him. There was no sign of Rachel or the impostor.

He opened the connecting door to cross to the second car. As he stepped outside, the train lurched and he lost his balance. He grabbed for one of the chains serving as the only barrier preventing someone from falling between the cars. He almost dropped the gun, which would have plunged into the river far below. But he managed to hold onto both the chain and the gun. He righted himself and entered the car.

The emptiness of the second car yawned back at him. He felt a momentary surge of panic. There was no way they could have gotten off the train. So that meant they had to be in the lead car. He checked the automatic and walked quickly to the connecting door. Anger fed the adrenaline pumping into his system erasing the pain in his head and making him forget about his still bleeding head wound.

He crossed the barrier between the two cars without incident. He entered the lead car and stopped. Carefully, he scanned the interior. There were two males: the conductor, who took one look at DeLisa's gun and froze and a young black kid, who was lost in the sound blaring through his head from the headphones he wore. The other three occupants of the El train car were females. DeLisa frowned as he studied them. The confusion was evident on his face. Rachel and the impostor were not there.

Two of the women were seated on a bench together. They both appeared to be asleep. They were elderly; at least they looked older than DeLisa. One of them had her arms around a shopping bag and the other had her head resting on the shopping bag holder's shoulder. DeLisa studied the third woman in the car. She was younger than the other two. Much younger. Her hair was short and dark, but he was unable to see much of her face, as her chin rested in her palm with her fingers splayed across her cheek. She was staring out the window. She was also a stranger.

A knot of despair formed in the mobster's gut. He couldn't figure how he could have lost them.

"Hey, man, what's with the gun?" the conductor said, nervously.

"Shut up," DeLisa hissed.

One of the sleeping women stirred. It was the one whose head was on the other's shoulder. Her eyes opened momentarily and flicked in his direction, before she closed them again. But in that instant an incongruous recognition jolted him. There had been something familiar about this woman's gaze. Something damnably familiar. He started toward her.

The train decelerated as it pulled into a Loop station. The woman he was approaching sat up, but kept her head down. Ten people boarded the train at the Loop stop. Three of them got between DeLisa and the woman. Raising his gun, he shoved and swatted them out of the way. The conductor, who had opened the train doors when they pulled in, bolted from the car. The doors stayed open. DeLisa saw the old woman heading for the exit at the other end of the car. It was at this instant that he noticed that she was wearing designer jeans and tan boots exactly like Rachel's.

"Stop, Rachel," he shouted.

Another voice yelled, "Run. He's spotted you."

Rachel was wearing some of the facial makeup Judy Daniels had used to implement her disguise as Angelina Lupo. The latex strips that substituted for wrinkles across the forehead and under the eyes, had enough adhesive left to stick to Rachel's skin and change her appearance. To supplement the disguise Judy had given her the cheap beige raincoat she had worn and taken Rachel's suede jacket. The scarf Rachel had worn around her neck was transferred to her head. At the hands of Judy Daniels, the Mistress of Disguise/High Priestess of Mayhem, the transformation had taken seconds. If Rachel hadn't looked up at her father, the deception would have been successful.

DeLisa was concentrating so intensely on his daughter he forgot about the younger woman. Crossing the car, he was slammed with a body block. He was knocked backwards onto a bench. He went down, but he was agile and got back to his feet quickly. The young woman had thrown the block.

Judy leaped to her feet after throwing the block and raced for the door, but DeLisa was quicker. He caught her by the arm and yanked her back into the car.

"You're not going anywhere, Mrs. Lupo."

"Let me go." Judy began struggling, but he silenced her by jamming the muzzle of his gun against her head.

Some of the passengers who had boarded at the Loop station saw his gun and quickly left the car; however, far too many remained. He put his arm around the hostage's waist and backed toward the motorman's cab. He kept the gun against her head as he shouted, "Okay, everybody off."

The few riders remaining needed little additional coaxing, but four Hispanic lads sporting bright gang colors stared a challenge back at DeLisa. He fired a bullet into the ceiling of the car. The gang members were gone in an instant.

The gunshot brought the motorman out of his cab. Before he too could escape, DeLisa aimed the gun at him. "Move the train, now!"

"I can't," said the flushed-faced man in the pin-striped bib overalls. "The doors are still open."

"I don't give a shit about the doors," the mobster said. "Just move the train."

With his eyes darting between DeLisa and his hostage, the motorman returned to the cab and pushed the control lever. The train began rolling out of the station, traveling deeper into the Loop. The wail of police sirens echoed off the skyscrapers as the El train picked up speed.

94

News specials on Senator Harvey Banks's murder were being carried on each of the Chicago television stations. Running commentaries were provided from the anchor desks of news rooms interspersed with reports from man-on-the-street reporters located at various places around the city. To dress up the coverage the networks ran the senator's press conference in its entirety beginning at four o'clock.

In the remodeled mansion on South King Drive Ida Mae Stanton and her nurse watched the coverage on the console color television set in the living room. Mrs. Hudson had made a pitcher of ice tea and together the two women stared at the screen with horror while they sipped the beverage.

Finally, Ida Mae placed her glass down on an end table. Angrily, she thumped the tip of her cane on the floor. "If Reggie had been with Banks none of this would have happened."

"It's probably a plot, Ida," the nurse said. "They got Reggie away from him on some phony trip to Washington and then—"

"Wasn't nothing phony about Reggie having to go to Washington, Helen. That was his job calling. Uncle Sam's the one paying his salary. It was legitimate and I don't want you running around saying it wasn't."

"Well, I'm sorry. I just meant—"

"Oh, woman, you don't know what you meant. That man is

dead and, now that I think about it, I'm not so sure if even my Reggie could have prevented what happened today. It was too slick."

The doorbell rang.

Helen Hudson got up to answer it. She was gone long enough for Ida to miss her. The old woman was turning around to call for the nurse when Helen stepped up beside her. Ida took one look at the nurse's puzzled expression and said, "What's wrong?"

"There's a man outside to see you. I wouldn't open the door and I was about to tell him you were resting and couldn't be disturbed. Then he said that he's Ernst Steiger's nephew."

Ida's only reaction was a slight widening of her eyes. She turned from Helen Hudson to stare at the television. She sat rigidly still. "What does he want?"

"I told you, Ida. He wants to see you."

The old woman continued to stare at the screen.

"Do you want me to tell him to go away?"

Ida hesitated a moment and then, using her cane for support, stood up. Helen stepped back as she walked past. The nurse followed the old woman to the front door.

He was visible through the glass and metal window of the heavy wooden outer door. Ida stepped as close as she could to the glass and peered through it at him. What she saw wasn't sufficient to convince her.

"Open the door, Helen."

With a confused frown, the nurse stepped forward and unbolted the door. The young man outside made no move to enter.

"Mrs. Stanton?" he asked.

"Yes."

"My name is Ernest Steiger."

"Come in."

He crossed the threshold and stood under the ceiling lamp in the hallway. Ida studied his face. Then she let out a gasp and said, "You don't look anything like Ernst, but you're the spitting image of Karl."

"Yes, ma'am," he said with a slight bow. "That is the reason I'm here. My father has been hurt. I need to bring him inside."

"Why don't you take him to a hospital?" Helen said.

The look Ernest gave her was chilling. When he turned back to Ida, the old woman understood all to well why Karl Steiger could not be taken to a hospital. Her mind raced. She was torn between two worlds; that which was when her daughter Adele was alive and that which existed in the here and now with her grandson Reggie. This would be no easy decision.

"Where is Karl?" Ida asked.

"In a car down the block," Ernest explained. "He's been shot."

"Ida, we can't . . ." Helen began.

"You've got to go with him, Helen," Ida said. "I would do it myself, but I'm not strong enough."

"I'm not getting involved in this," Helen protested. "It's against the law."

The old woman stepped forward and grasped her nurse's arm. "You've got to help him, Helen. The man in that car is Reggie's father."

Her statement not only stunned the nurse, but also Ernest Steiger.

"Who is Reggie?" he said with open confusion.

"This is no time for a family reunion. She's going to help you bring your father inside. Now go."

Like sleepwalkers, the nurse and the assassin turned from the old woman. Then a renewed urgency overcame Ernest and he hurried out the door. Reluctantly, Helen Hudson followed him.

95

MARCH 7, 1994
4:30 P.M.

The Meigs Field Tower on the lakefront received a transmission from a military aircraft approaching Chicago.

"Meigs Tower, this is Air Force Flight sixteen zero nine Zebra requesting landing instructions."

"Sixteen zero nine Zebra," the air traffic controller responded, "are you a military flight?"

"That is affirmative, Meigs. My passenger is a VIP on a priority assignment for the F.B.I."

"What type of aircraft are you flying, sixteen zero nine Zebra?"

"An F-Four Phantom Jet with full armament."

"Be advised, sixteen zero nine Zebra, that this is not a military airport and we do not have a runway capable of landing your aircraft. You are to divert to O'Hare Airport's military field. Do you copy?"

"That's a negative, Meigs Tower. My passenger says we must land at your airport. Please clear all traffic and prepare for my approach."

"Sixteen zero nine Zebra, you must divert to O'Hare! You can't land here!"

The F-4 Phantom banked over Lake Shore Drive to fly south toward the tiny lakefront airport. As the fighter approached, the harried controller cleared the minimal air traffic in the area and sounded the alarm alerting the emergency ground crew to a potential disaster in the making. Then he sat back to watch a plane crash in progress.

Motorists on Lake Shore Drive and residents in the high rises in the downtown area were surprised to see a military jet flying this low over the city. Usually, this only happened during the annual air show. However, this was March and the air show was a midsummer event.

In the Phantom's narrow cockpit the young pilot spoke to his rear seat passenger over the intercom. "I can see the field now, sir. It does look a bit small."

"You can land on it and take off without any problem," Reggie Stanton said. "Just remember to cut your power the instant we touch down. Also, you're going to have to rev it a bit for takeoff."

"Sounds like you've done some flying."

"I've done a lot of things," Stanton said. "You never know when a particular skill will come in handy."

"I agree. Well, here we go. Hold on."

The fighter dropped toward the air field passing the downtown

area and Grant Park, zipping over the Shedd Aquarium and the
Adler Planetarium. At the outer marker, the pilot lowered the landing gear and flaps. The fighter dropped onto the short runway like a
rock. A very fast rock.

Cutting back on power, popping the drag chute and using his
brakes and full flaps, the pilot wrestled with the spirited, needle-
nosed beast as it continued to rocket down the runway, passing the
tower and the emergency vehicles to approach the far end of the cement surface, which abruptly ended where the lake began. Through
the shadows of approaching twilight the Air Force pilot and his
F.B.I. agent passenger could see green water lapping the stone pillars at the end of the runway. The water seemed to be beckoning the
steel bird.

Smoke spewed from the wheels as the tires scorched on the runway. The plane slowed, but the pilot began having his doubts as to
whether it would stop before they hit the water. Then, with only a
matter of scant feet left, the Phantom halted.

Exhaling a sigh of relief, the pilot turned the plane around and
taxied back toward the terminal.

"I knew you could do it," Stanton said.

But the pilot was badly frightened. He had no idea how he would
ever muster up the nerve to fly the plane out of here.

96

MARCH 7, 1994
4:32 P.M.

Chicago-based F.B.I. agents Donnelley and Prentiss were waiting in the Meigs Field terminal. They had been alerted to expect an agent on a priority assignment from Washington to arrive
by military jet. They were in the dog house with Dave Franklin, so
the job of acting as escorts, or as Donnelley called it "flunkies," had
fallen to them.

They had figured this was going to be a short assignment when the Phantom jet raced past the terminal on its way to what they expected to be its final resting place in Lake Michigan. But somehow the plane had survived the landing. They watched it taxi back to the terminal and the pilot open the canopy.

"I know this guy from somewhere," Donnelley said, as Stanton climbed from the aircraft and removed his helmet and flight suit.

"Did you ever work with him before?" Prentiss asked.

"No," Donnelley said. "but I've seen him before. I just can't place the when and where."

Stanton shook the pilot's hand and turned to enter the terminal just as a group of outraged airport officials converged on the plane.

"He's a big guy," Prentiss said, noticing the way Stanton filled out the double-breasted, charcoal gray suit. "Looks like a boxer."

"Yeah, but he sure as hell don't look like any agent that I've ever seen," Donnelley said.

Inside the terminal Stanton spied them. He recognized the type. He flashed his identification. "I believe you're waiting for me."

"Yes, sir," Prentiss said, making a move to take the attache case Stanton carried.

"I can handle it," Stanton said, staring past the young agent at Donnelley. "Do you have your instructions?"

Donnelley shrugged in a gesture transmitting that what he'd been told had little importance to him. It was obvious from his posture and expression that this lack of regard also extended to the black agent.

"I want to be taken directly to Chicago Police Headquarters," Stanton said. "You think you can manage that?"

"Oh, yes, sir," Prentiss said. "Right away, sir."

Stanton didn't move. He continued to stare at Donnelley. "I want to hear him say it."

Donnelley wilted under Stanton's gaze. He looked down at the floor. "Yeah," he mumbled.

"Yeah, what?" Stanton said, taking a menacing step toward him, as Prentiss blanched.

Donnelley tensed. "Yes, sir."

Stanton wasn't through yet. "Let me explain something to both of you. I'm on an important special assignment. This has been authorized in Washington. So either one of you screw around with me or fail to do exactly what I say when I say it, I'll not only have your asses on the spot, but I'll also make sure you get bounced out of the Bureau so fast your feet won't touch the ground until you hit the street. Do I make myself clear?"

Donnelley looked as if he was in extreme pain, but he managed to join Prentiss is a snappy, "Yes, sir."

97

MARCH 7, 1994
4:45 P.M.

The Chief of Detectives' Office had been turned into a command post. The afternoon's third watch crew had been augmented with detectives borrowed from the five areas around the city and a number of headquarters supervisory personnel had been called in to assist. A special field task force was on the street checking out leads on anything that looked promising.

Cole was in the cubicle he had occupied when he worked in Detective Division Headquarters under former Chief Riseman. The lieutenant he'd evicted, Marjorie Kotter, had voluntarily taken Govich's secretary's desk. Every report coming in concerning suspicious incidents around the city or possible sightings of the suspected assassins had been faxed to headquarters and was being personally reviewed by Cole.

So far, of the numerous reports he'd received, Cole had put aside two for closer scrutiny: the expressway shootout and a "shots fired and threats" call on a Loop-bound C.T.A. train. What particularly interested Cole about this last case was that the gunman fit the general description of Tuxedo Tony DeLisa. The description of the hostage was confusing. Some said she was a middle-aged woman, others reported her as being younger. The gunman had commandeered the train and forced the engineer to operate it with the doors open. At the next station on the line the gunman and his hostage had gotten off. By the time the police arrived, they were gone.

Cole leaned back and tried to form a picture in his mind of what had happened since the senator's death. It was like trying to assemble a jigsaw puzzle under water. Some pieces fit easily. Other wouldn't connect at all. He realized he simply didn't have enough to go on at this point. He planned to stay here all night, if necessary, until he was able to put it all together.

Lou Bronson crossed the office toward Cole. Bronson had been following up on the El train shooting.

"I might have something here, boss."

Cole motioned the detective to a chair inside the cubicle.

Bronson held a pocket-sized notebook in his hand, from which he read. "The Twelfth District responded to the first call at the Harrison and Morgan C.T.A. Station. A couple of women jumped the turnstile. The faretaker hit the alarm. Before the car got there a guy comes in with a gun and follows the women down onto the platform. They all boarded an inbound Loop train. The cops from Twelve radioed ahead to have the train stopped downtown."

"That's probably the same train we received reports on about a man holding a woman hostage," Cole said.

"I agree, but the thing that got me interested was a car they found abandoned outside the station. It was a new Lincoln, which had been abandoned after the driver smashed it into a concrete abutment. There was a lot of damage to the front and the keys were still in the ignition. It's registered to Antonio DeLisa."

"Blackie," Cole called across the office bay to where Blackie was sitting at one of the desks.

The sergeant came on the double.

"I think we've got a lead on your Mistress of Disguise/High Priestess of Mayhem."

98

Chief Govich was in his office. Cole was handling everything, so he found there was really nothing for him to do but sit back and wait. Periodically, like just about every fifteen minutes, he went out and checked on the progress of the investigation. Finally, things hit a plateau and he found that he was being given the same reports over and over. The last time he retreated back into his office and vowed not to leave it again for at least an hour or until new developments surfaced. Cole would keep him apprised of any progress. The commander was good. That was why Govich had picked him for the original Banks's investigation.

Alone, Govich felt at once inadequate and unnecessary. He considered going out into the field to lead the investigation like an urban George S. Patton. He quickly rejected this. He was the chief of detectives, not a street cop. His place was where he was, not out there getting in the way of other people trying to do their jobs.

He paced the office for a time, flopped down in his desk chair, but just as quickly got up to pace again. Then his private line rang.

"Govich."

It was the superintendent. *"I need to see you and Larry Cole in my office right away."*

They were ushered into the large fourth-floor office by the superintendent's administrative aide. Cole was startled when he saw the man seated across from the superintendent.

Reggie Stanton stood up and turned to face Govich and Cole.

"The commander and I have already met, superintendent,"

Stanton said. "I neglected to tell you earlier that I was once with the CPD."

"Is that right?" the superintendent said with surprise. "I guess that makes you a member of the family."

When they were all seated, the superintendent said, "Agent Stanton's going to help us with the investigation into Senator Banks's death. He informed me that the Bureau's got some leads they're going to share with us. He also has the same opinion we do about Tuxedo Tony DeLisa being involved. I want you to give him everything that we've come up with so far."

"I assume we'll be getting all the data that the Bureau has on DeLisa in return?" Govich asked.

"Of course," Stanton said. "But I don't think we have very much at this point."

"Oh, I don't know about that, Reggie," Cole said. "My understanding is that your Chicago office has been conducting a round-the-clock surveillance on DeLisa and his operation."

"We'll be glad to share anything we have with you, Larry," Stanton said with ease. "I'll make sure you get it as soon as I talk to the special agent-in-charge. However, since I'm already here, maybe you can fill me in from your end first."

Cole looked at Govich. The chief nodded. The commander began with Judy Daniels.

Washington, D.C.   **99**

MARCH 7, 1994
6:15 P.M.

H*e was supposed to be home an hour ago,"* Arlene Connors said to the operator in the F.B.I.'s Washington, D.C. office. *"We have a dinner engagement at eight. Could you possibly get in touch with him?"*

The operator knew who Connors was and also that his wife carried her own share of political weight up on Capital Hill. Apparently there had been a near foul-up with the deputy director earlier or the D.C. S.A.C. wouldn't have been so testy when Connors called. A complaint from Mrs. Connors, behind what had happened earlier, could really develop into something ugly.

"Do you have a number I can call you back at, ma'am?" the operator said.

After recording the number and disconnecting, the operator searched the waste paper basket for the piece of paper she'd discarded earlier bearing the address the trace on Connors's call had revealed. After finding it she punched a direct line button on her console. "D.C. Police, this is the Washington, D.C. office of the F.B.I. We'd like to request your assistance."

Chicago, Illinois # 100

MARCH 7, 1994
5:30 P.M.

R achel DeLisa had been roaming the streets aimlessly. She finally pulled herself together long enough to duck into the public toilet of a service station. There she removed the makeup the woman disguised as Angelina Lupo had applied on the El train. She discarded it and the scarf in the washroom trash container.

Outside was a public telephone. She stopped and stared at it. Something urged her to keep walking and get out of Chicago as fast as she could. But something else wouldn't permit her to forget the woman who had helped her. The woman who had given her lemonade and supper last night, and breakfast that morning. The woman who had held her while she cried.

Rachel walked over to the phone. She fished coins out of her pocket and dropped them in the slot before dialing her father's Oak Park mansion.

After one ring it was answered. *"Hello?"* Attorney Frank Kirschstein's voice came over the line.

"Mr. Kirschstein, this is Rachel."

"Where are you, Rachel?"

The phone was grabbed by her father. *"Rachel, where in the hell are you?"*

"Stop yelling, Papa."

He took a deep breath. *"Okay, baby. Where are you? Why did you run away?"*

"Where is the woman who helped me?"

"I asked you a question, Rachel."

"Listen to me, Papa. I want to know what happened to the woman who helped me. Tell me the truth or I'll hang up and you'll never hear from me again."

"Wait a minute, honey. What are you . . . ?"

"Papa, I'm only going to ask you once more before I hang up. What happened to the woman who helped me?"

"She's fine. I've got her downstairs. She's not hurt. I swear it."

"You locked her in that room where you—"

"Rachel, stop it. This is an open line. We don't talk on open lines."

"Papa, you get her out of there and bring her to the phone right now."

"Wait a minute. Just wait a minute."

"No, you wait, Papa. Get her, like I said, or I'm hanging up."

"Okay, but you stay on the line. Do you hear me?"

There was a brief rustling noise and then Kirschstein was back. *"Hold on, Rachel. Your father went to get Mrs. Lupo."*

"That's not her name," Rachel said, suddenly feeling drained.

In a purring voice the lawyer said, *"We've got to watch what we say on these phones, dear. You know that."*

Rachel wanted to scream. Everything they touched was underhanded and dirty. Nothing could be honest. Nothing could be done out in the light of day where normal people lived and loved.

"You know your father is very worried about you. Why don't you come home and talk to him? I'm sure the two of you can work this out."

"Mr. Kirschstein, if you don't shut up I'm going to hang up this phone. Then you can explain to Papa what happened."

"Rachel, please . . . you can't . . ."

She hit one of the buttons on the key pad. The noise made the lawyer gasp. He didn't say another word.

A moment later her father's voice came back over the line. *"Rachel, are you still there?"*

"I'm here."

"Hold on, baby." She caught a vicious, *"Here,"* which was cut off by a hand being jammed over the mouthpiece. She guessed that papa had called her rescuer a name. Rachel was not concerned about this as long as he didn't hurt her.

"Hello?" The woman's voice was strong, but she sounded scared.

"This is Rachel. Are you okay?"

"So far so good, but I don't know how long that's going to last."

"I'm not going to let Papa hurt you. I promise that."

"Well, I wish you could see him. He doesn't look like he's in much of a mood to listen to you."

"Don't worry. He'll do as I say." Rachel paused a moment. "I wanted to thank you for helping me, but I don't even know your name."

"My name is unimportant right now. The fact that I'm a police officer, however, is—"

The phone was yanked away from her.

"Okay, now you've talked to her," Papa said. *"When are you coming home?"*

"I'm not, Papa. At least not right now, but I'm going to call back later to talk to the officer. I don't want anything to happen to her. If it does you'll never see me again."

She hung up.

101

K arl Steiger was fading in and out of consciousness. He was in a great deal of pain. Lingering on the edge of a coma, he relived a number of the events of his life. The dreams were so real he felt he was actually back in the past.

He was eleven and wearing ragged clothing as he ran through the snow in Germany. He held his father's hand tightly, as two Russian soldiers pursued them. The soldiers wore brown uniforms and carried machine guns with round magazines. Suddenly, there was a burst of gunfire and his father pitched forward into the snow. Karl fell beside him.

His father, Johann, wore the uniform of a major in the SS. Karl remembered how Johann and Uncle Ernst had quarreled about the section of the SS to which his father was assigned. Uncle Ernest referred to Johann's fellow SS members as, "a den of pigs." Johann had warned Ernst that comments like that could lead to even one of Otto Skorzeny's war heroes being shot.

Now his father was lying beside the young Karl Steiger. Unhurt, Karl rolled away. The Russians caught up. One of them, a boy who looked no older than fifteen, struck Karl a backhanded blow to the head. The German youth was knocked back into the snow. The other Russian, who was much older and heavier than his companion, began bludgeoning Johann Steiger's lifeless body with the butt of his machine gun.

The young soldier was so absorbed by the spectacle of the brutality, he ignored Karl. The click of the sleeve dagger snapping into Karl's hand made the Russian turn around. His eyes went wide in alarm, but by that time it was too late. The dagger lodged deep in the Russian's chest. Karl leaped forward before the Russian hit the ground and snatched the machine gun from his hands. The other soldier spun in time to catch a burst of bullets in the face. Karl kept firing long after the Russian was dead.

In a snow-covered field in the middle of Nazi Germany at the end of World War II, eleven-year-old Karl Steiger dropped the empty Russian weapon, replaced his sleeve dagger, knelt down in the snow beside his dead father, and cried.

A tear rolled down the cheek of the wounded, unconscious Karl Steiger in 1994.

"How is he?" Ernest Steiger said over Helen Hudson's shoulder.

They were in the basement of the Stanton house. The basement that had once been the exclusive domain of Ernst Steiger and his nephew Reggie. The basement that had been preserved to be the same as it had been the day Uncle Ernst died.

The nurse bristled, "This man could die at any second. He has bullets inside of him. There could be massive internal injuries. He needs to be in a hospital."

Ernest looked from her to his father. Karl was so pale his blond hair looked dark in contrast to his skin. But there were certain rules of the trade that were to be followed at all times. A wounded comrade could never be taken to an unsecured or unfriendly medical facility. It was better to die than be captured. It would also maintain the security of the mission. Karl Steiger had taught his son this precept.

Ernest looked around him. He was particularly drawn to the photographs lining the walls. Pictures of Uncle Ernst, whom Ernest recognized from those he had seen when he was growing up. In each photo Ernest was with a younger man. *Reggie,* Mrs. Stanton had called him. For the first time in his life Ernest discovered that he had a brother. He didn't know whether to be elated or alarmed.

While Mrs. Hudson watched over his father, Ernest walked around. He had once been in the old von Steiger hunting lodge in Austria. This place reminded him of it. This was a man's place; a distinctively German place. Even the beer steins were German. Then there was Reggie. Ernest stepped closer to one of the photographs. It was a picture of Reggie Stanton in his police uniform fifteen years ago. Ernest was forced to remark to himself that Reggie looked more like his father than he did.

"Who was Adele?" Ernest asked Mrs. Hudson.

"Ask Mrs. Stanton," the nurse snapped.

"I'll be back," he said.

"Don't be too long. He can't last."

Upstairs Ernest found Mrs. Stanton in the living room. The television set was off and the only illumination was from a table lamp beside her chair. Also on the table there was a crystal decanter. Ida Mae held a glass containing the same brown liquid that was in the decanter. Ernest smelled the whiskey.

"I want to thank you for everything you've done, Mrs. Stanton."

The old woman looked up at him with eyes brimming with a host of emotions. Then she looked away and took a pull from her glass of straight whiskey.

"Your father tell you to bring him here?"

"In a way. He was in a great deal of pain after he was shot and he kept repeating 'Adele's house.' I finally managed to get an address out of him." Ernest paused a moment. "Who was Adele, Mrs. Stanton?"

"She was my daughter."

"Reggie's mother?"

She took another drink. "Yes."

"Does Reggie know about me and my father?"

"No." She said the word so vehemently some of the whiskey spilled. "Reggie thinks his father's dead. I didn't know anything about you until you showed up here."

Ernest stood in silence for a time. "I've got to leave, Mrs. Stanton. I trust that you and Mrs. Hudson will take care of my father until I return."

Ida merely nodded.

"If he should . . . " but the word stuck in Ernest's throat. He swallowed with difficulty and managed to say, "die, I'll understand. I don't want to leave, but there are some things I must do."

The old woman stared at him. She recognized the look on Ernest Steiger's face. She had seen looks very much like this on the face of her grandson. Ernest was going out to kill.

He was turning for the door when her voice stopped him. "You and your father were responsible for the death of Senator Banks." It was not a question.

Without turning around he answered, "Yes, we were."

She didn't reply. He let himself out of the brownstone.

102

MARCH 7, 1994
5:42 P.M.

I think the Bureau needs to review any available information we have on Mr. DeLisa before we mount any action against him, gentlemen," Stanton said.

"And how long will this review take?" Govich asked.

"At least twenty-four hours."

Cole sat forward. "Begging your pardon, Superintendent, but we've got an undercover police officer involved in this. There's every indication that she's in danger right now."

The superintendent looked from Cole to Stanton.

The F.B.I. agent kept his eyes on Cole. "I'm as concerned for the welfare of your officer as you are, Commander, but I think we've got to weigh our options very carefully."

"I don't understand what could be more important than a police officer's life," Cole said.

"You don't have one solid piece of evidence connecting DeLisa with the senator's death," Stanton countered.

"Our undercover might."

"You don't know that. All you would be doing is charging out to DeLisa's house in violation of a court order barring harassment from local as well as federal authorities and end up compromising any chance we might have of nailing him with Harvey Banks's assassination."

Cole's jaw muscles rippled as he said, "Banks is dead, Stanton. Judy Daniels could still be alive."

"At ease, Commander," the superintendent said softly.

Cole managed to barely muzzle his anger.

Govich cleared his throat before saying, "With all due respect to the Bureau, Agent Stanton, I don't understand why you need twenty-four hours to make a decision on this. You've had DeLisa under surveillance for weeks, perhaps even months. In your files I'm quite sure you've got enough to tie him in tight to the senator's death."

"Suppose we don't."

"You don't really believe that, do you?" Govich said.

The Superintendent put an end to the argument. "The decision's been made, gentlemen. Agent Stanton has been placed in charge of this case by Washington according to a fax I received from the agent-in-charge of the D.C. office. As such, I suggest that we let him handle it."

"Thank you, Superintendent," Stanton said rising.

Govich and Cole also stood, but made no comment.

Back in Govich's office Cole said, "Something stinks to the high heavens here, Chief. No federal agency sticks its neck out to get involved in an investigation like this, especially the F.B.I. On top of that, senator or no senator, Harvey Banks's murder was in our jurisdiction and belongs to us."

"You're right, Larry, but we've got to be careful with this. The superintendent's trying to minimize the political fallout. With the F.B.I. taking over, he can make them the fall guys when the press starts making accusations of negligence. Didn't you say that Stanton told you he was the senator's bodyguard?"

Cole was pacing the floor in front of Govich's desk like a caged animal. "That's what he said. But every time I run into this guy something crazy happens. He's like something out of a nightmare."

Govich picked up the phone. "Let me see if I can get in touch with Dave Franklin. Maybe he can shed some light on this."

A few minutes later Govich hung up the phone. "His office says he's out of town and can't be reached. All I get is the answering machine at his apartment. I could try calling Martha Grimes, but she probably won't be able to tell us much."

"Maybe I could try something," Cole said.

"Be my guest. I'm out of options anyway."

Picking up Govich's phone, Cole dialed a number from memory. "First Deputy, how are you, sir? Fine, fine. I hope I'm not disturbing you. Oh, you heard. Yes, in a way. I'd like to talk to you about something that might be connected to it. I was thinking of driving out to see you. Yeah, in about a half an hour."

"That was the first deputy?" Govich said with a raised eyebrow.

"Retired. William Riseman. He was sitting in your seat fifteen years ago when I conducted investigations into four homicides in which Stanton was a possible suspect. They were transferred to the I.A.D. from the Detective Division at Riseman's request."

"That doesn't make sense."

"I know," Cole said. "The next time I heard from Stanton he was with the F.B.I."

"You think Riseman can fill in the blanks?"

"I hope so, Chief."

"Where does he live?"

Cole headed for the door. "In Oak Park about a mile from DeLisa's place."

103

R eggie Stanton walked out of police headquarters onto State Street. The unmarked F.B.I. car with Agent Tom Prentiss at the wheel was parked across the street. When the baby agent saw Stanton, he cranked a hard U-turn and skidded to a stop in front of the door. Donnelley was in the back seat. Stanton opened the door and got in.

The interior of the car was hazy with cigarette smoke. Without turning around Stanton said, "Dump the butt and don't light up again as long as you're with me."

With a frown Donnelley opened the window and flipped the still smoldering cigarette onto the sidewalk in front of headquarters. Before anyone noticed the infraction, Prentiss rocketed away.

"You want to go to the office, sir?" Prentiss asked.

Stanton remained silent for two blocks. When they reached Harrison Street he said, "Stop the car."

Prentiss complied so abruptly Stanton and Donnelley were thrown forward.

"I want you two to go into the office," Stanton ordered. "I understand there's a blanket surveillance on Antonio DeLisa."

"That's a little above our level, sir," Donnelley said. The sneer in his voice was evident.

"I can understand that," Stanton said. "But I want the surveillance on DeLisa canceled. Use my authority from Washington to do it."

Donnelley whistled. "That's a pretty tall order, boss."

Stanton turned around to look the agent in the face. "But you will do it, won't you?"

"Oh, yes, sir," Donnelley said, nervously. "Right away."

Stanton surprised them by opening the door and getting out of the car. He looked back at them. "I'll check with you in an hour to see if you've done what I told you. Don't disappoint me."

"We won't, sir," Prentiss said.

Stanton waited for Donnelley's nod before slamming the door and descending the steps to the subway station beneath State Street.

"Where's he going?" Prentiss asked.

"To hell I hope," Donnelley answered, getting out of the car and lighting a cigarette. As he got in the front seat he said, "Let's go do what the man ordered."

Washington, D.C.   **104**

MARCH 7, 1994
7:05 P.M.

Deputy Director Connors had been alone in the basement of the house on First and F Streets for nearly an hour. He had strained and pulled against the ropes until his flesh was raw and he was drenched with sweat from the exertion. However, he found himself as securely bound as he had been the moment he regained consciousness an eternity ago.

There was no doubt in his mind that Stanton planned to kill him. Had he been in the shadow agent's shoes he would do the same thing. Connors had forced him into the Bureau because Stanton was a natural. A virtuoso at the art of murder. A master who never showed any emotion nor had any compunction about killing. As long as Connors was on the aiming end, things had been fine. Now that he was on the receiving end he was terrified.

Then he heard a faint noise coming from somewhere above him. It was a dull thumping sound. He listened and the thumps were repeated. Someone was knocking on a door.

The noise became louder. Connors considered calling out, but that could bring Stanton or the little black man down on him. Then he heard shouts.

The words were muffled to the volume of a whisper by the walls and his position in the basement of the house. He strained with all his might to hear what was being said. He caught only one word: "Police!"

"I'm here! Help! Help me!"

The thumping and shouting stopped. Connors was afraid they hadn't heard him and were going away. He screamed, "Help!"

Chicago, Illinois **105**

MARCH 7, 1994
6:12 P.M.

A rmand Hagar was dropped off in front of the Haggerty House. He squeezed out of the Ford sedan, driven by another DeLisa henchman, that had tailed the Steigers from the Hyde Park Hotel onto the Kennedy Expressway. From the Ford, Hagar had used a CB radio to position the Mack truck and back-up white van. The plan to shove the Steigers through the guardrail was his idea. He had anticipated watching the two Krauts plummet to their deaths with a nearly sexual excitement. Then everything had gone wrong.

The car drove away as Hagar limped up the stone steps of the old house. His foot felt as if it had swollen to the size of a basketball. He unlocked the door and struggled inside. He hopped to the first floor bathroom and threw open the medicine cabinet. The bottle of pain pills was on the bottom shelf. Clutching the bottle he moved as quickly as he could to the water cooler in the kitchen.

Hagar had given no more thought to the Steigers after the shoot-out on the expressway. He figured the pretty boy and his daddy would be running for their lives now, even if they had managed to scatter the bodies of three of DeLisa's top lieutenants all over the Kennedy.

He shook two of the pills into his hand, popped them in his mouth and chased them with a paper cup of water drawn from the cooler. He refilled the cup. He was raising it to his lips when he caught movement out of the corner of his eye. The movement was so slight as to be almost imperceptible. It had come from the kitchen entrance. He jerked around and saw a dark, shadowy figure standing there. Hagar could only make out the silhouette of a man clad in black with a hooded mask over his face. Startled, Hagar dropped the cup and grasped the handle of the revolver in his waistband. He attempted to pull the gun, but it was too late.

The wounded killer felt a constriction in his throat. It was as if something he was attempting to swallow had gotten stuck there. He tried to force the object down, but his entire throat was frozen in pain. He dropped the gun and his hands came up to make contact with the handle of a dagger which had been hurled across the room to penetrate his Adam's apple.

Strangling on his own blood, Armand Hagar, aka Andrew Haggerty, collapsed to the floor.

The man in black slowly moved across the kitchen. As Hagar's life ebbed away, he became aware of his killer standing over him. A gloved hand reached up and removed the mask. Ernest Steiger stared down at Hagar.

"I found the hidden compartment you used to spy on me and my father. I also saw you in the car following us. That was terribly sloppy work. DeLisa should have known better."

Hagar continued to stare at his killer for a few seconds longer then, with a terrible gurgling gasp, blood bubbled out of his mouth and his eyes glazed over in death.

106

Reggie drove his BMW from the Illinois Institute of Technology parking lot. He sped south toward the brownstone on King Drive. He planned to track the two men who had assassinated the senator. However, he had no more interest in their deaths than he had in Butcher's and Cappeletti's. The assassins were merely hired killers. They didn't matter, but their boss, DeLisa, did. The mobster would die first, then the assassins. He intended to find them even if it was the last thing he ever did.

His fingers gripped the steering wheel tightly. He was stopped for a red light at Thirty-ninth Street. The senator being dead kept coming back to him with the impact of a sledgehammer blow to the chest. If only Banks had listened. Only allowed Reggie to protect him.

The light changed. As he raced across the intersection he felt moisture on his cheeks. He reached up with the back of his hand to brush it away. It was only then that he realized he was crying.

Reggie Stanton never cried. He never laughed either. He felt things like lust, hunger and anger, and he loved his grandmother. He had also loved Uncle Ernst. He had possessed a deep affection and respect for Harvey Banks. But he had never outwardly displayed any open emotions to anyone with the exception of Ida Mae, whom he periodically embraced. When Uncle Ernst died he didn't shed a tear. Now he was crying for Harvey Banks, a man who had no blood ties to him at all. He realized that in some ways Banks had meant more to him than Uncle Ernst. Initially, this thought seemed like a familial blasphemy; however, the more he thought about it the more he realized that it was true.

Reggie scolded himself. This was not the time for remorse. Now was the time for action.

He pulled up in front of the brownstone and bounded out of the car. He let himself in and headed for the basement where his weapons were secured in a special hidden closet Uncle Ernst had built. He was passing the entrance to the living room when his grandmother's voice stopped him. He was in such a hurry he hadn't noticed her sitting in the dark.

"Grandma, what are you doing?" he said when he saw the whiskey decanter on the end table and the glass in her hand. "You know what the doctor said."

"I got no time for stupid doctors' opinions tonight." There was a slight slur in her speech.

"Next you'll be telling me you want a cigarette." He crossed the room with the intention of confiscating the whiskey.

"If I had a cigarette, I'd smoke it," she said. "I need to talk to you."

He halted. Her tone alarmed him. The last time he saw her like this was the day Ernst Steiger died. The task of telling him had fallen to her.

"Sit down," she said, nodding to the couch across from her.

Slowly, forgetting the whiskey and his imminent mission of revenge against DeLisa, Reggie sat.

107

MARCH 7, 1994
7:25 P.M.

Judy Daniels was scared, but she felt she was handling the situation well. At least so far. Of course, she was certain things would get worse very soon.

They were holding her in the library. Prior to Rachel's phone call she had been locked in a dark, foul-smelling basement. DeLisa had threatened her with everything from dismemberment to being flayed alive, yet, other than a little rough treatment when he forced her off the El train and into a taxi downtown, she was still unharmed.

After Rachel called they had kept her upstairs. DeLisa, who had a habit of staring at her like a taxidermist with a fresh carcass, made her nervous, but she refused to show it. A couple of times, when he had to leave the room, Frank Kirschstein, whom she recognized from having seen him in Chicago court rooms, stayed with her.

She was bound to a chair with a set of Smith and Wesson handcuffs. Now she and the lawyer were once more alone.

"You know," he said in a voice which was almost melodious with the way he made vowels and consonants ring, "there is a standing court order barring any police agency from spying on or otherwise interfering with Mr. DeLisa or his business."

She glared at him. "Is this how you enforce violations of court orders nowadays, Counselor?"

Momentarily, Kirschstein appeared at a loss for words.

"You know my people know I'm here," Judy said.

"That's merely wishful thinking on your part," he said with a forced smile.

"Is it? Then why do you and Tony the Penguin speak in riddles every time you talk on the telephone? Who do you think's listening in, the Easter Bunny?"

At the reference to DeLisa as "the Penguin" Kirschstein paled and looked nervously at the closed library door.

"You could still get out of this," she said. "You've got to have a few million dollars stashed away. With what you know about DeLisa's operation, the government could easily slip you into the Witness Protection Program. That could solve a lot of the problems you're going to have very soon."

"It looks like you're the one having problems, officer."

She pressed on. "Your number one problem is going to be back any minute now."

"Tony's my client and he pays very well. That's the kind of problem I like."

"DeLisa's going to be the death of you, Mr. Kirschstein, and you know it."

They heard DeLisa's footsteps echoing on the alcove floor. Kirschstein froze into a rigid silence. Judy's back was to the door and she made no attempt to turn around when it opened.

DeLisa walked in and came around to sit behind the desk facing them. He had applied a strip of gauze secured with surgical tape to the bridge of his nose. There was some swelling and his eyes were beginning to blacken. The effect made him look like a ghoul who'd just climbed out of a grave.

"What's going on?" he said to the lawyer.

"Nothing, Tony," Kirschstein said quickly.

"What were you two talking about?" the mobster demanded.

"Talking? Who us?" The lawyer sounded so frightened Judy actually felt sorry for him.

"Goddammit, Frank," DeLisa shouted, "I heard the two of you talking when I walked across the alcove. Now I want to know what you were talking about!"

The desk telephone rang. Kirschstein jumped to answer it. *Saved by the bell,* Judy thought. *But for how long?*

"It's for you," he said, extending the instrument to DeLisa.

"Who is it?"

Kirschstein shook his head and nodded toward Judy. It was apparently someone whose identity he didn't want revealed in front of her. *And I thought we were becoming such pals.*

DeLisa snatched the receiver and barked, "Yeah."

Whoever was on the other end did all of the talking. The look that descended on DeLisa's face terrified Judy. She figured that when he hung up she was dead or would at least begin to die. However, when the conversation ended nothing happened. The mobster simply stared blankly at the far wall.

"What is it, Tony?" Kirschstein asked.

"Shut up, Frank."

The silence in the study stretched to an eternity. Finally, DeLisa said, "That was my man on the other side. The Feds are pulling the surveillance off of me. Phones, the house, the warehouse, everything."

"Well, that's good news," the lawyer began. "I mean you don't have to . . ."

DeLisa pulled the automatic from his waist band. In one motion he cocked the weapon and placed the barrel against the lawyer's forehead.

"The only reason I don't blow your fucking brains out right now is because what you've got in there ain't worth the price of a bullet."

"Please, Tony," Kirschstein pleaded while keeping his eyes tightly shut. He began to tremble violently.

A cruel smile spread across DeLisa's face. "Hey, lady cop, would you look at this? Big shot lawyer, six-figure retainer, never lost a case because he's got the motion to fix in tight. Now he's about to crap in his pants because he's afraid to die."

There was nothing Judy could do but watch.

Abruptly, DeLisa lowered the gun and laughed. "What's the matter, Frank? Can't you take a joke?"

Kirschstein's eyes popped open. His skin had turned a greenish shade of pale and his trembling had not abated. Still staring at DeLisa, he bent forward slightly and his hands flew up to his mouth.

"Oh, shit, not in here, Frank!"

The mobster snatched the lawyer by his shirt collar and propelled him across the room to the secret passage. Judy could no longer see them, but she did hear the false bookcase swing open. There came the sound of feet descending the steps Judy had been down earlier. Then silence. A short time later DeLisa came back into the library alone.

"You know, you can never really tell about people," he said in a maddeningly conversational tone. "Now take Frank. Put him in a courtroom with a judge, jury and bunch of shit-eating deputy sheriffs to protect him, and he's fearless. Won't take crap off of any man. He'll make most people look like damn fools when he gets them on a witness stand. But out here in the real world, you put a gun to his head and he goes to pieces."

"What did you do with him?" Judy asked.

DeLisa looked at her as if he was seeing her for the first time. Pulling his gun he walked around to stand in front of her.

"Well, Officer . . . " he began. "I didn't catch your name."

"Does it matter?" she managed with a bravado she really didn't feel.

He shrugged. "I guess not. But what I was going to say, Miss Lady Cop, was that you shouldn't really worry about Frank. You should be concerned about what I'm going to do to you."

DeLisa raised the gun and placed the cold muzzle flush against her forehead, as he had done with the lawyer. Although the housing partially obstructed her vision, she refused to take her eyes off him. He stared back with amusement.

For a very long time there was no sound in the room. Then, with a soft mirthless chuckle, he lowered the gun. "Like I said, you can never tell about people. Maybe you're acting so tough because you figure Rachel's your ace. I wouldn't stretch that too far. But then it actually might not matter in the long run. The Feds didn't pull off me because they think I'm a nice guy. They're up to something. I figure they're coming to get you. It won't be anything spectacular, like SWAT. Probably something much simpler. Well, I'm kind of a simple guy myself when it comes to these things. Also, I didn't get where I am today being a pussy for anybody and that includes my daughter. So you just sit tight while I go and change into something more suitable in which to greet our uninvited guests. Then you and I are going to make up a little reception party for them."

He walked past her. She heard the study door open and close. Exhausted, Judy slumped forward in her chair.

108

MARCH 7, 1994
7:30 P.M.

Reggie was seated on the bed on which Uncle Ernst had died and looked down into the face of his father. Standing behind him were his grandmother, leaning heavily on her cane, and the nurse.

"Why did Uncle Ernst tell me he was dead?" Reggie said so softly the two women could barely hear him.

"The F.B.I. hounded Karl out of the University of Chicago where he and your mother met," Ida said. "Everywhere he went they'd show up and tell everyone that he was the nephew of the war criminal Ernst von Steiger. Swastikas were painted on his dormitory room doors and he was spat at and called a Nazi wherever he went. When he transferred to Georgetown University in Washington, your mother went to meet him.

"It was January of nineteen sixty," Ida said crossing the basement and sitting down heavily in Uncle Ernst's old leather armchair. "Your mother flew there to meet him. She was pregnant with you. I knew it, but Karl didn't. When she arrived Karl wasn't there to meet her. She spent the next week trying to find him. It was winter and she got sick. She never got over it. Later we discovered that the F.B.I. had arrested Karl and held him incommunicado on some trumped up charge all the time Adele was there."

Reggie turned to look at his grandmother. "Did he know about me?"

Slowly, she shook her head. "After the Washington incident they had him deported. It took years for him to get the decision reversed. He wrote, but I kept the letters from Adele. Karl even called from Germany once. I answered the phone, but when he asked to speak to your mother, I hung up."

"Why, Grandma? I don't understand."

"Because it wasn't right. Your mother was a brilliant girl. Beautiful on top of it. Had a scholarship to the University of Chicago. Had the chance to get out of this neighborhood and out from under being poor like I was. All she was doing with him was throwing her life away. What chance would she, or for that matter you, have had with a D.P. ex-Nazi?"

"So she died thinking he had abandoned her?" Reggie questioned.

"Yes. I always thought she would recover from that cough, but it just kept getting worse. When she was gone, the rest really didn't matter." Ida's voice trailed off.

"Why did you let Uncle Ernst come to live with us?"

Ida began twisting the head of her cane. "I couldn't be both mama and daddy to you. I saw what you were becoming and I didn't like it. You ran from fights, let people take advantage of you. Ernst was tired of running and needed a place to hide where no one would think to look for him. Karl had written him about me and you could say that he had no place else to go. To keep him safe, Ernst vowed to never get in touch with him again. Right before he died he was about to break that vow, but he never got the chance. For his part, Karl had no idea Ernst was here."

"So you did everything for me and my mother?" Reggie said bitterly.

"You have no right to say that to me, Reggie. No right. I loved Adele. I love you, too. I was just trying to take care of my own as best I could."

Reggie turned back to study the dying man's face. With a great effort he managed to reach out and touch the skin of his cheek. It was ice cold.

At Reggie's touch Karl opened his eyes. He looked up at Reggie. For an instant recognition dawned. He managed a smile and tried to speak, but the effort was too great and he lapsed back into unconsciousness.

"Mrs. Hudson," Reggie said.

The nurse stepped around him and gently probed the wounded man's neck for a pulse. She found none. After checking his vital signs she said solemnly, "He's gone."

Reggie didn't move. He sat looking down into the face of the man whom he had dreamed about so many times in his life. A man whom he never got the chance to talk to. Finally, he leaned over and kissed his father's cheek. Then he stood up.

"Where is the other one?"

"He's your brother, Reggie," Ida said.

"I know who he is, Grandma! I want to know where he is."

Frightened, she said, "He's gone after the man who is responsible for this."

Reggie nodded. He took one last look at his dead father before going to Uncle Ernst's weapons closet.

109

The alert beeper sounded on the radar set in the state police car patrolling the Eisenhower Expressway. Trooper Karen McNamara's eyes widened when she saw the speed on the digital readout. Ninety-three miles per hour and accelerating.

Slamming the police cruiser into drive and activating her emergency equipment, she pulled off the shoulder of the road. The license plate number of the approaching vehicle also flashed on the display. She hit a button, making a permanent record of both it and the clocked speed. Then she made visual contact with the speeder.

She had reached sixty-five miles an hour when the black convertible Corvette zipped by her as if she was standing still. She glanced at the readout. One hundred one miles an hour. Traffic on the expressway was light and moving fast in the outbound lanes. She cranked up her cruiser to ninety-five and then one hundred. Snatching up the microphone she called her dispatcher.

"This is Car three one-twelve. I've got a speeder traveling in excess of a hundred miles an hour on the Eisenhower westbound from Pulaski Road. I am requesting assistance."

"Stand by, Car three one-twelve."

Trooper McNamara could see the sleek black car up ahead as she topped 105 to begin closing the distance between them. The driver of the Corvette had to hear the siren and see the red lights of the police car behind it. That meant he was either crazy, drunk or had a snoot full of shit. There was no way she planned to let him get away.

"Car 3-112, we have units responding from the interstate and Illinois two ninety west of your position. Their ETA is three minutes. What is your current location?"

They were already past Cicero flying west toward the Austin and Harlem exits. It was at this point that the Corvette again began accelerating. The numbers on Trooper McNamara's radar set began flipping upwards.

115 . . . 122 . . . 125 . . . 130.

She grit her teeth. "I can do that too, bucko. Little Karen's not letting you go that easy."

She jammed the accelerator to the floor. The needle inched over 110 and began climbing to 115. The cars they were passing became a blur. She had never driven this fast before and the intensity of the experience was almost sexual.

The body of the police car began vibrating. The howl of the engine was loud enough to block out the reception on her police radio. The trooper had gotten all she could out of the cruiser. However, the Corvette continued jetting into the night. She kept her foot on the accelerator until a yellow warning light began flashing on the dash SERVICE ENGINE IMMEDIATELY. At Harlem Avenue she decelerated. The Corvette was gone.

"Car three one-twelve," she said into her walkie-talkie. "I lost the vehicle I was pursuing in the vicinity of I-two ninety and the Harlem exit in Oak Park. Have all units be alert for a late model, black Corvette convertible bearing Illinois License SCJ one nine four."

She pulled onto the shoulder of the expressway and tapped the number into her mobile computer. As the registration came back she read it to herself. "Andrew Haggerty, eighteen fifty-nine South Prairie Avenue, Chicago, nineteen ninety-four Chevrolet Corvette. Well, Mr. Haggerty, you're in a lot of trouble. Nobody runs from me and gets away with it."

But Trooper Karen McNamara was wrong. Exactly twelve minutes later, after she had returned to her assigned Radar Monitoring station in the westbound lanes east of Pulaski Road, a silver BMW performed the exact same maneuver as the Corvette. She also lost it in the same area of Harlem Avenue and the expressway. As she announced the description of the second vehicle to her dispatcher she figured that it simply wasn't her night.

110

A re you making any progress on the senator's assassination?"
William Riseman asked, as he led Cole through his Oak Park
home.

Riseman's house was large for a confirmed bachelor who lived
alone. In a study, dominated by a word processor and the book
manuscript the former first deputy superintendent was writing on
criminology, Riseman walked over to the bar.

"What are you drinking?"

"Orange juice on the rocks will be fine."

Riseman opened a refrigerator beneath the bar and held up a
carton of orange juice. "This okay?"

"Yes, sir."

Riseman poured and handed Cole a glass. He fixed himself a
bourbon and water before leading Cole to a pair of armchairs on the
other side of the room. When they were seated the retired cop said,
"So, how can I help you with the investigation?"

"The F.B.I.'s involved in this thing, sir."

"The F.B.I.?" Riseman responded with a raised eyebrow. "Now
that's one for the books. What are they doing, acting as advisors?"

"No. They've taken over the entire case."

Riseman's face went blank. "Either things have changed radi-
cally in the short time I've been away from the department or there's
something very wrong here."

"I agree," Cole said, placing his glass down on a cocktail table
coaster. "There's an agent named Stanton running the show. A couple of days ago he claimed he was Senator Banks's bodyguard."

"He didn't do his job very well."

"No, he didn't. Stanton's also an ex–Chicago cop. Do you recall assigning me to a series of homicides on the southside about fifteen years ago? I had a young cop as my number one suspect."

A smile played at the corners of Riseman's mouth. He drained off some of his bourbon, swirled the cubes around in the glass and said, "Reginald E. Stanton. Rookie in the Sixth District. Supposedly knifed four people. Used three throwing knives and something called a needle knife. As I remember, you were getting close to something. In another day or so you'd probably have had it. Instead the case got taken away from you."

Cole smiled as he recalled that Riseman had always possessed near total recall when it came to facts and figures connected with police work.

Riseman continued, "So you want to know what happened as far as this Reggie Stanton went?"

Cole nodded. "It might help shed some light on what's happening now."

"I doubt that, but I guess there's no harm in telling you why we refused to go any farther with those knife murder investigations. In the words of the Godfather, 'They made us an offer we couldn't refuse.' "

"Who?" Cole asked.

"The F.B.I. Back then, the late seventies, early eighties, the Feds were investigating the department on a continuing basis. It had taken nearly half a century to begin dispelling that mob-owned town image. But there were still a lot of people, and no small number of them cops, who felt there was still a chance to turn an illegal buck in Chicago now and then.

"There were your individual operators we used to call 'Bandits in Blue,' who did such things as traffic shakedowns, drug confiscations that went into their own pockets, and even occasional armed robberies of known criminals. The Feds weren't so much interested in that type as they were the organized corruption on an official level. You could say we had our share of that too."

"Commander Charles Howard and that pair he had bodyguarding Big Willie McCoy?" Cole asked.

Riseman nodded. "The F.B.I. had a blanket surveillance on McCoy's Seventy-ninth Street operation. They had Howard, an alderman and a bunch of cops in line for federal indictments. There were strong indications that McCoy's bribes went all the way to City Hall. When it broke the scandal was going to rock the very foundations of city government, not to mention throwing more mud on a department that already looked dirty enough."

"But there was never any corruption scandal in Six," Cole said. "I heard some rumors and, if I remember it right, there were enough indications of crooked cops, but that was all there was."

"The F.B.I. handed us the whole thing. Videotapes, marked money transactions, undercover operatives, everything. We handled it ourselves. There were a few local indictments, but nothing spectacular. For the most part, the administration hushed things up. Howard was dumped from being a commander and quietly allowed to retire as a captain. It was handled very discreetly."

"That was awfully generous of the Bureau," Cole said, skeptically.

"Maybe not," Riseman said, taking a pull of his drink.

"I don't understand."

Riseman set his glass down on the table beside Cole's and said, "They got your Reggie Stanton in return."

111

MARCH 7, 1994
8:12 P.M.

Despite the fear and tension surrounding her, Judy had dozed off. She was awakened by DeLisa unlocking her handcuffs. She jerked at his touch.

"Take it easy, lady cop," he said. "We're going to a party."

She stared at him in amazement. He was completely outfitted in a black tuxedo with all the accessories to include a pair of black patent leather oxfords and a cummerbund. His hair was combed and he looked alert and refreshed.

"I'm sorry to have to do this," he said, stepping behind her and snapping the cuffs in place to bind her arms behind her back. "But then we will be on different sides of this little conflict to the end."

She stood there until he finished. Then he draped something over her shoulders. Judy was stunned when she saw that it was a full length, black Ranch mink coat. Not even in her wildest dreams had she ever thought it possible for her to wear anything like this.

"It's all I could come up with on short notice," he said, "but it'll serve the purpose."

"What purpose?" she asked, as he took her arm and escorted her from the library.

"I told you, we're going to throw a little reception party for your friends. I wouldn't call it anything elaborate, but it will have some spectacular results."

They crossed the alcove and entered a set of double doors adjacent to the main staircase. On the other side were winding carpeted stairs leading down. DeLisa held her arm as they descended.

At the bottom a corridor stretched perpendicular to the stairs. The smell of chlorine in the air was strong.

"That's from the pool," DeLisa explained. "There's also a bowling alley down here. But that's not where we're going."

He urged her down the corridor toward a wall constructed of sheet metal. As they approached there was a static crackling noise in the dry air.

"That's an electrical field," DeLisa explained. "On TV they would call it a force field. I call it a security rip-off. Costs an arm and a leg to install and a fortune to operate. Gives out about as much juice as a charge from a car battery, but then, if you're exposed long enough I guess it could curl your hair."

Removing a device resembling a small TV remote from his pocket, he pressed a button. Simultaneously the humming stopped and the sheet metal wall swung upwards to reveal a dark room beyond. He hit another button and overhead lights went on illuminating a sophisticated command center.

DeLisa led Judy over to a raised, backless chair and sat her down. The room was cool so he adjusted her coat. He did not remove the handcuffs. On a table next to the chair was a bottle of champagne in an ice bucket and two long stem glasses. He was prepared for the party.

He uncorked the champagne. "Tell me, lady cop, what does this place remind you of?"

Judy looked around. The console was set up so it could be operated by a single person. There were screens, dials, knobs and levers everywhere she looked.

"It resembles something out of a spy movie I saw once on late-night television."

DeLisa's face became animated with excitement. He poured Judy a glass of champagne and attempted to hand it to her. She gave him an exasperated look. How was she supposed to drink it with her hands cuffed behind her back?

"Of course," he apologized. "Allow me."

He held the glass to her lips. She took a sip. It was expensive and dry.

"Go on," he said. "Tell me more about what this reminds you of."

She shrugged. "There's no more for me to tell. This place looks like something out of a cheap spy movie."

He slapped her hard across the face with his open palm, knocking her to the floor. He snatched her back into the chair and straightened her coat. Her head spun and she tasted blood.

"Let's not go calling things we have no understanding of 'cheap,'" he said. "Everything you see here not only costs, but is very real. I got the idea from a James Bond movie. In fact, a number of Bond movies. I was always a big fan of the villains: Blofeld, Goldfinger, Drax, the whole bunch."

He turned away and placed her glass back on the table. He picked up a full one and with it in hand he began activating the various systems. The console lit up like a Christmas tree.

"I had the weapons and defense systems constructed by the same people who made the F.B.I. surveillance equipment they've been using to keep tabs on me."

He pushed a button and a big screen monitor went on above the console. It looked more like a small movie screen than a television monitor and the definition was startling. Displayed was a view from the front of the mansion looking down the driveway in the direction of the front gate. DeLisa manipulated a dial and the picture zoomed to take in the house across the street. It was dark.

"That's where your buddies, the Feds, were," he said. "By the way, are you federal or local?"

She started not to answer him until he raised his palm to slap her again. "Local. I'm local," she said, turning her head away in case he did follow through with the blow.

He went on in the same casual tone as before. "I had as much information about them as they had on me. But now they're gone and I figure we'll be having company shortly. Whoever comes will be in for quite a surprise."

DeLisa sat down at the console. "Each of these readouts has a function. This one displays the distance from the machine guns on top of the house to the designated target. This one adjusts the range of the mortars on the roof. And this one . . . ," he turned to look at Judy. He noticed the blood on her face. Standing up he removed his handkerchief and used it to dab the blood away from the corner of her mouth. "We'll let that last one be a surprise."

He returned to the console. "Let's take a look around the neighborhood and see what's stirring."

The scenes on the large monitor began changing rapidly. Each displayed a dark suburban street; however, each view was enhanced by an infrared lens.

"Now that's interesting," DeLisa said, stopping at a particular scene. A sports car was parked haphazardly on the side of the road beneath a tree. "That's a late-model Corvette. Parked in the middle of nowhere. Not the smart thing to do. Somebody'll come along and rip it off. That's if the owner really cares. Shall we take a better look around?" He was now speaking more to himself that to Judy. "No, I've got a better idea. Let's activate our perimeter detectors and take a look-see at what's going on down at the front gate." He turned to look at her again. "You've got to admit it, lady cop, this is exciting, isn't it?"

With her face swelling from the blow and the taste of blood in her mouth, Judy Daniels managed a weak nod.

112

MARCH 7, 1994
8:18 P.M.

The guard at the front gate was the youngest and smallest in stature of DeLisa's henchmen. As he bounced from foot to foot to keep warm, he watched his breath vaporize in the cool night air. The temperature had dropped into the thirties. He figured that DeLisa had probably forgotten he was out here. He was about to walk up to the house when he felt the sharp tip of a knife jammed against the side of his neck. He went rigid.

The guard attempted to see his assailant, but he remained in shadow. The guard was searched and his .357 magnum removed from its shoulder rig. He heard it clatter to the ground on the other side of the fence.

"How many are in the house?" a muffled voice demanded.

The guard started to turn in the direction of his interrogator. The pressure of the knife point broke the skin and the guard cried out.

"Shut up and don't turn around again. Now, I asked you a question. How many are in the house?"

"Three, maybe four."

"Okay, we're going to take a walk up there. I'll be right behind you." The knife vanished. "I've got a machine gun at your back so don't try anything stupid."

The guard turned and walked through the gate. He could feel the man with the knife behind him. The burning sensation at the side of his neck, where he'd been stuck, turned to a painful throb.

As they approached, the house was dark. They were halfway there when suddenly a bank of bright lights flashed on blinding them. The staccatto chatter of a machine gun split the air. The guard was not aware that he was hit until he found himself on the ground, stitched across the chest with machine gun rounds. He turned to see his attacker rolling across the lawn firing an automatic weapon at the house. The last thought the young mobster had was that this guy was indeed crazy to be going up against Tony DeLisa.

113

MARCH 7, 1994
8:20 P.M.

B ill Riseman's telephone rang. He answered it. "Riseman. Well, hello, Jack. How are . . . ? Yes, he's right here. Hold on."

Riseman extended the phone to Cole. "It's Govich. He sounds like he's ready for a straightjacket."

Cole took the phone. When he hung up he said to his host, "Stanton's going after whoever killed Senator Banks and I guess that starts with Tuxedo Tony DeLisa. Stanton even had the F.B.I. surveillance pulled off DeLisa's house. The F.B.I. is denying any offer to take over the investigation from us and some official spokesman in Washington has already criticized us to the media for being duped."

"What are they doing about DeLisa?"

"The F.B.I. has got some agents headed this way," Cole said, grimly, "but I don't give a rat's ass about him. Judy Daniels could be in real danger right now."

"What are you going to do?"

"Govich is sending Blackie with help. He's also trying to get the

Oak Park PD to pitch in, but they've got a major chemical warehouse fire that has a lot of their people tied up. I guess it's going to be just me for awhile."

"Going in there alone is not real smart, Larry," Riseman said with a frown. "For all you know, Stanton could be in with DeLisa. Even if he's not, you're still going to be at a big disadvantage."

Cole looked at his former boss. "At this point I really don't have a choice."

114

MARCH 7, 1994
8:21 P.M.

Reggie Stanton drove into the neighborhood of expensive homes where Antonio DeLisa lived. He was about to leave his car in the spot where Naomi had waited for him when he dropped Butcher and Cappeletti on DeLisa's doorstep the other night. Then he heard the unmistakable rattle of machine gun fire coming from a short distance away. He sped to the end of the street and turned the corner. He was two blocks away, but could easily see the floodlights illuminating the property. And under those lights there was a shooting war going on.

Stanton stopped a hundred feet from the gate. Hopping out and snatching the canvas bag he had carried from the basement of the brownstone in Chicago, he ran to the driveway entrance. The reverberations of mortar rounds detonating shook the ground. He flattened himself against one of the stone fence pillars and peered across the lawn.

All the fire was coming from the house. Machine guns, operated from ten locations, were ripping holes in the turf, while mortar rounds blasted foxhole-size craters in the ground. Stanton figured DeLisa had to have a small army in there to initiate such withering fire. Then, through the dense smoke enveloping the small battlefield, Stanton saw the target of the attack.

The figure in black was exposed in the middle of the lawn. There was no cover anywhere around him. The shots were being aimed to strike close without actually hitting him. Stanton found it hard to believe that any group of marksmen could be this skillful.

He took a moment to study the prone figure on the lawn. He knew who this was. The black outfit and hooded mask revealed little about him. However, there was no doubt in the F.B.I. assassin's mind that he had to help this man.

At this point the sniper's game became more deadly. Bullets zipped closer to the trapped target. A bullet nicked him in the leg. Another grazed an arm. The fly snared in the spider's web cried out.

Quickly, Stanton snatched open his bag and removed one of the old weapons Uncle Ernst had preserved over the years, a Carl-Gustav gun. It was made in Sweden, looked like a bazooka and had been designed as an anti-tank weapon. With little difficulty Stanton loaded it and hefted it onto his right shoulder. He stepped from the safety of the stone pillar out into the middle of the driveway. This placed him in full view of the house. He sighted the weapon on the mansion's upper floor.

Instantly, the fire was directed at him, the bullets dangerously close. Stanton fired the anti-tank weapon. The deafening discharge knocked him down.

115

MARCH 7, 1994
9:01 P.M.

L ook at this asshole," DeLisa shouted. "All he can do is eat dirt and die."

Too bad about the bodyguard, DeLisa reflected, but he had been forced to kill him in order to get to the man in black.

DeLisa tracked the target with the computer and let the guns do their work. No hits at first. Just a bit of fun. An occasional mortar blast to add a little flavor to the affair. Soon he grew bored.

"Hey, lady cop, watch this," he said without turning to look at Judy.

He punched control buttons which narrowed the field of fire around his human target. He sliced it to millimeters before letting the guns nip at the legs and arms of his victim. DeLisa was enjoying the sadistic spectacle so much that he didn't see the man at the gate until he aimed the bazooka at the house.

Frantically, DeLisa swung the guns toward the newcomer, but it was too late. A round exploded from the bazooka and rocketed toward the house to slam into the second floor. The impact knocked DeLisa and Judy to the floor. The house shook violently and dust flew through the air. The lights dimmed, went out and then blinked back on.

Ignoring the policewoman, DeLisa jumped to his feet. The external floodlights had been destroyed by the blast. A number of console readouts were dead. All remote firing had ceased. DeLisa pushed the buttons to operate the mortars. Nothing happened.

He laughed. "You sonofabitch. But it's not over. Not by a damn sight."

116

MARCH 7, 1994
9:04 P.M.

Ernest Steiger heard the blast of the bazooka, but thought it was simply more fire being directed at him. Then the house exploded, the lights went out and the shooting stopped. He looked around. A short time later the firing started again, but in a greatly reduced volume than what had been the case before. He was no longer the object of the attack, as the bullets were being concentrated at the gate.

Ernest realized there were only two ways he could go: toward the house, which was suicide, or toward the six-foot fence surrounding the property, which was thirty feet away.

He realized he was hit—two wounds in his left leg and one in his right arm—but he believed he was still ambulatory.

He tried to leap, but collapsed into a half crouch before falling back to the ground.

"Move, dammit," he muttered against the pain.

Ernest managed to stand even as the pains shot through his body, and hobble toward the fence.

He reached the driveway just as three .50 caliber machine gun bullets, fired from the house, slammed into him. Pitching forward, he landed on the asphalt surface. The shock of the rounds muted the pain.

"Stay down!" a voice called from the shadows beyond the front gate. "I'm coming to get you."

This was followed by machine gun fire being directed from the direction of the voice back to the house. Superior fire was returned as bullets hammered the stone pillars on either side of the entrance.

Suddenly, the shooting on both sides stopped. Ernest could feel blood from his wounds soaking through his clothing. He expected gunfire from the house to resume at any second and end it for him. Then he heard the sound of a car starting out on the street. The engine revved, followed by squealing tires. A gray car, its headlights extinguished, roared into the driveway and raced toward the injured man.

117

J udy Daniels was lying on the floor of DeLisa's command center. She had not moved since the impact of the blast knocked her out of the chair. The mink coat covered most of her body. DeLisa hadn't turned to look at her since he recovered from the blast and returned to his remotes. She was not seriously injured, but she was angry. As angry as she'd ever been in her life.

The mobster was totally occupied with the events outside. He screamed obscenities at the monitor screen, which had become grainy with static. She watched DeLisa's back as she began inching her arms behind her and curling her knees into her chest. Her intention was to swing the handcuffs around in front of her.

118

D eLisa couldn't see who was out there on the lawn, but he planned to kill them anyway. He guessed that the intent of the second attack was to provide a diversion to rescue the man in black. He figured both attacks had been mounted by the Steigers. One was hit and trying to save the other. Well, Tuxedo Tony planned to get both of them, even though Hagar had told him they'd got the old man on the expressway. He would later decide on an appropriate fate for the bungling biker. Now he planned to dispose of whoever was out there on the lawn. He managed to get a couple more of the remote machine guns working and was leveling them at the last place he'd seen the man who'd fired the bazooka, when a gray car sped onto the grounds.

With a roar of triumph, DeLisa smashed his fist down on a red button on top of the console.

On the screen the car was visible racing up the driveway toward the wounded figure in black. Then, as if a gigantic hand had reached down and grabbed it, the car was lifted into the air, flipped over and dropped on its hood. Briefly, flames flared beneath the undercarriage before the report of an explosion rocked the damaged mansion.

DeLisa howled with excitement. "I installed an anti-tank landmine under the driveway. It's activated by a remote detonator, you asshole. How do you like them apples?"

There was a noise behind him. DeLisa spun in time to catch the steel bracelet of one of Judy's handcuffs in the face. The blow drove his front teeth through his upper lip. He covered his face with his hands and she quickly changed her point of attack. Stepping closer to him, she kneed him in the groin. The air rushed from his lungs with an agonized groan and he bent over just as she formed her cuffed hands into fists and struck him in the face again. Barely conscious he was knocked back into the console.

She continued to press the attack.

119

R eggie Stanton was disoriented and in pain. He was hanging upside down in his car. He was held in place by his seat belt. He reached up to undo the clasp with his right hand. A sharp pain shooting through his wrist made him cry out. Slowly, he raised his injured arm and held it tight against his side. He tried to reach the clasp with his other hand, but his shoulder wouldn't operate properly.

Finally, he managed to unbuckle the seat belt. He collapsed to the roof of the upside-down car. He landed on his injured shoulder. The pain was so intense it made him dizzy. The strong, acrid smell of gasoline permeated the car. With a tremendous effort he got the door open and rolled onto the lawn. He made it about fifteen feet before the car caught fire with a dull thump followed by the roar of an explosion. Stanton felt the flames singe his clothing as he continued to roll away.

He bumped into a body. He turned to find the man he'd attempted to rescue lying on the ground beside him. Both of them were now in full view of the house. Their position was illuminated by the flames from the burning car.

120

DeLisa went down on his hands and knees. His face was covered with blood. He glanced up and saw the policewoman's foot swing up. It caught him in the forehead. The force spun him sideways. He fought through the haze of pain and disorientation to anticipate her next kick. She aimed it at his side. He reached out, caught her foot and twisted it. She lost her balance and fell heavily to the floor. He scrambled forward and grabbed her by the throat.

"You're dead, bitch!" he said through smashed lips. "I should have done you the minute we got back. Now your ass is mine."

He increased the pressure and watched her eyes bulge as her face darkened. He wanted to prolong this. To make her die slowly.

Her hands drifted away. Her eyes glazed over, but now he wanted the moment to last. To keep her from dying he relaxed his grip. Her eyes came back into focus and she looked at him. He started to choke her again when he felt her hands at his groin. She got a firm grip on his bruised privates and squeezed. He screamed and rolled off her. His agony was unbelievable and he was certain he was going to pass out. He tried to think through the pain, but his whole being became concentrated on what she was doing. Then she released him.

He opened his eyes and saw her running across what was left of his control center. She was having trouble keeping her balance with her hands cuffed in front of her. She was heading back upstairs. He struggled to his feet and went after her.

121

L arry Cole drove slowly through the streets of Oak Park. Twice he'd gotten lost. As he turned onto DeLisa's street, he heard what he initially thought was thunder coming from off in the distance. He gave it little further thought as he began searching for a street sign. The next noise told him that what he'd heard was not thunder, but a very powerful explosion.

122

J udy was exhausted. Adrenaline and fear had fed her fury during her attack on DeLisa, but then when he had choked her she'd been forced to use her last reserves of strength in order to escape. Now she barely had the energy to climb the stairs.

The smell of smoke filled the air, as she pushed open the door leading into the entrance alcove. Dust was thick in the air and fallen plaster and debris littered the floor. Up on the second floor flames danced off corridor walls. The front of the mansion had been destroyed.

She could hear DeLisa coming after her. She started for the front door, stumbling once and falling, when the door was kicked open.

Judy saw a horrible apparition struggle into the house. It looked like a two-headed creature with four eyes, two arms and four legs. It headed straight for her. She turned to run back the way she had come when DeLisa lurched into the alcove behind her.

The mobster shakily held a gun in his hand. He stared first at Judy and then at the two-headed monster. DeLisa's face looked as if it had been shoved into a car fan. One eye was closed and blood streamed from cuts and gashes all over.

"Your friends first and then you, bitch," he lisped through smashed lips.

She screamed as a machine gun rattled sharply. Stunned, DeLisa dropped his gun. He held his hands out in a gesture of surrender.

The two-headed monster made its way from the door across the alcove. Actually it was two men, with one carrying the other. The one being carried was bleeding heavily, leaving a thick trail of blood across the floor. The carrier was much bigger. She also noticed that he held a sausage-barreled, side-loading machine gun in his free hand. Both of them wore hooded masks and black outfits.

"Okay, Steiger," DeLisa mumbled. "We can settle this. You're messed up pretty bad. So's the kid. I can help you."

The big one allowed the wounded man to slump to the floor. He collapsed in a lifeless heap.

"C'mon, man," DeLisa said with a bravado Judy found maddening after all he had done. "We're professionals. We don't kill like this. The niggers and spics do that. We're not going to sink to their level."

The machine gun was held dead steady. With a painful effort the man in black reached up and pulled off his hood.

When DeLisa saw the face he gasped, "Who are you?"

The unmasked man's voice was filled with pain. "That's my brother lying on the floor. Karl Steiger was my father. Because of you, they're both dead. Like you said, we kill like animals. Now it's your turn, DeLisa."

"Freeze, Stanton!" Cole shouted from the door.

Judy spun around. She recognized the commander and saw the 9 mm. automatic he had trained on the big man in black.

"Don't interfere in this, Cole," Stanton said without taking the gun off of DeLisa.

"Drop the gun, Reggie. I mean that," Cole said taking a couple of steps forward.

"I can't. DeLisa's responsible for the deaths of Senator Banks, my father and my brother."

Judy could no longer control herself. "Let him do it, Commander!"

"Shut up, Daniels," Cole snapped. "Now drop the gun, Reggie."

For a brief instant, Stanton wavered. DeLisa took the opportunity to make a dive for the basement stairs. Stanton fired at him and missed. Cole fired at Stanton and didn't. Judy Daniels screamed.

CHICAGO BLUES

They call it Windy City,
'Cause the wind there has no pity,
Like a freight train roarin' toward you,
Like its whistle blowin' through you,
Through your heart, through your heart,
through your heart.
Chicago blues,
Chicago blues,
Chicago blues.

It's a wolf pack in the park.
It's a switchblade oh-so-sharp.
It's a hooker's cold, cold heart.
It's Chicago after dark,
After dark, after dark, after dark.
Chicago blues,
Chicago blues,
Chicago blues.

Its North Side leaves you grievin'.
Its South Side leaves you bleedin'.

It's cheatin' and it's lyin'.
It's the gun's-eye-view of dyin'.
View of dyin', view of dyin', view of dyin'.
Chicago blues,
Chicago blues,
Chicago blues.

EPILOGUE

MARCH 10, 1994
12:27 P.M.

Senator Harvey Banks was buried following a solemn high mass at Holy Name Cathedral. The daytime temperature dropped below freezing and snow flurries blew through the air. The coffin was carried down the Cathedral steps by eight pallbearers consisting of members of the upper and lower houses of Congress, the Governor of the state of Illinois and the mayor of Chicago. Also attending the funeral mass, which was celebrated by the Archbishop of Chicago, were selected members of the Chicago Police Department. The superintendent of police was in attendance. Chief of Detectives Jack Govich and Commander Larry Cole were also there.

Govich and Cole were squeezed into a pew near the back of the church. They were in full dress uniform with military style overcoats, which made them uncomfortable in the overcrowded church. They were actually glad when the services ended, and they were able to escape into the cold air.

The funeral procession headed for the Oakwood Cemetery, where Mayor Harold Washington was buried, stretched for miles. Govich and Cole served as part of an honor guard on the steps of the Cathedral before watching the lead cars of the procession pull away. Then they walked to Cole's police car, which was parked on Chestnut near Lake Shore Drive.

"Has the superintendent said anything to you?" Cole asked as they walked through the cold.

"No, he's been pretty quiet about the whole thing. The F.B.I. coming in and taking over took the heat off him."

Cole shook his head. "They did a real quick about-face on this one. Too quick if you ask me. I came close to cold-cocking that Agent Donnelley when he tried to force me and Daniels out of DeLisa's house."

"So what's there to worry about?" Govich said. "They took the assassins' and Stanton's bodies, and arrested DeLisa. We didn't even have to fill out a miscellaneous incident card on it. You can't beat that for simplicity."

"I still don't like it," Cole said.

They said little else until they reached Cole's car. Standing outside of it, waiting for them in full uniform, stood Blackie Silvestri. He looked out of place in the heavy coat and cap that never seemed to fit right.

As the three of them climbed inside for the ride downtown, Blackie said, "Manny started eating solid food this morning, boss. Looks like Lauren'll be kicking him out of that hospital bed before the end of the week."

"Good," Cole said. "We'll look in on him later."

"There's one other thing," Blackie said. "The Feds let Tuxedo Tony out on bond a little while ago. His mouthpiece Kirschstein held a news conference in front of the Federal Building. He's talking about suing everybody from the janitor at police headquarters to the president of the United States for everything from violating a court order to attempted murder. From what I heard, Judy did quite a job on DeLisa."

"She beat the crap out of him," Cole said. "He'll take those scars to his grave."

"She should have killed the bastard," Govich said quietly. "Would have saved everybody a lot of trouble."

Cole and Blackie were so surprised by Govich's words neither of them said a word.

After dropping Govich at police headquarters, they headed for the Area One Detective Division office. It seemed like a long time since either of them had been there.

A young blonde policewoman with a stunning figure stuffed into a smartly pressed uniform was sitting at Blackie's desk. She stood up and snapped to attention as they approached. Cole looked quizzically at Blackie, but said nothing. The sergeant didn't return the commander's look.

Inside his office, Cole examined his messages. There was nearly a week's worth. He scanned the most important ones and placed them on the side. He was about to begin returning calls when he noticed that all the ones for today were taken by someone with the initials "J. D."

"Oh, no," Cole said, just as there was a knock on his office door.

He looked up as the policewoman stuck her head inside. "There are two women to see you, Commander. The older one says she's Reggie Stanton's grandmother. They have a package for you. Something that he left."

Cole studied the policewoman. It couldn't be. It just couldn't be. This woman was more fair-skinned, had blue eyes, was better built and even taller than . . . then he noticed the name tag over the right breast of the uniform shirt. It read DANIELS.

"Shall I send them in, Commander?"

"Yes. But I need to know something first."

She again snapped to attention. "I hope I can assist the Commander."

"Are you Judy Daniels?"

She gave him a conspiratorial look. "Better known as the Mistress of Disguise/High Priestess of Mayhem. My face is still bruised from DeLisa's slap. I was applying makeup this morning and guess I got carried away. Dr. Drake put me on convalescent duty for a week. Sergeant Silvestri assigned me to be your secretary."

She turned to leave.

"Can I expect a different look every day?"

She smiled. "Definitely, Commander. I couldn't really do it any other way."

When she was gone he said into the emptiness of his office, "Why me?"

Ida Mae Stanton was accompanied by Billie Smith, Reggie's half Vietnamese half African American girlfriend. They sat down across from him. The grandmother did the talking.

"You were Reggie's friend. I know because every so often over the years he'd mention you. He never had nobody else except Ernst Steiger, me and the senator. But there was nobody he could call a real friend. Maybe he didn't want one, but he liked you."

Cole didn't know whether he was supposed to be flattered or feel guilty. He decided to remain mute.

"He wanted me to give this to you." She nodded to Billie. The young woman removed a thick brown envelope from her oversized purse. She laid it on Cole's desk.

"What's that?" he asked.

"Those are Reggie's files," Ida Mae explained. "Just like Hoover, he kept his own. Everything he did for the F.B.I. going back to his first . . . " she hesitated before saying, ". . . job back in nineteen eighty. It's all there. Names, dates and places. He's got photos and dossiers given to him by the F.B.I."

"What am I supposed to do with them?"

Her face hardened. "You too smart a black man to have gotten where you are today without knowing the answer to that, but let me say this. There's another copy of those. A Professor Ronald Hakim has it. He's gone to ground, but you can bet that someday he's going to use what's in that envelope. What you do between now and then is up to you, Commander. Let's go, Billie."

When they had left the office, Cole stared at the envelope. Finally, he got up the nerve to open it.

Martha Grimes buzzed Dave Franklin, the SAC of the Chicago Office of the F.B.I.

"Jack Govich is on line three, sir."

"I really don't feel like talking to him. Take a message."

"I think you'd better, sir. He said something about having 'Stanton's files.' "

"What?"

" 'Stanton's files.' I don't know what that means, but it sounds serious. You still want me to take a message?"

"No, I'll talk to him."

Franklin pushed the button over the blinking light. "What is it, Jack?"

"I want to make you an offer you can't refuse. I give you something you want, you give me something that I want."

"Okay, I'll play. What do I have that you want?"

"Tuxedo Tony DeLisa."

Franklin laughed. "Haven't you had enough trouble out of DeLisa? You keep this up and he's going to own the CPD."

"But you don't know what I have that you want."

"Okay, what?"

DeLisa was registered in a suite on the fourteenth floor of the Palmer House in downtown Chicago while his mansion was being repaired. He had hired a private security firm with political connections to guard him. Six men occupied the rooms on either side of the suite and guards were always on duty in the hall in front of the suite door and at the elevators.

"We got trouble!" The voice of the guard stationed at the elevators crackled over the walkie-talkie. *"There's a bunch of cops with search and arrest warrants on the way."*

The guard at the suite door leaped to his feet. He hammered on the doors to either side and on the one where the principal was located. The four other guards came out of the two rooms to stand shoulder to shoulder with their buddy. They blocked the entire corridor like the offensive line of the Chicago Bears.

With Cole and Govich in the lead, Blackie Silvestri, Lou Bronson and a squad of eight of the biggest, meanest cops Govich could find on short notice, rounded a corner in the corridor and headed straight for the guards. Cole held the legal documents over his head.

"We've got search and arrest warrants for Antonio DeLisa and Frank Kirschstein. Anyone interfering with the service of these instruments will be arrested and charged with obstructing justice."

As the cops came face to face with the guards, Govich said, "Along with getting their asses kicked."

The guards decided that discretion was the better part of valor and got out of the way.

"Who's in there?" Cole asked the guard who looked to be in charge.

"Just Mr. DeLisa and Mr. Kirschstein," he said, and then added. "Oh, yeah, the kid came back a couple of hours ago."

"What kid?" Cole asked.

"Mr. DeLisa's daughter. Rachel. She's in there with them. Mr. DeLisa was real glad to see her."

Cole and Govich exchanged looks. With her in the picture they would have to be careful. It would have to be strictly by the book.

Cole stepped to the suite door and knocked. There was no response. He looked back at the guard.

"They're in there," he said to the cop. "I know it."

"Key?" Govich said to the guard.

He hesitated momentarily before handing it over. "Please don't tell him it was me who gave it to you. It'll be my ass."

They found the attorney first. He was sitting on a sofa in the expansive living room overlooking State Street far below. His head looked like someone had spilled a strawberry pie all over it. He had been dead for at least an hour. Maybe more. Whoever had done this had come up behind him with a blunt instrument.

Blackie had gone with Bronson to check the bedroom. His voice boomed from the back of the suite, "Boss!"

The panic there brought Cole at a dead run. Govich was right behind him.

In the bedroom they found Rachel still at work. How long she'd been at it was anybody's guess. Methodically, she lifted the metal pipe over her head and slammed it down into the pulpy, bloody mass on the bed. Again, again and again.

Cole nodded to Blackie and Bronson. They stepped forward and grabbed her arms, stopping her in midswing from continuing in the overkill of her father. She did not resist.

They led her from the room.

Cole and Govich approached the bed. It would take an autopsy to tell if what was left had been Tuxedo Tony DeLisa. Now it didn't even look human.

"Fitting," Govich said.

"Yeah," Cole added.